Black Sands & Toitoi

Dedication

To my dear wife Jan who corrected grammar and
encouraged me during the many re-writes. Also to
my children, Kiri and Paul and to my grandchildren,
Emma, Alisha, Lucas and Ava. I hope this story
inspires you to delve into the fascinating world
of make believe. Please forgive the violence and
bad language, it is part of some peoples' lives.

Synopsis

To escape winter blues, three Canadian ladies holiday
in New Zealand. Offsetting the air-fare, they stay at
a cheap but quaint West Coast hotel and befriend
local artists. Socialising at a pub, they cross paths
with a motorcycle gang. Unsuspecting, they become
involved in a drug network that has its beginnings
on the edge of the Gobi Desert, continues through
Hong Kong to the South Pacific islands.

This is an international story that links Hong Kong
Triads with New Zealand gangs and China's attempts
to colonise the South Pacific with economic stealth.
The Cook Islands, with its maritime zone of two
million square kilometres, is a prime target. With
naval bases in Pago Pago and Guam, America seeks the
intervention of New Zealand, the Islands' protector.

The tribes of Rarotonga play an integral part in the final
outcome, as does a black and white collie dog named Lady.

Chapters

BLACK SANDS & TOITOI

PETER PEDROTTI

On the West Coast of New Zealand,
black iron sand bakes hard in the summer sun.
Above it, wispy white toitoi waft in the sea breeze.
This is the story of contrast and conflict.
Love versus hate.
Good versus evil.

CHAPTER 1

Rarotonga and the Case of the Cold KFC

It is summertime in the Cook Islands. As always, the eastern side of Rarotonga receives the first glow of the rising sun and that's when the roosters start to crow. It is circular like the face of a clock and like clockwork, every morning, the cocks crow progressively as they welcome the sun. The last to crow are those on the western side where they are shaded by high volcanic peaks. By the time the sun is overhead, the crowing stops, that's when the dogs start to bark!

This early morning ritual is comforting to the locals, but for Ah Chung it is a never ending source of annoyance. Even with windows shut tight and the air-conditioner on high, the first crows at four in the morning have him awake and listening. In Hong Kong, the distant rumble of a gathering storm would have lulled him back to sleep. Even the crackle of lightening or the boom of thunder was soothing compared to these cacophonous cocks.

Ah Chung waits until he hears the nearby shrill crow of an immature wannabe, followed immediately by the louder authoritative crow of its master, before he pokes Miriama Maana's slender brown back with the tips of his fingers.

Miriama, his tall, beautiful PA, interpreter, comforter and sex mate is so competent and compliant that he has not wanted any other female companion during his five years as Pacific Rim Manager of Chan Chemicals International. The chemical company is seriously wealthy being the world's leading supplier of natural ephedrine and pseudo-ephedrine. Its headquarters are located in an impressive building on Bonham Street near the wharves of old Hong Kong. Its Board is powerful, with links to the Chinese Government and to the Triad movement of Hong Kong.

A few years previously, after an international crackdown on the illegal use of some of their drugs, the Board decided to invigorate its management. They started at the bottom by sacking their elderly Pacific Rim Manager based in Rarotonga. The replacement they were seeking had to be energetic and innovative with the ability to mix with multi-nationals. Above all they wanted loyalty and the capability of finding new ways of selling their products, discretely, without international complications and they chose a rising star named Ah Chung. They were aware that Ah's family had a long association with the English and that he had earned a Masters of Commerce degree at Oxford University. More persuasive than those attributes is the family's connection with the Wo Shing Wo Triad gang of Hong Kong.

Like Miriama, Ah Chung is tall, dark haired and slender. Although in his mid-twenties, his outward bearing is confident and mature and all his decisions are measured. But don't mistake that for softness as his deep seated genes hark back to the ruthless age of the Mandarin. On his frequent visits to Hong Kong he frustrates his mother by skillfully parrying the advances of another beautiful Chinese bride as the last thing he wants at the moment is the complications of a wife.

Miriama is ideal. Not only a perfect PA, but true to her Cook Island upbringing, has respectfully and patiently taught him about life on her island. His Oxford schooling and intellect were of little use in this small, sparsely populated tropical paradise and at the start he was indecisive and confused. Hiring Miriama was the smartest thing he ever did and this would not have surprised his

Manager who had deliberated carefully over his selection.

For some time, the Operations Manager had been under pressure to find new ways of delivering Chinese medicines to the world, particularly the most difficult and the most lucrative, an alkaloid extracted from a plant that grows naturally on the edges of the Gobi Desert. Its botanical name is ephedra sinica and its potent alkaloid is called ma huang or ephedrine, the precursor of methamphetamine.

Ah Chung circumvented the internationally imposed restrictions more easily than he expected. He bought a small warehouse next to Chan Chemicals in Avarua and started a new business, The Chung Coffee Company. Like his chemical business, it has a legitimate side and also a secret side, that enables him to distribute non documented drugs to the South Pacific.

The coffee is grown and processed on a nearby island and because Ah Chung pays well, the farmers have seen their profits double over previous years. Now he is able to buy small amounts of green beans, something that other buyers have been denied. It is the green beans that interest him the most. Much to his surprise, his legitimate coffee enterprise is booming, making it easier to hide the relatively few bags containing the drugs.

On arrival in New Zealand the bags of green beans are delivered to a coffee factory for roasting. The factory is owned by JS Holdings Limited or more specifically Johnny Schmidt Holdings Limited. Johnny being the leader of the Satan's Sons gang.

The accounts for the roasting and sale of the coffee beans are open to inspection and scrupulously accurate. The same applies to Chan Chemical's legitimate sales of pseudo-ephedrine and ephedrine to the major chemical companies of New Zealand and Australia. Payment is by electronic transfer directly to Chan Chemicals in Hong Kong and there is no attempt to conceal the information. The clandestine shipments however, are paid for in cash, and that is hand delivered to Ah Chung in Rarotonga. This is a risk and involves the exchange of huge amounts of money.

No one in Airport Customs is on the take, as word would spread too easily. Instead, Ah Chung relies on the trusting nature of the officers and their tendency not to upset their main source of income, the tourists. Basically it comes down to risk management.

Ah Chung limited the risk, at the inception of his coffee company, by deliberately hiring island workers with tribal connection to local Members of Parliament. His other employees are four muscular Triad supervisors from Hong Kong who are more skilled at martial arts than the import and export of green coffee beans.

Today he is expecting two million dollars from one of the syndicated Auckland gangs. It will be the second monthly payment of the year and chaperoned by a smartly dressed gang member from the Satan's Sons.

Ah Chung prods Miriama again, and she yawns then throws open the closed shutters. After five years she has become conditioned to the artificially cooled air, but still feels unnaturally confined. It makes her throat and eyes dry, but it doesn't last once she emerges into the warm, moist, perfumed air of her tropical home.

Created by volcanoes, her island has limited flat land for an airport. The eastern end of the runway is as close to the town of Avarua as safety allows while the western end has been pushed out into the lagoon, past the coral reef to the edge of the deep blue water of the Pacific Ocean.

It is like landing on an aircraft carrier for the pilot of the Air New Zealand Boeing 777 and he guides the plane down on a long slow approach over the sea. The winds are from the West and that means Dan Henare, born in Rarotonga and now a Satan's Sons gang member will get a close look at the harbour and the main business centre of the island. It is an honour and a reward to be picked as the money runner. The money is concealed beneath a bulk delivery of KFC. The chicken is always welcomed by his iwi and Dan smiles at the thought of the good times at the party tonight!

Delivery of the chicken is shared among the seven largest Auckland gangs that have formed the syndicate, at Ah's request, to make the handling and distribution of contraband drugs more efficient.

Now it's his turn so he gets to visit almost once a year. He knows there is a risk that the money secreted beneath the cold fatty chicken may be detected, but the risk pales against the everyday risks of being a gang member, *'Shit! all that can happen is I'm locked up in*

jail for a few months making fuckin' ukuleles, that's better than being beaten or dead!" He doesn't know that he is smuggling two million dollars and that will mean a long time in jail, depending on how freely he will talk!

The central volcanic peaks rise up to meet the plane and then the palm covered slopes speed by the windows before there is the customary 'bump' as the wheels hit the runway. As if angry at being stopped, the wheels squeal when braked and the engines scream in protest at reverse thrust, before the slow roll up to the airport terminal.

The plane soon empties with steps locked against the front and the tail. Emerging into the bright sunshine, Dan welcomes the mouldy wet warmth of his tropical homeland. The ukulele man with a band of plastic frangipani on his straw hat, strums a tune and the passengers waiting to clear Customs are cajoled into shedding their big city stresses.

Dan waves when he spots his mother in the Welcome Pavilion, what he doesn't see are two young thick-set Chinese standing a few paces back on the sidewalk.

As he waits beside the carousel, his knapsack soon appears, but his two large styro-foam boxes secured with bands of packing tape are no-where to be seen. More and more luggage pushes through the rubber straps onto the carousel until only unclaimed bags make a second circuit. For the first time Dan becomes worried. Looking up and down the carousel there are now only a few bags left and he frowns. The ukulele music is now an annoyance as his anxiety grows. A quick glance to his left and then right informs him that there seem to be more Police and security officers hovering nearby. His smile returns, when he sees the first of his two taped boxes, push through the heavy rubber straps. Breathing a sigh of relief, he places it on his trolley. That's when he notices that one corner of the box has been broken and then patched with wide yellow tape printed with recurring words, 'COOK ISLAND CUSTOMS.' He senses the two Policemen on either side, a moment before he feels firm restraining hands on each arm!

One of the two Chinese, out in the Welcome Pavilion, moves close to the open doors and raises a camera with a telephoto lens and snaps multiple shots.

The first real decision Ah Chung made five years before was to pressure his Hong Kong manager into providing funds to build a new house high on the hills overlooking the golf course and the airport at Avarua. The huge cream plastered building with a red tiled roof is more than just an expensive residential property as it contains not only expansive living quarters for himself and Miriama but also a restaurant sized kitchen, a large dining room, a conference room and an office. In a separate building there is housing for his warehouse supervisors who double as security and two locally hired guards manning the front gate. The complex is surrounded by a cream plastered wall that matches the houses and topped with circular rolls of razor wire and security cameras. The money for the complex came from the Chinese Government, Chan Chemicals and Shan Chun, Mountain Master of the Triads. Under Cook Island law, the land cannot be bought, but the Government granted Ah a sixty-year lease, more than enough time to complete his legal and illegal business transactions. More funds were required for his expensive taste in cars, furnishings, kitchen and internet security, but money was not a problem. At seven dollars an hour, the minimum wage, Ah Chung employs four ground staff and a kitchen hand, Leilani Henare, sister of Dan the money-runner. Wah Lee, an experienced Chinese cook, is paid ten times that amount, but he is from Ah's home town of Tung Chung in Hong Kong and is a friend of the family.

From his vantage point in his second floor office, Ah sees the 777 land and discharge its passengers and then receives the worrisome phone call.

Now sitting facing him, with their backs to the window are his four warehouse supervisors. This is the first time a delivery of money has been confiscated and they are interested in how their young boss is going to handle the situation.

Looking at the alert, strained faces in front of him, Ah decides to lighten the mood, "Well the Police and Customs will be eating a lot of KFC tonight!"

The supervisors smile and relax back into their chairs.

Ah knows that there is a long way to go before he will accept that the money is lost. This money is gone, but it will be replaced! He

smiles a cynical smile as he thinks how the cash strapped Cook Island Government has just made a two-million-dollar windfall. He is not smiling however, with the thoughts of how he is going to pressure the syndicate of Auckland gangs into sending more. Deep in thought, he picks up one of the photographs off his desk and studies Dan Henare closely. He is looking at a healthy young Rarotongan man with a distinctive circular koru tattoo just visible below a ring in his ear and partially covered by his collar. He doesn't know of Dan's family connection with Miriama, Leilani his kitchen hand and Pita at the front gate, those are trifling domestics matters.

Northward and not far away, the Cook Island Police Headquarters, opposite Trader Jacks, is an imposing two story building faced with grey polished stone. It is out of character with the usual flimsy island structures and definitely out of character with the island's laissez faire style of living. The architecture is too stern and colonial and a blue Cook Island flag with its Union Jack and circle of stars hangs limply at the top of the flagpole out in the middle of the court yard. The building is air-conditioned but it is no match for the oppressive afternoon heat.

Inside, a long line of impatient tourists wait to be processed for their Drivers' Licenses. A further irritant is that there are no pens on the ends of the chains at the writing desks!

At the rear of Police Headquarters are the cells, only one of them is occupied.

Dan Henare is agitated. Denied cigarettes and a fix, he alternates between sitting on the bed, the plastic chair and pacing the four by six metre room. He knows he is entitled to a phone call and has already decided to call his brother in New Zealand. That will get a message to Johnny, he'll know what to do. In the meantime, he reasons, if he keeps his mouth shut he'll be jailed for a short time and then be free!

Without P for two days his thought process is not sharp, if it was, he might start to worry about who would want his silence to be permanent!

CHAPTER 2

Julia, Wendy and Robyn

In stark contrast to the warmth of a tropical island, Toronto is in the grip of a harsh winter. For the past two months the temperature has been below zero and the snow banks on the sides of the road are grey with soot, sand and salt.

Canadians enjoy the change of season, the miracle of spring, the hot summer, fall colours and the first fluffy white snowfall, but no one enjoys the long freezing winter!

It is just before dawn and warm humidified air hisses from the ceiling vents in Julia's bedroom. Julia Johansson has pushed aside her duvet and her long blonde hair is spread over a satin pillow. Under closed lids, her eyes move rapidly from side to side as she watches her dream.

Wendy Howard, across the hall in their rented apartment is also asleep. Wendy and Julia are in their late twenties. What binds them as friends is their freedom of spirit, love of adventure and a quick laugh. These qualities and their age are the only similarities.

Julia, elegantly tall, slim and Scandinavian is cool and composed and sometimes extraordinarily determined.

Wendy, of medium height, is very English. Her round face is

framed by black curly hair and her complexion makes her appear cherubic. She is energetic, composed and lives an orderly life as a Television Production Assistant.

That suits Legal Executive Julia just fine, as she prefers not to get involved with the mundane.

Beside Julia's bed a digital radio clock clicks over to 6:30am and after a short fanfare a male announcer's voice booms. "It is six thirty and this is CBC Radio One... Watch out folks it's getting tropical out there.... The weather office is calling for a three degree rise making it a balmy minus seven... Yowee!... Grab your lotion and UV glasses it's a burn up in the GTA, and yes, the sun will rise this morning, that's in half an hour, so it's going to be a sunny, happy thirteenth day of February and I guess I don't have to tell you... IT'S MONDAY!"

Julia with eyes shut, reaches over and bangs downward a few times until she hits the 'snooze' button and the annoying voice fades away. Stretching one elegant arm above her head, she flicks on the light. Yawning, she sits up then swings her legs over the edge of the bed and feels for her slippers. With eyes half closed, she shuffles out of the room into the cool of the dark hallway. Feeling with her hand she locates the light switch then flinches at the sudden stab of light.

A beeping alarm can be heard coming from Wendy's bedroom. There is a 'click' and the beeping stops.

Julia listens for movement then gently knocks on the closed door. Turning the knob, she pushes it open. The light from the hallway floods into the room.

Wendy, feigning sleep, has the blankets pulled up to her chin. She stirs and with eyes squeezed shut, turns her head and frowns before raising her eyebrows up and down as if her lids are stuck together. Blinking them open, she immediately clamps them shut again and pulls her pillow over her head smothering a groan.

Julia moves close to the bed and lifts the pillow. "Good morning English rose, it's time to get up and stoke the fire, feed the chickens and milk the cow." There is no response, "Hey sleeping beauty…. you asked me to wake you no matter what, because you are going

to have a shit-of-a-day."

Wendy opens her eyes and sighs, "Go away Jules." Pulling the blankets over her head, she turns her back on Julia. After a moment she mumbles, "I've changed my mind, I'm going to have a sick-and-tired day!" She rolls back towards Julia, "That's me sick and tired of television!"

Julia laughs, steps forward and pulls the blankets half way down the bed.

Wendy grabs the pillow and places it over her face.

"It's going to be a bit warmer Wens, only minus seven!"

A muffled raspberry comes from the middle of the pillow.

Julia crosses over the hall to the bathroom and turns on the shower as Wendy sighs, gets out of bed wrapping herself in a soft blue dressing gown that matches her slippers, then walks down the hallway to the kitchen.

Breakfast preparations are repetitive. Muesli in two bowls then a carton of trim milk beside a smaller carton of half and half for coffee. Fresh squeezed orange juice into two glasses, a tub of margarine, a jar of jam, two coffee mugs, Tim Horton coffee in the coffee maker and finally matching bread and butter plates beside the bowls. That's the routine, she thrives on being orderly. Walking to the kitchen window, she is intrigued that her view is obscured by a layer of frozen crystals.

Julia glides into the kitchen wrapping her hair in a towel as her pink satin slippers make a slithering sound on the tile floor. "That shower head is hopeless it keeps pointing at my feet. Didn't the supe say he had fixed it? God he is hopeless! The building is freezing and now the shower won't work!"

Wendy gets up from the table. "My turn!"

Julia puts whole grain bread in the toaster, takes the lid off the margarine and pours milk on her muesli. Glancing at the frosted window she sighs, then pulls her dressing gown tighter around her legs before pouring a coffee.

Wendy calls from the bathroom. "It's okay, I've fixed it, the nozzle was loose."

Julia picks up a remote and switches on a TV on the kitchen

bench. A rotating news banner appears with a stab of music then a voice over. "It's seven o'clock, time for the CBLT Morning Report, brought to you by Pacific Travels." A commercial plays showing a picture of palm trees and a sandy beach accompanied by strumming guitars and bongo beats. The music fades, "Have you ever dreamed of a romantic holiday on some far distant island? Then dream no more! We have the destinations, you supply the romance! Call us now at Pacific Travels for your great escape... Phone free at this number, or visit our website... Pacific Travels dot ca."

The News continues as Wendy returns partially dressed, drying her hair. "Hey Jules, we need a holiday, where would you like to go?"

Julia, eating toast, pauses, deep in thought. "I guess a place far away.... Not commercial, natural, lots of warm sunshine." She points to the TV, "Maybe a beach, yeah nice and warm." She shakes her head, "No, it should be hot, yeah, stinking, stinking f'n hot!"

Wendy raises her eye brows. "F'n hot?"

"You bet!" Her happy smile changes to a frown when she looks at the time on the TV, "Damn, you start dreaming and half an hour slips by, oh well back to the real world of sweat and tears and f'n law suits."

Wendy nods. "And frozen f'n sidewalks."

Julia snorts then sips her coffee.

Wendy is aware of Julia's stresses and stops drying her hair. "Speaking of sweat and tears and law suits, how's your job?"

Julia grimaces. "The job's fine! I really like helping people but working with the partners is a real pain. Like right now, John and Joe have decided to stay an extra week in Mexico, just like that, no beg pardons. I've got a mountain of contracts waiting to be signed and clients wanting answers." She turns to look at Wendy, "You remember Greg the junior partner, he's no help at all, he won't sign anything and takes two hour lunches which includes a game of squash a sauna and a massage, while I'm stuck in the office. I feel like walking out and letting the phones ring, it's just not fair… you know, like I'm a chattel, not an employee!" Julia pushes her plate away and stands looking down at Wendy, "Anyway enough of me,

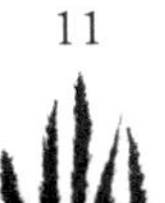

how's the mad mad world of television?"

Wendy continues to brush her damp, curly black hair then stops and looks up. "Jim doesn't take two hour lunches, but I'm mother, sister, confessional priest, slave and secretary and fighting off being his next conquest!" She pauses then grimaces, "He's got hands all over the place! Yuck!... Oh for a holiday somewhere nice and quiet, away from the city!" She stands clasping her breakfast bowl and empty coffee mug.

Julia holds out her hand, "Hey, leave the dishes, go and get dressed…. I'll load the dishwasher."

Fifteen minutes later, with collars tight against their chins and trying not to slip, they hurry away from the building. The banks of snow are taller than the pedestrians, white and icy on the side of the sidewalk, but grey with streaks of black from vehicle exhausts, on the road side.

At an intersection, Julia and Wendy cross over through a valley cut in the bank and enter the subway, jostled by other commuters trying to escape the cold.

Robyn Petheridge, best friend of Wendy and Julia, is already at her desk. The entrance to her auto insurance company is narrow, typical of most of the businesses and shop entrances on Dundas Street. Situated between Little Italy and Little Greece, the insurance company is little in enterprise and little in stature. Behind the narrow closed door however is a large lineup of irate customers.

Robyn is one of three harassed clerks trying to manage the situation. She is not exactly portly, neither is she slim, her pale skin makes her freckles obvious under concealing makeup. At thirty, her conservative clothing and short cut red hair makes her look much older. Being slightly older than her friends, Robyn provides the glue that binds them together. She is a good listener and loves them equally and will not take sides. They look upon Robyn as an older sister and are comfortable that she doesn't challenge their own good looks.

At this moment Robyn is trying to explain to a new immigrant that he cannot make a claim as he is seriously behind in his payments and his contract has been cancelled.

The man who pretends not to understand, refuses to take, 'no' as an answer.

Finally exhausted she asks her supervisor to intervene.

As the grumbling client departs she takes a deep breath and beckons the next antagonist who seats himself saying. "I'm gonna sue you guys!"

Eastward at University and Bloor, Julia unlocks the door of an office that has a bronze plaque announcing GILFILLAN & EPSTEIN, MATRIMONIAL ATTORNEYS AT LAW'. To her right, covering most of the front window is a large banner, GET A BETTER PRENUPT HERE! Entering the building, she is about to sit down, when a heavily rouged, middle aged lady rushes in shouting. "That low down slimy bastard's done a runner!"

Julia sighs and slumps deeper into her chair.

Down town, closer to the lake, TorontoTV is in an imposing red building at the foot of the CN Tower. The once bustling edifice with all its departments packed to overflowing is now like a morgue as the recession bites into the advertising dollar. Redundancies have stripped the fun out of the business and humourless accountants now have the power to dismiss old hands and to strangle the contracts of the expensive 'arty' types. Those same workers, with years of audio visual experience are exactly what TorontoTV needs to survive.

The Chief Financial Officer, instead of looking at the long term future of free-to-air television, where home-made content will be its saviour, has one eye on his bonus and the other on a future telecom career. He listens to newly employed, smart young executives who say that the future is via the internet. But the internet is a delivery system not a content maker. It is understandable that they think this way, as desk top computers, iPhones, iPads, androids, tablets, notepads, laptops and shoot-em-up-games are all that they have ever known!

Wendy Howard is caught in this financial squeeze. The pressure on her and her production staff is to be more and more cost effective.

Hanging up her coat, she checks the answer phone messages and is met with a torrent of requests from her producer, *'Doesn't he ever sleep?'* Ignoring the recorded messages, she decides to look at e-mails instead. Monday is always difficult. The tidy up after the weekend requires a quick flick through production error reports, then a deeper analysis just in case some other department has tried to pass the buck. The inter-department meeting is warfare with no prisoners taken and Jim expects her to have all the answers and if not, she must fall on her sword! Her psychosomatic wounds are so numerous that she survives on codeine, massages and glasses of wine.

After a revisit to the answer phone messages and the e-mails, Wendy thinks she will survive this Monday!

Pressing an auto dial number on her desk phone, she waits for it to be answered. "Hi Jules, how about lunch?... Tides?... Okay, see you at one, stay on the line while I check with Robyn." She presses another button, "Hi Robyn, I'm meeting Jules at Tides at one, do you want to join us?....... Great, see you there."

Tides restaurant at the Toronto waterfront is bucking the recession and doing a booming midday business. Wendy orders her meal then looks at her friends. "I don't know about you two, but I need a holiday! If I don't get away soon, I'll go bonkers. I have trouble getting to sleep and when I do, I have nightmares. What about you guys, do you think it's the winter blues?"

Julia shakes her head. "It's called stress and very harmful!"

Robyn nods. "We all need a holiday it's as simple as that."

They pause as their wine order arrives.

Wendy swirls a chardonnay then takes a sip. "But where? Let's think about it and see what we can come up with. It'll be great if we can all get away together.... There I'm feeling better already."

At the end of the day, Julia enters the subway thankful to escape the biting wind that funnels down Yonge Street. On the wall across the tracks is a large poster advertising New Zealand spring lamb.

Now seated on the train, the poster slides past and she wonders about a country that has four million people and fifty million sheep and is 100% pure. The thought of green fields and bouncing lambs returns as she trudges through ankle deep snow to her high rise apartment. Removing her heavy overcoat, mittens, scarf and beret, she opens the door to the lounge where Wendy is curled up on the couch under a large quilt, reading a novel.

She looks up and smiles. "Hi Jules!"

"Hi Wens, you know that poster in the subway advertising New Zealand spring lamb?"

"Oh, something about fifty million sheep, yeah, why?"

"Well, I was thinking about New Zealand. It's about as far away from Canada as we can get on this planet and down there it's the middle of summer, what do you know about the place?"

Wendy places her book on the arm of the sofa, "As you say, it's a long way away. In-fact it's a bloody long way away!" She pauses for moment thinking, "What do I know about New Zealand?... Not much, but it is subtropical, English speaking.... lots of sheep, must be green."

Wendy makes room as Julia sits down beside her, "They're an out-doorsy sort of people.... Like their sport. They won the America's Cup, that's a sailing trophy and they have a rugby team called the All Blacks.... They play cricket, that's also an English game." She turns to look at Julia, "I remember back home we always had New Zealand spring lamb at Christmas and their wines are divine." She thinks for a moment, "Not much else, oh yeah the natives have tattoos on their faces and they do a haka.".

"A what?"

"A haka, it's a war dance, it's quite famous."

Julia frowns. "Never heard of it!"

Wendy studies Julia for a moment. "Do you think we should go there for our holiday? The airfare would be expensive."

Julia has a habit of wiggling closed lips when she wants something, and is doing it now. "The exchange rate makes it slightly cheaper, it's something like six cents on the dollar."

Wendy shrugs. "I suppose it's better than the other way around. Any saving is better than none."

Julia nods and Wendy shrugs again, "Not sure about the long flight, it will cost heaps, we'd better check prices first... I mean why not fly to Florida or Bermuda instead?"

"You remember how that worked out last time."

Wendy grimaces. "Yeah, not so good, what about Mexico or Cuba?"

"Let's check package plans, I'm guessing the flights to New Zealand will be much more expensive, but accommodation much cheaper, maybe one balances out the other?"

Wendy shrugs, not convinced. "Let's call Robyn, she'll know."

Julia nods and flips open her cell phone. "Hi Robyn, Jules... am I interrupting anything?" She presses 'speaker' and both hear her say.

"Nope, only TV."

"You know the holiday we were talking about at Tides?"

"Yep!"

"How would you like to go to New Zealand?"

"Where?"

"New Zealand, you know, down under, next to Australia."

"The fifty million sheep place?"

"Right, you've seen the subway poster too."

Robyn is silent for a moment, thinking. "It's a long way, have you checked prices?"

"No, we thought you might know?"

"No I don't."

"I think the accommodation will be cheaper than Mexico or Cuba, everyone and their dog are heading that way."

"Maybe, do you want me to check it out, how long should we stay?"

"What do you reckon, three weeks, is that long enough?"

"It's never long enough when you're on holiday, what about Wendy, can she get away?"

Julia looks down at Wendy who nods. "Wens is okay."

Robyn smiles. "What an original idea Jules, all the way to New Zealand for a holiday. I've always wondered about that place. So isolated, so distant from our politics and the Middle East... Spectacular scenery, you know "Lord of the Rings" and all that, it would be really different."

"Yeah that's what I thought! Do you mind checking out a package plan? I wouldn't mind slumming a few weeks at a backpackers if we had to do that."

"Now that is something we haven't tried, I'll get back to you tomorrow."

Julia gives the thumbs up to Wendy then turns back to her phone, "One place you could check is Pacific Travels, they do a lot of advertising on TV."

"Yeah I've seen their ad., I'll give you a call tomorrow, bye Jules."

Wendy calls out. "Bye Robyn."

Julia clicks off her phone as Wendy stands throwing off the quilt. "What the hell, in for a penny in for a pound!"

Julia smiles. "That's very British of you Wens!"

CHAPTER 3

Tane, Mike and Lady

New Zealand, at the bottom of the globe, is sweltering after a long hot summer. The Hawkes Bay hills are ochre with slashes of puriri green in the valleys. Out of sight, the shorn sheep cluster under the leafy branches escaping the sun. The farmers are worried as their ponds turn avocado green and only the holiday makers and the vintners rejoice about the hole in the ozone!

Northward, on the other coast, nature is kinder. At least once a week water laden clouds collide with the Waitakere Ranges, change direction upward and discharge their load. The plants, responding to this nurturing, raise their leafy branches ever higher. This thick, lush, vegetation covers the Ranges down it's slopes to Auckland City to the East, and to the Tasman Sea to the West. At its base, on the western side, sits an old bushman's cottage, just before the high black sand dunes of Karekare beach. The cottage, with its roof of rusty corrugated iron and planked with grey kauri timber, shelters under the canopy of a large puriri tree. Not a misfit, the weathered cottage belongs in the bush and doesn't compete with the natural beauty of the surrounding foliage. Above the tree tops, wispy white smoke curls from a tin chimney, disturbing the stillness.

It is a calm morning with the faintest of sea breezes and the sounds of the bush are everywhere. The never-ending 'rasp' of the cicadas, the occasional chimes of the bellbirds, the varying call of the tui, the 'cheep', 'cheep' of the fantail and the rhythmical, 'thump', 'thump', 'thump' of the ocean surf.

The cottage is owned by Tane Lendic a potter and he shares it with his best friend and landscape painter, Mike Robinson. While Mike is fair skinned and blonde, Tane is dark. His mother is Maori and his father, half Maori and half Dalmatian. He is descended from gum diggers who arrived in New Zealand just before the turn of the century. These settlers from the Mediterranean, toughened by their homeland's rocky terrain and hot sun were not afraid of hard work. In their new home, the Northland swamps, they dug deep ditches and then prodded the drained marshes for clumps of solidified kauri gum.

Tane's grandfather was one of those gum diggers who seized the opportunity to make a living from the world's demand for varnish. The amber nuggets were as precious to the gum diggers as gold and it was extracted by the new immigrants, locally born European and the Maori, both men and women. Naturally the close association of the races produced many brown eyed, brown skin offspring.

Tane's grandmother is Ngapuhi, a feared warrior tribe and he inherited their strength. From his grandfather, he inherited ancient Persian genes, the same found in Alexander the Great! The need for money drew the two unlikely cultures together and Tane's grandmother taught her husband how to survive. She showed him how to cut, strip and make long strands from the tall native flax, harakeke, then to weave the strands into ropes, mats, bags and cloaks. She taught him how to make a temporary shelter out of raupo, a swamp land reed and shared her knowledge of plants that would heal. Boiled kumarahou and koromiko leaves as a tonic for asthma and bronchitis and the deadly swamp disease, tuberculosis.

When his hands blistered from using the long metal prods, she took him into the forest and showed him the heart shaped kawakawa leaves and made a poultice for his sores. Boiling the leaves, she made him drink the bitter tea, telling him that it would cure him of mate pukupuku, now known as cancer.

Mostly, she taught him kiakaha, to be strong, so that he could survive the festering water, the mud, the sandflies, the mosquitos and the back breaking work. Only the fittest survived those years in the swamps and Tane is a product of those times. He is handsome with soft amber skin and short, jet black, wavy hair. His lips curl at the corners and when parted, display white even teeth. He is a picture of health, in the prime of life and proud of his dual ancestry.

On this fine summer morning he is asleep, face down with one arm dangling over the side of a large bed. He shares everything with Mike, except the only bedroom in the cottage. As the owner, that is his privilege.

Lady, his dog, a Border Collie, pushes open the door and licks his face.

Opening one eye he smiles then mumbles. "Okay girl, let's go." Sitting up, he slips his feet into his jandals, stands, yawns and stretches his brown muscular arms above his head.

Each morning it is part of his waking routine to pull open the curtains and look down on the black sand dunes and the long sweep of Karekare Beach. He never tires of the changing view. One morning it may be blowing a storm, the flax and the toitoi fronds whipping in the wind and the dark green waves frothing and crashing onto the beach. Another, like today, it will be sunny and gentle with blue skies and calm blue green water.

As he massages his hair with his fingers, Lady pushes her nose against the back of his leg until he moves into the living room full of half-finished paintings.

Against the inside wall is an old metal framed double bed and on it, face down, Mike Robinson is asleep. Spread-eagle and nude, his long blonde hair drapes over the pillow. With his head to one side you can see an evenly clipped beard, but no moustache above his parted lips. The neat beard is a surprise as it doesn't match the rest of his casual appearance. But that is Mike Robinson, at thirty years of age he is still boyishly handsome and trying to ignore deeply instilled proper attitudes. No matter how casual he would like to appear, he cannot conceal a pampered upbringing.

As in Tane's bedroom, the early morning sun sends spears of light through the edges of the faded curtains facing the beach. In the half light, Tane moves over to an easel in the centre of the room and studies a large seascape with a tall craggy island in the background. He moves to the window and pulls back the curtains. Sunlight streams in and the magnificent panorama of the beach is on display. Turning, he walks back to Mike who is now awake and blinking at the sudden intrusion of bright light. "Wakey wakey rise and shine, meet the day with a smile you great creator, or should I say great boozer!"

Mike mumbles. "Caruso was a drunk, so were Dylan Thomas and Vincent Van Gogh!" He rolls over onto his back, "So was his dwarf friend, Toulouse Lautrec, so I'm in bloody good company."

"Yeah but not Michael Angelo or Da Vinci, what about all that fitness bullshit last night at the pub? Wake me at six, I'm going for a run, was that bottle talk or just to impress the ladies?"

Mike stifles a yawn. "Both!"

"Okay, five minutes and then I'm off….. Lady won't wait."

At the mention of her name Lady starts to whine.

Mike sits up and waves them towards the door. "Don't wait for me, I'll make breakfast."

As Tane moves past the painting he stops and studies it again, with his head to one side. He is interrupted by Lady's demanding bark. "Okay, okay, we're off."

The painting is very good. Mike has captured the rugged coastline with bold strokes and earthy colours, and he didn't miss Tane's brief nod of approval. Over the years he has come to rely on his artistic opinion. Although Tane is a potter, Mike admires his precise painting skills and his intuitive colour sense and knows his critiques are usually right! He studies his painting trying to see it through Tane's eyes, then moves over to the window and watches as Tane and Lady leave duel tracks in the black sand dunes under the gently waving toitoi fronds.

Tane and Lady always enjoy their early morning run. The bright orange rays of the sun sparkle on the crests of the wind formed waves of black sand and highlight the nearby pods of red flax flowers where noisy tuis clutch the long stalks, inserting their beaks to drink the sweet nectar. On golden mornings like today, the sights and sounds never change. Mingled with the calls of the tui are the distant squawks of the kaka parrots in the pohutukawa trees, their chatter reverberating off the sandstone of the cliff face. The trees, somehow thriving in the cracks, still display splashes of crimson although it is well past Christmas. Everywhere is a symphony of sound and colour. The rustle of the toitoi, like brush strokes on a kettle drum. The flute, clarinet and oboe of the song birds and the staccato castanets of the cicadas. Rhythmically pulsing through all is the double bass, 'boom', 'boom' of the pounding surf.

Like city folk who have grown accustomed to the constant hum of traffic, Mike, standing nude under the outdoor shower is not aware of the sounds of the bush or the distant surf. The shower beside the back door is screened from the road by the cottage and by the overhanging puriri tree at the rear. He is enjoying the feel of the warm water squirting out of the large shower head and full of the joy of living, he starts to sing. His pleasant melodic voice silences the tuis who stop to listen. Turning off the shower he slips on his jandals and unclips the wooden pegs off a large beach towel hanging on the line. After drying himself he returns it to the same place on the line. Life is simple and good.

Waiting for him on an up-side-down beer crate are faded Dan Carter underpants and black rugby shorts. Once dressed, he enters the kitchen and hears the faint scratching of the scarlet bougain-villea vine scraping against the glass of the kitchen window. The breeze also flaps the net curtains and the sun illuminates a square patch of light on the wooden bench.

The kitchen, although basic, is neat and clean and practical. Copper pots hang from a beam above a wood fired stove. Picking up a metal rod he inserts the hooked end into a matching slot on top of the stove and lifts one of four circular metal plates and places it beside the hole. Poking the embers underneath he adds a handful of tea-tree sticks, then hooks the plate back into place again. Hanging the rod on a nail beside the stove he selects a large cast iron frying pan and adds fat from a pot that sits at the back of the stove.

Soon the pan is sizzling and giving off smells of lard, dripping, olive oil and smoky bacon.

Opening an old Kelvinator refrigerator, he removes a leg of ham and a tray of large brown eggs. Closing the door with an educated backward kick, he uses his hunting knife to cut slices of ham into the pan. Immediately the ham starts to splutter and sizzle and using his knife makes room for four golden yoked eggs. The same sharp knife slices four wedges of sour dough bread which are then placed on each side of a many holed pyramid tin toaster. Poking his knife in a hole at the top, he lifts it into position over the open hole on the stove top. Soon the room is filled with the smell of ham and eggs and toast and freshly perking coffee.

Mike's breakfast preparations are interrupted by scratching at the door and he opens it to Lady who looks up panting. Her mouth is open and her pink tongue hanging out the side. "Beat him again eh, let's see what we have for the dog person this morning."

Opening the fridge, he pulls out a beef leg bone, "Beef cordon bleu for the Lady, extra rare!"

She jumps up and takes it from his hand, rushing out the door just as Tane arrives.

Wiping the perspiration off his face, neck and shoulders with a towel, he pours two mugs of coffee. "There's something about coffee that I can never understand, it always smells better than it tastes, why is that?

After breakfast, a whistling kettle announces that the water is ready for the dishes which are neatly stacked in the sink. They debated buying a dishwasher but decided it was simpler doing it the old fashioned way. Whoever cooks, dries, so Tane pours the bubbling water over a cake of Taniwha soap in a perforated tin. With an "ouch" "ouch" he removes the tin and begins scrubbing the plates with a brush, rinsing them in a plastic pail of hot water before placing them on a leaner for Mike to dry.

Tane is the practical one of the household and he also keeps the finances straight. Although the owner, he is relaxed about housing his friend. They have a simple arrangement. Mike doesn't pay any rent but pays half of the running costs. Food and drink comes out of the kitty…. an old Buzzy Bee cookie jar. They have total trust so there are no disputes.

Nearing the end of the wash-up, Tane feels around in the soapy

water for the few remaining knives and forks, gives them a quick brush and then swirls them in the rinsing water before depositing them on the bench top. He pulls the rubber plug and gives the sides of the sink a wipe then dries his hands on a tea towel hanging on a line over the stove. "The kitty's getting low, only twenty dollars, so we'll need to top up soon, how're you fixed?"

Mike scowls and snaps his tea towel like a whip. "Bloody money!"

Tane shrugs, meaning there's nothing much he or they can do about it.

Mike puts his hand in his pocket, pulls out his phone and searches his contacts list. While it is connecting, he looks at Tane, "Jenny called last week and said they had sold two paintings, so there will be money coming to my account. I'll check. She mentioned something about a corporate job as well.... I'll see how that's going."

His phone, now on speaker, can be heard ringing and then answered by a bright female voice. "Hi Mike, how're you doing out there at the beach? It must be magic on a sunny morning... I'll have to come and visit, any more paintings?"

"It still throws me when you know who's calling, good thing I'm not on 'Chat', Tane and I are standing here in the nude!" He winks at Tane as they hear her say. "Next time call me on 'Messenger', much prefer face-to-face."

"Maybe, but you know how bad the reception is out here in the bush, ls 'Messenger' free?"

"Well it comes with your package plan, but nothing's free."

"You're right, that's why I'm phoning, you know, paying the bloody bills and all that!"

"I do know, boy do I know! Hey, a thousand dollars should be in your account today or tomorrow, that should help, eh!"

"Yeah sure will, thanks."

"No need for thanks, I'm getting my commission. Speaking of commission the Auckland Council want five of your paintings, five hundred dollars each. I've got the contract. Do you want to come in and sign it, I'll treat you to lunch, how about tomorrow?"

Mike turns to Tane and raises his eyebrows.

Tane gives him the thumbs up and Mike puts the phone back beside his ear, forgetting it's still on speaker, "Hey, that's great and sure, I'll come in tomorrow for lunch." He winks at Tane again, "Starving artists and all that, see you tomorrow, bye."

Dropping his cell phone into his pocket, he turns to Tane, "Fancy that five paintings for the City Council, great!"

Tane pulls a tea towel off the overhead line and snaps it like a whip toward Mike. "What about the luncheon oh starving artist, and what about Jenny's commission lover boy?"

Laughing, the two carry on a tea towel duel until one of the copper pots flies off the overhead beam.

Still laughing, Mike retrieves it and then turns back to Tane, "Speaking of money, how close are you to your next firing?"

"I need some help loading today. I guess I can wait for you to return for the unload. Just remember," He points an accusative finger, "While you are enjoying crayfish and champagne I'll be on Weetbix and water!"

Mike looks at him for a moment and then places an imaginary violin under his chin and starts to bow.

Departing the back door which is never locked, the boys are joined by Lady. who circles the men until she knows where they are going then takes the lead.

As they amble along the track they disturb the fantails that are hunting sandflies in a glade of pukapuka trees. It is only a short track and they soon emerge from the muted light and earthy smells into the sunshine of a clearing where the kiln sits next to Tane's pottery studio.

The homemade kiln is hive shaped and built of fire bricks. Being a furnace there are no windows only a chimney and a floor-to-roof rusting iron doorway that is just high enough for the men to enter without stooping.

The studio, a few steps further up the glade was once the New Lynn Railway Station. Braced and then cut into three sections, it was transported by horse and cart to its new location and used as a bushman's house. Now fitted with new windows along the front and a glass door, Tane gained more light by replacing two sheets of corrugated iron in the middle of the roof with corrugated plastic.

To heat the studio during winter, he used the left over bricks from the kiln to construct a not-too-straight chimney for a fireplace at the far end. Against the wall, opposite the front windows, are rows of shelving with drying pottery.

On the floor, linoleum sits on top of hardboard, to cover the uneven and worn planks making it easier to walk and clean.

In the centre of the room is a splattered, treadle powered, potter's wheel and two large lidded tubs of grey clay. A piece of hose pipe with a tap dangles above the wheel and runs the length of the rafters to the rear wall where it connects to an external tank filled with roof water.

Tane loves his studio and feels creative and at peace when working at the wheel or seated at his bench under the windows.

At this moment, covering the length of the bench is a fifty-piece dinner set of hand painted porcelain waiting for its final firing. This is exactly what attracted Tane to become a potter. It fulfilled his need to create. From the start he realised that he had an unusual talent in shaping clay into works of art. It was simple and effortless, as if his hands were being guided by an unknown force. He didn't know why he had the talent but knew that the creating of beautiful wares left him feeling complete and satisfied. Tempering this joy was always the fear that his creations would fail. Not because of his lack of skill, but because of other influences that would make his glazes run or bubble, or at worse, make his pottery explode!

Placing a stack of empty plastic bread containers on the bench under the window, he helps Mike load then carry them out to the kiln.

Lady knows that she is not allowed to nip at their heels at this time, so she keeps her distance and chases her tail, yipping with delight.

CHAPTER 4

The Satan's Sons Gang

Not far from Tane's pottery shed, but on the North facing slopes of the Waitakere Ranges is the headquarters of the Satan's Sons gang.

At the bush end of Henderson Valley Road, it is perfect for their clandestine meetings. At right angles to a country road, a winding gravel driveway snakes up a neglected ten acre farm to a level cutting where an old house has a commanding view of the valley below. Behind it is a large red corrugated iron barn with double doors and a small door leading to an attached side room. To its right is a pig pen and a milking shed. The house and the barn are in use, but the other buildings are overgrown with long tendrils of kikuyu grass.

Surrounding the cutting is a corrugated iron fence and a gate, all topped with rows of barbed wire. The compound's secluded, elevated position makes it an ideal fortress. Security cameras are placed among the ramshackle buildings and along the driveway. The control room, on the side of the barn is manned by an unpatched gang member. The control panel is networked to a matching one in Johnny's office. The security installation cost him more than he expected, but ongoing maintenance is now quick and cheap as he arranged sex for the married installer, then continues to blackmail him with the video evidence.

That is the way gang leader Johnny Ray Schmidt connives his way through life.

The house is for his use and his money man, Joey Moser and Sergeant and enforcer, Butch Gueber and two sex slaves, Carla and Kylie who share a bedroom beside the kitchen, where they also prepare meals.

Carla and Kylie are happy to do domestic as well as sexual duties as directed for and by Johnny. He makes sure his gang is evenly rewarded for their loyalty and financial contributions, but he is careful to rotate the favours making it an infrequent reward.

Carla Rae in appearance is what you would call nondescript, even mousey.

Kylie Temata, on the other hand, with her long shiny black hair, olive skin and big brown eyes is beautiful.

You may wonder why they would choose this way of life, but their up-bringing is typical of most of the girls who choose to become prostitutes. Both were sexually abused, frequently, at a young age by a much older person they trusted. This makes intimate sexual relationship confusing. What is the meaning of love? How does it relate to sex? Without loving parents or care-givers to guide them, they continue to make bad life choices and now under the influence of alcohol and drugs and easy money, they are easily manipulated. They don't complain about their obligations within the gang but there is a difference between the two.

Carla has no ties and welcomes the money, drugs and sex, while Kylie, a single mum, has two dependent children, Wiremu who is almost five and Caitlin four.

Kylie is biding her time until she has enough money to escape.

Johnny senses this, and gives her just enough money and drugs to keep her in check.

Both Kylie and Carla share the same need for physical and monetary security and it is hard to leave when they know that life with the gang is half the work for double the money out on the streets.

Joey is the newest employee, hired to manage the burgeoning legitimate businesses. Johnny knows this is a risk and does his best

to isolate him from his illegal dealings.

Neither Joey nor Butch, Johnny's enforcer, have wives or girl-friends, that is a condition of their employment. It is not a problem for Butch, who takes sex when and how he wants it. Cohabiting with another human being never crosses his mind. Joey on the other hand is desperate for female companionship but curbs his desires as he is concealing a dangerous secret. A secret that may be compromised by frequent intimacies.

Financially the gang's most lucrative venture is the manufacture and distribution of an opaque crystal with the pharmacological name of methamphetamine. In New Zealand where there is a tendency to shorten names as a sign of affection, methamphetamine becomes 'P'. Its origins come from a cynical usage of the nation's tourism brand, '100% Pure, New Zealand.' The fact is, P is not pure but one of the dirtiest drugs on the black market.

When the part of the brain that controls the conscience is blocked, a drugged person feels no remorse at committing the most heinous of crimes. The drug stimulates the brain so that the user is super alert and all senses are functioning to capacity. So much so that the user feels superior to all other slow witted humans. So on one hand they are functioning as a super human and on the other, without conscience.

Not only are the actions of the P user potentially deadly for the victims, but also for the users themselves! Highly addictive, exces-sive use will inflict long term mental injury as well as leading to convulsions, heart attack, stroke and death!

The Satan's Sons gang has other streams of illegal income; the sale of cocaine; marijuana and an ever growing list of artificial psycho stimulants. Prostitution is legal and that is also profitable and managed by Joey, Johnny's Bookkeeper. Cash is flowing in so fast that Johnny is forced to launder his money by buying legitimate businesses. Those also are in Joey's domain. Some of Johnny's business is neither legal nor illegal like the protection business and seemingly honest institutions that control poker machines!

Out of the same mould that made Adolf Hitler, Mussolini and

Muammar Gaddafi, Johnny Ray Schmidt controls his North and West Auckland empires without mercy or conscience. His determination to succeed is fueled by paranoia and a clinically low self-esteem. Also, like many tyrants, Johnny is not book learned but he is not stupid either. Often hampered by alcohol, P keeps him sharp and energised and compliments his superior intuition and people skills. The negative side is that his blood pressure is often dangerously high and that causes frequent headaches.

Early that morning, Johnny instructed Joey to purchase a beach house at Piha, a few bays north of Karekare.

Now midmorning, he steers his new BMW around another of the never-ending bends of Scenic Drive and sees at last the magnificent sweep of the beach, eight hundred feet below. It is one of his favourite places and he lowers the window to catch the smell of the sea and a better view of Lion Rock standing guard out in the bay.

Often, just to get away from Johnny and Butch he would drive to Piha and walk along the wide stretch of black sand enjoying the roar of the surf and the buffeting of the ocean wind. Always he would return refreshed as if somehow it had blown away his angst. Today he is on gang business, but that doesn't stop him from enjoying the view.

Johnny said the beach house was for R and R, but Joey knows it is for a more sinister purpose.

On the seat beside him is a suitcase containing a bank cheque for two hundred thousand dollars and two hundred thousand dollars in cash! The cash is on his mind, *'It's the amount that is going to secure my freedom and it is sitting beside me right now! Why not take the money and run? Is it a safer bet?'* He teases himself with the thought, but reason prevails, *'Yeah and every gang in New Zealand and Australia will bounty hunt my head!'* He sighs then says out aloud, "Forget it Joey, stay with the plan!"

Now at beach level, he is jerked back to reality by his GPS's authoritative but pleasant female voice. "Turn right on Glenesk Road, fifty metres."

He makes the turn and meanders inland along a sparsely populated valley that ends at the base of the ranges.

Earlier, when he was instructed to buy a house in the bush, Johnny made it clear that it had to be isolated from other buildings, the more remote the better.

Now, slowing at a straight piece of road, he pulls over to the side and reaching over lifts a piece of paper off the top of the suitcase to remind himself of the property's details. It is a printout from a Trade-me auction.

The three bedroom settler style house is owned by a local celebrity who writes popular children's books. Having never dealt with arty types before, he wonders if it will be easier or harder to buy her house?

The online auction did not reach the reserve of four hundred thousand, so he is hoping the same with cheque and cash will make for a quick sale. The gang's Lawyer, Keaton O'Nally QC searched the title and prepared papers for the author to sign.

Joey called the owner the previous day and told her that JS Holdings Limited was willing to pay the reserve price and asked when it would be a good time to visit. He didn't tell her that the four hundred thousand dollars would be half cash and the other half a bank cheque. Neither did he tell her the documents will show the purchase price as two hundred thousand dollars, not four. He knows he will have to convince her that it is a tax dodge for his company and not to be concerned. Most sellers are mystified, but usually agree. Every month he buys properties and businesses the same way. It sounds odd and it is, but it's his job to launder the bundles of cash that continue to grow. As he drives towards the house he knows that the property has been on the market for three years and she will be anxious to sell.

Escape to the Sun

At the bottom of Toronto, at Yonge and Queen, the travel agency is two levels below the arctic blast. An escalator takes you down to the shops servicing the commuters on their way to the subway station. It is ironic that Pacific Travels resides in this underworld as it relies entirely on artificial light and heat and pictures on the wall to create a tropical environment. The white light does no favours for a pasty faced agent who turns his attention away from a computer screen and then back to the expectant faces of the three ladies seated on the opposite side of his desk. "A good choice ladies, clean, green and very affordable!" Asking their names, he hands each of them a travel folder that contains tickets and an itinerary. Returning to his computer he takes a breath and then launches into a rapid monologue of their flight details. At its conclusion, out of breath, he looks up expectantly but is met with blank stares.

Julia realises that he is waiting for confirmation, so she nods.

Satisfied, he turns back to his screen, "As requested, the first night you are booked into the Auckland Backpackers Hotel, Queen Street." Again he looks up, "Are you sure you don't want to book other accommodation during your stay?.....no?...okay!"

With the business side over, he relaxes back into his chair, "I've

been to New Zealand and loved the place. I enjoyed the sun, surf, great food and the lifestyle. I wish I was going with you." Standing, he shakes their hands, "Thanks for choosing Pacific Travels, have a great holiday."

They depart clutching their escape tickets for three weeks of freedom and an exciting fifteen thousand kilometre leap into the unknown.

With a four-hour stopover in Vancouver, the nineteen-hour journey was more grueling than they expected as economy class leg room caused discomfort. Arriving in Auckland, stiff and tired, they vaguely acknowledge the cheery farewells of their airline stewards.

Jet lagged and lethargic, they push their no charge luggage trolleys out into a summer's morning. The piercing light jolts them awake. Never before have they experienced such bright light! Hurriedly donning sun glasses they make their way to a taxi van with a covered trailer attached.

The driver, a middle aged rotund Maori man, greets them with a friendly smile. "Where to ladies?"

Wendy, always the organiser, steps forward. "Backpackers Hotel, Queen Street please."

"No problem!" He extends his hand towards Wendy, "Hi, my name is Danny Topu, pleased to meet you."

Wendy with her English up-bringing is used to this formality and shakes his hand. The others find it a bit strange. Whenever do you shake the hand of a taxi driver?

As he swings the suitcases into the trailer he notices the luggage tags, "Canada eh, getting away from the cold. Don't blame you a bit!" He slides open the side door and gestures for them to get in.

Robyn and Wendy climb into the back while Julia opens the front door and pulls herself up into the passenger's seat.

Danny likes the boldness of the pretty girl, "Where you from?"

"Toronto."

"Great city! I've been there with a Golden Oldies rugby team. Went up the CN Tower." He turns and points towards the city, "We've got one of our own now." Realising that they can't see the tower from the airport, he turns back to Julia, "Good people Canadians, just like us Kiwis!" His laughter shakes his belly,

"Played at King City, you know it?…. About forty minutes North of Toronto."

Julia and Robyn nod.

There is silence for a few minutes as they absorb the sights and sounds of a summers day down under. They notice the traffic driving on the wrong side of the road. The men in shorts and colourful island shirts. The palm trees and brown skinned island women dressed in sarongs with a flower tucked above their ear, all very different from their own snow bound homeland.

Danny likes the look of his passengers and decides to help them. He glances briefly at Julia sitting beside him. "Holidaying or work?"

"Holiday."

"Good on you, glad you have chosen New Zealand." He nods, "We'll look after you."

Julia is not so sure she wants to be, 'looked after', but is too tired to protest.

Danny knows he's intruding on their privacy but persists knowing that he can help them to enjoy New Zealand, "How long?"

"Three weeks."

He nods. "That should be enough to see some of our country."

He is silent for a few minutes as he forces his way into the airport traffic.

Now on the outskirts, they pass by a huge sign that displays the words. 'Nau Mai Ki Aotearoa'. Beneath it in smaller letters, "Welcome to New Zealand." It is a reminder that at last they are really here, far from their frozen northern hemisphere homeland.

With the windows down, the warm breeze carries occasional wafts of unfamiliar but pleasant floral smells from an amazing variety of flowering shrubs and creepers. Everywhere they look the landscape is new and wonderful and they begin to relax.

Clearing the airport roads, they are soon on a major highway heading North to Auckland City.

Danny turns to Julia again. "Have you made big plans? Rotorua? Queenstown? Bay of Islands?"

She shakes her head. "We haven't planned anything Danny. The air fares were expensive so we have decided on a budget holiday, if you know what I mean."

He nods, enjoying her honesty,

"We'll go where it is inexpensive, has a beach and where the sun shines. We looked up Auckland on 'Google Earth'. There seems to be sandy beaches and harbours everywhere, like this!" She points out the window towards the waters of the Manukau flowing under their harbour bridge, "See what I mean!"

Danny laughs. "You can see better beaches than on the muddy Manukau." He looks upward into his rear view mirror, appraising Wendy and Robyn, then makes up his mind, "I know a place that's not far from here on the West Coast." He points to his left towards the harbour entrance, "It's called Karekare Beach and you can stay at Fahey's Homestay, have you heard of a Homestay?"

They shake their heads,

"It's like a bed and breakfast but with full meals. Not as large as a hotel and usually you have to share bathroom facilities." He is silent for a few moments allowing them time to think, "Been to Jean's place myself with the missus a few times. You have your own room and the place is almost on the beach. It's been there for years. Jean Fahey runs it on her own. Her husband died a few years back and she's a great cook, home style meals, if you know what I mean." He winks at Julia, teasing her with her own words.

She gives him a brief smile and he continues, "The meals are just like that!.. Not skimpy little fancy servings but real meals." He shakes his head, "You'll never leave the table hungry, no siree!" His thoughts take him back to the delicious roast lamb dinner during his last stay.

He glances at Wendy and Robyn again in his mirror, "I don't usually tell tourists about Jean's place because it's not really what they are looking for....... Somehow I think you will love it there. Jean is so hospitable, she treats you like family. There is one other thing you need to know about Karekare Beach, it has black sand, not your usual white stuff, but it's still sand!"

Julia is interested. "What makes the sand black? I've never heard of it."

"A volcanic eruption."

For the first time Julia realises there is more to Danny than a taxi driver. "A volcanic eruption?"

He points to his right. "Like One Tree Hill over there. It's a volcanic cone."

"I don't see a tree?"

"It was chopped down as a protest."

"Can't imagine that helping any protest. An innocent tree being chopped down!"

"It was one man's protest, a Maori protest. It's complicated."

Julia is interested and continues to stare at Danny.

He shrugs, "It was about land confiscation many years ago. The Council has planted replacement trees but they are still too small."

Julia can see that Danny is dark skinned so she suppresses her curiosity. "What about the volcanic eruption, did that happen in recent time? I mean, there's not likely to be another while we're here is there?"

He shakes his head. "Nah, nothing to worry about. No active volcanoes. Not in Auckland anyway!" He has researched many of the questions asked by the tourists over the years and enjoys giving them the answers. "Millions of years ago a volcano erupted out in the ocean just up from Karekare beach. The red hot iron lava on contact with the salt water exploded into sand and small rocks that eventually washed up onto the beaches of the West Coast." He glances in the mirror at Robyn and Wendy to include them in his story, "If you've come to New Zealand looking for heat, Karekare beach will give you that in bucket loads! The black iron sands get really hot in the afternoon. Anyway, just think about it and give me a call and I'll try and arrange it with Jean." He hands Julia his business card from off his dashboard, "It will cost you eighty dollars for the taxi ride over the Waitakere Ranges to the beach. It's about a two hour drive and I think Jean charges about sixty dollars per person per night, including meals."

They are silent for a moment and surprisingly it is Robyn who speaks first. "I've never seen black sand before, I think it will be worth a shot!"

Julia swivels to face her friends. "Okay with me, what do you think Wens?"

"I'm easy.... Sixty dollars for room and meal is very cheap... Converting to our dollar, it's even cheaper." She frowns looking at Danny in the mirror, "Danny are the beds okay, like they're not full of bugs and stuff? Are the rooms clean?"

He chuckles. "Nah and Yeah. There are no bugs and yes the rooms are extra clean. Jean would be soon out of business if they weren't She changes the sheets every day and the mattresses every two years. They're huge, super king size. I have always had a good night's sleep and the missus and I are not exactly feather weights." Again his belly shakes.

The ladies warm to his happy disposition and like his self-effacing humour.

Julia turns towards her friends. "If we can book in tomorrow, how long do you think we should stay?"

Wendy shrugs. "What about a week? I'm thinking it will take a few days just to get our feet on the ground. Lying on a hot sandy beach sounds pretty good to me, no matter what the colour."

Danny can sense her questioning eyes in the mirror again and looks up, "Danny, how basic is Faheys?... I mean it is a proper hotel?"

His protruding tummy vibrates again with laughter. "Wait till you meet Jean you'll see why you shouldn't ask that question. Look it's not the Royal York, but it is homey and spotless." He shrugs, "She may be full, I don't know. Do you want me to give her a call?"

Again Robyn takes the initiative. "Yes please."

Danny selects a number on his hands-free phone and it can be heard ringing.

The Fahey Homestay is an old eight bedroom kauri villa set high above a small tidal creek to allow for winter run off. It is painted white with a green corrugated iron roof. Protruding upward from the central ridge are brick chimneys painted green like the roof and at ground level a verandah runs the full length of the building. The house was built on one of the few flat patches in the valley and a small wooden bridge, without side rails, connects it to the main road. To the South is the beach and to the North the steep bush-clad slopes of the Waitakere Ranges.

Between the beach and the Homestay is Tane's cottage, with the kiln and work shed only a short walk away from her back yard.

Jean, portly and middle aged, is pegging clothes on the line when she hears her phone ringing in the kitchen. It is stridently mechanical and out of place with nature's more pleasant sounds. Hurrying, she enters through the screen door that closes with a bang and picks up the hand piece off the wall. Although out of breath, she still answers with a happy. "Fahey's Homestay, Jean Fahey speaking."

"Hi Jean, this is Danny Topu, remember me the taxi driver?"

"Of course I do Danny and your wife, uhmm…. Moana. How're you guys doing? Do you want a room?"

"We're fine thanks Jean and no, I wish we could! Listen, I've got three nice Canadian ladies with me just off the plane, they're looking for some relaxation, Kiwi style, for a few days. How're you placed and what are your rates these days?"

There is a slight pause. "We're not so busy now, so there is no problem with rooms. If they stay a week it will be sixty dollars a night including meals. If they stay two weeks I'll make it fifty-five a night, ask them how that sounds?"

"Don't need to Jean, I'm on speaker phone so they can hear you, pretty nifty eh!"

Jean screws up her face. "Oh dear this modern stuff, you've got to watch what you say!"

Danny teases. "And how you look!"

She instinctively brushes hair off her face and looks inquiringly at her phone. "Oh no, you can't see me, can you?"

He laughs. "Nah, just teasing, your equipment's not that flash!"

"Are you talking about me, or my phone?"

Danny chuckles and then looks at Wendy and Robyn in the mirror and then sideways at Julia. "So what do you think, do you want to make a decision right now?"

They look at each other and there are no objections, so Julia leans toward the phone. "Hi Jean, I'm Julia, nice to talk with you. We haven't really made any plans yet. Is it okay if we stay a week and then let you know if we want to stay longer?"

Jean likes the sound of the Canadian twang and knows she is

going to enjoy getting to know her guests. "Of course it's okay."

Wendy leans forward. "Hi Jean I'm Wendy. As you can hear, I'm English not Canadian, I live with Julia in Toronto."

Jean hears more than just an English accent, she hears a privileged upbringing.

Robin, seated next to the window, behind Danny, needs to speak a little louder. "I'm Robyn, Jean… the other Canadian."

"Welcome to New Zealand Robyn, I guess you must be pretty tired after your long flight. I'll make your stay as comfy as I can. When would you like to book in?"

The three look at each other.

Julia suggests. "Tomorrow?"

They nod and so she turns back to Danny, "Can you take us tomorrow?"

"No problem."

She leans towards the phone again. "It all sounds great Jean, we'll see you tomorrow, thanks for the welcome."

"Looking forward to meeting you, bye for now."

Danny adds. "Bye Jean."

"Bye Danny."

They both switch off.

Jean returns to her clothes line and unknowingly hums a happy tune. As she said, she's going to enjoy looking after her Canadian guests. It is a cruel irony of nature that those people who would make the best parents are often denied children of their own.

CHAPTER 6

The Potter, the Painter, the Romance Maker

Mike's nose is almost touching the canvas as he adds highlights with his palette knife. All his paintings are of the West Coast and its surroundings. He has experimented with other subjects and media, but each time returns to thick oils, the coastline, the surf and the black sands. Everywhere he looks there is another creation. He loves the contrasting colours of the coast and the freedom and the mystery of Karekare beach. It gives him joy and frustration as he attempts to copy nature with imperfect tools.

After years of experimenting, he has shortened the process. He instinctively knows which browns, yellows, orange, reds, purple, and black, capture the rocky cliffs and the craggy island sentinel out in the bay. He knows the many shades of green and the type of strokes required for the nikau; the silver and black ponga; the puriri, karaka and the fine straight edges of red for the pohutukawa; the rata and the broader swivel stroke for the kaka beak flowers.

Mike's talent is known throughout New Zealand, even though he has not entered competitions. He prefers the anonymity and luxury of being his own worst critic as his parents are rich. Being fearsomely independent, he never seeks their support, but it helps,

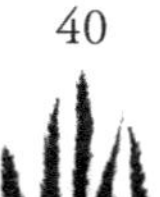

Swiveling away from his large canvas, he rinses his knife, wipes it clean and returns it to the paint box. Standing, he studies his work then mutters. "Something's missing." He studies it again and shakes his head. Looking down he notices Lady's quizzical look, "Okay let's go visit Tane."

Waiting for them at the pottery studio is the newly fired fifty piece dinner set arranged on the bench. The artwork is bold, simple and strong, with the dominant colour a wide ring of royal blue near the edge of all the pieces. At the edge is a thin band of bright orange that matches the orange streaks on the yellow nasturtium flowers, the central feature. The orange band is not hard up against the band of blue but separated by a thin width of white allowing the colours their own individual glory.

Tane, with his back to the door is so preoccupied with checking each piece that he doesn't hear them enter.

"What do you reckon you'll get for that lot?"

Almost dropping a bowl, he places it on the bench, then turns. "You gave me a fright!"

"Sorry, I thought you'd seen us coming." He moves closer to the glistening pieces and nods, "It looks really good, better than the nikau set, what did that sell for?

"Five hundred."

"You'll get seven fifty for this!"

"Maybe?.... If I was selling in New York, I'd get a thousand. Here, maybe five hundred. Again, hard to say, there are so many cheap sets around, even the Italians and Spanish are selling cheap." He shakes his head, "But they are crap quality. I bought a soup mug the other day and chipped off a piece of the glaze with my thumb nail, underneath was soft brick clay." Picking up a plate, he flicks it with his finger, "This is hard porcelain!" Stretching to take the kink out of his back, he continues, "Our market is so small, but I'm still getting sales. I think people are starting to choose quality over quantity."

Mike takes the plate out of his hand. "And bloody good art work!"

Tane smiles appreciating his friend's support. Sweeping his hand over the china he sighs, "Jenny tries her best I know it must be hard for her. How's your painting going?"

"It's finished, but there's something missing." He shrugs, "Do you mind taking a look?"

"Sure."

"I wonder if we should try and sell overseas, I'd like to give it a go."

Tane nods then stands. "Worth a try."

"Anyway, I'm good for finances for a couple of months, thanks to the City Council."

Tane nods again as Mike reappraises the beautiful display of china, "Go for a grand, it's worth it, and you're right we need to try overseas."

"My greatest need right now is for one of Jean's coffees, let's go!"

The track that leads from the pottery shed to the back of Jean's Homestay is a two minute walk. As usual, Lady who knows where they are going is already under the manuka branches. To hurry-up the slow-pokes, she stops often and waits for them to catch up before racing off with the thought of another delicious hand out.

Jean, looking out the kitchen window, sees Lady and hurries to open the screen door. Lady bounds up the steps and pushes her head into the kitchen. She knows she is not allowed inside, but at least she manages to block the door from closing and her nose has already told her what was cooked the night before. The smell is her favourite, roast beef. Saliva drips from the end of her protruding tongue onto the lino on the floor.

Messes like that never bother Jean as she really enjoys their company. From a motherly perspective, she thinks of them as boys and not as men and is grateful for their help with heavy chores and the occasional grocery item. Their reward is a big roast meal every Sunday evening. It never was an arrangement it just happened.

They have been friends for five years but it wasn't always that way. At first when she heard that a Maori boy had bought the cottage, old prejudices clouded her judgment and she was apprehensive. Now that she knows Tane and Mike, she realises that she was wrong, and treats them more like sons than friends and is impressed by their creative skills. The feeling is mutual, as the boys enjoy her motherly warmth and always look forward to her gastronomic meals. At the slightest excuse you will find them in her big kitchen chatting over a cup of tea or coffee and enjoying a plateful of home baked cookies. One day it might be sweet crunchy Anzac biscuits. Another, Afghans with a swirl of cocoa icing and half a walnut on top. Their favorite is hot left over scones smothered in strawberry jam and whipped cream. She doesn't only satisfy their sweet tooth. Sometimes she plays cupid for unattached females staying at the Homestay.

Tane and Mike push past Lady and enter the kitchen, seating themselves at a small table covered with a plastic, red and white chequered cloth. The table doubles as Jean's preparation area. Beside it, out in the formal dining area, is a much larger table and chairs made from solid kauri. This eight legged, sixteen seater is Jean's pride and joy.

She hands them a mug of coffee and then returns with fresh cream in a pitcher, a sugar bowl and two teaspoons. "Roast lamb on Sunday. I hope you will keep a good appetite and look respectable. We have three Canadian lasses coming to dinner and you might as well bring Gary, but spruce him up a bit.... Have you ever seen him use a comb?"

Mike cups his hands. "This is what he does. He fills his hands with water, splashes it over his head, then using both hands brushes backwards a couple of times. I don't think he uses a comb."

"Does he like girls, you know, date them?... I've introduced some pretty cute ones to him, but nothing seems to happen."

Tane laughs and shakes his head. "If you're asking if he's gay, no he's not!" He shakes his head again, "Nah, not Gary, he's just awkward around women. His mother walked out on his family when he was young. With two older brothers, I suppose being raised in an all male family made females seem strange, even a little frightening. I've watched him at the pub and the rugby clubs trying to chat them up." He pauses drinking his coffee, "He's bloody shy, that's all I can say."

Mike nods as Jean rises from the table. "That's too bad, well anyway buy him a comb and a toothbrush, now that I think about it, you know, small steps."

"It will take giant leaps for Gary kind." They laugh then sip their coffees and spread jam on yesterday's scones.

Next morning, Auckland city is again bathed in sunshine as Danny's taxi arrives at the Queen Street Backpackers Hotel.

Julia, Wendy and Robyn are already at the curb with their bags.

Danny jumps out and greets them with a wave of his hand, "Oha atu ki a koutou katoa."

As usual it is Julia who is direct. "Sorry Danny but I don't understand a word you're saying!"

He laughs. "You've never heard a Maori welcome before? It means welcome to you all."

Robyn asks. "Are you fluent in Maori?"

He nods.

"I like the sound of your language, it's kind of musical, almost like Italian"

"Actually oha atu ki a koutou katoa, is more than just welcome. It means that you are as welcome as one of our tribe."

"I like that too!"

Opening the side door of the luggage trailer, he swings Robyn's trundler and backpack up and in with ease.

This time she decides it's her turn to sit in the front, so Wendy and Julia climb in the back.

Having lifted the other bags into the trailer Danny closes the lid and locks it before pulling himself up onto the driver's seat and is pleased to see Robyn sitting beside him. There is an uncomplicated softness about Robyn that he likes.

Soon they are on a motorway that heads West out of the city. As he drives he takes a quick look at each of his passengers and notices the tell-tale puffiness under their eyes. "Did you sleep well last night?"

There is stony silence,

"Okay I'll change the subject." He looks at Julia in his rear view mirror, "Remember yesterday you asked me about volcanoes?"

She nods,

"Well those three hills over there." He points ahead, "They are volcanic cones about six hundred years old. The European settlers named them after their gentry." He points to the closest hill, "That's Mount Hobson." He points again, "That's Mount Eden... and there's Mount Albert.... English names eh!" Again he looks

in his mirror, this time at Wendy remembering that she is English, "We named them centuries before your ancestors arrived. There are a lot of places in New Zealand that have a Maori name as well as an English name."

"Do you mind that?"

"If it's a biggy, we get it changed. If not, it doesn't matter. You know the old saying, 'You can call me by any name as long as you don't call me late for dinner.' " He winks at her and again his tummy shakes with laughter.

Having left the lowlands of the CBD, ahead of them to the West is a long line of hills that extend across the horizon. He points, "Those are the Waitakere Ranges. We're going over the top and then down the other side to the coast. At the top there's a good view of the city and also the Tasman Sea, where we are heading." He nods his head towards the ranges. "Once we're up there, you'll get a close look at our native bush," He pauses to look in his rear view mirror again to see if they are listening.

They nod, so he turns to Robyn, "The Waitakeres are a protected forest and that means you'll get to see many of our centuries old indigenous plants and trees, I'll point them out to you."

With Auckland's volcanic cones beneath them, the taxi continues its climb up past the small township of Titirangi and onto Scenic Drive. The foliage is now so dense that the bitumen road, snaking its way up and around the bends is constantly under a canopy of various shapes and shades of green. Growing on the carved banks of the roadside, facing the sun, are bushes of blue and white flowering koromiko mixed with yellow honey suckle. Just above the smaller shrubs and ferns are fuchsia shrubs with their pink and purple lantern flowers and higher up, under the dark green of the puriri tree hang clusters of shiny deep red berries enticing the wood pigeons to eat. It is one of nature's cycles. The puriri trees feed the pigeons and their seed filled droppings sprout new growth.

Other than fishing, the bush is Danny's delight. From an early age he was taught bush craft and lore and now that he is an elder in his tribe, it is his job to hand on that knowledge to the next generation. He knows the Maori names of most of the plants, their food value and their medicinal uses.

Robyn, Wendy and Julia appreciate this unexpected tutorial and mile after mile find themselves becoming fascinated with the surprises of the forest.

The taxi is now high into the ranges and they catch occasional glimpses of the distant blue green waters of the Tasman Sea. Starting their descent around the many serpentine bends, Danny points to a massive tree on the edge of the road. "That tree is the king of the forest. It is called a kauri tree. Its origins are prehistoric." Danny senses their interest, "They were here when dinosaurs roamed the forests, you know, millions of years ago."

Robyn has a clear view, while Wendy and Julia are obscured by Danny's large back. Robyn is impressed. "What a huge tree! It does look prehistoric. Look at its bark, grey like the skin of a lizard."

Danny nods, enjoying her excitement. "That one is only a baby, maybe four hundred years old. The largest is up north in the Waipoua forest, it's called Tane Mahuta, meaning God of the forest."

Julia asks, "Do you know how tall it is?"

"Tane Mahuta?" He glances at her in the mirror and she nods, "I have driven tourists up to Tane many times, so I know the answer, it's one hundred and sixty-eight feet tall and forty-five feet around its trunk. I don't know what that is in metres or centimetres."

Robin asks. "Do you know how old it is?" He glances sideways at her appreciating her interest. "I've been asked that too. The experts aren't sure because they would have to cut it down and count the rings to get an accurate age. They guess it's somewhere between twelve hundred and fifty, and two thousand five hundred years old."

She nods. "That's about the same age as our redwoods in B.C."

He nods. "We have many ancient trees that you won't find in Canada, also insects and birds and a tuatara lizard that is older than many dinosaurs, in fact it is a dinosaur."

Robyn has a nasty thought. "Do they bite?"

He shakes his head, smiling. "Nah, it's small, about two feet long and eats moths, grubs and insects.... I must admit it is a pretty fearsome looking creature, something like those sea dragons of the Galapagos Islands." He glances in the mirror to see if they know what he is talking about.

Wendy and Julia nod as he continues,

"It's very unlikely that you will see one, they're on protected islands off the coast."

Robyn is relieved. She doesn't like the sound of the lizard, even if it doesn't bite!

Danny drives toward another much taller kauri tree that protrudes out onto the edge of the road. He points, "You can see why the tree is great for milling timber," He looks up, "See, there are no branches until near the top."

The ladies from their position in the van, have difficulty looking up, except Robyn, who lowers the window and pokes out her head. With the window of their air conditioned van down for the first time, the ladies are able to feel the warm moist air and smell the damp of the rotting vegetation. They hear the bird songs of the forest and the clatter of millions of cicadas.

The van passes close to the enormous trunk of the kauri tree and Robyn can almost reach out and touch it. With a last look at the green canopy high above, she withdraws her head and raises the window. Turning to Danny she nods, sharing his awe of the tree.

Catching her nod, out of the corner of his eye, he continues,

"It was almost milled to extinction at the turn of the century. As a protected tree it is now recovering, but it is facing an even bigger threat from tourists, like yourselves."

This causes a frown on all their faces. Typically, Julia asks the question. "Why us?"

"Thousands of tourists a day walk the tracks to the giant kauri trees. They don't know it, but fungus on the soles of their shoes is causing die back, a disease that is killing the kauri as surely as the early woodchoppers." Conservationists, both Pakeha and Maori are trying to close the tracks. If the die back continues, you won't be treated to the sight of one of our most precious treasures. We use the word taonga."

Wendy, always looking for a simple and practical answer, says, "Could we build boardwalks around the trees, or find an anti-bacterial spray?"

Danny likes her intelligence. "Smack on Wendy, that's exactly what is happening now. Who knows if will be enough to save the specie?" He pauses for a moment and wonders whether he should say more, knowing that his thoughts are taking him into the spiritual side of being a Maori. Glancing at Robyn again, then at Julia and Wendy in the mirror, he decides that they may understand, "You know, my people believe that all the trees are living creatures and protected by a God, Tane Mahuta."

Robyn turns to look at him, "Yes, the same name as the giant kauri tree up North. Before we kill anything in the forest we ask for forgiveness. I know that is hard for you to understand, but is part of our culture and beliefs." He looks at Robyn who nods, "To us the early settlers seemed barbaric the way they insulted our God. It made for trouble, as it did then and does now!" Danny, knowing that he has stepped way beyond the usual relationship between a taxi driver and clients who happen to be tourists, is silent for some time as he drives down toward the sea.

Soon the horizon is a long line of blue green water and clouds. Robyn sighs. "What a view, this is magic!".

Not far away, Tane, Mike and Lady slip and slide down a black sand dune at Karekare Beach. As always Lady bounds on ahead and then races back to playfully nip at their heels. They are happy in each-others company uniting in the freedom of the morning and the deserted beach.

They splash through the frothing surf to cool off before heading up the beach to the track that leads to their cottage, just visible over the tall toitoi grass.

Lady leads the way but turns off the track towards the creek where she laps the cool water. The sound of a van arriving at Jean's makes her stop, and as inquisitive as ever, decides to investigate.

Danny turns off the road and crosses over a small bridge and stops in the car park below the Homestay. The girls, not knowing what to expect, are fascinated by the old but tidy building. They clamber out as Jean comes bustling down the wide front stairs to welcome them.

It only takes a brief look at her guests to know that she will enjoy their company and that they will depart friends. She is gifted with this ability and is rarely wrong. Approaching the van, she greets Danny with the usual handshake. "Danny, good to see you again."

"It has been too long. I still think about your Sunday roasts!"

She taps Danny's protruding belly. "You don't look like you are fading away!"

He laughs. "Hey! I'm on a liquid diet, but it doesn't seem to be working!"

She wags her finger. "Beer is not a liquid diet, way too much sugar and it makes you hungry."

He taps his tightly closed lips. "Shsss, they will get the wrong impression, anyway Jean, meet your Canadian guests."

Wendy pushes herself forward. "Hi Jean I'm Wendy. Reaching forward she shakes Jean's hand."

Wendy turns towards her friends, "This is Julia, and this is Robyn."

They shake hands.

Julia and Robyn continue to struggle with this quaint and persistent handshaking.

Robyn blushes at the contact and Julia, even more reserved, is the last to offer her hand.

Jean notices all this without comment, just as Lady, with a welcoming, "woof!" bounds around the side of the van.

Robyn, at the sight of the fast approaching dog, lets out a shriek and cowers behind Danny.

Lady ignores Robyn and looks up at Danny with her tail wagging so vigorously that it makes her hind quarters sway.

He reaches down and strokes her black and white mane. "Don't be afraid of Lady, she's a lovely girl!"

Lady continues to wag her tail, sniffing up and down Danny's leg.

He turns to look at Robyn who is still afraid, "She won't hurt you Robyn, in fact quite the opposite, she'll protect you. She'll want to be your friend. Don't mind her sniffing. Her nose tells her everything; where you have come from; what you have eaten, and most importantly, what animals have been near you; she's just being nosy!" He laughs at his own joke as Robyn continues to peek out from behind.

She decides to explain her fear. "When I was young, a dog bit me

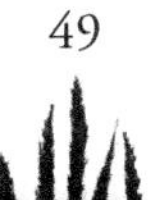

on the arm and I had stitches. I've still got the scars." She holds up her arm, "Since then I've been afraid of dogs. I can't even walk past one without breaking into a sweat."

Danny nods. "Lady probably senses your fear and is curious… Lady say hello to Robyn."

Lady has been watching him and when he points, she slowly approaches Robyn wagging her tail.

Robyn has her arms stiff at her sides and Lady licks one of her hands. Although her insides are screaming, she tentatively strokes Lady's neck, then when her courage fails, pulls away horrified with what she has done.

Danny smiles, "See, that wasn't so bad, by the time you leave here, you two will be great friends!"

Julia turns to Jean. "Is she your dog Jean?"

"No, I wish she was. She belongs to Tane a Maori boy and a very successful potter who lives over there." She turns and points towards the beach.

Julia, always wanting to buy something new and unique, is intrigued. "Can we buy some pottery from him?"

"You can ask him yourself on Sunday, he's coming to dinner with his mate, an artist friend." She turns and beckons with her hand, "Come on up, I'll show you to your rooms."

As Danny and Jean help carry the bags up the front steps to the veranda, Lady, satisfied with the new arrivals, ambles off in search of new adventures.

The ladies, approaching the heavy wooden door with its shiny brass knocker, stop to admire the old stained glass panels on either side. The yesteryear design of twisting vines with red roses and green leaves adds a welcoming touch. The door is open and the group step into a black and white tiled vestibule. It is as if they have turned back the clock to the nineteenth century. In front of them is a dark stained hat and coat stand with a small drawer in the middle and a head high oval mirror above. Up each side of the stand are polished brass coat hooks and on either side of the drawer are the handles of umbrellas with their points sitting in two copper tins on a lower shelf.

Jean points to the umbrellas. "It rains a lot in winter, you need those!"

They turn right, down a long hallway with a white domed ceiling edged with ornate cornices and see four closed doors on each side and one open at the end. It is the communal toilet and bathroom.

Julia is about to comment on this possible inconvenience, when Jean leads them into the first bedroom on the right. The room captivates them with its antiquated elegance. Apart from the modern rimu headboard of the king sized bed, it is as if they are in a room of a Charlotte Bronte novel. On the bed is a hand stitched Dresden Plate patchwork quilt and above it, suspended from the ceiling, is a Tiffany lamp. Everywhere there is new oldness. On each side of the bed are two matching, hand woven oriental scatter rugs, sitting on a varnished rimu floor. The skirting at the base of the walls is sculptured kauri boards that have been painstakingly scraped of their layers of old paint to expose their original golden grain. Above the skirting, vertical tongue and groove kauri boards, also scraped and varnished, extend upwards a third of the way. The remaining two-thirds is covered with embossed pink floral wall paper. It is not tight but rippling, being on top of many layers of wallpaper glued to the original hessian scrim.

To the left of the group is a black cast-iron fireplace surrounded by ceramic tiles that match the leaf and grape design of the lamp shade. The windows that look out onto the veranda are slightly open, held in place by cast-iron counter weights, concealed behind the sashes.

Before Julia can claim the room, Wendy sits on the bed and thinking of her previous sleepless night, bounces up and down. "This is mine!" Sighing she stretches out and sinks into its firm softness.

Leaving Wendy luxuriating on the bed, Jean takes Julia and Robyn into the room across the hall. It is identical, except the quilt is a Log Cabin and the view from the window looks out toward the bush-clad Waitakere Ranges. In the foreground, above the mown kikuyu grass is a long row of white sheets gently flapping in the breeze and propped up by a tall 'Y' shaped kanuka pole.

Julia, forgetting the inconvenience of a shared toilet and bath,

stretches out on the bed. "This will be just fine thanks Jean."

Jean, standing in the doorway, looks at Robyn and then points up the hallway past Wendy's room. "I guess that one will be yours, Robyn, I replaced the mattress yesterday so you are the first to use it." With a conspiratorial wink she grasps her elbow and guides her into the room, "Sometimes it's not at all bad to be last, oh, by-the-way, do you mind telling the others that the only booking I have this week has been cancelled so I'm all yours for the next few days. Actually I prefer it. I've been much too busy this summer… When you're ready come on down to the kitchen and have a cup of coffee or tea so we can get to know each other better. I've made some fresh scones and I think you will like my strawberry jam."

As Jean walks back down the hallway Danny appears having delivered the bags to the rooms. "I keep telling them that we don't tip in New Zealand, we are paid to do our job and that's enough."

"They're just used to it."

"Yeah but it seems wrong. I don't know, it seems somehow to cheapen my service."

Jean places an arm around his large back. "Can you stay for lunch?"

He chuckles. "I thought you'd never ask!"

Happily chatting they walk arm-in-arm into the kitchen.

It is later in the afternoon and the sun has moved onto its downward path and is now blasting through the side windows of Tane's cottage. This is ideal light for Mike to add the finishing touches to his painting of the beach. His concentration is broken by chatter and laughter. Looking up he sees three ladies in bikinis with rolled towels under their arms climbing the sand dunes. He moves to the window for a better look and they see him and wave. Taken aback, as if caught out, he returns the wave.

Wendy walks backwards so that she can have a longer look at the handsome blonde man in the window. "Do you think that is the potter Jean was talking about? He looks younger than I expected."

Julia pokes her with her towel. "And pretty darn cute eh!"

Robyn kicks the sand as she walks. "Look at this sand will you, isn't it strange, black as coal." She shifts from one foot to the other,

"Danny was right, this stuff is really hot!"

Soon they reach the top of the last dune. Stretched out before them is the long curve of Karekare beach with its flat black sand disappearing into the surf.

Wendy raises her arms above her head and pirouettes, "It's a day made by the Gods, look at that surf, isn't this heavenly. So remote and uninhabited, it's like we're castaways on an island, like Robinson Crusoe!"

Julia smirks. "If it's make believe, I'll settle for a Man Friday!"

Wendy turns and studies Julia for a moment. "Jules do you have a secret fantasy?" Wendy moves around in front of her and teasingly looks up into her face, "What romantic thoughts have you been concealing from me Jules girl, tell me more!"

Julia gives her a shove that causes her to tumble backwards, then races down the dune with Wendy in pursuit. At the bottom they continue to be showered by black sand from Robyn's bottom bumping descent above them.

Brushing off the clingy sand, Julia shouts. "Come on, I'll race you to the water." Discarding their towels, they run down the gentle slope of the beach enjoying the unfamiliar feel of hard wet sand under their toes.

Julia is the most athletic and with golden hair streaming behind her she looks like a Palomino horse.

Wendy is more like a Mustang with her shorter legs pumping hard.

Lagging behind is Robyn, and like a Shetland pony, is reluctant to run for anything.

They reach the surf and dive under the curling waves. This is what they came for and now like a dream it has come true!

Earlier, without being seen, Lady followed them as they passed by the cottage. Now lying on top of a dune she watches their play and can't resist joining them. Plunging down, she races across the sand and into the water barking and jumping and biting at the foam.

Wendy and Julia greet her with happy shouts, while Robyn pretends she isn't there.

Not far away, Tane at his potter's wheel hears Lady's faint playing bark. Knowing that Mike is painting, he is curious. Placing a wet cloth over a piece of green pottery, he leaves the shed and ambles down the track to the cottage. As usual the door is open so he enters the studio unannounced.

This time Mike is startled.

Tane moves past him to the window and watches the girls at play.

Mike, now aware of Lady's barking, puts down his palette knife and joins him at the window.

Tane turns to Mike. "Those must be Jean's Canadians. Lady might be making a nuisance of herself, I'd better check. Do you want to come?"

Mike shrugs. "Oh why not!"

As he passes his painting he stops and studies the same sweep of beach that he has painted in all its varying moods and realises he has never added a human component. Maybe that's what's missing? Shrugging he leaves the cottage and follows Tane along the track to the beach.

Now seated at the bottom the dune, beside the ladies' towels, they watch Lady encouraging Wendy and Julia to play the never-ending-game of throwing the stick into the sea. Having found a small piece of driftwood she is generously allowing them to take turns. Never tiring of the game she swims out, grabs the wood in her mouth and returns, dropping it beside their legs. Wanting to add more people to her game, she splashes over to Robyn who squeals and runs away. She thinks that is just great and chases after her which makes Robyn shriek even louder.

Tane stands and placing his fingers in his mouth, whistles a 'stop' command.

Lady immediately turns and races up the beach dropping the stick at his feet. Imploring him with her eyes, she doesn't understand his inaction, or why she should be told to 'stay', so she picks up the stick again and runs back to where it is much more fun.

With their backs to the dunes, the ladies did not see the men arrive until Tane's whistle. They see that the two men are tanned and that one is dark and the other fair. They recognise the man in the window. There is no mistake, they are attractive males and must be Jean's potter and painter friends.

Julia asks. "Shall we go and get our towels?" It is a rhetorical question as they adjust their bikinis and leave the water.

Lady doesn't like this change in the game and races toward them dropping the stick at Wendy's feet who obliges by turning and throwing it as far as she can out into the surf. By the time she returns, they are half way up the beach and she knows the game is over.

The men stand as the ladies approach.

Mike shakes the sand off a towel and holds it out to Wendy who is first to arrive. "This yours?"

"Doesn't matter they belong to the hotel, thanks, I'm Wendy." She takes the towel and makes a show of drying each of her short but shapely legs.

Mike waits until she straightens. "I'm Mike and this is my mate, Tane."

Tane picks up the remaining towels and hands one to Julia and the other to Robyn who is the last to arrive.

Julia smiles up at him. "Thanks, I'm Julia." She turns to Robyn, "This is my good friend, Robyn." She wraps the towel around her back, under her arms and then tucks it firmly in the front. Firm enough to push up her breasts so that they bulge out at the top.

Tane politely averts his eyes, a nicety not missed by Julia.

Lady, still hopeful, joins them with the stick in her mouth and drops it beside Robyn.

Tane walks over, bends down in front of Robyn and picks it up. Looking down at his muscular brown back, she hopes that her blushes are not obvious. Straightening, he smiles at her. "Lady will do that all day if you let her." She nods, returning the smile.

Julia walks over drying her hair. "Are you Tane the potter?"

He is surprised. "Yes, I am! I guess Jean has been talking and you must be her Canadian guests."

It's Julia's turn to be surprised and then trying to sound like John Wayne, drawls, "Word gets around fast in them thar hills."

Mike brushes wisps of blonde hair out of his eyes and decides to join in the fun. "Yeah, it's called bush telegraph." Sweeping his muscular arm around towards the green encroaching hills of the Waitakere Ranges, he tries his own drawl, "Yes pretty lady and we have plenty of bush around them thar hills!"

Everyone laughs and Julia turns to Tane. "I wouldn't have been at all surprised if your name had been Friday!"

"Friday?"

"Oh, it's okay, just a private joke!"

Still not understanding, he shrugs and decides it's not worth pursuing.

Wendy has now finished drying herself and copies Julia by wrapping the towel under her arms and around her large breasts and then squeezes suntan lotion onto her arms, legs and neck.

The ladies take turns helping each other to cover their inaccessible parts. When they are done, Wendy screws the cap onto the tube and walks over to Mike. "You said that Tane is your mate. In Canada and my country, England, it would mean you two are an item, you know, more than just good friends! Is that what you are? I'm sorry for being so direct, but I don't want to say the wrong thing."

Mike looks at her for a moment and then at Tane who is chuckling.

Wendy blushes knowing she has asked a very personal question.

Mike sees her discomfort and puts her at ease by shaking his head. "Mate in New Zealand means best friend. Partner on the other hand means something very different. As you say, more than just good friends! But seriously Wendy I don't mind you asking." He looks toward Tane, "And I'm sure Tane doesn't mind either. We don't care about that sort of thing, some of our best friends are gay."

Secretly, the girls are relieved as their good looks adds an unexpected excitement to their stay at the beach.

To change the subject, Julia looks around and opens her arms wide capturing the breadth of the beach. "This is heavenly, Mike. Fancy having all this beauty to ourselves." Bending down, she grabs a handful of black sand and watches as it slips through her fingers, "This black sand is amazing!" Looking up she points to a clump of tall white topped grasses swaying in the breeze, "What are those tall fluffy things called? They look like horses' manes."

Mike follows her gaze. "The common name is Prince-of-Wale's feathers. Tane calls them toitoi, that's their Maori name."

She stands and studies Tane closely, looking at his dark skin. "Jean says you are a Maori, Tane, but you look kind of European."

Tane is surprised once again by such a direct comment. "Wow you Canadians don't beat about the bush do you and yes I'm Maori with Dalmation on my father's side."

Mike decides to tease his friend. "This beach is owned by Tane and his tribe, the Ngapuhi, you are supposed to get his approval to be here."

Curiosity aroused, Robyn looks up at Tane. "Really, you own this beach?"

He shakes his head. "No, we look after the beach. We don't believe anyone can own a beach. It's like a living person. The sand is its skin and the sand hills are its body. The grasses and shrubs its hair and the rivers it's veins. The tide comes in when it is awake and goes out when it sleeps and it storms when it is angry."

He shakes his head again, "You can't sell a living body, or put a fence around it or own it! The slave traders tried that and you know how that ended." He turns towards Mike, frowning, "Mike is just taking the piss!"

Julia frowns. "What does, taking the piss mean?"

"It means taking the mickey. Have you heard of taking the mickey?"

"Oh sure, but taking the piss is a very strange expression, where did it come from?"

Tane looks at Mike who shrugs. Neither of them had ever thought about it before. "We haven't a clue, hey I'm not boring you with my Maori stuff am I?"

Julia shrugs. "How can we be bored. Here we are under your sun on a magical beach miles from anywhere with two interesting guys telling us about their land and ancestry, what's to be bored about." She looks at her feet, "The only thing that is making me uncomfortable is this sand, it's getting a bit warm for my tender Canadian tootsies, can we cool off in the water?"

As the group move toward the wet sand, Lady who has been sleeping in the shade of a toitoi plant, slides down the slope and grabs the piece of driftwood from out of Tane's hand and then circles them ready to play again.

Whether it was intended or not, Julia has gravitated towards Tane and Wendy towards Mike. Robyn has the company of Lady, who continues to try and include her in her game. Time after time she drops the stick at Robyn's feet and then is forced to retrieve it herself. Eventually they arrive at the water's edge and at last Robyn condescends to throw the stick into the water. It is not a very good throw, but Lady thinks it's wonderful.

With the cooling water surging around their feet, Tane turns and points northward toward the end of the beach. "Just around the corner is Bethell's Beach, named after a Pakeha family that cleared the land. Before that it was on the maps as Waitakere Bay, but the local Maori say neither is right and that its proper name is Te Henga, meaning the sand that looks like an upside down canoe."

Julia asks. "What does Pakeha mean?"

"Anyone who is not a Maori, or of Polynesian descent."

"The Maori do seem to have the naming rights."

Mike turns to her with a grin. "You and Tane are going to get on just fine!... But seriously, while you're in New Zealand, I'd stay away from talking about racial things, there are some nutters out there."

Robyn, who is standing close, nods. "You're right, boy do we know all about nutters!"

The girls laugh.

Robyn sees Tane's frown and touches him on the arm, "Hey, the nutters are not you two, heavens no, we're talking about the ones we left behind in Canada!"

Tane is relieved, worried that he had devulged too much of his ancestral heritage.

A large cloud momentarily blocks the sun making Robyn aware of the close by cliffs. She points. "I find the cliffs kind-of threatening, like they're watching us!" She shrugs, "Maybe it's all this talk about your Maori beliefs Tane."

He nods, "You are not wrong. We feel it too, that's what attracts us to this place. It's a sanctuary yet dangerous. I have often sensed a strange foreboding.... Maybe it's because I know an ancient story about this beach. You wouldn't know it, but this beach is tapu, which means it's sacred. We believe the spirits of the dead still haunt this beach."

Engrossed in his story, with his black wavy hair, gently moving in the sea breeze, Julia is entranced by his dark good looks and can picture him as a Maori warrior.

He turns and points to the southern end of the beach, "See that peak in the distance above the cliffs. Many centuries ago there was a Maori fort there named Kaka Pa. The daughter of the Chief of the Pa fell in love with a young warrior from another tribe. Unfortunately the other tribe was their enemy.... I guess it was something like Romeo and Juliet in Maoridom.... Anyway the affair was not only unacceptable but punishable by death! The two lovers had to plan their meetings with care." He pauses and looks at Julia. "A high price for love, eh!"

She nods.

"Although at great cost, they devised a plan so that they could meet each other. The boyfriend would sneak down to this beach at night, burying himself in the sand and breathing through a hollow reed. Each morning the Chief's daughter would look for the reed, sit beside it covering it with her cloak. By raking the sand away from his face, they kissed and made plans to runaway together. Her father became suspicious of her strange morning ritual and spied on her for a few days. It was the unusual spreading of her cloak and strange movements that gave her away. At last understanding what was going on, he rushed down to the beach and pulling her aside drove his spear into the sand killing her lover."

Turning towards a high rocky island out in the bay, he continues "That island out there was built by her as a cairn for her lover, it's called Tikinui. Over the centuries, erosion has moved the beach back to where we are now."

Julia frowns. "That is not a nice story Tane, I hope it is not true."

He nods. "There's usually some truth in Maori legends."

Wendy, feeling uncomfortable, looks up at the sun. "This sun is too hot for my winter skin, we'd better get back to Jean's." She looks shyly up at Mike, "Maybe we could see you tomorrow?"

Tane, concerned that he may have again said too much, says to

Julia. "We've got a seven-a-side tournament tomorrow. Would you like to come?"

"Seven-a-side, what is that?"

"It's summer rugby, a shorter version of our winter game."

Wendy nods. "It's played all around the world, something like CFL but without padding and helmets."

Julia wrinkles her nose. "That primitive, I should have guessed. Sounds like a typical man's game."

Mike corrects her. "Actually women play it too. In-fact Canada has very good men's and women's representative teams, I'm surprised you haven't seen them on TV."

The ladies shake their heads, "If you would like to come, we'll take two cars and some unfortunates are going to have to travel with Gary our wild mate."

Robyn slightly concerned, asks. "How wild?"

"He's unique, seeing's believing."

Both men laugh which leaves her still not any the wiser, "The tournament is being played at Helensville a country town about an hour north of here. If you want to join us we'll pick you up after lunch at twelve thirty, how does that sound?"

They look at each other and nod.

Tane is relieved, making a mental note to curb his story telling. He has another thought, "Oh and bring your togs, we usually go to the hot pools for a soak."

Julia asks. "What sort of hot pools? Are they man made heated water or natural spring water?"

Tane looks down into Julia's wide blue eyes and appreciates her faultless features. "Yeah they're natural. Hot mineral water bubbles up from underground. Everyone says the waters have healing properties, but who knows?... Whatever, it is really relaxing, I'm sure you will like it."

Julia nods as Wendy says. "Love hot pools!"

Robyn asks with a frown. "What are togs?"

"I guess you'd call them bathing suits or swimming trunks."

Julia laughs. "How about bikinis?"

Tane knowing he is being teased, punches her lightly on the shoulder.

Robyn still frowning, adds. "Togs? Sounds more Roman than Kiwi!"

In single file the group leave the beach, while Lady, already bored with all the talk, is chasing the screeching red beak gulls at the edge of the surf.

CHAPTER 7

Ukuleles and a Murder

On an inner road on the north-western side of Rarotonga is a hand painted sign wired to a fence with an arrow pointing inland to the base of the hills, 'PRISON CRAFTS FOR SALE'. As the permanent population of the Cook Islands is only fourteen thousand it is not a large prison.

A paved exercise yard is surrounded by buildings on three sides. The largest, to the South, is for administration. To the West are sixteen cells facing inwards. The third block, to the North, is for ablutions and a large work room where ukuleles are made for the tourist trade.

Surrounding the whole complex is a high-wire perimeter fence, more to keep visitors out than to keep prisoners in. Escapes are rare as there are few places to hide on the small island. To the West, towering above, is Hospital Hill covered in thick tropical growth.

Already the word is out that Dan has arrived at the prison. It is no surprise as the Henares have always been trouble makers. For generations their name has been linked with ill temper and no regard for authority. Some of the current inmates are his relatives and the whispers already have the amount of smuggled money as five million dollars! So Dan is a bit of a celebrity and there is an excited buzz around the cells.

Over the past few hours at Police Headquarters, Detectives brow beat, cajoled, threatened and even offered protection if he would confess to the knowledge of the money. Having talked to Inspector Robert Vaiili, head of gang control Auckland, and younger brother of their own Commissioner, they even pretended to know exactly where the two million dollars came from and where it was going!

Dan's silence is partly a Christian belief! At the arrival of the Missionaries, the Cook Islanders, being spiritual by nature, embraced Christianity and wove it into their daily lives. In his youth Dan was an altar boy at Saint Mary's Catholic Church at Aorangi and now, subjected to interrogation, remembers his Priest's teaching. "Let what you say be simply 'yes' or 'no', anything else is of the Devil!" His silence was being even more obedient to God than to his New Zealand gang. The Police, mistaking his silence and angelic smile as insolence, decide a spell in prison will loosen his tongue. A snitch will relay everything they want to know anyway.

Convenient for Ah Chung, but disastrous for Dan, the lead story on Cook Island TV that night was the confiscation of a reported six million dollars and the internment of the suspected smuggler in the local jail. It only takes a moment of thought before Ah phones his cousin, Tattoo Chung, one of his supervisors and enforcers and asks him to come and have a chat.

The following morning, the roosters are crowing, but there is still only half-light when Tattoo checks that there is no movement at the rear of the property and then quickly makes his way to the spiked rear entrance gate. Disarming the alarm, he opens it just wide enough to squeeze his chubby body through, then shuts it with the faintest of 'clicks'.

With his camouflaged rifle bag slung over his shoulder and dressed in matching Red Army fatigues and a floppy hat, he soon disappears into the undergrowth and moves up the hill beside the road. It would be easier for him to use the road, winding its way up to the hospital, but he can't afford the risk of being seen. His year of intensive training with the Chinese Army in sniper warfare, returns, stripping him of any emotion or conscience and he is now a focused killer. There is no hurry, as he has been told that the prisoners regularly exercise in the courtyard at eight o'clock. Clicking open the lid on his night watch, he calculates that he has three hours to get himself into position. It is fortuitous that his cousin built on the North side of Hospital Hill, not far from the hospital parking lot with a track leading down the South side to the prison below.

Nobody sees or hears Tattoo's progress through the bush as there are no dwellings except for the Hospital on top of the hill and at this hour of the morning even the patients are asleep.

Half way down the track on the south-side, he finds what he is looking for. The clearing is up a bank, just high enough to be out of sight, with only the branches of an overhanging flame tree obstructing his view of the prison, five hundred metres below. Unzipping the bag that contains the British made sniper rifle, he is reminded of how much heavier it is than the more familiar gas fired Chinese rifles.

It was brilliant of Ah to decide to use the foreign rifle as the 8.5ml. bullet, once found, will point to Big Ben not Beijing.

Pulling the folded butt out of the bag, he sees the small red, white and blue of a Union Jack stuck on the side. It reminds him that he is holding a weapon that is proven in Afghanistan, Syria and Iraq and capable of killing silently with pinpoint accuracy from a distance of fifteen hundred metres.

Now prone, he reaches forward and re-arranges the barrel mounted bi-pod so that the telescopic sight is level with his eye, then adjusts the focus. The distant white basketball court markings on the central enclosure are now sharp and clear. He is so focused on his deadly preparations that he is not aware of the fragrant smells of the overhead flame tree, frangipani and cassia flowers on either side, or the agitated squabbling of a flock of mynah birds close by.

After an hour, the still, clear, Rarotonga morning, typical for this time of the year, has clouded over with the start of an ocean breeze. That suits Tattoo just fine. He checks and adjusts and checks again the telescopic sight and the strength of the breeze and then uses the remaining time to cut branches with his machete to construct a bower around the shooting sight.

With the camouflage complete, he is satisfied that a passer-by will not detect anything amiss.

Half an hour later, the sun is now well above the horizon and he can feel the heat under his army shirt and he begins to sweat. Opening the lid on his watch he sees that it is now eight o'clock and there is activity starting in the court yard below. In ones and twos the prisoners emerge into the sunlight and then back into the shade of the building walls as they circle around enjoying their relative freedom and the morning sun. Their movements are slow so he can focus with ease on their faces and can see their silent speech, hi-jinks and laughter.

One prisoner emerges on his own and stops and seems to look directly up at him, but Tattoo knows that he is looking at the hospital, perched high above.

Zooming in, he sees the koru on his neck and he knows that he has found his man. Slowing his breathing, he twists the stock beneath the barrel slightly to the left with his left hand and then right with the other, so that the rifle is locked firmly in his grip.

Pulling the butt tight into his shoulder he is now ready to shoot.

Suddenly a group of young men descend on Dan, slapping him on the back and shaking his hand and his target is momentarily obscured.

Tattoo swivels the rifle on its bipod as he follows the progress of the group. They move out of sight for a few moments as they pass in front of the ablutions and ukulele block and then emerge into the sunshine in front of the cells and administration.

Three times the close knit group circle the basketball court and there is no clear shot. Breaking the routine, a basketball is bounced to Dan and he takes a couple of paces and shoots a jump shot that misses. He laughs and calls out for the ball again and positions himself at the top of the circle, bounces the ball twice and then shapes to shoot.

He is looking straight at the rifle when the bullet flicks through his forehead with just the smallest of holes but shattering his skull at the rear. The basketball stays in his hands as he slumps to the ground.

Dan is instantly dead.

Tattoo adjusts the rifle downwards and studies his victim, searching for any sign of life. His close scrutiny is interrupted by the arrival of stunned and bewildered prisoners and a guard.

Dismantling and then packing the still warm rifle into its bag, he scatters the branches of the bower, pockets the spent shell, checks for further evidence and then moves quickly up the track toward the hospital.

Twenty minutes later, just before he reaches the car park, he moves into the undergrowth and cautiously descends through the bush to the back gate of the house. Safe behind the high protecting walls, he begins to relax.

Opening the rear door next to the kitchen he enters the food storage room, turning briefly to wave to Wah Lee the cook who is stirring scrambled eggs in a large wok. Behind Wah Lee is Leilani Henare, kitchen hand, who is loading bread into a toast machine. She has her head down so he is sure she hasn't seen him, but he is wrong! Closing the door, he removes the bag off his shoulder and props it against the wall as he searches for a suitable hiding place. Deciding on the moveable vegetable bin, he pulls it away from the wall, places the bag underneath then pushes it back into place.

Leilani saw Tattoo as he entered through the back door and something about his furtive movements made her drop her stare when he turned to look in her direction. She has never liked Tattoo Chung. Whether it is the way he looks at her or the fact that he never smiles, or whether it is just that her intuition tells her that he is dangerous, whatever the reason, she keeps her distance. So she is curious about what he is up to and even with the door shut, hears the squeak of the roller wheels of the bin when it is moved and then again when it is pushed back into place. She knows it is odd that he is in that room, as he has never been in there before! Glancing up as he exits the room, she sees that he no-longer has the long thin bag on his shoulder.

On returning home that evening, she hears the dreadful news that her brother Dan has been shot that morning in the prison courtyard over the back of Hospital Hill and not far from the kitchen where she works!

Going to bed early she stays awake thinking about Tattoo Chung. Her instincts tell her that Tattoo's furtive behaviour has something to do with her brother's death. Tossing and turning she eventually drifts into a fitful dream filled sleep and wakes suddenly when a gun explodes close to her face.

It is still dark and her pounding heart subsides once she realises that it is only a nightmare. Now fully awake she has an urgent curiosity to find out what was in that long thin bag. Dressing quickly, she slips out of the house before the cocks start to crow.

The gates at the front of Ah Chung's house are opened by her cousin Pita. He waves to her from inside the guard house and wonders why she is pushing her Vespa down the driveway to the kitchen. She must have run out of petrol again. Helped by the half-light of early morning, she inserts her key into the lock of the kitchen door. Knowing that she has half-an-hour before the cook arrives, she finds the cupboard with the torch inside and switching it on, points it at the floor then follows its circle through the kitchen into the hallway by the back door. Gently opening the door of the food storage room, she closes it carefully behind her. She is immediately enveloped by the pungent smells of ginger, garlic, onions and bananas and the sweeter smell of jasmine wafting in through a small slatted window. Pointing the torch to the left she sees the large rectangular storage bin with its sloping lid. The unit is supported by caster wheels that she heard squeaking yesterday morning. With effort she slowly pulls one end of the bin away from the wall and out into the centre of the room. Kneeling behind it, she shines the torch under the bin, nothing there!

As she stands, the torch shines on the sloping underside of the shelving and she sees that it creates an alcove with the base of the bin. Her heart skips a beat, there is the bag resting on the base. Shocked by the discovery and its meaning, the colour drains from her face. Switching off the torch, she listens for any noises coming from the interior of the house. Knowing she is in danger, she turns her head left and right straining to hear even the faintest of sounds.

Nothing!

Her nerves are on edge and she is afraid, knowing that her worst fears are about to come true that the bag contains a rifle!

Leaving the torch off, she bends down and pulls the canvas bag out and places it on the floor.

Studying it in the early morning light, she can see it has a shoulder strap and a handle in the middle and two small leather straps with buckles fastening a flap at the top. Untying them, she holds the middle handle with one hand while pulling the folded butt of the rifle out with the other. The large telescopic sight catches on the bag, but she perseveres and soon the empty bag falls to the floor.

Placing the rifle on top of the bag, she moves over to the door and listens, holding her breath.

All is quiet so she returns to the rifle and kneeling, picks up the torch and switches it on. On the side of the folded butt, is a small Union Jack with the maker's name below, 'Accuracy International' and under that, 'Model-L115A3'.

Reaching into the pocket of her shorts she pulls out a restaurant order pad with a small pencil attached and copies the make and model number onto the cardboard at the back.

The quiet of the night is suddenly shattered by a rooster crow close to the window. Startled, her heart starts to race which galvanizes her into action. Sliding the silencer on the end of the barrel back into the bag, she pulls the bag up and over the stock and then covers the folded butt, buckling the straps. Bending, she returns the bag to its hiding place.

As quietly as she can, she pushes the heavy bin back against the wall, then gently opens and closes the storage room door behind her. Crossing to the kitchen, she returns the torch to the cupboard and then turns on the lights not bothering to silence her usual noisy breakfast preparations.

The day seems longer than usual and she can't wait for her fifteen hour shift to end. Her last duties are to load the dishwasher, wipe down the benches and sweep the floor. At eight thirty, she hangs up her apron, makes sure her pad is in her back pocket and leaves the kitchen, locking the back door before departing the car park.

All day she has been wondering what she should do. Should she tell her cousin Miriama who hired her? Should she tell her cousin, Pita, at the front gate? Should she tell her mother or father who are still shocked and mourning the death of their son? She is hardly aware of the other traffic as she zips along on her Vespa scooter.

Throughout her young life, whenever Leilani is troubled she always turns to the wisest and most caring person she knows and that is her grandfather and Chief, George Henare. She always knew that he was named after the English King, the ruler of the British Dominion and Emperor of India, but to her, he is far more important than that.

Although late in the evening, she can see that he is watching TV, so she parks by the front steps and seats herself on the tiled floor, resting her back against the padded front of his sofa chair. Without speaking they watch their favourite show, an old rerun of Home and Away.

George knows that something is bothering her, as it is unusual for her to visit so late. Reaching forward he strokes her hair, something that he has done since she was a small child, now grown up, she still enjoys his loving touch.

Closing her eyes, she can feel her tension ease and for the first time in two days, begins to relax.

Since her grandmother's death a year ago, she has visited him during the weekends and spent time doing household chores, cooking meals and washing clothes. For her they were not chores but an opportunity to give back some of the unconditional love that he has given to her over the years. She knows he is lonely, but he never complains.

Home and Away fades to black and a commercial starts so she swivels around to face him. "Granddad, you know how Dan was shot at the jail."

Looking down at her anxious face, he raises questioning eyebrows and then nods, "Well I think I know who shot him, and I don't know who to tell."

George picks up the remote and switches off the TV, then pats

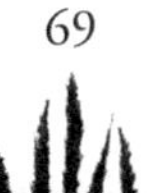

the sofa beside him. When she is seated, he reaches over and holds onto her small hand. "That is serious stuff Leilani, you'd better tell me all about it."

"Well, yesterday morning I was in the kitchen at the Chinaman's house when Tattoo Chung came through the back door dressed in army clothes and he had a long bag over his shoulder." She reaches over and squeezes his arm with her other hand, "You remember Tattoo? I told you before how he is really scary."

He nods.

"There's something about him that frightens me!"

George nods again, wondering where she is heading.

"Well I was at the other end of the kitchen by the toaster and I don't think he saw me.... It was the way that he sneaked through the back door that made me suspicious. I knew he was up to something. Anyway he goes into the store room next to the kitchen and shuts the door. I could hear a bin being pulled out and then pushed back again. When he came out he didn't have the bag. I didn't think anything of it at the time until I heard about Dan being shot!.... I couldn't sleep last night so this morning I sneaked a look behind the bin and found a rifle inside that same bag. I have its name and number."

She reaches behind and hands him the pad.

George studies the scribbled message for a moment and then lifts and drops their clasped hands. "Can I keep this?"

"Sure thing.... what should I do granddad?"

"Leave it with me, don't worry yourself any longer, I'll make a few inquiries and then decide what to do.... Have you told anyone else about the rifle? What about your mum and dad?"

She shakes her head. "No one knows, only you!"

"Good, keep it that way, I'll talk to your mum and dad myself."

He pauses thinking, "Do you mind telling me what the rifle looked like? Did it have a telescope? Did it have a silencer on the end of the barrel? Can you remember any of that?"

She nods. "Yes it had a telescope and a thing on the end of the barrel and it had a couple of short legs folded under, I had trouble pulling the bag off it."

Leo nods again and gently taps her on the leg. "Go and have a good night's sleep... okay?"

She nods and he kisses her on the top of her head.

Leilani, with the load lifted off her shoulders, stands and kisses him on each cheek, not minding being scratched by his whiskers. Stopping at the bottom of the front steps, she turns and waves goodbye before roaring off down the coconut palmed driveway on her noisy beat up scooter.

George looks at his watch and decides it's not too late to call Leo Maana, the Paramount Chief. "Hi Leo, sorry to call so late, but I think we need to talk. It's about my grandson's death in the jail.... Is it too late to come over?"

"Not at all George, it will be nice to see you again. It's terrible news about Dan... Come over as quickly as you can."

"Okay, I'm on my way."

George turns the key in the ignition of his old Corolla, a surprise Christmas gift from Dan and as he grips the steering wheel, memories of his grandson tear at his heart. Tears flow from his eyes and he shakes his head as he thinks of how that lively, happy Altar Boy is now stiff and silent in a body bag in the mortuary.

Leo Maana's house is inland, high up on the sides of Mount Raemaru and built on old tribal land. Befitting his Paramount Chief status, his house is modern by island standards. It is built in the traditional shape of a vaka and because of its elevation there are few biting insects and other low-land pests. With most of its folding doors along the veranda open, he has a clear view of George's car lights below him on the ancient coral road of Ara Metua.

As a lower Chief, George greets his Ariki with eyes averted.

Once formalities are over, Leo, still holding George's hand, requests him to talk with him as an old friend. With protocol removed, the two look at each other directly and their smiling eyes greet one another with the combined memories of one hundred and twenty years. Unspoken is the bond of their Puaikura ancestry, their personal likes and dislikes, their weaknesses and their strengths and above all, their love for each other.

Leo has always liked, but more often been annoyed at the spark of non-conformity in the Henare family.

George in turn understands and admires the quick decision making and ruthlessness of Leo when he is forced to take incisive action. Contrary to public perception, the Ariki of the Cook Islands still controls the popular thought and culture of the people, just as it was in the ancient times, before the Missionaries. Never mind that the Papa'a democratic system reduces their powers.

Two white wicker chairs, facing each other, sit on an old finely woven moenga under the gentle 'woosh' 'woosh' of an overhead fan. Leo points to one of the floral patterned cushions and then seats himself on the other. "So my old friend what do you want to tell me about Dan Henare?"

George looks at him for a moment, as he organises his thoughts. Reaching into the pocket of his shorts he pulls out Leilani's order pad. Reversing it so that the cardboard back is exposed, he hands it to him. "That is the make of a rifle and its number that my granddaughter, Leilani found at the Chinaman's house. Miriama your granddaughter hired her to work in the kitchen." Leo nods as George continues, "She found the rifle just after Dan was shot yesterday morning. I asked her what it looked like and she described a sniper's rifle."

Leo studies the scribbled information and then taps his finger tips on the cardboard as he considers his next move, "Albert has been asked to investigate the shooting. I have already talked to him. There is little information at this time except that he knows that it was probably a sniper bullet that killed Dan. You know that Dan belonged to the Satan's Sons motorcycle gang in New Zealand don't you?"

George nods.

Leo gestures with both hands, "Maybe the gang wanted him dead, who knows? Two million dollars is a lot of money!"

"I thought it was five."

"No, two million…. that is what Albert says."

They are silent for some time thinking about the shooting.

Eventually Leo clears his throat, "I'll give my son a call." Reaching over, he picks up a cell phone from a side table and selects a number. Without an apology for calling so late, he greets his son and then comes straight to the point, "Have you found the bullet that killed Dan?"

Without hesitation Albert replies, "Yeah we have, and it has been sent to New Zealand for a forensic report. We should have an answer back tomorrow." There is a moments silence, "Why do you ask dad, do you know something?"

"Well maybe..... Dan's sister, Leilani who works for the Chinaman Ah Chung found a sniper's rifle at the house and wrote down a description of its make and beneath it a number. I have them with me, do you want them?"

"Yes please…. very interesting….. Just a minute I'll grab a pen and paper." Again there is silence, "Okay, shoot!"

"The rifle has a small Union Jack on its butt and beneath it the words, International Accuracy and a serial number, L one one five A three." Leo can hear his son's deep breathing as he writes. "Give me that number again."

"L-one-one-five-A-three."

"Got it. I'll let you know tomorrow, it may be something, it may not. We have to be a bit careful with the Chinese, they have connections right up to the Prime Minister. So you're going to have to keep this to yourself, is that okay?"

"Sure son, thanks." He looks over at George and then turns back to his phone, "Keep Leilani out of it if you can…. she could be in danger."

"No problem, I'll talk to you apopo, papa. Meitaki, aerera." The phone clicks off and Leo places it on the side table, then sits up and looks at George. "Between you and me, if the bullet and the rifle match and my son and the Police don't take action, we'll do the job ourselves. Okay?"

George nods then stands, shaking Leo's hand as he departs.

Leo follows and then waves from the veranda calling out to George as he opens the car door, "Aere ra George."

CHAPTER 8

Rugby, Pool and Julia's Story

Out front of the Homestay, two open top Jeeps come to a sliding halt, showering stones and clouds of dust. Lady, standing on the back seat of Tane's Jeep adds her barks to the welcoming beeps.

Julia, Wendy and Robyn, sitting on a swing chair on the veranda, wave then walk down the curved concrete path to the carpark. Julia goes directly to Lady and gives her a welcoming rub, so Lady licks her face. Grimacing, then removing the moisture, she climbs up onto the front seat beside Tane.

Lady doesn't like this arrangement and quickly sticks her head between the two.

Gary is already seated beside Mike in the other Wrangler, so Wendy and Robyn climb in back.

Mike turns and greets them with a cheery. "Morning ladies, this is our mate Gary."

Half turning, he mutters a muffled greeting. Having accomplished what he had been dreading, he disengages by looking out the window.

Robyn is attracted by his shyness and taps him on the arm. "Tell me about your seven-a-side game Gary, what's it all about?"

Caught off guard, his mind is blank until he sees the rugby ball at his feet. Lifting it up with his foot he clasps it in two hands pointing one end towards her. "Well you have this ball, see, that you run with and try and get it to the other end and the other team try to stop you. If you get the ball over the line more times than the other team then you win the game". Expertly rotating the ball, he makes a passing movement, "You can't throw it forward like in gridiron, only sideways and backwards... Oh, I guess you can win with penalty goals and conversions as well!"

Robyn, ignoring the last complications, leans over and takes the ball out of his hands. With difficulty she spins the ball. "Seems simple enough."

He rocks his head from side to side, meaning yes and no. "Well yeah, nah, you get smashed sometimes."

She frowns. "Don't you get hurt?"

"Nah, only at the start of the season, like now when the ground is hard."

Mike turns, smiling. "No brain no pain!" Reaching over he gives him a playful slap on the back of his head.

Jolted, Gary returns the smile, happy to be the butt of a joke. Robyn doesn't like that. "I'm not sure I would like to see you getting smashed Gary. He wobbles his head again. "Yeah, nah, it's not so bad, it just looks worse than it really is. When you're playing you don't feel the knocks. It only hurts when you get a bad injury like a hammy or kicked in the guts."

She raises her eyebrows. "Kicked in the guts, doesn't sound like fun. What's a hammy?"

Mike answers. "Pulling or tearing the large muscle that connects the rear of the knee to the pelvic bone. It's very painful and means you are sidelined for three or four months."

Wendy asks. "Do you have a good team Mike?"

"It's okay, but we're always short of players. There's not many of us out here in the bush. We rely on a lot of ring-ins. We have a retired All Black playing for us today, Mark Elias, he's still pretty quick, we'll need him!"

Gary interjects. "Mark may have been an All Black, but Mike

and Tane are still the best players in our team."

Mike laughs. "I don't think Mark would agree."

Lady, losing patience with the chatter and inaction begins to yip, so Tane calls out to Mike. "All set?"

Mike nods. They reverse out of the car park with engines revving and race over the little bridge turning left onto a loose stoned road leaving trails of dust that drifts slowly towards Jean's sheets hanging on the line.

The open top Jeeps provide little protection from the wind and the girls soon give up trying to keep their hair in order, or to chat, so they relax and abandon themselves to the fun of the ride.

They feel more than hear the heavy beat coming from the car's stereo. This is freedom and they wave their arms above their heads in time with the music. Happiness is what they have been seeking and it is like a balm for their winterised souls.

By the time the cars turn into the Helensville Rugby Club, they are relaxed, wind burnt, refreshed and ready for new excitement.

The club's building is typical of many rugby clubs throughout New Zealand. A large hall sits above cement block rooms. These ill lit, spartan catacombs house equipment, showers, toilets and changing rooms. Exterior, anchored to the block wall, facing the playing fields are concrete steps planked for seating. The building, painted in the club's colours of yellow, orange, red and white is garish, but it adds a bright splash to the otherwise monotonous greens of the rural valley.

In one corner, under the stand and closest to the car park, is the tuck shop manned every weekend by volunteers from the Junior Club. As the cost of the yearly subscription is deliberately low, the tuck shop and weekly meat raffles are the main source of income. This income also helps the slim finances of the Senior Club. The tuck shop is always well patronised. On offer is scalding hot coffee and tea, hot meat pies, deep fried chips and battered hotdogs on a stick with free tomato sauce. Only the best locally made pies are sold and it takes special skill to eat one without burning your lips.

Everyone enjoys the tuck shop as it provides some fun on a bleak winter's morning. The tuck shop is a much loved Kiwi icon, just as important as the BBQ, a game of touch, or cricket on the beach, fishing for snapper, blue cod and crayfish, or eating pavlova.

The Waitakere team's changing room is alive with happy chatter and the 'clip-ity-clip' of cleats on the concrete floor. Seated shoulder to shoulder in the small room, the players are in various stages of undress, exuding smells of sweat, dirty socks, liniment and a variety of deodorants. The team is a mixture of differing ages, size and nationality. This is the strength of rugby in New Zealand, where race, religion, sexuality or social standing have no part in the enjoyment and camaraderie of the game.

Tane, Mike and Gary receive the expected insults for being late and Gary pulls and pushes a few of his team mates aside to make room.

As youngsters, Tane and Gary were in the same classrooms at Waipu, a small beach community North of Auckland. But it was the love of rugby that made them best friends. During the winter months, they arrived early to school for a game of touch. Then again at lunch and finally a quick game after school until the bus driver tooted.

While the northern hemisphere kids are kicking soccer balls, New Zealand kids are honing skills that will one day make them All Blacks, rugby League players and Black Ferns.

Tane, always the captain of one of the teams, would choose Gary because he was his friend and because of his size and strength.

Gary returned the favour by never missing a touch; vigorously competing for the ball and then passing it to his nimble footed captain.

Years later when Tane left for the city, Gary followed. Although different types of people with different skills, they still remain friends and they still play rugby together.

At first, when Mike joined them at the cottage, Gary was jealous but that soon passed and the fun began. What binds the threesome is their mutual happiness; zest for living and the expectation that the world's their oyster.

After a while, Mike needed more room for his paintings so Gary bought a cottage next door, returning most evenings to watch TV or play cards at the kitchen table. When he is with them, he is content, although confused why they accept him as their friend.

For their part, there is nothing about Gary that they don't like. His job as a builder's labourer is physical but stress free. He is funny, reliable and honest and his likes are their likes and he epitomises K. I. S. S. Keep it simple, stupid.

In winter, the rugby fields are long grassed with frequent patches of mud, but in summer the clay soil mixed with river sand is baked hard and the grass cropped close to the ground. The conditions are ideal for fast, open, sevens rugby, but unforgiving when a player hits the ground.

The Helensville tournament involves eight teams and there is a winner's and loser's competition, so that each team plays three games. Because of the hot conditions, the large playing field, and only seven players per team, the game lasts only fourteen minutes. With two fields, side by side the competition is over in three hours. This suits the dairy farmers who can play and socialise and still be home for their evening milking.

The Waitakere team have drawn the home side for their first game and as Tane, Mike and Gary run onto the field, the girls clap and cheer. Not used to the noise, the large cows in a nearby paddock lift their heads with dull eyed surprise.

The game is hard and fast, and the boys, aware of the girls watching, play with heightened power and guile.

Robyn, Wendy and Julia, caught up in the exciting ebb and flow of the game, jump, clap and shout their support. They are surprised at the guys' unexpected athleticism and strength which adds to the occasion.

Gary has never played better and keeps checking to see if Robyn is watching. She is and not only enjoys his prowess but also the way he protects his friends from over-zealous play.

The full time hooter goes and the teams straggle off the field.

Waitakere win the game, with Tane and Mike scoring most of the points.

Tane is still breathing hard when Julia joins him on the field, placing her arm in his. "That was really exciting Tane. I never guessed. You really are a star!" He nods vigorously, still trying to catch his breath, which makes them both laugh. Enjoying the feel of her arm in his, he turns towards her. "You know, that is the first time we have beaten Helensville, you brought us luck." He smiles down at her happy face, "Do you like our game?"

"It's great, there's a freedom to it. Not structured like Canadian football. I can see why you like it. I'd give it a go!"

He nods. "I've seen you run, you'd be a natural. Our next game is against either Mahurangi or Wellsford." He points to her watch, "What's the time?"

She pushes her wrist up toward his face and he nods again, "We only have ten minutes between games, so I'd better get back to the guys."

Not far away, Wendy has singled out Mike and like Julia, links her arm with his. Being considerably shorter, she is forced to quicken her step to match his longer stride. "It's terrific the way you three play, like an ice hockey line."

He smiles down at her. "That's part of the fun, we understand each other's moves, it's a great feeling."

Wendy teases. "Will you teach me some moves, maybe I'd like the feeling?"

He laughs then gives her arm a squeeze. "You would!"

Robyn, watching her friends, approaches Gary, who is dawdling behind. He gets alarmed when he sees her coming. "Gary you were terrific you're just as good a player as Mike and Tane." He kicks his boot into the grass. "Aw, I dunno, it's my job to set them up for the tries."

"I bet you could score just as many if you really wanted too!"

"Yeah I guess I could, but it doesn't matter we won anyway!"

"I was cheering for you, did you hear me?"

He nods, smiling down at her. "Yeah, I was playing for you, thanks!"

She holds up a bottle of juice. "I've got orange juice, do you want it?"

The offer and the look in her eyes, reminds him of his mother who many years ago gave him a wedge of orange at half time. Not used to any kind of affection during those early years, the memory was stored away. "Hey, I'm not used to that, thanks a lot!" Confused by his emotions he looks over at Mike and Tane and starts to move away. "I'd better join the guys, see you later."

Robyn calls out. "Have a good game, play well, bye!"

He turns and waves with the bottle of orange juice in his hand and an unfamiliar glow in his heart.

The Waitakere team link arms forming a circle around their coach as he talks about their semifinal opponent, Mahurangi. They disengage with the usual 'hoop-laa' and high fives before running out onto the playing field.

As artistic celebrities, Tane and Mike often mingle with the rich and famous. At a recent party they met Mark Elias, ex All Black who is always available for a friendly game. He agrees, with the bribery of free beers, to join them in the tournament. Four years out of international rugby, Mark still likes to keep fit, renew old acquaintances and of course enjoy a beer or two. That is the usual payola for being a favourite son of an adoring public.

With the addition of a fourth good player, the Waitakere team are too fast and strong for Mahurangi who form a line after the game and clap their opponents off the field.

Gary is asked to lead as he uncharacteristically scores the most tries!

The final, which is twenty minutes in duration, is against a composite team from Whangarei. With a much larger population, their starting lineup and their bench is far too strong for Waitakere. A team of four good players against a team of seven good players will always lose. Whangarei speed up the game and Waitakere are pushed to exhaustion.

The final whistle blows and it is Waitakere's turn to clap the victors off the field.

When Robyn approaches Gary, he mumbles an apology. "Sorry we lost Robyn."

She strokes his arm. "You were great Gary, I was amazed how hard you played, you must be exhausted."

He nods. "Thanks, but I hate to lose"

"Hey, you won two out of three and you are the runners up!"

"Yeah! I guess you're right…. That's the best we have ever done!"

Robyn clenches her small fist and punches him lightly on the arm. "There you go!"

As the group walk towards the grandstand, Tane turns to the ladies. "We won't be long, grab yourselves a drink at the bar. Oh, and you'll have to sign the visitor's book at the door, liquor regulations and all that!"

Upstairs a large crowd is gathered. The attractive ladies with their Canadian twang are soon the centre of attention.

Julia, not used to open faced flirting is defensive but secretly flattered. The hopefuls soon drift away when the men arrive smelling of shampoo and deodorant.

Mike points to their large handles of beer. "You could have bought smaller ones you know."

Wendy frowns. "Why should we?" She raises her mug towards Julia and Robyn who do the same and they clink them together, "Cheers!"

At the bar, a group of fans surround Mark Elias, hoping to relate a story to their work mates. Cocooned by all this reverie, over the next three hours he will slip into a state of happy inebriation.

After another round of drinks, Mike suggests they head for the Parakai Hot Pools, they all agree.

The hot therapeutic water has been enjoyed by New Zealanders for many generations. The park like grounds in front of the two large pools are shaded by huge magnolia trees. Their white satin, plate sized flowers decorate the horse shoe driveway leading to the entrance. The original wood lined pools and shacks of the eighteen eighties have long since been replaced by two large, modern concrete pools, one outdoors and the other enclosed.

The men already up to their necks in the hot water of the covered pool, watch the hesitant entry of the girls down the steps. They grip the central railing as if that somehow will reduce the stinging heat. Dressed in their bikinis, their "oooh!" and "aaahs!" are not the only thing that attracts the attention of the other bathers. Gary, Mike and Tane are aware of the appreciative looks and enjoy that these are their ladies.

Gary has eyes only for Robyn, feeling a possessive pride he has never felt before.

There are envious looks as they sidle up to their men who are supporting themselves with arms outstretched on the edge of the pool.

Julia rests against Tane's arm. "Hey Maori boy are you trying to cook me?"

"It's great eh!" Scooping a handful of water, he watches as it spills out of his palm, "These are miracle waters. No more aches or pains, and yes you would be tasty with a side dish of kumara and puha!"

"What are kumara and puha?"

"Maori food. Kumara is a sweet potato and puha a type of thistle. It tastes a bit like bitter spinach. Jean always cooks kumara with her roasts, so you'll get a taste. Hey, we're joining you for a roast at Jean's tomorrow night."

"Great!"

She leans forward and turns towards Wendy and Robyn. "Hey guys, the boys are coming for dinner tomorrow night, it's a roast meal and we'll get to eat a Maori sweet potato."

Tane adds. "It's called kumara."

The girls repeat the word, "koo-mah-rah" and enjoy the way it rolls off the tongue.

Wendy hearing Julia's comment about being cooked, is sure she was taught that the Maori were cannibals. Turning to Tane. she asks. "Didn't you used to eat us.... you know, cannibals."

He is surprised by the question. "Yes we did, but that was a long time ago.... We were always short of meat, but the real reason why we ate our enemies was to gain their mana and strength and protection from their ancestors." He gently pokes her with his finger,

"You white folk taste like pork!"

"You're having me on!"

Gary enjoys the banter. "No he's not, it's true!"

Mike stretches out and kicks his legs a few times before turning around and pulling himself out of the water. "Tomorrow will be roast lamb, no Pakeha!"

Robyn smiles. "Well, that's a relief, I don't fancy my mouth being stuffed with an apple!"

Gary wonders what Robyn would taste like, and then realises that it is an inappropriate thought and looks away.

The soothing waters relax their tired muscles and the bright chatter gives way to occasional small talk and then silence.

Gary turns to Robyn. "Would you like to try the water slide?"

She asks cautiously. "What is that?"

"I think you'll like it. You sit on a rubber mat and shoot down a twisty tube."

"Well I'm not sure, but I'll have a look and see!"

Wendy and Julia are surprised because that is so not timid Robyn.

Julia lifts her hand out of the water. "Look my hand is wrinkled, I'm ready to go sliding!"

Wendy says. "Me too!"

Outside, towering over the two pools are large, twisting, plastic tubes. Hot mineral water is pumped to the top and it swirls downward at an ever increasing speed. To reach the top, the sliders have to carry their rubber mats up a spiral staircase.

Robyn picks up a mat, to the surprise of her friends, as they can all hear the muffled screams of the sliders in the tube.

Gary stays behind Robyn and by the time they reach the top the others have already been shown how to hold and sit on their mats. Close beneath them, large volumes of steaming water cascades down the opening of the tube.

Julia holding onto the top of the mat dives in first and her scream is soon swallowed by the first bend.

Tane jumps in next, followed by Wendy and Mike.

Robyn listens with apprehension to Gary's instructions, takes a deep breath and dives in. She is so afraid that her scream chokes in her throat as she is swept away.

Concerned, Gary follows, yelling. "Hold onto the mat Robyn!"

They twist and turn and bump against the sides as the flow of water pushes them ever faster until like corks out of a bottle they are jettisoned into the pool below.

Laughing and spluttering, Julia clambers out first. "That was fun, I'm going again!" Just behind her, Wendy pulls her bikini bottom into place and yells. "Wait for me!"

As the two hurrying bodies climb the stairs, Robyn puts her hand on Gary's chest, shaking her head. "Half way down I flipped up-side-down and every time I tried to breath, I swallowed water.... I tell you, it was no fun, I'm not going again!"

Gary takes her hand off his chest and holds it at his side. "Hey, I'm not fussed, it's kids' stuff anyway, I'm happy to stay with you."

She moves close to him and clasping his other hand, provocatively looks up into his hazel eyes. "Don't let me spoil your fun Gary!"

Only his mother had ever held his hands like that before, and it stirs up long forgotten memories. "You're not spoiling my fun Robyn…. I'd rather be here with you." He shrugs, "Than anywhere else! I'm really sorry I talked you into going on the slide."

"It was my choice. Julia and Wendy have been telling me that I should be more adventurous, so for once I was, thanks to you." She squeezes his hands again, "You know something, you are a very nice man!"

"I am?"

"Yes, I like you more than I can say."

At that exquisite moment, the Devil-may-care Gary becomes serious. "And I like you too, Robyn. You are only the second person to say that to me."

"You have a girlfriend?"

He laughs, squeezing her hands. "No silly, my mother."

They are silent for a few moments before he asks, "How long are you staying in New Zealand?"

"Three weeks, why?"

"I'd like to spend as much of that time with you as I can."

Suddenly feeling insecure, he adds, "If that is okay with you?"

"Silly you, of course it is!" Removing her hands she possessively links her arm with his, "Let's get a coffee and wait for the others."

Once seated in the coffee shop beside the pool, Gary asks. "Are you hungry?"

She nods. "That's what holidays do to me, I'm hungry all the time!"

"Good, there's a pub across the road that has great food. Have you eaten in a Kiwi pub before?"

She shakes her head,

"It's an experience, piles of food and cheap!" He has a sudden thought, "Is Jean expecting you back for dinner tonight?"

"She asked us that before we left. We guessed we would be eating out. I think she was expecting it." She shakes her head, "You know what, she told us to be careful! Fancy that, just like a mother!"

He nods. "She's like a mother to all of us. I'll get the coffees, what do you want?"

"A trim milk cafe latte with extra trim milk on the side please!"

Gary gets up with a frown, rehearsing under his breath. "Trim-milk-cafe-latte-with-trim-milk-on-the-side."

An hour later, the group enter the large dining room of the Parakai pub. It is clean but sparsely decorated. Everything is either chrome or white and red, like the ceramic tiles on the floor, or plastic like the red flowers at the centre of the tables. Red and white were the favoured colours in the sixties and every new owner of the pub saw no reason to change. Now half a century later, it has returned to fashion as art deco.

Marie the Maori kitchen hand is standing behind the counter with pen and paper ready to take their order. Behind her is the cook, Hinemoa. While Marie is young, pretty and lithe, Hinemoa is large, middle aged, and very much in charge. The menu looks appetising and Wendy orders crumbed snapper.

Robyn avoids the deep fried food and chooses teriyaki chicken salad.

Julia goes for the more robust beef stroganoff, while the men order the special, T Bone steaks, eggs, onions and chips. Not asked for, but added is a small portion of mesclun salad with orange nasturtium flowers on top, an unexpected nicety.

Hinemoa, in an oversized white chef's jacket covering the top of

her large jeans is wearing sanitary gloves and her long black hair is trapped inside a plastic cap. Wiping her hands on a towel, she waddles over to the counter. "Hi yous guys, I'm Hinemoa the cook. The meals will be ready in about half an hour. Go and have a drink, I'll send Marie when they're ready." She studies them for a moment, "I'd recommend the private bar for yous lot, the other's pretty rough." She waits a moment for her warning to sink in, "There's a motorbike gang in the public bar, you'd think they owned the bloody place the way they carry on!"

From where they are sitting, they can see the small private bar with a number of retirees playing poker machines. Ignoring her advice, Julia leads them past the private bar and into the busy public bar. It has a T.A.B. with a large TV showing horse racing and on one wall a row of closed dart boards. What attracted her attention is a faded pool table in the middle of the room, and that is the game she loves. As the cook warned, many of the patrons are gang members. There is also a splattering of farmers, a few rugby players from the tournament and the unemployed.

There is a noticeable drop in chatter as they size up the new comers.

Once the assessment is over, the usual boisterous hub-bub returns, punctuated every so often by loud intoxicated laughter.

To discourage the group from staying, two gang members, play-ing at the pool table, stop to offer their opinion on how lovely the ladies look and that they would be better lovers than the faggots with them. This is accompanied by leering, sneering and bent wrists. As the newcomers do not react they return to their game.

Mike, Tane and Gary are uncomfortable knowing that they are placing their women in danger.

Tane grasps Julia by the elbow. "I think we should go to the other bar!"

Mike nods. "I agree!"

Gary, who is not afraid of anyone, says nothing, but is aware that Robyn has moved closer to his side.

To the surprise of the men, except Wendy and Robyn, Julia says. "This is okay, this is fun, I haven't played pool for yonks and I have every right to be here. Who'll buy me a beer?"

Gary is quick to offer. "I will."

Julia smiles. "Thanks, I'll have that Liberty beer we had at the rugby club."

Wendy nods. "Same for me!"

Robyn asks for a glass of sauvignon blanc and then hands him some money which he is too polite to refuse.

As he departs, Julia turns and studies the tough looking men at the pool table. The biggest, who seems to be the leader, is a blue eyed Caucasian with grey hair pulled back and tied in a ponytail. His grey streaked moustache is tobacco stained like his gold capped teeth. Beneath his mouth is a thinning, clipped, V shaped beard. He has few tattoos apart from black dots on each of his knuckles, but he has many rings in his ears and eyebrows and a couple in the side of his nose. His shoulders and neck are covered with long grey hair which protrudes from under a faded black singlet and his track pants disappear into the top of black leather motorcycle boots. He exudes aggressive authority. Sensing the gaze, he stops lining up a shot and looks up glaring at Julia until she looks away. Then he says in a voice loud enough for all to hear. "Broads make me nervous!" Sighting along his cue stick, he knocks the black ball into the opposite corner, and as he returns to his stool, he picks up one of two twenty dollar bills from the end of the table.

Gary returns with a tray of drinks and Julia ambles over and places a twenty dollar bill against the other.

Tane starts to get off his stool but is stopped by Wendy. "It's okay, she knows how to play, she's very good, wait and see."

The big man, who is Johnny Ray Schmidt, gang leader of the Satan's Sons, is surprised by the challenge. He smiles at her but his eyes are cold. "You want to play with me little lady?" Again the gang laugh, "The rules are, you set up then break. If you lose I keep the money and you come home to my place, clean the dishes and wash my undies." Getting off his stool, he bends over and scratches his backside. The gang laugh as he turns to face her again to see if she has changed her mind and also any sign of fear. Annoyed by her unwavering stare he adds softly, "Yeah, you'd pretty up my place, real fuckin' good!"

Unfazed, Julia racks up the balls then turns to him. "Does that mean I can choose my own stick?"

Johnny, now seated on his stool taps his cue on the wooden floor a few times, eyeing her from head to toe. The chatter in the pub subsides.

After a moment, with a circular motion of his arm, he theatrically waves towards the cue sticks on the wall. "Little lady, be my fuckin' guest."

The pub returns to its usual boisterous self as she takes her time sighting along each of the sticks. They are all warped and the tips worn. Shaking her head she knows that the only straight stick is in Johnny's hands.

He starts to tap the handle on the floor again as she approaches. The tapping becomes faster and louder the closer she gets, then stops abruptly when she holds out her hand. "In that case, I choose that one, please!"

The pub patrons are now aware of the drama that is unfolding and conversation has stopped. For the first time the rapid fire mono-toned commentary of a horse race can be heard coming from the TV.

Johnny's sneering face turns red with anger. Before he says anything, Butch his Sergeant and enforcer moves so intimidatingly close to Julia that she can smell his beery breath. "That's Johnny's stick, bitch, choose another!"

Ignoring him, Julia continues to stare at Johnny with her hand held out in front. Again she points to the stick in his hands. "Are you afraid to use another cue stick Johnny?... Doesn't that one belong to the pub?"

There are subdued mutterings and quiet chuckles from some of the patrons as another frowning gang member strides towards her. "Bitch, that cue stick and this pub belong to Johnny. If he doesn't want you to have his stick then you'd better listen…. You deaf bitch? You heard the man!"

Chatter stops again and the race results can be heard as well as the 'ping' of the till and the tinkling music from the poker machines. Johnny gets off his stool and waves his men away. "It's okay Butch, Karl, no fuckin' sweat!" He pushes forward his cue stick,

"Here Yankee Doodle, play with my stick, foreign bitches turn me on!" There is uneasy laughter.

Expressionless, Julia walks forward a few paces and clasps the cue stick in two hands, lifts it horizontal and sights along it, rotating it left and right. Without expression on her face, she nods and then looks at Johnny, "As I thought, this is the only straight stick in the pub, thanks for the lend anyway!"

There is muted jeering from a few of the patrons, admiring her pluck but afraid of what will happen next.

Tane, Mike and Gary move quickly to Julia's side as Butch and Karl advance menacingly towards her. Before anything can happen, Johnny stands and aggressively bangs the table with a closed fist, "Break the fuckin' balls lady, not mine!"

Julia moves to the end of the table and then in a clear voice directed at Johnny, "Johnny, I'll leave you one shot, that's all, one shot!"

By now the whole pub has moved closer to the table so that Julia and Johnny are surrounded by a crowd. Bets are taken, not whether she will win, but how many shots Johnny will be left to play. It is intriguing for the spectators as they anticipate watching the unlikely spectacle of a pretty North American girl challenging one of the toughest gang leaders in New Zealand. They see the confidence of the girl as she calmly chalks the tip and then strikes the cue ball with surprising force spreading the cluster evenly around the table. Looking in the two end pockets, she sees that there is an 'under' in one and an 'over' in the other. After a brief scrutiny of the remaining balls on the table she turns to Johnny. "Unders!"

With clinical precision and skillful repositioning of the white, one after the other she sinks the 'under' balls. Her control is so exceptional that the non-gang members applaud each of her amazing plays. Once, when snookered, she even jumps the ball to complete her shot. Never before has the bar seen such a high standard of pool, certainly not from Johnny and he is the champ!

Johnny stays expressionless, but his flushed face and a throbbing vein in his neck shows that he is under pressure.

When there are only the 'overs' left, she runs the cue ball gently up to the black pushing it against the cushion. Without looking at Johnny, she returns to her friends, taking a long drink from her mug of beer.

Tane is watching her closely, stunned by her skill.

When she looks up at him he sees a steely glint in her eyes, something that he has not seen before and wonders about his Canadian lady.

By now Johnny has stalked the table on all sides taking imaginary shots, but mostly wondering where he should leave the cue ball if he misses. With pressure of time he decides on a yellow ball that only needs a gentle nudge to drop it into the middle pocket. It is not a hard shot, but his blood pressure is high and he is having trouble focusing. He is so preoccupied with hiding the cue ball that instead of 'kissing' the yellow, he strikes it fuller than intended and it is propelled hard into the front edge of the hole. The yellow doesn't drop but springs back striking the cue ball sending it back to where it came from, next to the black.

All Julia has to do is to run the black into the corner pocket to win the game.

That is a precision shot but Johnny has seen her skill and knows that she will probably make it. He is beaten even before she moves into position. Lining up the shot she stops and turns to him. "I told you I would give you only one shot!"

Johnny gets off his stool reverses his stick and whacks the remaining balls off the table. His gang have seen his violent eruptions before so they are not surprised. Walking past Julia he stops and picks up the two twenty dollar bills, turns and walks slowly back handing his cue stick to Butch. Reaching forward he rips open her blouse exposing her bra and shoves the bills down with his fingers between the cleavage of her breasts.

Taken by surprise she crosses her arms in front of her torn blouse as he raises his hand as if to slap her face. There is horrified silence as he changes his hand to the shape of a pistol, points it at her head and says softly. "Bang!" Glaring into her eyes he lowers his hand then turns abruptly and signals to his gang to follow him out the back door.

Once the repetitive banging of the door stops, the bar is half empty and subdued.

Julia removes the money from between her breasts, pockets it, then does her best to re button her blouse before tucking it into the top of her shorts.

Tane is amazed to see that she is smiling as she reaches down and picks up the cue stick off the floor. Holding it in the middle in one hand she lifts it above her head announcing in a loud voice. "This stick is now public property!"

That breaks the subdued mood and as she returns it to the rack on the wall there is clapping and whistling. The clapping follows her as she walks over to her friends who are still too shocked and relieved to join in. Sighting her beer she hurries over to the table and drinks more than she intends, causing her eyes to water.

They laugh as she wipes her eyes with the back of her hand. "Well that felt good. What an arse-hole!... Did you see what he did?" She looks at the missing buttons on her blouse then up at Tane, "I guess it could have been worse! He's one freaky guy."

Giving her a friendly punch on the shoulder he says. "Wow, lady, I'm impressed, good on you!" He shakes his head, "Who would've guessed that you were a champion pool player, do you have other secret talents?"

"That's for you to find out!" Moving closer she looks up teasingly into his eyes and locks both arms around his waist. He does the same. For a long moment they are close together before he whispers in her ear. "You are one gutsy lady, for a moment I was very afraid! Crikey, you could play pro!" He shakes his head, "You just don't look like a pool player!"

She pulls away from his arms, afraid that he may feel the pounding of her heart. She is not aware that his own heart is racing leaving him strangely light-headed. Confused by her emotions she sits down beside him next to Mike. Across the table she can see the questioning in the eyes of her friends. They knew she was good at pool, but now realise that she had concealed her true ability. What they don't know is that she is very protective about her personal life as it revives uncomfortable memories of her father as a professional pool player and the life that they lived.

Whether it was the adrenaline of the game, or the unexpected bonding with Tane, or the sudden intake of alcohol, or all three,

she feels it is the right time to tell them something about herself. Clasping Tane's hand in hers she looks across at Wendy, Robyn and Gary. "I'd like to explain why I'm so good at pool." She pauses then turns to Tane, "You mentioned that I could be a pro. I never have been, but my dad was, that is how he earned his living going from town to town throughout Ontario and Quebec." She takes a long drink from her mug before placing it back on the table and lightly running her finger around the rim, "As a baby and for most of my younger years, mum and I traveled with him staying in cheap motels, mostly about a month. That's when the locals learned that they could only beat dad when he wanted to be beaten and they would call him names like 'cheat' and 'hustler.' Sometimes he was attacked and beaten up."

She looks across at Wendy and Robyn, "Those were the scariest moments seeing blood coming out his nose and mouth. Mum would clean his face with a wet towel then stroke his hair and rock him like a baby."

Julia's eyes become haunted with a far-away look, "Those were not pleasant memories! Whenever dad was beaten up I knew we would be on the move again."

Studying her beer, there is an awkward silence before she brightens and looks up at Tane, "But there were happier times too. Like when he would challenge me to a game, I loved that. He made me a short cue stick and I used to stand on a chair so that I could see over the rim." She looks over at the now vacant pool table, "The more dad played the better he became and he was able to win high paying tournaments. It was great being taken to the flashest restaurants and ordering anything that I wanted. Those were the happy times."

Staring sightlessly into her beer mug for quite some time, the group wonder if she will continue, she does, "Eventually dad bought a camper van and life became simpler. Far better than living out of a suitcase. Mum had been home schooled so she knew how to teach me geography, math, English and patois French." She nods, "I had better schooling than many of my own age, but of course what was missing was contact with other girls and boys." She looks directly at Wendy, "I know that I'm selfish sometimes and prefer my own company."

Wendy shrugs as she continues, "Maybe that is because of my years of being alone." She turns to Tane, "Most of the time that is." Looking across at Wendy and Robyn she continues, "The trailer parks were full of children living the same sort of life as my own so I had brief friendships. I know I often cried when we had to move." She shakes her head, "Those friendships were important to me."

Wendy and Robyn are captivated by Julia's story. Whenever they had asked about her past she would politely evade their questions.

After taking another sip Julia holds her mug up towards the overhead light illuminating the golden bubbles, "This beer is too warm, don't you drink it colder?"

Gary knows his beer better than most. "Our tap beer is not very cold, bottles are colder."

Julia shrugs. "When you're thirsty I guess it doesn't matter. In Canada we like to feel a cold bite in the throat."

Wendy changes the subject. "Jules you have a degree so moving around didn't seem to harm your education."

She shrugs. The personal inspection is starting to make her uncomfortable. "There's not much more to tell, except that mum told dad that I had to go to a proper school when I reached ten. Dad bought a cheap cottage beside a lake in the Ottawa Valley and I traveled to school on the school bus. I liked that ride and going to school because it got me out of the cottage. At first it was strange, so many kids and the fear that I wouldn't know enough. I soon found I was ahead of most of my class and from then on enjoyed school."

Julia remains silent again with the same far-away look in her eyes, then she continues, "Dad's arrival and departure was still the focus of our lives. Sometimes he wouldn't return for a month or two and it was cold and lonely in the winter. Most of the other cabin owners left at the first snow fall, so we had few neighbours. Our cabin was not winterised so it was hard to keep warm." She looks across at Gary knowing he is a builder, "The exterior cladding was very old, it was called Ten-test. Do you know what that is?"

He shakes his head. "Never heard of it."

"Must be a Canadian thing. I guess it passed ten tests of some kind." She shakes her head, "It was only sheets of thick tar paper coated with fine chips of red stone to make it look like bricks. When the cladding was new, it probably lived up to its name, but after years of blizzards and hot summers, it became cracked. I used to help dad seal it with hot tar and a brush. It was a messy job and I can remember the smell." She shakes her head again, "But that didn't stop the freeze from pushing through the walls. Mum and I were forever chopping wood to feed the stove. It was great that stove, it not only heated the cabin but it also cooked meals and heated water. I soon learned which woods would split easily, which were fast burners and which were slow."

Tane looks down at her long elegant fingers still clasped in his hand. He sees the manicured nails and can't image her chopping wood. He turns to her. "You must have been freezing most of the time. Do you know how cold it got Jules?"

She is warmed by his first use of her pet name. "The coldest I can remember was minus forty degrees and that was so cold that you had to breathe through your fingers, like this." Clasping her hands together, she places them over her nose and mouth, then removes her hands, "Otherwise your nostrils would freeze together and you could get ice patches on your lungs. That could kill you! It was very scary!"

Mike shakes his head. "Not for me!"

Gary says. "I've never seen snow. I'd like to, but I'm not sure about those ice patches on your lungs."

Robyn is uncomfortable, as if somehow her homeland is under attack. "Snow can be beautiful and fun when it is falling gently, you'd like that Gary."

He shrugs, still trying to imagine what it would be like to have frozen lungs. Tane asks, "So what happened next? How long did you live by the lake?"

"Seven years. It wasn't all bad. Summers were fun and in winter we blatted around on an old skidoo and I made a skating rink by the cabin. But winter in Canada does seem to last forever." She shakes her head, "Dad was away longer and longer and there was never enough money. In the middle of winter mum and I would catch fish to change our diet of smoked meats and pickled cabbage." Gary loves fishing, after rugby it is his favourite sport and Julia's words spike his interest. "What sort of fish were in the lake Julia?" She is about to answer when another thought pops into his head, "Wasn't the lake frozen? I mean how could you catch fish?"

"Have you heard of an ice hut?"

"Is it an igloo?"

"No it's an insulated hut that sits on a sled. It looks a bit like an out-house with a chimney. We had our own hut on the edge of the lake waiting for winter. When the ice was hard enough, we towed it out with our skidoo." She pauses for a moment, "Do you know what a skidoo is?"

Gary nods. "Yeah I have seen them racing on SKY Sports. They have snow jumps just like the jumps made for dirt tracking, it looks like fun. We have something here called a Seadoo that floats on the water. It looks like your skidoo but it has a propeller not a belted track. I have fished from one of those, they're fun!"

Mike asks. "How do you know when the ice is hard enough to stand the weight of a skidoo?"

"You can tell by its colour. If it's clear and black or blue, then it is okay but if it's full of bubbles it's way too thin." She holds up her hand showing a two inch gap between her thumb and finger, "You can walk on the ice when it's this thick." Using both hands to show a greater thickness, she continues, "Six inches and you can pull the hut with the Skidoo. When it is three feet thick you can land a plane!"

Tane is impressed. "How do you know those sort of things?"

Julia laughs. "Easy, it's in the Farmer's Almanac. Everything you need to know is in that magazine." She shakes her head, "For Canadians it's more than just a magazine, it's a way of life!"

Gary has a puzzled look on his face. "I suppose you have to crack the ice somehow to get at the fish."

"Sure do. It's not difficult. We share a post hole driller with the other hut owners. After the hole is drilled we position the ice hut so that it is in the middle."

Julia's fishing story is interrupted by Robyn and Wendy who are bored by the subject and offer to buy another round of drinks.

Julia pulls one of the two twenty dollar bills out of her shorts, "On me!"

After they have gone, she moves her chair opposite Gary and points to a square coaster, "Say that's the floor of the ice hut." Next she points to two sides opposite each other. "On each wall there are boards attached for seating. Against the back wall, is a gas heater with its bottle outside for safety. Opposite that is the door. It's pretty basic but cosy. It gets so warm you can take off your gloves and jacket, very odd when you are on a slab of ice! Great for keeping the drinks cold though. Mum and I liked to drink rum and coke, the guys usually drank beer."

At the mention of beer, they all lift their mugs and take a drink.

Julia places her mug on the table and shakes her head, "Definitely not cold enough." She looks at Gary, "The biggest fish I ever caught was a musky." Lifting her arms she stretches them as wide as she can, "This big!..... Mum and I were fishing alone, so while I kept the line tight she rolled up her sleeves, pushed her arms into the hole and put her fingers into its gills. It was so heavy she struggled to stand, even then its tail was still in the hole. We were eating musky steaks for weeks!"

Gary asks. "What sort of fish is a musky, is it like a big salmon?"

"No it's the largest of the pike family. Do you catch pike here?" Gary shakes his head, so she continues,

"It's proper name is muskellunge. You can see why we shorten it to musky, much easier, eh!.... It's quite special to catch one. Usually we catch the smaller northern pike or the good eating pickerel. To catch those we use live shiners or flat heads, a kind of small minnow that we buy at sport shops."

She looks at the guys to see if they are bored, but they are not, "The most common fish we catch is perch and the small and large mouth bass, but you use different bait for them..... So that's how we catch fish in winter."

Gary nods. "I'd like to do that and I'd like to drive one of those, what do you call them?"

"Skidoos."

"Yeah, skidoos."

Julia smiles, knowing that he would have the time of his life. She can see him zooming around on the snow clad fields and frozen lakes of Sebastopol in the Ottawa Valley. So different from the green pastures of temperate New Zealand.

Robyn and Wendy return with the drinks, and Julia changes seats, back beside Tane.

Mike teases Wendy. "You missed hearing how Julia caught a giant musky."

Wendy mutters. "Not that fond of fishing."

"That's a shame. I was thinking of teaching you how to surf cast off the beach at Karekare!"

Wendy reaches over and taps his hand. "So maybe I can be persuaded!" Turning to Julia she asks, "You had other food besides fish in winter, didn't you?"

"Oh sure we had a cellar full of smoked meats and baskets of root vegetables, potatoes, carrots, turnips and long twists of onions. The veges that wouldn't last were either pickled or cooked inside preserving jars. We also had all sorts of preserved fruit. In late summer I picked apples, peaches and pears growing in the orchard. Or searched for wild strawberries, blueberries and raspberries. We had to watch for the bears. Dad did bring sacks of flour and sugar and mum made oven bread with yeast or sourdough. Breakfast on Sundays was special. Stacks of pancakes and long rashes of smoky bacon smothered in dark maple syrup and fresh brewed coffee. We didn't have a cow, so we were often short of butter, milk and cream." A decade of memories flash through her mind as she stares into her beer.

When she looks up, she is flushed and homesick, "I left home when I was seventeen. Dad and mum came to my High School graduation where I was presented with a scholarship to attend Montreal University. But it was only mum who waved goodbye when I left on the Grey Coach bus, I cried most of the way."

Julia is again silent for some-time with the same far-away look in her eyes.

Tane is the first to break the silence. "Do you mind telling us what happened to your dad, is he still playing pool?"

Reaching down, she lifts up her shoulder bag, opens it and removes a fat envelope. "Would you like to see some photos?"

They nod, so she hands a photo to Tane who studies it for a moment. "He's quite fair like you."

"Yes, his parents were born in Sweden. That's where the Johansson name comes from."

Wendy who has never seen photos of Julia's family, reaches over and takes it from Tane. "He looks like a happy guy!" "That was taken after he had a big win. It was always extremes with dad, feast or famine! When he came home the world would suddenly come right. There he would be larger than life, all smiles and smelling of whiskey, with perfume or bath salts for mum and a toy for me. I was way past that but it was good to see him again. I don't think he knew how hard it was for us to survive." Picking up her mug, she taps it with her finger nail, "Drink got to dad in the end. At first it affected his judgment, his eye sight, his co-ordination and finally his heart. He died quite suddenly when I was in my second year at University. He left two legacies, a life insurance policy giving mum and me some security and his pool table which filled the largest room at the cottage. After the funeral I returned to the cottage and played game after game. It was if I was obsessed. Day after day I played. If I missed a shot, I would play it over and over again, just as dad taught me. I didn't want to stop, it made me feel like I was with him again." She looks across at Wendy and Robyn, "I felt as if dad was with me tonight, helping me, it was very strange. I felt invincible!"

Looking towards the pool table, she wonders if he is there now watching her and wishing that somehow he would miraculously appear.

Shaking her head she looks down at the photo in her hand, "Mum understood how I was hurting and never said a word!"

She turns to Tane, "So that explains why I never want to be a professional pool player, ever, also why I'm so good."

It's Robyn's turn to look at the photo, she has seen others, but this one is new. "So this is your mum?"

"Yes and that's a new dress and evening coat bought by dad."

"She is very pretty. What did she do after he was gone?"

Julia looks at the bubbles on top of her beer then swirls them around. "Mum was confused and lethargic for six months, but one day she phoned me and I could tell that she was her old bright self again. She asked me to come home for a few days but wouldn't tell me why. That made me curious. When I arrived, the first thing she said was, 'Jules, do you remember Edie Schweibert who owns the farm across the lake?' I said, 'of course I do. He was a nice man and used to help us when things got tough. But why do you ask?' She touched me gently on the cheek. 'I have been seeing him quite a lot over the past few months and the other day he took me out for a meal and asked me to marry him! What a shock!... I wanted to talk to you first.... Is it okay with you Jules? I know how close you were to your dad.'"

Julia looks across at her two friends, aware that she had never confided with them as she is doing now, "Of course I was surprised and delighted and gave her another hug. I told her that it was the best news I'd heard all year and we hugged and cried." There are tears in Julia's eyes, threatening to spill, but she continues, "I can't praise Edie enough for his care. He is a wonderful man, like a guardian angel. After every storm he would arrive with his plough and dig us out, or drop off a leg of ham or bacon or a pail of milk. He made sure the wood bin was always full. Mum never contacted him or asked for help, it was if he knew when we were struggling. What is most endearing is that he is quietly spoken and unassuming, never staying long and saying very little... Now that I think about it, I guess he and mum had something unspoken going on and little was needed to be said. He had been a widower for a number of years and it was natural that he was lonely, I guess we gave him a reason to live." She straightens and wipes the moisture from under her eyes, "Anyway they got married just over a year after dad died and mum is still happily re-organising the farm house."

She looks across at Wendy, "As you know, I phone her often. I don't think they will ever learn how to use the internet. It would make my life so much easier."

Turning to Tane, sitting beside her, she continues, "Wendy and Robyn were kind enough to travel North with me to say goodbye before we left on our holiday. Mum was very concerned about us travelling so far away and to a strange country. A long journey to her is from the lake to Montreal. Overseas is across the Saint Lawrence River…"

Julia's story is interrupted by Marie from the kitchen telling them that their meals are ready.

Gary is the first off his stool. "Food, great, I'm starving!"

As the group move toward the restaurant, Tane remembers Lady out on her own in the car park. "Go get your meals, Lady needs water and a feed, I'll be back in a tick."

As the others enter the dining room he exits through the back door and is greeted by Lady's agitated barking.

Now outside he sees the bright orange glow of the setting sun silhouetting the surrounding hills and also the German style helmets of the Satan's Sons gang clustered around their bikes. Tane unties Lady from the roll bar and then holds onto her collar as she jumps to the ground. She lifts her head and places her muzzle in his hand as she tries to tell him with moans and whines that she is desperate to relieve herself, is hungry and thirsty and that she is worried about the gang. He strokes her neck to calm her, then bends down close to her ears. "Shoosh Lady, I know they are bad bastards, don't worry they don't scare me." Unclipping her lead she rushes off to the nearest tree. Returning, she alternates glancing towards the gang with growls, chomping on dog biscuits, and lapping water. When she is finished he taps the back seat and she jumps up, staying still as she is clipped onto the roll bar again. Without looking at the gang Tane strolls nonchalantly back towards the rear door.

The gang have been silent watching him. Now that he is closer, Johnny taunts. "Hey lover boy, I'm going to take your fuckin' Yankee bitch, she's mine!"

There is sniggering as Butch calls out. "Get your cards ready bro, we're going to play poke-her tonight!" Only a slight hesitation in Tane's step indicates that he has heard. The jeering is lost behind the bang of the closing door and he composes himself before joining the others who have already started their meals.

Ten minutes later, Hinemoa the cook, concerned for the safety of her guests, decides to serve the desserts herself and enters the dining room with plates of apple pie topped with whipped cream. Placing the tray on a table beside them, she asks. "Ready for your dessert? How're your meals, okay?"

They look up smiling and nodding.

Removing their plates, she serves the pies.

Robyn dips her finger into the whipped cream and puts it in her mouth. "Wow real cream, back home this would be mock cream or ice cream."

Julia sighs with eyes closed. "This is dreamy but very fattening!"

Wendy says. "Right now, I don't care!" As she scoops a spoonful into her mouth.

While they are eating, Hinemoa approaches their table again. "Look it's none of my business, but I'm really concerned for yous lot, being tourists and all that." She turns to Julia. "I heard how you taught that pig of a man a lesson. Good on you girl, but there's trouble brewing." She walks around the table collecting the empty bowls and places them on a trolley then turns to Julia, "You probably don't know it, but a gang man's mana is everything to these bastards." She shakes her head frowning, "Maybe it's because they don't have anything else going for them? Anyway Johnny Schmidt will want revenge!"

Julia is genuinely surprised. "Just because I beat him in a game of pool?"

"No, you didn't just beat him girl, you humiliated him."

Julia shrugs as Hinemoa continues, "It's serious stuff. He won't harm you himself, no he's too smart for that! He'll use one of his un-patched members. They'll do anything to join his gang, they might even kill you!"

Julia frowns. "Really, that's crazy!"

"They ARE crazy! What with P and weed and booze. Who knows how crazy!" Hinemoa, with her arms folded, looks down at the men, "And guys that means you too!... Look I can tell when troubles brewing, I've been in this business too long. The manager didn't want to know anything about it so I phoned the cops, they should be here soon."

Tane nods. "Thanks Hinemoa we appreciate your concern." He looks at the others, "I didn't want to spoil your meals, but I can tell you that the gang are waiting for us out back." He turns his head in the direction of the car park then back again, "What was worrying me was how we were going to get out of this place in one piece!"

Hinemoa unfolds her arms. "With the cops here you'll be safe, after they go, who knows? ….. Look I think I can help. I'm knocking off shortly and my car is parked by the kitchen door. It will be a bit of a squeeze with three in the front and four in the back. You can stay over night at my house if you like."

As Wendy and Robyn nod in agreement, Tane declines with a shake of his head. "I appreciate the offer, but our Jeeps and my dog are in the car park. I can't just leave her and the Jeeps with the gang! They might kill her or worse turn her into a fighting dog, they may even torch our cars."

Hinemoa nods.

After a moments silence, Mike adds. "We'll take the Jeeps home after the cops come and the gang has gone…. Just in case we are followed, the girls should go home with you, Hinemoa, we'll pick them up later."

She is not convinced. "What if the gang follow you?"

Tane shakes his head. "If the cops are with us, there will be no trouble. If not, this is dirt track country and you are looking at last year's champions. I'm sure we can give them the slip."

She reluctantly nods. "Okay…. My house is just before the Waimauku bridge on highway sixteen, number four, nine, nine. Do you know where I mean?"

The men nod, so she continues, "Look for the tall bamboos on the right, the driveway's just past them. Got it?" Tane nods. "Four, nine, nine, past the bamboos on the right and just before the Waimauku bridge." He looks around the table and everyone seems to be in agreement except Julia who has that same determined look in her eyes that he has seen before.

She shakes her head. "Not so fast, I'm the one that got you guys into this mess, I'm staying."

Mike frowns. "Julia, you may be a terrific pool player but you know nothing about off road racing. It is an extreme sport and very dangerous."

Julia straightens, folding her arms. "I'm staying!"

Wendy reaches over and squeezes her arm. "Please Jules I wish you would come with us."

Julia shakes her head looking directly at Tane.

After a moment, he sighs and then shrugs. "Okay, you're with me. Gary can ride with Mike. Look after Lady for me will you?"

Mike frowns. "Sure,… but why?"

Tane points toward Julia. "They're after her and it will be safer for Lady."

Mike nods, so Tane continues, "What I was thinking, we'll try and lose them in the Woodhill Forest. If we can't shake them we'll take them over the dune jump to the beach." Mike and Gary look surprised as Tane continues, "Yeah the first night dune jump ever! If nothing happens, then it will be a nice ride along the beach to Muriwai anyway."

Hinemoa has been listening without comment, now she steps closer to Julia. "Young lady I admire your guts, but I wipe my hands of what could happen! If you survive the chase the gang will finish you off anyway. Don't be so stupid!" The harsh words make Julia even more determined and she shakes her head.

Hinemoa sighs and turns to Robyn and Wendy again, "Can't you talk some sense into her?"

Robyn looks directly at Julia. "What would your mother say Jules?"

"As my daddy used to say, 'What the eye doesn't see, the heart doesn't grieve for!'"

Without showing it, Hinemoa admires Julia's courage, "Okay, good luck to you, young lady, see you later at my place." She turns to Wendy and Robyn, "Come on, let's go!"

Beckoning them to follow, she picks up the dishes and pushes open the swinging doors to the kitchen.

Within minutes, two Police cars drive into the car park and stop with their headlights pointing towards the gang. The unexpected arrival, forces Johnny to change his plans. Not knowing the direction the Jeeps will go he sends a scout northward on Highway 16 and another southward past the turn off to Helensville. There are explosions after explosion as the hogs are kicked into life. Johnny leads the remainder of his gang over the bridge towards Hellensville and stops in the industrial section bellow the town. All exits are now covered. He could have stayed and confronted the cops, because in his mind he thinks he has done nothing wrong, just a few ripped buttons on a blouse, more of a prank than a serious offence. Certainly not physical assault! But he is not sure of the Yankee bitch, she could be trouble! With major gang issues to solve, he doesn't want time wasting court issues.

Thinking again about her mocking blue eyes, he revs the engine of his Harley wanting to turn that look into fear.

Once the gang have gone, Hinemoa leaves the kitchen, unlocks her car and opens the rear door.

Wendy and Robyn come running and end up on top of each other on the back seat. As they untangle themselves Wendy starts to laugh followed by Robyn and then Hinemoa who adds a surprisingly high pitched giggle.

Looking in the rear view mirror she says. "You know that was fun, I haven't felt this good in years. It just shows you need a bit of excitement in your life sometimes."

CHAPTER 9

The Chase

With Julia sandwiched between Tane and Mike, they hurry out the rear door of the pub.

Tane unties Lady and leads her, reluctantly, to the back of Mike's car.

Gary, seated beside Mike, turns and rubs under her collar. He can feel her agitation and strokes her ears which she usually likes, but not tonight. Eyeing him, she pulls away with a sharp bark. It is impossible to explain to her family that she knows that the gang are trouble and also that she doesn't like riding in Mike's car, no amount of petting will change that!

The doors of the Police cars open and two policemen walk toward the Jeeps. The first to arrive shines his torch on Tane's face. "Hi I'm Senior Sergeant Pringle of the Helensville Community Police and with me is Senior Constable Mulligan of the Waitakere Police.... You guys okay?"

Shining his torch on Julia, he sees her torn blouse, "You okay miss?"

"Yes, I'm fine officer!"

"Are you a tourist?"

"Yes, from Canada."

"Are you Julia the pool player that was assaulted in the pub?"

"Well not exactly assaulted, maybe molested, or more correctly, man-handled, my blouse was torn, that's all,..no biggy!"

He studies her for a moment then opens and reads his notebook. "From what I've been told, you WERE assaulted, which IS a biggy! Do you want to press charges?"

"No!"

"Are you sure?"

"I'm sure.... I'm a Legal Executive so I know about criminal charges and their outcomes. What Johnny will probably get, if convicted, is some sort of community service with home detention." She shakes her head, "I don't want that to spoil my holiday."

"Okay, but for the record I'll need a statement from each of you, we may lay charges anyway... Did you know that Johnny Schmidt, that's his name, is a gang leader? He is a very violent man, in fact he has a number of convictions and has been in and out of jail." He shakes his head, "You shouldn't be playing pool with that sort of person."

Julia tries to look penitent as he steps back from the jeep, "Do you mind coming with me to my car it will be easier to take notes." He points to Mike and Gary, "Do you mind going with Constable Mulligan to his car, please."

After ten minutes of questioning, the Senior Sergeant reports to his Communications Centre then approaches the Jeeps again, "I suppose you are heading South on Highway Sixteen?"

Tane nods and the Sergeant continues, "I have to head North to Shelly Beach, there's a bit of a domestic. Senior Constable Mulligan will escort you out of town." He turns to Julia with a smile, "You must be some pool player lady, beating Johnny Schmidt, but please stay out of public bars, particularly those owned by gangs, not the place for tourists......... enjoy the rest of your holiday in New Zealand." Julia smiles back. "Thanks officer." He touches his cap and returns to his car, departing with lights flashing.

Julia turns to Tane. "Nice guy!"

"We have good cops in New Zealand." Reversing, he leads the way out of the car park with the Constable following at the rear.

A few kilometers out of Parakai, just before the round-about to Helensville, Constable Mulligan receives a call to attend a fatality on Old North Road, a few kilometres south. Flashing his headlights, the Jeeps ahead pull over and stop. Knowing it is a risk to leave them unprotected, the Constable checks with dispatch. They instruct him to go to the fatal crash as it takes priority.

Putting on his hat he walks to the two Jeeps and tells them that he has just received new orders.

Mike and Tane reassure him that they will be okay.

Convinced that the gang have gone elsewhere, Constable Mulligan returns to his car and accelerates past the two Jeeps with his siren blasting and disappears over the bridge towards Helensville township.

Johnny and his gang hiding in the dark of an industrial car park below the town are advised by their scout, on Highway 16, that he has just sighted the two Jeeps. The distant sounds of the Police siren is soon replaced by the angry crackle of motorbike engines.

Shortly after, Mike in the rear Jeep becomes aware of a single headlight shining in his rear view mirror. As it is still a distance behind, he is unable to tell if it is a motorbike or a car with faulty lights. Pressing a *'phone'* icon on his dashboard screen he leans toward the display and says "Tane." When Tane's face appears in the centre of a circle, he says *'Dial'*

Almost immediately Tane replies. "What's up bro?"

"There's a headlight behind me, could be a motorbike, could be one of the gang."

Tane studies his mirror. "Yeah I see it, let's go the Woodhill route anyway, better get our helmets on." He turns to Julia and points over his shoulder toward the back seat, "There's two helmets in a bag, can you grab them?"

Julia pulls the travel bag over the seat. Both helmets are black with a silver fern. One has the lettering, 'Head Job'. She turns the lettering towards him. "Now let me guess, this one's yours!"

"Yeah sorry about that, I have never had a female navigator before."

"Right now I'm no lady or navigator, I'm a unisex co-driver." She clasps the chrome roll bar above her head, "Let's go Joe!"

He has seen that look before in the pub and shakes his head.

In the other Wrangler, Gary and Mike have also put on their helmets.

Tane speaks into his phone again. "I'll need some time to cut the chain at the forest gate, can you slow them down somehow?" Mike thinks for a moment, then nods. "Go open the gate, I'll let you know if it's the gang behind us." He looks in his side mirror again at the now fast approaching head light. In the distance are many more lights, "I can see more lights, I'm sure it is the gang! Why don't you turn off your lights just before going up Foresthill Road, the gang will follow me, not you, okay?"

"Sure thing, good idea Mike."

"I'll take these guys on a little detour to Lone Kauri Road, then I'll double back. That should work, what-do-you-reckon?"

Knowing what to expect, Tane smiles, "I like it, thanks." He waves his hand above his head, "See you later bro."

Julia is slammed back into her seat as he accelerates down the highway and it excites her.

Very soon they see the sign pointing towards the Woodhill Forest. Tane cuts the lights and for a moment they are racing blindly through the night and just in time their eyes adjust to safely make the turn.

Behind them Mike slows until the leading bike is a hundred metres in the rear.

Gary frowns then turns to Mike. "Lone Kauri Road has a dead end."

"Exactly!" Mike waits until he is sure that it is a motorbike and that the following lights are also bikes before he pushes down hard on the accelerator. Hurtling along the flat highway for a kilometer, they slow to take a bend. The gang's scout closes fast until he is just behind. Now at the bend, Mike swings wide then brakes hard, turning in the direction of the slide. The locked rear tyres cause clouds of white smoke creating a smoke screen. Blinded the scout is forced to take the inside lane next to the bank. Too late he sees the trap. There is no room between the Jeep and the fast approaching clay bank. Narrowing the gap even further, Mike jerks the steering wheel hard to the left and the tail of the Wrangler snakes around and the front bumper contacts the bike and a black leather boot. The cry of surprise and pain is lost in the roar of the engines, showers of sparks, and the shrill metallic scream of metal on metal. Correcting the slide, Mike presses down hard on the accelerator leaving behind a crumpled body and a bouncing black German helmet that continues to give chase.

Mike and Gary do hi-fives while Lady who has been buffeted by the collision, whimpers and growls until she realises that her family are celebrating, so she joins in the fun.

Mike turns to Gary. "One down, that'll slow them a bit!"

"Yeah, as slow as a swarm of angry hornets!"

Lady has stopped barking, but her growl is now coming from deep inside her belly. Gary reaches backwards and rubs her ears and again she eyes him followed by a shake of her head.

Mike asks. "Have you actually driven along Lone Kauri Road before?"

"Sure, it ends with a turn-around just before the cliffs."

Mike nods. "My plan is to lead them to the end of the road as fast as I can. I'm hoping they don't know the road!"

Gary raises his eyebrows. "Your timing's got to be good!"

"You bet. There's a wooden barrier at the end and you wouldn't want to hit it at speed, it's a long way down!" Mike leans forward and uses voice recognition again and Tane answers. "You guys okay?"

"No problems. Just to let you know that it IS the gang chasing us. Their count is now minus one!"

Julia answers, "Good job, I hope it was Johnny!"

"Don't know."

Gary leans forward, "How're-you-doin'-Julia?"

"Don't worry about me mate, this is the best fun I've had in years! It sure as hell beats sitting in a stuffy office!"

Both Mike and Gary look at each other. Gary shouts to Mike. "Did you hear that, she called us mate!.... Bloody hell, she's a Kiwi already!"

Mike leans toward the phone. "We're not far from Lone Kauri

Road, the gang is just behind, I've got a surprise for them, see you soon."

Tane says. "Good luck." And they both switch off.

Mike continues to watch behind, then slows until the gang's headlights flood his side mirror again. Suddenly there is a 'THUMP' that jolts the car and a hole appears in the middle of the back seat, just above Lady's head. The bullet passes between Gary and Mike and the front windshield shatters in a shower of glass! They all jump with fright. Mike turns to look at Gary and then over his shoulder at Lady. The wind blasts in and Mike has to shout to be heard. "WOWEE, you okay?" Gary nods. Mike gestures toward the back with his thumb, "How's Lady?"

Restrained by his straps, Gary turns as far as he can and anxiously studies her. Swiveling back, he nods. "She seems okay, she has her nose stuck in a fuckin' big hole in the back seat." He checks his own limbs, brushing chunks of glass off his legs and arms.

Mike immediately guns the jeep trying to distance themselves from further shootings. With no resistance to the blast of the wind, their skin is stretched tight and when they open their mouths to speak their cheeks puff open exposing their teeth in an unnatural grin. They find that squinting is the only way to stop their eyes from watering.

Gary reaches forward and pulls open the glove compartment removing two pair of old fashioned round driving goggles. "We'd better put these on!"

Looking like something out of a yesteryear racing magazine, they start to laugh. Mike's laugh doesn't last long as he thinks about the gun shot. '*That was a close call, a little lower to the right or left and we would have been dead!*' He shouts towards Gary. "They sure-as-hell are playing for keeps!" Checking in his rear view mirror, he can see the leading gang member closing fast with a pistol pointing forwards and he yells, "Hold on tight they're aiming again."

Yanking the steering wheel to the left and then to the right, in quick succession, he almost causes the Jeep to roll. Two wheels on one side bite into the gravel, while the other two, up in the air, are frantically spinning. After a moment they bump down and the Jeep slides in the direction of the turned front wheels. They hear the sharp, 'crack!', 'crack!' of the pistol above the clatter of loose gravel. With the weaving then sliding, the bullets pass harmlessly into the bush on the sides of the road.

A rapidly approaching sign on the left, points the way to Lone Kauri Road on the right. Mike expertly slides off the main road and then slows to make sure they are still being followed. Turning his head, he shouts again, "I'm going to turn off the lights, get the spotlight ready." He points under Gary's seat. Gary loosens his restraining straps, lifts up the lamp and plugs it into the cigarette lighter on the dash. He has done it many times before on possum and rabbit shoots, but this time they are the hunted.

Mike points at the spotlight. "We'll blind them with it."

Gary nods.

Mike turns off the headlights and the sudden darkness is frightening as they try to adjust. The tea-tree, nikau and ponga trees on the sides of the narrow road rush past at a frantic pace. Mike knowing that there is a steep drop to the right favours the left, causing them to bump against the bank a few times.

With no red tail lights or headlights to follow the gang slows.

At the last bend before the end of the road Mike turns his headlights on again and the gang race to catch up. The white painted posts and railings at the end of the road can be plainly seen. Mike switches off the car's lights again and they hurtle into darkness towards the edge of the cliff.

Lady, crouching low in the back, whimpers as she senses Mike and Gary's fear. Mike counts out aloud. "One… two… three, hold on tight, this is it!" Jerking the steering wheel hard to the left the Jeep slides sideways on the loose gravel. Propelled by the momentum, the boot swings around to face the fast approaching retainer posts. Mike and Gary and Lady are now facing towards the on-coming bikes. Mike brakes hard with his foot, then pulls on the hand brake.

Loose stones ricochet off tree trunks as it shudders and shakes with the opposing forces. Sliding to a halt, it stops at the edge of the cliff with just the softest *'bump'* against the railing. Mike, Gary and Lady expecting a bone shaking jolt, relax back into their seats.

The quiet idling of the motor is suddenly drowned by the roar of the bikes rounding the bend. Mike's voice is strained as he tells Gary to get the spotlight ready. When the first bike's light strikes the Wrangler, he shouts, "NOW!" They charge forward with headlights on full and Gary's spotlight trained on the front biker, who, unable to see and with no time to react, instinctively swerves and finds himself being catapulted over his handle bars and the barricade at the end of the road. Like a large floppy doll, he wraps around the trunk of a kauri tree while his bike cart-wheels down the steep slope. The remainder of the gang rush past aware of the danger but unable to stop. Bikes slide horizontally on the loose gravel and there is the squeal of locked brakes, followed by the metallic crashing sounds of bike on bike and the louder thumping noise of bike on posts, on tree trunks, and the louder crunch of metal on unmoving rock.

Now around the bend, Mike, breathless, squeezes out a long sigh through clenched teeth.

Gary removes his goggles and wipes the lenses and the sweat from his brow. Smiling with relief, they do a high five, only to be reminded that the night is not over as they hear a few of the motors behind them being kicked into life.

Further up the coast, Tane and Julia drive up to a triangular swing gate that blocks the entrance to the forest. Their headlights light up the sentry like columns of tall pine trees behind, and also the padlocked chain, which is soon removed with a bolt cutter. Driving on through, they park on a grass verge waiting to hear from Mike and Gary.

Worried, they sit in silence.

As they wait, an intimate force surrounds them. It is unfamiliar, strange and powerful. A force that they both can feel. It is quite extraordinary and very real, like a magnetic force swirling between them. Taken by surprise, the encounter leaves them confused.

Tane reaches over and strokes Julia's arm lightly, running his fingers down from her elbow to her hand which he gently clasps. Being a potter, his finger tips are sensitive and he marvels at the feel of her silky skin and her soft golden hair.

Julia squeezes his hand in return.

Struggling to speak he breaks the intimacy. "It's not right!"

She is surprised by his words. "What is not right?"

Taking hold of both of her hands, he shakes his head. "I've put you in danger!... You are a guest in my country and here you are being chased by a gang!"

Still holding his hands, she pulls him as close to her as the restraining straps will allow. "Tane, I'm the one that started all this, it's not your fault.... Hey what's more important is what is happening between us right now! Can you feel what I'm feeling?"

He nods, and she continues, "What an extraordinary feeling, I want it to last. I have never felt this way before! It's like we are being locked together."

Tane nods again. "Yes, it's crazy. I can't explain it either, but it sure as hell is real!" The moment is broken by the ringing of the dashboard phone.

Julia can see that it is from Mike and she presses the 'talk' button. "Hi Mike, what's keeping you?"

"About fifteen gang members, minus a few…. You sound happy?"

"Tane and I are getting bored, you know, nothing to talk about!"

"That's hard to believe, anyway we'll be with you soon. We're just turning off the main road onto Woodhills, have you got the gate open cause we've still got company."

Tane leans towards the phone. "The gates are open, are you guys okay?"

Gary says. "Yeah we're okay, but watch out the gang means business, they're shooting at us."

Tane turns to look at Julia to see her reaction.

Julia remains poker faced, so he adjusts his side mirror and listens for Mike's engine. All he can hear, in the distance, is the high pitched whine of motorbikes. Turning to Julia he nods. "They're coming!"

Moments later Mike and Gary and a wide eyed Lady roar past with horn beeping.

Julia jumps out and swings the gate closed wrapping the severed chain with its padlock around the gate post. Jumping back in, she turns to Tane. "That'll keep them for a couple of minutes!"

He nods, engaging the gears.

As they chase after Mike and Gary, Lady who is standing watching from the back seat, is still wondering why she is not in the other Jeep.

Fighting the bucking, swaying vehicle, Tane steers along the twin track that follows the natural lay of the land. Twisting and turning, it curves around rocky outcrops and drops suddenly down the sides of steep hills. Tall pines flash past like rows of soldiers and startled rabbits scatter and possums freeze, when caught in the headlights, mesmerized into inaction.

The two vehicles are now one behind the other, but they are not alone. Tane keeps seeing flashes of headlights in his mirror getting closer and closer.

As they race towards Muriwai beach, the track straightens and changes to soft sandy loam which sprays out behind them. Accelerating over the flatter terrain, the Jeeps become airborne, launching over small humps and hollows. Tane and Mike fight the unpredictable sudden jerks of the steering wheel. With difficulty Tane leans towards the phone and calls Mike.

Gary has to grip the handle on the dash to answer. "Hi Tane, what's up?"

"Turn right at the next intersection and head for the hill climb." Mike nods, shouting. "Gotcha! Hey Julia, hold on tight, you're in for a very bumpy ride!"

She frowns, fighting to stay on her seat. "So this is not bumpy?"

"You've seen bucking broncos, right?"

"That bad!"

"Yep, that bad. Hey Tane, there are only a few of the gang left, but they are as mad as hell, we messed them up pretty good on Lone Kauri Road!"

He can see the damage to the rear seat and the missing wind screen and also that Mike and Gary are wearing goggles. "You look like you have been through a war zone, is that a bullet hole in the rear seat?"

Gary puts the phone close to his mouth to try and nullify the noise of the motor and the wind and the 'flap', 'flap' of his goggle straps. "Lady is a little bruised, Mike and I need a change of under-wear, other than that, all is well…. I have to tell you there's one hell of a mess back there though, it was like something out of a movie and yes, they have guns!"

Julia and Tane look at each other again. Tane to see if Julia is scared and Julia to show she is not.

Julia says. "Well there's two of us now, that will give them double trouble!"

Gary tries to talk between the bounces and finds it difficult to keep close to the phone. "Hey, Jules, mate, welcome to off street racing Kiwi style."

Tane leans forward again, shouting. "I'm going to slow a bit to let the gang catch up. I'm picking they haven't been here before…. We'll join you on the climb up to the first jump!" Tane turns to Julia, "There's water at the bottom of each of the jumps, they'll have to be bloody good to handle that lot!" Just as he says this, the road ahead is momentarily lit and then plunged back to darkness again, then lit again by the chasing head lights of the gang. This on again, off again, lighting is matched by the rise and fall of the high pitched crackle of the motorbike exhausts.

Suddenly an intersection races into view and they veer right and the track rises and falls like rolling waves. At each crest they are lifted off their seats, then slammed down on impact. Ahead is a much steeper hill and almost immediately Julia feels herself being pressed back harder and harder into her seat until they reach the top and at the descent she is thrown violently forward. Although restrained by her harness, she bangs her helmet on the dash board. Instead of being afraid, she loves the exhilarating feeling of being suddenly plunged downward and lets out a whoop.

Tane is surprised and smiles, shaking his head. "That is just the start of the jumps, there's a huge one coming, hold on tight to the handle on the dash!"

Not knowing what to expect, Julia says happily. "I'm holding, I'm holding!"

The track widens, allowing the two RVs to climb the steep hill together. There is another flash of light as the interior is lit by the head lights of the gang behind as they also start their climb.

Gary gives a thumbs up to Tane and Julia, beside him in the other jeep, then quickly returns to his two handed grip on the handle on the dash.

Higher and higher they climb with headlights soaring into the sky until they reach the crest at the same time and become airborne as their momentum propels them horizontal for a brief few seconds. Gravity soon tilts them downwards and their headlights light up the flat surface of the water below. With two huge splashes they dive into the shallow pond together. The front wheels penetrate the soft mud and the bull bars, the radiators and the lights propel a wave of slush forward. Then the rear wheels bump down, churning a fountain of slurry behind them. Within seconds the mud splattered Wranglers are up and out the other side.

The gang are unprepared for what happens next, bikes fly through the air before crashing down on each other, the same as at Lone Kauri Road. There is impact of bike on bike and rider on rider, but this time the wet, thick mud, chokes the life out of the smoking engines.

What was ear splitting noise one moment is suddenly reduced to sloshing, cursing and moans and the idling of motors at the top of the hill where the remainder of the gang throttle back in time.

Cautiously they make their descent down the sides of the hill to the bloody, muddy tangle of bodies and bikes at the bottom. Johnny Schmidt, in the middle of the pack has escaped the plunge and now takes charge. He checks the damage… No deaths this time! With difficulty the gang extract the bikes removing as much of the mud as they can. Some start, some don't. Instructing four of his able bodied men to assist the four injured members back to the gate, Johnny phones the Saint John Ambulance Service. That leaves only three, including himself, to avenge the harm done to his gang.

Having sniffed heroin while waiting at Helensville he is primed for the fight and ready to kill! Now, looking up at the top of the hill, he can see that the two Jeeps have stopped and are watching. Cursing, he reaches behind and unstraps a sawn-off shot gun, aims and pulls the trigger but the Wranglers are already on the move and the deadly pellets fly harmlessly into the night. Reloading both barrels, he returns the shotgun to its pouch and signals his other two gang members to give chase.

Tane glances at Julia. "You okay Julia, no broken bones?"

She shakes her head, not willing to admit that the jolt had just about put her backbone through the top of her head, and that being covered in mud was anything but fun! Bruised by the jolting and huge centrifugal forces, she wonders how she could have been so thrilled, just a moment before. Secretly she is wishing that she could be soaking in a warm bath and then snuggling under the blankets of a soft bed. Pushing those thoughts aside, she straightens and looks at herself in the rear view mirror to see if there are any outward signs of injury. As she studies herself, the headlights of the gang bikes flash into her eyes and with dismay shakes her head. "Amazing they are coming again!"

Tane looks in his side mirror. "Let's see how they handle the beach jump!"

She whispers through clenched teeth. "Can't wait!"

Descending down toward the coast, the road meanders around the base of the black sand dunes. The trees have already given way to toitoi, flax and stunted shrubs, when a startled deer jumps out in front of their Jeep.

Tane jerks the Wrangler to one side, so that for a moment the deer and the vehicle race side by side. The abrupt movement has put the car into a slide close to the frightened deer, so close that Julia can almost reach out and touch the flared nose and the scared red flecked eyes. Fighting to regain control, Tane over corrects and the Jeep slithers around so that the rear now leads the way.

Julia gasps, as the centrifugal force again presses her hard into her restraining harness and then slams her back into her seat as the Jeep slithers around. Finding it painful to breathe, she knows there is damage to her chest.

Slowing, Tane turns the car sideways and then accelerates hard to straighten, just as the deer sidesteps and disappears into the night.

Reaching over, he strokes her arm. "Are you still with us?"

Julia exhales slowly trying to hide the pain. "Just!" He knows that she is hurting. "We should give them the slip pretty soon, hang in there Julia." Reaching forward, he calls Mike and Gary.

Gary answers with difficulty. "Hi Tane... what's up?"

"You guys okay?"

There is a moments silence as Mike corrects a slide, then leans forward, yelling. "All okay.... Lady is whimpering..... I think she may be bruised.... I've counted only three headlights behind so we have whittled them down!... What do you reckon next?"

"We're going to have to gun it over the soft sand just before the beach jump. Once over, turn south towards the river. I'm hoping it's not too deep, it's usually okay this time of the year. Good luck guys, see you on the other side."

As Mike hangs up he wonders if he should joke about Tane's meaning of '*the other side*', but he guesses right that Julia is not in a joking mood right now.

The engines are racing at full throttle, and there is a smell of hot oil, as they sway left and right over the soft sand. Immediately ahead is a cutting in the dunes high above the hard flat sands of the beach.

A moment later, Julia can feel herself being catapulted once again into space, and this time the free fall seems endless.

As if time is suspended, faintly in the distance she can make out the white lines of the surf and hear the pounding waves under the louder roar of the motor. The Jeep hits the sand with another bone breaking jolt, throwing her forward and then backwards, as it accelerates away. Although restrained, Julia's helmet bangs onto the windscreen and she is yanked downwards as if a giant hand has slapped her back into her seat. She feels something trickling down her chin and tastes blood in her mouth. The Jeep slides sideways, and looking over, she sees that Tane is slumped against the steering wheel. The engine is screaming as it starts to do figure eights in the sand. This throws Julia against the car door and away from the lifeless Tane. Using all her strength, she reaches over and pushes him off the steering wheel, then kicks with her heel, dislodging his shoe from the accelerator pedal. Immediately the mad careering slows and grasping the steering wheel in both hands she is able to hold it to a single slide.

Tane moans and shakes his head, just as the second Jeep crashes onto the sand behind them. Sitting up, he looks around, bemused why Julia is pushing across him, with her hands on the steering wheel. She lets go when it is obvious that he has regained his senses. Blinking, he shakes his head which only induces more pain! Still confused, he turns to her with a frown. "What happened, was I out?"

She nods. "Hell Tane, I thought you were dead, you scared the crap out of me, you must have bumped your head!"

He nods feeling the ache in his head, then becomes concerned when he sees blood trickling down her chin. "You've got blood on your chin. Are you all right?"

"I'm okay… I think I bit my tongue!"

By now the two vehicles have come to a stop some distance from the cut in the dunes. Tane reaches over and lightly strokes her bloodied face. "My poor Julia." He gently kisses her on the lips leaving a bloody smudge on his chin.

Julia sits up straight. "See I'm cured already!"

Having weathered the jump a little better, Mike motors up beside them and shouts. "Sorry to interrupt you two, but we'd better get moving." He points his thumb over his shoulder towards the cutting.

With headlights blazing and by the light of the moon, one after the other, three bikes expertly bang down on the black sand and then turn towards them.

Tane counts the lights. "One, two, three, we'd better get to the river pronto!"

Mike nods and they both race off down the beach towards the distant silver ribbon that starts narrow at the dunes and then fans out until it disappears into the surf.

Now that the bikes are on flat hard sand, they slowly gain on the two Wranglers. When in shooting range, Johnny reaches behind and pulls out his sawn-off shot gun from its holster. Already the two other gang members have pistols in their hands pointing forward. Johnny rests the shot gun on top of the high handle bar, pulls the butt tight into his shoulder, directs the barrels towards one of the Wranglers, then pulls one of the triggers. The unstable position causes the shotgun to kick upwards so the pellets zing over the top of Mike's car which is now only thirty metres ahead.

Although the pellets have long gone, the roar of the gun makes everyone duck, including Lady, who has found a safe haven on the floor. The pistol shooting is more accurate and two slugs whack into the spare tire on the back, behind Julia and Tane and kick up splashes of sand as both Jeeps take evasive action. They zig-zag trying not to crash into each other. The maneuverings have slowed their progress towards the river allowing the bikes to press within twenty metres and the next discharge from the other barrel of the shot gun punctures holes in the back of Mike's car and Lady yelps. The men know she has been hit!

Holding tight with one hand, Gary reaches back and strokes her head with the other, trying to soothe her, but knowing that there is little else he can do.

Mike, concentrating on zig zagging and pushing the Wrangler as hard as he can, shouts at Gary. "How is she? Can you see anything?"

Gary shakes his head and then holds on with both hands as Mike yanks the car in another direction. Julia doesn't want to look behind, but focuses on the silvery strip of the river, willing it closer.

The shooting has slowed the gang and the Jeeps are now far enough ahead that the pistols are no-longer a threat. Returning their pistols to their jacket pockets, the gang concentrate on the chase. With the shooting stopped, it is now a straight out race and the bikes close again until they are just behind the Jeeps again. This time they know that they will not miss!

Julia sees the river closing fast, but is dismayed that it is not a gentle flowing stream but a rushing torrent of water.

Tane calls Mike on his phone. "Head up the beach towards the dunes where the river is deepest!"

Giving the thumbs up, Mike turns abruptly inland, following Tane just as the triggers are pulled and the volley of bullets ineffectually zing down the beach. Everyone hears the 'crack' 'crack' of the pistols close behind. Julia's knuckles turn white as she tightens her grip on the handle in front of her, and she sees the river rushing towards them. Her inner mind shrieks, '*Oh no, not again!*'

The river, flowing through a gap in the dunes, has carved a three metre high bank on either side, before fanning out to thirty meters wide, but it is only one metre deep.

Mike's Jeep is the first to plunge into the water with a huge splash! Turning the wheels in the direction of the current, he drifts down towards the surf until the spinning wheels grip the soft river bed and propel him forward. Now in shallower water Mike is able to turn towards the bank and soon they are climbing up the other side.

In the other Jeep, Julia lifts her knees as the water swirls up and around her feet and she feels the vehicle aquaplane before it settles and then surges forward. At last she allows herself to turn and watch the gang, as two bikers who have followed them create huge splashes before tumbling over and over as they are swept away. Mike and Tane race onwards for another kilometer before stopping.

Julia touches Tane's arm and gives the thumbs up as Mike motors over and parks beside them. He calls out. "Tane, I think Lady has been hit, I'm going to take a look."

In an instant Tane is out of his car and anxiously looking down at Lady who is licking her bloodied left hind leg. Leaning into the car, he gently strokes her head. "My poor girl, are you hurt? Is it your leg?"

Lady looks up and whimpers.

Tane turns to Mike, "She doesn't seem to be bleeding much." He studies her for a moment, "We may harm her if she is moved. We'll have to get her to a Vet as soon as, there's one at Waimauku. You take her and I'll go and pick up Wendy and Robyn from Hinemoa's house."

Mike nods as Tane jogs back to his Jeep and removes Lady's blanket from the back seat and returns and wraps it around her.

She is beginning to shiver.

Climbing back into his car, he waves his hand and Julia does the same.

The Wranglers race off to the beach head at Muriwai, leaving behind bruised and very wet gang members and two bumps in the moonlit water.

CHAPTER 10

The Police Communications Centre

Earlier that evening, the Auckland Police Communications Centre is surprisingly quiet for a Saturday night. Constable Mary Clarke, seated in front of her screen at Northern Dispatch notes that it is eight o'clock. *'So far so good, six hours to go.'* She knows that it is too early for the usual cluster of noisy-neighbour complaints that will keep her busy. Apart from one serious crash on Old North Road; the expected drunk-in-charge reports from the road blocks and a gang related incident at the Parakai pub, it is strangely quiet. *'Shall I have water, Milo or another coffee?..... Don't know about coffee, it's supposed to be good for your heart but bad for your nerves, or is it the other way around? That's the trouble with all this new found medical stuff!'*

She decides to wait half an hour before choosing a drink. Sighing, she reaches for the latest NZ Woman's Weekly with a half-finished crossword puzzle, *'24 across, Angelina _ _ _ _ _?'*

As she is counting the letters in *'Jolie'*, she is interrupted by new information appearing on her screen.

'Ambos report possible gang incidents. 1 At the end of Lone Kauri Road. 2 At Old Woodhills Rd, halfway to beach. Possible deaths, many injured. Gang related? Time delay 5 minutes.'

Mary instantly sheds her lethargy. She knows that this is high priority and her actions will be under scrutiny. Acknowledging, she sends, '*RRR*' and follows up with the question. '*Name and contact details of Ambos informant?*'

Back comes the reply. '*Schmidt/Johnny, calling from mobile number UK. Ambos advise he sounded stressed. Said road accident. He has disconnected. NNNN. Ambos will call back if any further. They are requesting a safe forward point.*'

Mary Sends, '*RRR*' *again,* then presses the '*ND*' button which alerts her boss that he is needed at her North Dispatch desk. In the few seconds it takes the Inspector to arrive, Mary alerts her two incident cars and the Sergeant at Henderson Police Station.

Her boss for the night, Inspector Ronnie Vaiili is typical of most of the Polynesians in the New Zealand Police Force. He is softly spoken and quick to laugh, but that does not make him slow of thought. His team respect him as a smart and perceptive law enforcer. Ronnie is a people person and they like the way he empowers them to make decisions.

He knows it must be important as Mary is quite capable of handling most of the emergency calls on her own. Now, looking over her shoulder, he reads the report and points to the screen. "I know Johnny Schmidt, he's the leader of the Satan's Sons gang." He frowns, "This can't be gang warfare, the largest gangs have just formed a drug syndicate." He shakes his head, "This doesn't make sense!"

Mary is surprised that the gangs have become syndicated and is flattered that her boss has entrusted her with this information. "I've looked him up in the system, sir, there's a mobile number listed, I'll give it a call."

He nods.

After a moment, "No luck there, it goes straight to voicemail, I'll leave a message."

Again he nods.

At the 'beep' she leaves her message, "This is Constable Mary Clarke of the Police Communication Centre, we've received a one, one, one, call from this phone, please call again so that we can be of assistance, thank you." Again she looks up, "I've got two cars going to the two locations, both have firearms and Tasers. I have a dog unit and a Sergeant from Henderson. I don't think we have enough information to call the AOS or the chopper at this stage, what do you think?"

"All good Mary. Find out the names of the units involved and let me know when they are in position. In the meantime, I'll talk to Max."

Max Henderson, the District Superintendent is at the Aotea Centre with his daughter watching Swan Lake when his phone vibrates in his pocket. He is a distinguished looking forty-year veteran, married once, but now a long time divorcee. He removes his phone from his pocket and whispers. "Hi Ronnie, must be important?"

Ronnie can hear the orchestra playing Tchaikovsky's music and knows he is intruding on a special occasion. "Sorry to call you boss, but I thought it important to let you know that the Satan's Sons have just been involved in some sort of stoush resulting in death and injury."

Max, conscious of the sharp looks to his right, whispers again. "I'll call you back." As politely as he can, he excuses himself past numerous knees until he is out in the foyer. This time there is an edge to his voice and it is not from the annoyance of the phone call. "It's me again, what sort of stoush? Who with? How many deaths and injuries?"

Ronnie, who can still hear the faint strains of ballet music, shakes his head. "Sorry boss not clear yet, all I have is that the Ambos say the call came from Johnny Schmidt himself. That is unusual, why would he make the call and not one of his side kicks? He must be involved. It must be serious!" He pauses for a moment, frowns, then shakes his head, "It doesn't make sense, Joey would have let us know, I'm on my way to check it out."

Max nods, also frowning. "You're right, this is very strange, thanks for keeping me in the loop. I'm at the ballet with my daughter and I don't care diddly squat about a dying swan!" He is quiet for some time as he thinks about the gang.

If it wasn't for the faint music in the background, Ronnie would have thought that he had been disconnected.

Eventually Max makes a decision and continues, "You know, this is unfortunate, we are so close to busting that gang! Try to keep the lid on the whole thing as best you can. Be discreet and keep the media away, on second thoughts, refer them to me, somehow I'll have to play this down, we've invested too much time and money to stop now." He pauses again.

Ronnie waits a moment and then suggests. "Maybe this has something to do with the two million dollars in Rarotonga? That amount of money usually stirs up trouble."

"Interesting thought Ronnie, see what you can suss out with your Raro brother, and Joey, keep me informed no matter what the hour, okay?"

"Sure boss."

"Call me Max! We're both too long in the tooth for that malarkey".

" Okay… Max I'll talk to you later."

CHAPTER 11

The Morning After.

Outside Julia's open window a tui sits on the highest branch of a flowering pohutukawa tree and delivers a Parson's sermon using chattery squawks intermingled with surprisingly sweet bell like sounds. The loud, persistent, unfamiliar noise penetrates her sleep, and startled she sits up pulling the duvet up to her chin. The fear of the night before is still with her until she sees the sunshine and the beauty of a new day.

Yawning, she stretches her arms above her head, not a good move with bruised ribs. Getting out of bed she shuffles toward an old oak wardrobe that has a mirror. Pulling up her pyjama top she rotates left and right studying the purple and yellow patches under her breasts. "Well, at least that's a blessing."

"I'd say you have two beautiful blessings!" Says Wendy from the doorway.

Startled, Julia drops her top. "Don't scare me like that, I was checking my bruises. You wouldn't believe the battering I took last night!"

Wendy hurries into the room and sits on the edge of the bed. "Tell me Jules, what happened after we left? I mean that was one freaky night. First you kicked a gang man in the goolies and next

you're off on some sort of wild road chase!"

Julia, now standing beside the bed, nods, as Wendy continues, "When Tane arrived at Hinemoa's place, both of you looked like death warmed over! Hell Jules I was scared for you from the start, what happened last night?" She pats the mattress beside her and Julia sits down, tucking her legs under.

Nestled side by side, Julia can feel Wendy's warmth and is comforted by her best friend's concern. "I know I was silly last night but I had no idea that the gang would be so violent. Somehow it seemed like a game, but of course it wasn't. It was as bad as Hinemoa warned!" She shrugs, "I know you all tried to warn me but after the pool game I was on a high. Somehow I felt that I was kind-of invincible! It was as if I was protected! It's hard to explain but I felt like I could conquer the world!" She shakes her head, "I don't know why I felt like that? Maybe it was the beer, or perhaps homesick, or missing my dad." She shrugs, "The whole night seemed unreal, as if in a dream."

Wendy puts an arm around her shoulders and gives her a hug which hurts Julia's ribs and she yelps.

"Sorry Jules, are you still hurting?"

She nods. "It was really bad. The gang were shooting at us! I've never been shot at before. I was really scared!"

She turns towards Wendy, "I thought it was fun at first, but that soon changed! No matter what the men tried, the gang wouldn't give up, they really wanted to hurt us."

Shaking her head she stares down at the floor reliving the chase, "You wouldn't believe what we did to try and escape, it was Hell! We even drove up a steep hill and then splashed into a lake at the bottom. They had pistols and a shot gun and they put a hole in the back of Mike's Jeep smashing his windscreen. Bullets were kicking up sand as we zigged zagged along the beach trying to escape!"

She shakes her head again, "It was no game!"

Remembering Tane being unconscious behind the wheel, she taps Wendy on the leg, "When we jumped from the sand dunes to the beach, Tane got knocked out and I had to steer from my side of the car, it was not easy!"

Wendy opens her eyes wide. "Say what, you were shot at and

Tane was unconscious! Do you mean you were in the Jeep and Tane was out to it? How did you manage to survive?"

Julia is about to explain, when Robyn enters the room and jumps onto the bed.

Julia lets out a yelp.

Robyn studies Julia closely. "Sorry Jules are you all-right? Did you get hurt last night?"

She nods as Wendy puts her arm around Julia's waist and then leans forward, looking at Robyn. "Jules was just telling me how she had to steer Tane's Jeep from the passenger's side because he was unconscious!"

Turning back to Julia she asks with a frown, "How did you stop the Jeep?"

"I kicked his foot off the accelerator that seemed to wake him up. He was groggy for a bit, then he took the wheel as if nothing had happened!... I tell you it was real freaky!"

Robyn is still concerned about Julia's injuries. "How did you get hurt Jules?"

"They were shooting at us!"

Robyn places a handover her mouth then removes it. "They were shooting at you! Oh my God, it sounds like the wild west!" Getting off the bed she kneels in front of her and looks up and down noticing the bruising around her mouth, "You didn't get shot, did you?"

She shakes her head and is thankful for her friends' concern. "No, it was the jolting of the Jeep over the hilly road and also when we hit the hard sand at the beach. We were strapped into our seats, that saved our lives but the straps cut into my chest... Thank God I was wearing a helmet. Oh, I just remembered, Lady was shot and was taken to a Vet, that's why Mike didn't stop at Hinemoa's house. Tane and I were so exhausted and you lot were so sleepy we didn't want to talk about it, we just wanted to get back to the Homestay."

Wendy frowns. "Is Mike okay?"

Robyn interjects. "Yeah and what about Gary?"

Julia pauses, looking from one to the other with a smile. "They are both okay but I bet Tane's got one hell of a headache." She shakes her head, "I'm not sure about Lady?"

Robyn stands, folding her arms. "They shouldn't have taken her with them, she could have come with us, it was really dumb… I hope she is okay?"

Julia smiles up at her. "I thought you didn't like dogs?"

"I agree with the boys, she's not a dog, she's a dog person and very special, oh dear, poor Lady, I hope she's all right, we'd better visit the guys and see how she is as soon as!"

They all nod and any further discussion is interrupted by Jean knocking on the open door. "Morning lovely ladies, I hope you had a good time last night and the boys behaved themselves." Being more of a polite comment than a serious question, she continues, "Breakfast will be ready in half an hour, I'm making kiwi style scrambled eggs and bacon."

She is greeted with blank stares,

"Have you had kiwi style scrambled eggs before?"

They look at each other, then in unison shake their heads, each thinking the same thought. '*We only want cereal, fruit and coffee!*' No one has the courage to speak up, so Robyn replies. "That will be wonderful thank you Jean, see you soon."

As Jean departs humming a happy tune, Wendy says with a questioning voice. "Kiwi style scrambled eggs?"

They shrug their shoulders and try to hide their giggles.

CHAPTER 12

Emma's Story and Hand Painted China

The Waimauku Veterinary Clinic is down a side road near a creek and far enough from the nearest house that the animal noises are not a problem. Emma Swift's clinic is a dream come true. Like most small town animal clinics it is a converted house. "The cheaper the better, I'll renovate," were the instructions to the Real Estate Agent who has heard that request many times before.

After graduating from Massey University, Emma wouldn't allow the worry of repaying her student loan to deter her from owning her own business. She is of the new generation that want it now, not tomorrow, not in the future, but now and she hopes that a small down deposit will be acceptable to a bank. It is not, and hears the same message over and over again. "You have just graduated as a Vet and we have no evidence of your ability to repay a business loan. Anyway we require a minimum of a forty percent deposit, Reserve Bank regulations, which you don't have!" Seeing her disappointment, they add, "Look Emma, work for a few years and reduce your student loan, by say, twenty-thousand dollars and then come back and see us again. If you do that we will reconsider your application." Standing as a signal that the interview is over, they offer platitudes, "Don't give up on your dreams Emma, we're always here to help, by-the-way, do you have Life or Contents Insurance? How about your car? We can save you money with a package plan!"

Thankfully Kiwibank is more helpful, offering a business loan that covers the deposit as well as the purchase of the house but no additional funds for setup costs. She knows that she is going to have to seek her parents help.

Paul Swift, now sitting opposite her at the kitchen table, leans forward and extends his hands, palms upward towards her. She places her hands in his and he asks. "How much do you want?"

That is the very question she has been dreading. Holding her breath, she whispers. "Thirty thousand dollars!" Finding it difficult to breathe, she continues quickly, "It's the cheapest house I could find in an area that needs a Vet. It's out in Waimauku. It's selling for four hundred thousand and I'm sure there will be enough income to cover the mortgage. Kiwibank will help me with the purchase of the building, but I don't have any money for equipment and remodeling the house. I can show how that money will be spent if you wish."

He shakes his head.

By now she is almost in tears and squeezes his hands, "Look dad I don't expect you and mum to give it to me as a gift, I'll pay you back with interest, but it might take me some time." Having said every-thing she wanted to say she is exhausted and can't stop fidgeting in her chair.

He looks at her as memories flash through his mind; her early childhood; her teenage years and more recently as a University student. Now at twenty-five she is a qualified Veterinarian and he looks at her with pride. He knows that she could have been a fashion model with her tall, blonde good looks and is pleased she chose a less frivolous career. His thoughts only take a few seconds, but for Emma it seems like an eternity.

"Emma, I'm going to tell you something about myself and your mother. It's something that I'm sure you won't forget because some-time in the future there is every chance that a child of yours will come to you asking for help." He straightens in his chair, "When your mother and I first arrived in Canada we stayed with your grandparents in their big house in Kitchener. The first night when Ed and I were alone, he said to me, 'Paul, you're going to need a car to get around. First thing tomorrow morning we'll go down to George Fleishman's car yard and see what we can find.'

I shouldn't have been surprised at Ed's quick decision making as he was a self-made man growing up in an Ottawa Valley lumber camp. When he was twenty-seven he moved to Kitchener with money in his pocket and bought a house. As-a-matter-of fact he bought the house before he started looking for a wife. Fancy that, quite a guy!... I asked him how he was able to earn that sort of money cutting down trees? He said, 'Paul, you don't know the half of it. There were thirteen in my family living in a one room cabin on a small farm in Sebastopol, a German community, on rocky land gifted by the Canadian Government. I knew it was hard for dad and mum to feed us, so I decided to leave home at thirteen. In those days there were no regulations about leaving school. If there were, they were ignored. George, my older brothers, teased me that I'd be back in a week. I told them I wouldn't return until spring, and that is what I did. The cook and the stable manager at the lumber camp taught me everything I needed to know. In a way I was like a son to the whole camp. They all looked after me and taught me how to become a lumber Jack. I also saw how some of the men drank and gambled away their earnings during those long winter nights and I vowed not to do the same. Years later I had saved enough to buy a car and to help out my mum and dad before I moved to Kitchener.'

Interesting as his story is, about her Canadian grandfather, Emma wonders what it has to do with her and the loan.

Paul becomes aware that they have been holding hands for quite some time so he releases them and then continues, "Your mother and I had a little money that we had saved, but after the cost of moving to Canada, buying a car would have left us with nothing. Anyway the following morning, punctual as ever, we were greeted by George as he opened the gates of his car yard. I didn't know it but Ed had already spoken to him about me and he led us straight to a car that he thought would suit. I guess they knew that I wouldn't have a clue about North American cars."

Paul shifts in his chair as he has a new thought, "Now that I think about it, Ed must have thought that I was pretty wet behind the ears and wondered why his youngest daughter had married someone with such a strange accent. I didn't know it, but my dad had written a letter to Ed asking him to look after me. Fancy that, I would never have guessed or expected him to do that! It was both nice but insulting all at the same time. I was given the letter as a keep-sake after Ed's death, it still brings tears to my eyes."

Paul holds out his hands to his daughter again, which she clasps, "So, there was this huge white Dodge Polara, sparkling in the morning sun. My car in New Zealand was a Morris Minor and if the two cars were placed side by side, the Morris would have looked like a pedal car! It was enormous and I felt way too insignificant to own something so grand.

George nonchalantly handed me the keys and said, 'Take it for a spin son and see if you like it'.

I sank into the full width front seat, behind a huge steering wheel. It was like sitting on a sofa! I tried to hide my lack of confidence as I inserted the key and started the motor, expecting a great roaring noise, instead it quietly purred! As another surprise, when I turned the steering wheel it was effortless, not like my old stiff mini. Power steering was so easy! It took me a few attempts to get used to spinning the wheel a full revolution, just to make a half turn. I loved the car, but couldn't see how I could afford it.

When we entered the sales office, I was uncomfortable about having to admit that I didn't have enough money. Ed handed a cheque to George for the full amount then had me sign as the owner. I will never forget Ed's kindness."

Releasing her hand he smiles at her, "I've been expecting you to come and ask for help to start up your business. I must admit I'm surprised it has happened as quickly as this, but it makes no difference. Just as Ed helped me and your mother, we will help you."

He turns and looks out the open sliding doors of the patio towards his wife who is kneeling on a weeding cushion beside their raised vegetable garden.

Standing, he moves to the doorway, "Jan!...... yooo-whooo!"

She looks towards the house.

"Emma is here, she wants our help."

Jan places the trowel on the edge of the box and stands removing her gloves, then brushes long strands of hair off her face.

As she enters the kitchen, Emma stands and notices a worried look on her face, "Hi mum, you okay?"

"Hi Em, I was going to ask you the same. What sort of help do you need? Are you okay?"

"Sure mum, I've just asked dad if you two will help me with some money to start my own practice."

Jan frowns again. "How much do you want?"

"Thirty thousand." She is about to explain the reasons, when her mother interrupts, surprised it is not for a whole lot more.

"It's fine with me dear, we'll have to cash a bond, but that's not a problem." She looks toward Paul who nods. Reaching up she kisses Emma on both sides of her cheeks, "I know you will be a great Vet, I'm so proud of you!" They begin to cry.

Paul waits for them to dry their eyes and to sit down. "Emma, we'd expect you to pay us back, just as we paid back your grandfather, but you set the repayments. There is no time limit and there won't be any interest….. We don't want it to be a hardship."

Tears start flowing down her cheeks again as she looks from one to the other. "Thanks dad and mum, you'll never know how much this means to me!"

Paul says with a half-smile. "Oh I think we do!"

Hugging her mum first, then her dad, she buries her face into his soft shoulder and feels once again like a small child safe and secure in his unconditional love.

Now, two years later, with a thriving business, Emma quietly opens the door of Lady's cage, trying not to disturb her.

Lady immediately lifts her head then tries to stand. Emma places a gentle but firm hand on her shoulder and pushes her back into her blanket.

She is still confused and rolls her head around looking at the cage and then back up at Emma.

"Hi Lady, you are a very brave girl! You got shot last night and I fixed you up."

Lady lets out a low "woof" to say she understands loving sounds and a friendly face even though her hands smell of disinfectant and cats!

Emma checks for abnormalities and is satisfied with her condition. Her breathing is slow and rhythmical and her eyes are bright and intelligent. This does not surprise her as the two shotgun pellets did not hit vital organs and only penetrated into the upper thigh muscle before lodging against the bone.

Removal of the pellets required simple surgery, but she knows that the wounds will take a few weeks to heal and that she will be uncomfortable for the next few days.

Gently as she can, she applies her stethoscope and is satisfied with the sounds of a heart beat that is slightly faster than normal, owing to the pain killer. This time she doesn't try to stop her from standing, which she does with difficulty.

Twisting backwards, Lady tries to lick her injured leg but finds that the bandaging is just too hard to remove and collapses back onto her blanket with a moan.

A few minutes later, the phone on the wall rings, and Emma answers. "Waimauku Vet Clinic, Emma speaking."

Tane holds a business card in his hand that says *'Emma Swift, Veterinary Surgeon'*. He is glad that he is speaking directly to the Vet. "Hi Emma, I'm Tane Lendic, Lady's owner, Mike dropped her off last night."

Lady "yips" when she hears his voice and he recognises her "yip" amongst the other animal noises. Apprehensively he asks, "How is she?"

Emma looks at Lady, who is trying to stand again. "All the signs are good Tane, I removed two shotgun pellets from her left rear leg. There doesn't appear to be any complications apart from damage to tissue and muscle. There is swelling around the incisions, but I expect those to heal quite quickly. I'll do another inspection this afternoon and if you don't hear from me, you can come and pick her up after four."

Without realising that he has been holding his breath, he exhales. "Phew, that is good news, thanks heaps Emma and sorry for the late night call, I owe you one!"

Emma smiles. "As a matter of a fact, you owe me one hundred and fifty ones to be exact!"

Still buoyed by the relief he decides to tease her. "How about a contra deal? Do you like hand painted china painted by a very famous artist?"

She smiles, liking the sound of his voice. "Money's good, see you later." She hangs up thinking, '*I won't mind seeing Mike again and Tane sounds pretty interesting as well!*' She leaves the room still smiling. Tane clicks off the phone and takes the glass domed coffee percolator off the stove and places it on a coaster in the middle of the table. Reaching up he removes three large mugs from their hooks, then holding down the lid of the percolator fills them with the steaming black liquid.

The smell soon brings sleep tousled Mike and Gary into the kitchen. Both are anxious to hear about Lady.

"The Vet says she's going to be okay, just superficial wounds." Tane pours milk from a plastic bottle into each of the mugs, "How'd you sleep last night?"

Gary is the first to reply. "I had the weirdest dreams, I still feel edgy!"

Mike sips his coffee, then nods. "Me too, that was one crazy night, we'd better check on Julia, she got whacked around pretty bad, how about a visit after breakfast?"

Tane and Gary nod. As they sip their coffee in silence, they think about the unforgettable terror of the chase.

A hundred metres inland, the ladies enter the dining room and are surprised at its size. What they are looking at is hours of planning and work by Jean and her husband, many years ago. They removed the wall between the dining room and the kitchen and the enlarged room now stretches from the front veranda to the rear of the house.

Hanging from the centre of the dining room ceiling is a large six armed brass lamp supporting milk glass shades, decorated with small blue forget-me-not flowers.

Under the hanging lamp is Jean's pride and joy, a fourteen seater, eight legged kauri table with red velvet covered chairs. It came with the boarding house, being too big to fit in a conventional dining room. The table and chairs sit at right angles to the kitchen. Patrons can see Jean when she is in the kitchen and she can see them, a fine arrangement for conversation.

There is also a smaller table in the kitchen that is used when there are only a few guests, like this morning.

The girls, as Jean always calls them, are seated at the table with their coffees and have a close view of the 'Kiwi style' scrambled egg as it is removed from the oven.

A large baking pan contains what looks like a brown flat cake and not like any scrambled egg they have ever seen before! With the oven door open they can smell and see, another baking pan filled with strips of bacon, on top of halved tomatoes stuffed with parmesan cheese and fresh oregano. The smell is delicious.

Removing four large white plates from the oven, Jean spreads butter on thick toasted ciabatta bread. Placing them on the plates she tops them with a square of baked egg. Next she adds the tomato and the crispy bacon on the side, decorating the egg with a sprig of parsley.

Jean doesn't offer a choice of cooked breakfasts as she is not aware of the eccentricity of North American appetites.

Gingerly forking the square, they notice that beneath the brown crust there is the familiar light yellow of the egg as well as an array of other colours. Green strips of chives and chopped parsley; orange chunks of cheese and small cubes of bright red tomato. Although it has an indifferent crust, the baked egg is delicious with a hint of thyme and spiced with white pepper and just the right amount of salt.

Jean's greatest pleasure is seeing her guests enjoy her cooking. As she watches them from her favourite place at the end of the table, she wonders if they are enjoying their stay in New Zealand. On refilling Julia's coffee cup she notices the telltale bruising around her mouth. "Did you have an accident last night Julia?"

Still agitated by the night's events, Julia is irritated, but tempers her reply with a simple. "Yes!"

Heads turn towards her and the table becomes quiet. She wonders how much she should tell. Surprising herself, she retells the whole story which somehow makes her feel better.

Jean's ever deepening frown is directed towards the beach and Tane's cottage. "They should not have placed you in danger! I'm really annoyed at the boys! Just wait until I see them tonight, silly boys!" She shakes her head, "What were they thinking!"

Julia is surprised at the intensity of her anger. "I wish you wouldn't Jean. Everything that happened last night was my fault! You will make me feel really ashamed." She shrugs, "Apart from a few bruises I'm fine and the guys were very brave!"

Jean is silent for a moment studying Julia and her bruises. "Okay I'll mind my own business, but for Heaven's sake be more careful, some of those motorcycle gangs can be really nasty!" Standing she collects the empty plates, "Lunch is at twelve and I'll make you a nice salmon salad with fresh sourdough bread, do you like home-made lemonade?" With all the questions they feel like children again and strangely it is not unpleasant.

Robyn asks. "Jean, we're going to visit the boys to check on Lady, how do we get to their cottage?"

Jean turns and points towards the back windows. "Follow the track through the bush it will take you to Tane's pottery shed then to the back door of his cottage." She turns to Robyn, "Gary's place is just past Tane's." She points to the right, "That way."

Robyn stands. "Come on let's go get our bikinis, we can go for a dip after our visit."

Julia nods wondering how much of her bruising will show.

Robyn is more interested in the guys' cottages. *I wonder how they live? This WILL be interesting!'*

Without Lady as a watch dog, the guys are surprised by the knock on the door that interrupts their breakfast. Hearing the happy chatter they react in different ways.

Tane checks that his fly is zipped.

Mike pushes his long blonde hair backwards with his fingers and strokes his moustache.

Gary, in underpants, leaps towards the lounge in search of his shorts.

Tane gets up from the table and opens the door.

Dressed only in shorts and bathed by the early morning sun, his tanned muscular body shines like polished copper and his black wavy hair contrasts with the clear unblemished white and blue of his eyes. His smiling lips are parted displaying white even teeth. He is the epitome of masculinity and Julia's heart skips a beat. Everything that she was going to say is forgotten leaving only the rhythmical surge of the surf and the excited chatter of a large cicada on the window sill.

Tane breaks the reverie by sweeping a theatrical arm into his cottage. "Welcome to our humble abode Ladies."

The weathered exterior makes them expect a shabby interior, but they are wrong. The kitchen is orderly and clean. Fascinated by its antiquity they notice the old fridge, the wood fired stove and copper pots hanging from hooks. The unpainted wood interior smells slightly smoky, blending nicely with the aroma of freshly brewed coffee coming from an old percolator on the back of the stove.

Mike is standing behind a large slab of wood that is the kitchen table, conference table, office desk, preparation area, and a bar.

Just as Julia was captivated by Tane, Wendy finds herself attracted to Mike.

Still sleepy, his long blonde hair is unruly, yet somehow becoming. Wearing a black singlet and black shorts, his muscular presence seems to fill his corner of the kitchen.

Willing her eyes away, she picks up a small perforated tin containing a yellow lump of soap beside the sink. "Is this what I think it is?"

Mike laughs. "That depends what you think it is."

"Maybe some sort of dish washing gizmo?"

"Right Einstein! That my dear lady is our dish washing machine. Nifty eh! No moving parts and cheap to replace."

"Doesn't it leave the dishes soapy?"

"Nope, not if you rinse!" Reaching down to a stack of plates he scratches his fingernail along the top plate, "See, squeaky clean!"

Gary enters the kitchen and the guys have trouble keeping a straight face. Not only has he slicked down his hair, but he is wearing Tane's jeans and a shirt that is two sizes too small. There is noticeable strain on the shirt buttons and on the zip of the fly. The trouser legs ride up to his ankles.

Robyn thinks he looks just fine and Gary notices no one else but Robyn. Both realise that they are staring at each other and simultaneously blush and look away.

Robyn stammers. "We came over to check on Lady, how is she?"

Tane, Mike and Gary answer together, not with the same words, but meaning the same. "She's fine..... she's okay..... she's good."

Julia sighs with relief. "Oh! that's great news, it kept me awake last night. I was worried about her, I even had a nightmare where she saved me from the gang, it was very real, can we visit her?"

Tane nods. "Sure, after four today, unless something goes wrong in the meantime, but it looks good for Lady." He turns so that he is directly facing Julia, "I was thinking about YOU all night. I kept remembering your bloodied face, but look at you now, you look amazingly...... well."

Julia punches him lightly on the chin. "I come from tough Canadian stock!"

Taking a step closer, he cradles her in his arms, stroking her hair. She doesn't move away, even though it is painful, snuggling even closer. Like the previous night, a surge of energy passes between them and both are surprised and pull away.

Seeking a distraction, Julia notices a set of hand painted dishes on a shelf. Lifting the closest plate, she turns it up-side-down searching for the artist's name and sees 'TL'. Turning it again she is captivated by the bright splash of colours and the unusual crimson flowers that decorate the plate. They look like a cluster of large red bottle brushes. Fascinated that a flower can look like that, she inspects it closely, noticing the fine, precise, brush strokes of the petals that are tipped with tiny black dots. Realising that this small piece of artistry is rare, she looks up at Tane with renewed fascination.

He also has been watching her closely.

"This is terrific art work Tane, I'm impressed."

He smiles down at her. "That is a reject from my pohutukawa series. I spent a long time experimenting with colours and shapes."

"Reject, I'm surprised, it looks fine to me."

He moves beside her, looking down at the plate in her hand. "I'm happy with the design but the glazing is slightly pock-marked." Pointing to a small cluster of dots he continues, "Do you see these little indentations in the glaze?"

She nods and then shakes her head. "I wouldn't have noticed, you really are a talent."

Pleased that she likes his work he moves to the shelf and selects more of his creations. "All of these are rejects, mainly because of firing defects." Taking the pohutukawa plate he gives her a new one, "This is from my nasturtium series."

The ladies cluster around admiring the bold colours of gold, yellow and orange,

"I have a few flower designs but mostly I like the combination of flowers, berries and birds." He hands her a new plate, "Like this one, puriri and kereru." Then points towards the back door, "That large tree out there Just behind the clothes line is a puriri tree." Cradling the plates in one arm he beckons with the other, "Come outside, I want to show you something."

They follow him under the large branches of the tree then stop close to its smooth trunk. Around them shafts of light penetrate through the dark green canopy highlighting patches of dried brown leaves at their feet.

Tane places a cautioning finger to his lips and then slowly moves around the trunk looking upwards, until he sees a huge wood pigeon feeding on clusters of deep purple berries. Pointing them he whispers, "That's a kereru, a wood pigeon... isn't it magnificent!" The wild pigeon is the largest they have ever seen. It is unique with dark green iridescent feathers and a patch of snow white underbelly, "They are only found in New Zealand and are a protected species. At one time they were almost extinct but are now on the increase. Look at its markings, isn't it fabulous. There's heaps of them throughout the Waitakere Ranges."

With heads looking up they watch the kereru feeding on the

berries, a few dislodge falling onto their heads and shoulders.

Tane whispers again, "They are real gluttons! They eat so much that they can hardly fly. The berries ferment in their stomach and they become quite tipsy and easy to catch. That is why they were almost hunted to extinction, listen to this." He hands the pile of plates to Julia, lifts a foot removing a rubber thong then whacks it hard against the side of the tree.

Startled, the pigeon looks down, turning its head from side to side then launches itself off the branch with its wings making a loud 'woosh' 'woosh' 'woosh' sound as it departs.

Tane smiles at the girls, "That is what I wanted you to hear. If you ever hear that sound you'll know a kereru is close by."

Julia nods. "I'll remember that sound and also this moment forever, damn, where is my camera?" Looking down at the plates in her hand, she taps the top one with her finger, "At least we've got your painting of the pigeon, the colours match perfectly, I love it!" She looks up with questioning eyes, "Can I buy it, please? I'll pay whatever you want."

He laughs. "Whatever I want?.... Nah, I don't sell seconds, but you can have it as a gift."

Clutching the plate to her breast she reaches up and kisses him on the lips. "I'll treasure it forever!"

He teases. "Forever is a long time."

"Not long enough!" Stepping away, she moves the top plate to the bottom exposing another design, "Tell me about this one please."

Taking the plate, he shows it to Wendy and Robyn. "This is a fantail on a honeysuckle vine. The fantail don't eat the nectar but eat the sand flies that live above the vines."

Wendy takes the plate and exclaims. "Fantail, so that's what you call those little birds we see everywhere, what a fitting name, they do have a fan like tail."

Mike steps forward. "I prefer its Maori name, piwakawaka because that's the sound it makes."

Remembering the shrill chirp, Wendy tries to imitate the sound. "Peewokawoka, peewokawoka." Her plumy English voice makes everyone laugh. Turning to Tane she asks, "Can I have this one please?"

"Sure thing." He takes the last three plates from Julia and walks over to Robyn. "If you like, you can have these three. Two of them you have seen, the pohutukawa and the nasturtium, but the last one is my favourite, kowhai and tui." As he hands the plates to her, Julia and Wendy complain.

Tane looks at Robyn and smiles. "They belong to me and I can give them to whoever I like."

Robyn agrees. "Of course you can!" Studying his favourite design, she runs a finger around the shape of the bird and the cascading flowers. She adores the design with its golden flowers and a large black bird feeding on the nectar, "What did you say this bird is called?"

"A tui and those flowers grow on a kowhai tree. There are clumps of them on the track near Jean's." Pointing to the black bird with its beak deep inside one of the trumpet like flowers, he continues, "This is quite a large bird and it is sometimes called a parson bird because of the white tuft under its beak, you know, like a parson's collar."

They huddle around Robyn to get a better look at the bird,

"Tuis are the noisiest birds in the forest, for some reason they like to mimic other birds, why I don't know, but you'll hear them every morning at Jean's."

Julia nods, remembering the loud bird that woke her up that morning. She looks again at her unexpected gift, a painting of a wood pigeon and puriri berries. "How do you plan your paintings?... I mean, do you do sketches or something before you start?"

"I suppose you could call them etchings... I have lots of them, in black and white."

With arms folded, still clutching her plate to her chest, Julia moves close to Tane again. "Do you mind showing me your etchings, talented man?"

"I don't mind if I do, but I can assure you they look better by candle light with a glass of wine!"

She points a finger under his nose. "That's a date oh great painter of flora and fauna!"

Wendy turns to Mike. "I believe you are the one with the terrific etchings!"

"Who says?"

"Jean, she said you sell them for thousands of dollars."

"Did she now, well I wish it was true… I suppose over five years I have sold a few thousand dollars worth, but I'm not rich, if that's what you think… Fancy Jean saying that!"

Tane elbows Mike playfully. "He could be if he painted faster!"

Mike clips him on the back of the head. "You can talk, you make only twenty sets a year! That's less than one set a fortnight! You wouldn't keep a job in a Chinese sweat shop."

"Exactly!"

Wendy gets between the two of them. "Anyone who is good enough to sell their work is someone special. There are too many of us non-creatives in the world." She turns to Mike, "Jean says you paint beach scenes, I would love to see your paintings, do you have some we can see, or is that against artists rules or something?"

"No I don't mind." He points towards the cottage, "I'll be pleased to show you a large one that is almost finished, right now if you like?"

The girls nod and Mike leads the way out from under the shade of the puriri tree into the bright sunshine.

Before they reach the cottage, Gary rushes past, remembering the mess in the lounge.

Quickly straightening the covers on the sofa bed he kicks his clothes underneath then lifts and closes the mattress accompanied by the sound of complaining springs. Just in time he repositions the cushions as Mike enters the room then turns to face the ladies. "Welcome to my studio, bedroom and bedsit."

A painting on an easel is in the middle of the room covered by a sheet.

Gary now seated on the sofa is ready to enjoy the girls' reactions. He is very proud of Tane and Mike's talents.

Tane joins him on the sofa as the ladies cluster around the easel.

Mike removes the sheet with a flourish and a loud. *"Taadaah!"*

The large oil on canvas painting of Karekare beach is revealed and there are gasps of delight. Using thick oils and a pallet knife, his bold strokes make the black sand seem blacker; the sea more blue than green and the craggy island out in the bay a triangle of black, browns, orange, yellow and purple. His colours are an exaggeration but his perspective and shadings are true.

Wendy is spellbound. She may deride her own artistic abilities, but she recognizes superior art and its worth. Studying Mike with new respect, she is aware that he has concealed his talents. She realises that his artistic maturity is deliberately hidden behind athleticism and his uninhibited joy of living.

For his part, Mike is comfortable with this shield as he often experiences the discomfort of probing questions from people who are mystified how he can produce such beautiful works of art. They prod and probe trying to discover what makes him tick. It makes him uncomfortable. On this occasion however, he enjoys her accolades and seizes the opportunity to tease her with a knowing grin.

Wendy realises that he is skillful at playing games and she suddenly becomes very serious. "Jean is right, you have a terrific talent and I wish I could share your talent with the world! This painting would fetch big money in Toronto. How about I become your agent?"

Mike takes a steps backwards. "Wooh, not so fast. I already have an agent and to send my paintings overseas would be a huge challenge."

Wendy is not put off. "It's not so difficult sending paintings over-seas! The only difficulties are in your mind. If you really want something to happen you just have to do it!" Her statements are so forceful, there is a moment of awkward silence.

Mike sees how determined Wendy can be. "Well okay Wendy, I'll think about it."

"And I won't let you stop thinking about it!"

Robyn, who now has a better appreciation of both of the mens' talents, looks from one to the other and then quietly speaks her mind. "Although a little direct, Wendy is right. Both of you should work towards having a combined exhibition in Toronto. With eight million people, it's the right place to do it! It's a big world out there and you shouldn't hide your talents down here."

Julia and Wendy nod in agreement as Robyn continues, "I'll help you if you decide to try your luck in our part of the world. I have a number of contacts in the gallery world and it would be a breeze to arrange a showing. Besides, what a great excuse to get you all to Toronto."

Turning to Gary she continues, "Gary you can organise transport and security."

She turns toward Tane and Mike, "Julia, Wendy and I will become your Canadian agents."

She turns to look at her friends, then back to the men, who are looking a little stunned, "Wendy is right in saying you just have to do it, it's as simple as that!"

Gary doesn't know what to think as it is way outside his philosophy of keeping it simple, stupid!

Tane and Mike look at each other and then shrug their shoulders in semi acceptance knowing they have a lot more to talk about before anything happens.

Julia, now with a financial commitment, wants to tidy up the loose ends and starts to propose time lines.

At that Tane gets up from the sofa. "We have lots of time to think about those details Julia. Right now I'm living for the moment. I can see you're wearing your togs and we'll join you for a swim. After that we'll pick up Lady and then dress for Jean's Sunday roast, what do you reckon?"

Julia nods. "Sounds like a plan!"

CHAPTER 13

Johnny Plots – The Truth about Joey!

Johnny Ray Schmidt is tired. The little sleep he had the night before was full of crazy dreams. Everything was out of control and he was being attacked but couldn't move. Now awake, he is exhausted and drenched in sweat. His head hurts but he knows the cure. Crouched over he stumbles into his office and flops down into his chair. Red faced he gasps for breath as he removes a rubber tourniquet and a syringe from the top drawer, pulls up his sleeve and injects himself with P.

Leaning back, with eyes closed, he feels his body being energized and his mind clearing. His breathing subsides and the intense pain in his head fades.

Opening his eyes, he contemplates what happened the night before, assessing the damage. The count was eight, two dead and six injured. All were important cogs in his business. One of the dead was his own brother! He had known for a time that he was undermining his leadership and plotting a coup, but his death, while solving a problem, was still an insult and had to be avenged, his gang was watching!

As a backstreet survivor, Johnny is cunningly creative. Now with his brain alert, he fantasizes what he is going to do to that arrogant Yankee bitch and the guys that have caused him so much trouble. He toys with his thoughts before addressing a more urgent problem, the loss of two million dollars! What will the syndicate say? Will they try and put the blame on him? Will they try and poison his relationship with the Chinese supplier in Rarotonga? Hell, they may even try and make him cough up the extra two million bucks out of his own pocket, that would hurt!

As the sole processor of ephedrine in Auckland he would have preferred that the other gangs did not communicate with Ah Chung at all, but it was a concession he had to make. Ah compounded that problem by supplying all the leaders with an untraceable Chinese cell phone to be used only in discussions relating to Chan Chemicals. When it rings, a password is entered that deciphers a nonsensical text message.

Yesterday, Johnny's red phone vibrated loudly and played its familiar chopsticks tune. The cryptic message read. *'Money confiscated at airport. Must have same within a week.'*

This initiated a flurry of calls. He knows that the loss, divided equally among the seven gangs will not be crippling, but he also knows that because it was his man that lost the money, the gangs will lever the situation to their advantage. That is exactly what he would have done! But what about Ah Chung's share of the loss?

The popular drinking hole, the Puhoi Pub, North of Auckland, is the venue for the meeting this afternoon. It has been agreed that each gang is to be represented by only its leader and a sergeant and no patches, guns or drugs, in case of a police raid.

As he sits on his sofa plotting, his escalating blood pressure turns his face red and the end of his cigar, tightly clenched between his teeth, is flat and soaked with saliva. He would be almost apoplectic if he had known that one of his most trusted and valued members, Dan Henare, is lying dead in a body bag in the Rarotonga mortuary!

To the right of his desk is a row of windows that gives him a view of Henderson Valley far below, and also for Joey Moser his book-keeper, the other occupant of the office, who sits at the opposite end of the room. No longer a lounge, the room could be the smart office of any Corporate Chief Executive with a sofa against the inner wall and a potted palm beside it. There are two huge Michael Robinson paintings of Karekare beach on the walls and at each desk an executive swivel chair, the largest being Johnny's.

Beside Joey's desk are two lockable filing cabinets. Not obvious is a floor safe under the carpet behind his chair and nowhere is there any incriminating documents, but there is a shredding machine next to his desk.

The elegant décor satisfies Johnny on two counts, his vanity and a reminder of his burgeoning wealth.

Making a decision, he moves back to his desk and turns on his computer. While it is firing up, he looks up at a large flat screen hanging from the ceiling with twenty pictures and matching sound from security cameras and microphones strategically placed around the complex. Using a remote, he selects the camera inside the barn. Johnny trusts nobody especially his controllers and he should be concerned as he knows they are ripping him off. But cash is coming in faster than he can spend and he can afford to turn a blind eye.

Resting against the side of his desk is a Black Panther baseball bat. Picking it up he taps it against the palm of his hand. At each tap there is a 'clicking' sound as it makes contact with the rings on his fingers. The bat is feared as he uses it to discipline, just like an old time school teacher would use a cane. The result is the same, the bruising fades but the fear remains!

Johnny for all his brutish behaviour is a surprisingly efficient book keeper, meticulously recording all transactions in his little black diary. The diary is his most treasured possession and it stays with him always, even when he sleeps. It tells him at any given instance his gross worth and most importantly his cash holdings, right now, two million dollars in one hundred dollar bills under his bed.

All his illicit costs are paid with illicit cash. What he doesn't know is that Joey Moser, who handles the day by day legitimate business, is skimming ten percent with a backhand to co-operating managers. It's a case of honour among thieves. Their book keeping is fiddled to be ten percent lighter than the actual profits. The bigger the payout to Joey, the bigger the backhand in return. It's a dangerous game stealing from Johnny, but who's to tell, and why should they when greed is the master?

In appearance, Joey Moser looks more Arabic than Aboriginal. He has dark skin, brown eyes, straight black hair and a hooked nose with slightly flared nostrils. Of average height, he is wiry with some muscle development from pushing weights. Even with his large nose, he is handsome in a virile, sexy way. His brown skin, build and nostril flare he inherited from his half Aboriginal mother, while the hook on his nose, his intense brown eyes and long black hair, from his Jewish father. His physical features, being the unlikely coupling of three races, came about owing to his father's unusual occupation and unusual location.

His father emigrated to Australia from Israel as a book keeper. To help his immigration application, he informed the department that he would be studying to become an accountant. Australia needed accountants, so he was accepted. It was a semi lie, in that it was a pipe dream. The reality was that he never had sufficient funds to study for four years, so he drifted from one menial job to another. One skill he had learned, from an early age, and now very useful, was his ability to ride a horse. Stock men were in demand on Northern Queensland cattle stations so he found employment at last.

Alinga, his half-caste wife, who worked in the station kitchen was the bastard offspring of one of the owner's sons. He married her because she was a good cook and it legitimised sex on demand.

Joey never liked his father, but he loved his mother and she loved him. He loathed seeing her being physically and mentally abused. Wanting to protect her, he often ended up being battered and bruised, so he knew he would have to wait until he was older and stronger.

Alinga found solace by wrapping herself in Roman Catholicism, taking confession with the Parish Priest on his monthly visits. She was scared for her son and pleaded with the Priest to send him to a Catholic boarding school for boys. Because of his unusual looks, she knew that Joey was being bullied at his small country school and was also afraid of her husband's increased violence towards him.

The Priest listened, and referred her request to the highest deity in Northern Queensland, the Bishop of Townsville. There were funds available for such cases and being the compassionate man that he was, he arranged for Joey to become a full time boarding student at the highly regarded Saint Joseph's Nudgee College. It's Mission Statement: 'To inspire young men, to live justly, and to ignite in them faith, compassion and the love of learning'.

The school did exactly that for young Joey, except for one gnawing exception, he could not forgive his father and that hatred festered, challenging his Christian beliefs.

The school boasted one of the best sporting curriculums of any school in Queensland and after the hardships of living on a cattle station, Joey thrived in its friendly environment. Being of small build he was unable to be selected as an aspiring rugby player, but he excelled in athletics and judo, gaining black belt status. His academic prowess was not so good, but he had inherited his father's ability with book keeping and he also enjoyed learning the skills, as an extramural activity, of being a locksmith. The thought of being able to break into any safe appealed to him.

After graduating from school as a confident, strong young man, he returned home to find his mother bruised and bleeding from the mouth. He waited until his father came home from the pub that night and beat him to death with an iron waratah pole.

Throughout the night, Joey and his mother clung to each other for comfort, until emotionally drained, they fell asleep still locked in each other's arms.

In the early hours of the morning, with her dead husband propped up on the toilet, Alinga carefully detached herself from Joey and began to pace backwards and forwards, praying for guidance.

Just before dawn, she knew what she had to do.

Now, smiling down at him, she remembers all the good times

they had together and how his love had enabled her to endure the hardships of being married to an evil man. With tears in her eyes, she sighs, wipes her cheeks with her palm and then gently shakes him awake.

"What's up mum?"

Seating herself on the end of the bed, she strokes his legs. "I've been thinking about what we're going to do Joey. You're going to leave Aussie until this blows over. I'll take the rap and plead self defence. The police know I have been beaten before and I'll only get a few years."

Joey is surprised and objects, but his mother persists,

"I have some money saved, it is for you anyway." Feeling under her mattress she pulls out a roll of bank notes and points it towards him, "It's a little over two thousand dollars, that will get you to New Zealand and give you a new start."

He looks at her for a moment and then pushes the money away, shaking his head. "It's not right mum!"

She leans closer and forces the roll into his hand. "It's the only way son, do it for me, not for you. Please, it's what I want!"

Reluctantly he takes the money and flees to Auckland.

After completing the immigration forms, he is accepted as a New Zealand Resident and becomes an apprentice locksmith. A year later, after night classes, he is rewarded with a diploma and being more capable than that, has had ample time to party and enjoy life. He is popular with his student friends who enjoy his Aussie banter and they keep him supplied with marijuana and party pills, but those come at a cost.

The drug sellers at the technical college work for the Satan's Sons gang and when he falls behind in payments, the gang leans on him to open a few safes. Inevitably he is caught by the police and spends time in jail.

The up-side is that the confinement forced him to slow down and to take stock of his helter-skelter, carefree life. Also it gave him the chance to sweat out his addiction to party pills. To his credit, he stayed away from the more dangerous heroin and P.

As an indication that he has matured, while in jail he accepted the opportunity to take part in a personal development course that encouraged him to continue his book keeping studies. His high school pass marks allowed him to start at year two of a four year University Accountancy Degree. The best thing was that it was paid for by a government loan.

The three years of off campus study went quickly. It helped fill the hours of boredom and he applied himself well. Throughout his studies, he was encouraged by his mother who rang him as often as she could afford. In a way, Joey treated his educational confinement as payback for his mother's five year sentence for manslaughter.

After graduating with Honours, Joey checked the 'Jobs' notice board at the University and read that the New Zealand Police were seeking applicants from graduating accountants. He applied, thinking it would be a gas to work for the cops.

As the first interview did not go well, he was surprised that he was asked to attend a second, this time with District Superintendent Max Henderson. Being a top cop, Joey was concerned that it may have something to do with the death of his father. Why else would someone that high up want to talk to him? He thought about re-turning to Australia but reasoned that if the cops knew something, they would have arrested him already, so he kept his appointment.

Max Henderson was polite and put him at ease. He told him that as he had a criminal conviction it was against the law for him to employ him as a full time policeman. However he could employ him on a short term contract as a non-sworn officer. After training, he would become an undercover agent and be paid three times the salary of the accountancy job.

Joey was interested.

Max told him that from leaks he knew that the Satan's Sons gang was wanting to hire a book keeper and with his criminal record and accountancy degree, he would be a shoe in!

What appealed to Max was Joey's confident deportment, his intelligence, and something else that he couldn't explain. Maybe he sensed some of Joey in himself? His intuition and instinct had never let him down before.

Joey didn't know it, but there was huge pressure on Max to solve the methamphetamine problem. That pressure was coming from as high up as the Prime Minister! Joey could be the answer, but Max was aware of the dangers he would face. His assignment was not only dangerous, but unpredictable, and there was a chance that he may not survive, but he was prepared to risk Joey's life because of the opportunity of having a mole at the heart of the gang's administration.

The drug problem was so huge and damaging that he would risk sacrificing police lives for the cause. It was warfare and Joey could be collateral damage!

Max studied Joey and wondered what it would take for him to accept the job. His many years of studying human nature told him that Joey was a gambler, so he tried to sweeten the deal with a lie! He had the authority to pay for six months undercover training as well as a fortnightly salary, the equivalent of a Senior Sergeant, but he knew that would not be enough to entice Joey to accept such a dangerous job.

Max was so desperate to have a mole in the Satan's Sons gang that he promised him not only a good salary, but also a reward of two hundred thousand dollars if he was able to provide sufficient evidence to convict Johnny of manufacturing and distributing P.

Max was sure the Commissioner of Police would back him and persuade the Minister to pay the reward.

The bottom line being that it would be a cheap fix and also a political goldmine.

When Joey showed no reaction to the offer, Max decided to lift the ante by telling him that he would also remove his conviction from their data base. Of course neither he nor anyone else had the rightful authority to do that!

Again he studied Joey and could see that he was surprised and was weighing up the risks. So he said, "Don't give me an answer right now Joey, go home and sleep on it and let me know tomorrow....

Oh and Joey, this is very important, what I have just said must never be repeated to anyone, ever. If I find out that you have, I will deny it and I'll track you down, do you understand?"

Joey nodded, fully aware that he had just been threatened with either imprisonment or even worse.

As he left Police Headquarters, he had already made up his mind to accept. It solved two immediate problems, finances and a return to Australia with a clean slate! His step was light, as he thought about the pleasures of repaying his mother ten fold, money that she could now spend, having been granted an early release from prison. He smiled as he imagined living with her again on the Gold Coast.

There is the rub! Now one year on Joey could have blown the whistle on Johnny a number of times, but the evidence was always too soft. Also he is making so much money that he can afford to wait. Another factor is that Johnny won't allow him into his world of illicit dealings. All his book keeping duties are to do with Johnny's booming legitimate businesses. The exception being when he is asked to purchase a business using half cheque and half cash.

Johnny gives him the cash and Joey knows it is not from his accounts. The vendor agrees to sell the business, on paper, for half its real value, the full GST component and the price paid never being disclosed. A snooping tax man would have difficulty relating the sudden wealth of a business owner with the sale of their business.

Joey is kept busy buying businesses and laundering large amounts of cash.

JS Holdings now owns brothels, tow trucks, garages, fun parks, liquor and party pill outlets; off shore fishing licences, various houses, a number of pubs and restaurants, and the sale of fresh coffee beans.

Disposing of cash this way has its risks, but it is always a direct deal between Joey and the seller and no Real Estate agent is involved, only Keaton O'Nally, QC, the gang's legal adviser. It is also Joey's job to subtly advise the seller that they are dealing with ruthless people and that it must remain private. Greed keeps them silent, they take the cash and run.

Johnny doesn't keep all the money to himself as he shares a small percentage of the profits of the legitimate businesses with Joey, it is making him rich.

Johnny also shares a small percentage of the illegal profits with his Controllers who have the job of rewarding their men. It all seems very transparent and fair, but of course it is not! Four times that amount comes in as non-accountable cash and that is shared with nobody! The laundering of the cash is evidence, but not the evidence Max wants, as it does not point directly at the manufacture and sale of methamphetamine!

Right now Joey can feel the squeeze between the police and the gang. Max could expose him at any time and Johnny could discover the truth, either way he is dead! He is caught in the proverbial, rock and a hard place.

In a way it has sharpened his attention to detail. His book keeping is immaculate with the bank statements and books balancing to the cent.

For Johnny, this is a never ending business, far more difficult than for any legitimate C.E.O. He can take a holiday at his peril, but that makes it not a holiday. There are no weekends off and if he screws up, he is not removed with a golden handshake but is dead! Life is too complicit to have a confidant, or the comforting arms of a wife or partner and too precarious and distracting to raise a family. Not that he doesn't have a brat or two that he has been forced to deny. If that doesn't work, he throws money at the mother who is then told not to return, if she does, the child will disappear…. That works!

Johnny turns away from the overhead TV satisfied that there appear to be no internal or external threats, so far! By now the iMac has booted up and in 'Chrome' he clicks, 'Bookmarks' and scrolls down to 'Carjam'. Looking at his palm, he reads a car registration number that he copied onto his skin the night before.

After firing both barrels, he was close enough to see the number plate on one of the Jeeps. He could also see the fast flowing river up ahead and was not sure that the bikes could cross. When the Jeeps suddenly changed direction and headed up towards the dunes, he signaled his men to follow. Braking, he removed a pen from his pocket and wrote the number plate on his palm. By the time he arrived at the river his two gang members and their bikes were being tumbled towards the surf.

It took a half hour for the salvage and then another hour to dry out, before continuing along Muriwai Beach to the beach head.

CHAPTER 14

Frolic at the Beach – Gary and Robyn's Story

While Gary, Mike and Tane change into their togs, Julia leads the girls along the track to the beach. They pass tall bushes of toitoi and coastal flax and through bunches of spiky oioi.

Closer to the beach, just before the dunes, they admire the sprawling Maori ice plant with its star-like mauve flower.

At the edge of the beach, they climb up, then down, the black sand dunes covered in exotic marram grass and dwindling patches of golden pingao.

Gary, wearing Mike's largest togs, follows the others and grabs a towel off the line. By the time they arrive, the girls are already splashing in the surf. The men drop their towels at the bottom of the dunes and then sprint down the beach to join in the fun.

Although the wind is blowing off the sea, it is a gentle breeze and the waves are moderate.

Julia and Wendy dive under the tepid waves as they roll in and then resurface after they have passed.

Robyn, however, jumping as high as she can, only just keeps her mouth above the water.

Gary swims towards her with powerful strokes as a large wave approaches. Firmly but gently he lifts her high out of the water then braces as the wave smashes over his head and tries to suck them towards the shore. He lowers her after the opaque bubbling tail departs, leaving them waste deep, still clasped together.

Robyn wraps her arms around his neck and whispers close to his ear. "Thanks lifesaver!" Pulling his head towards her she kisses him full on the lips. The unexpected and unplanned kiss is brief and tinged with shyness. Totally oblivious to their surroundings, they are not aware of another larger wave that crashes down, this time bowling them over. As a trained Life Saver and surfer, Gary has been dealt far harsher blows and reacts quickly, rolling under her so that his body absorbs the **'thump'** of the hard sand. Laughing, he stands, pulling her close and this time kissing her with far more passion and intensity without the least bit of embarrassment.

Robyn is happily helpless, surrounded by his strength and content to stay in his close embrace with her arms wrapped around his broad shoulders and her lips inches from his.

She has dreamed of this moment, but the closest she has ever come, was reading about it in a romance book! Now it is for real and more wonderful and exciting than she had ever imagined!

Not far away, Mike and Tane, like playful dolphins, join Julia and Wendy in the fun of diving under the curling waves.

Mike wipes the water off his face and long hair, then calls out to Wendy and Julia. "Do you know how to body surf?"

They shake their heads.

"Watch me." Turning, he waits until a wave is about to break immediately behind him, then dives forward matching its speed. His hunched shoulders catch the bubbling water and he becomes part of the movement that deposits him far up the beach.

Julia, the quickest to copy, after a few false starts, is soon zooming along matching the waves.

Wendy, unable to launch herself forward with sufficient speed, is left behind by the waves with increasing frustration.

Mike wades over to her, "Would you like a push?"

She nods.

Standing behind, he holds onto her slim waist, "When I say GO, dive forward."

She nods again, enjoying the feel of his hands around her waist.

He turns his head and watches for the next wave, "Here it comes, ready….. GO!" The wave curls above them and he throws her forward. At that instant, reaching behind, she clasps his wrist so that instead of joining the wave, she swings around and grabs him, just as the wave breaks. Now, standing locked together, she places both of her hands on the sides of his face and pulls him to her kissing him with an open mouth. Lost in their embrace, they are not aware of the buffeting water that is trying to tear them apart, conscious only of their hungry desires and the taste of salty lips.

Wendy reaches upward and supported by the water, locks her arms around his neck so that her hips are squeezed tight against his loins and she can feel his manhood swelling.

With mutual passion and pounding hearts, the kiss continues, until another larger wave knocks them over.

Spluttering and laughing they know that this is the start of something very special.

Meanwhile, Julia, captivated by the new found thrill of body surfing, is not aware of her friends' romantic escapades, until turning toward the waves she sees two pairs of bodies locked together.

Being the first real opportunity to get close to her, Tane decides on the direct approach. Timing his ride to zoom in towards her, he catches her around the waist and she squeals with delight as they are swept up the beach locked together.

Julia has long since forgotten about her bruised ribs as their companion wave passes them by and then retreats, accompanied by the tinkle of small crushed shells.

Still entwined on the wet sand, Tane rolls Julia over so that he is now on top of her and they gently kiss. Both respond to the extreme intimacy of lips on lips.

Julia feels the firmness of his body and opening her mouth wider, touches his lips with the tip of her tongue. Time stops for both of them. It is a magical moment and the most beautiful kiss of their lives. The pure passion of the kiss totally belongs with their natural surroundings. Clean clear water, the warm sun and the pleasant nautical smell of the beach.

As if nature decides they have had enough, a large wave surges over them accompanied again by the tinkle of shells. Spluttering and laughing, Tane helps Julia to stand, who then blows the water out of her nose and wrings it out of her long blonde hair. The excitement of the kiss has added an extra sparkle to her already beautiful clear blue eyes. They both decide right then and there that they are totally in love and totally belong to each other.

Tane strokes her face. "Julia you are the most beautiful woman I have ever met and I claim you as mine!"

Julia looks deep into his eyes and gently with her finger tips follows the contours of his forehead, along his nose, down and around his lips and then placing both hands on each side of his face pulls him toward her again so that their lips are only just touching. There they stay connected, motionless, as if in a trance until she pulls away needing to breathe. "That is my answer beautiful Maori man!" This time the kiss is firm and passionate, each desiring the other.

Against huge physical urges, they disengage, knowing that this is not the time or place to continue what is so natural in nature. Hand in hand and even though they have left the water, they float back up the beach to join their friends who are already toweling themselves at the bottom of the dunes.

After a while and in no great hurry, the couples saunter back to the cottage. The happy chatter eventually returns to Lady and they decide that they all want to go and pick her up.

Gary turns to Robyn. "Would you like to ride in my car?" When she nods, he explains to the others, "That will give more room for everyone else!"

Tane laughs. "Whatever! See you at Jean's in an hour."

The girls continue along the track, while Gary follows the road to his cottage, a few metres further up the beach.

Two hours later, showered and shaved and smelling of deodorant and after-shave, Mike and Tane rev their Wranglers just as Gary, waving, roars past in his old but immaculate Nissan Fairlady. The silver sports car is his pride and joy and he keeps it spotless. This is at odds with his usual careless and messy self.

You would think that growing up without a mother would have forced him to manage himself in an orderly way, but for some reason that has not happened. While he ignores piles of dishes in the sink and clothes on the floor, he spends hours removing bitumen specks from off the bonnet and sides of his beloved car.

Following the beach road to Jean's, the three cars arrive at the car park and the ladies, sitting on the swing chair, wave.

Robyn is pleasantly surprised at Gary's car, expecting a RV like his friends, or at worse, a beat up wreck.

Life is suddenly very exciting and they hurry down to greet their new found friends.

Gary, standing beside his open passenger door, enjoys watching Robyn as she sinks into the soft black leather seat. His heart skips a beat when she lifts her face and smiles up at him. Returning the smile, he thinks. '*This is perfect. I have my car and now I have my girl.*' Unknowingly, he continues his thoughts out aloud, "What else could a guy want?"

Robyn surprised at his unexpected words, shrugs. "That's for you to tell me?"

"Oh sorry Robyn, that sort of slipped out."

She reaches through the half open door and squeezes his hand. "Don't be sorry, I'm flattered, so romantic!" Pushing the door wider she beckons with her finger. As he bends, she reaches up pulling him closer and kisses him briefly on the lips. Releasing him, she sinks back into the comfort of the leather with a contented sigh.

Julia seats herself next to Tane and Wendy beside Mike.

Robyn, watching is reminded of their physical dissimilarities. Tane is medium height and dark and Julia tall and fair. Mike is tall and fair and Wendy short and dark. She turns to look at Gary and realises that they too are dissimilar. She is plump, freckled and a redhead. He is tall, tanned, with short cropped auburn hair, but they both have blue eyes. She smiles at a presumptuous thought, *'There will be no brown eyes in our family.'*

A waving arm catches her attention. It is Jean wearing her floral apron, standing in the doorway. Robyn waves back, *'How nice!'* It makes her feel great.

Gary selects a Johnny Cash CD and as Johnny's, gravelly voice fills the car, Robyn marvels at how close the two of them have become in such a short time. Surrounded by country music that she loves and with her new found man, for once in her life she is content. Not wanting the moment to end, they remain silent as the bush on the sides of the road flashes past. Both are wondering about their future together.

Robyn studies Gary's profile and then gently taps him on the hand that is resting on the T shift. "Tell me about yourself Gary and about your family?" He glances at her as she continues, "It's just that I know so little about you. I mean, I'm not trying to pry, I really want to know everything about you, even your secrets."

Smiling, he turns down the music, then squeezes her hand. "No, I don't mind, but I'm afraid it's not very exciting. I'm twenty-eight and was born in a small hospital at Paparoa, that's a country town on the North side of the Kaipara Harbour." With his attention back on the road, he again has a quick glance at Robyn and is aware that for the first time he is comfortable being alone with her, "That's the harbour near the hot pools, it's the biggest harbour in New Zealand."

Robyn nods and his thoughts go back to his childhood. Thoughts that he hasn't revisited for a long, long time. He is silent for a few seconds watching the road ahead. After another quick glance towards her, he continues, "Dad was a fisherman and owned a small plywood boat that was tied up at the Pahi wharf, close to where I was born. I have good memories and bad ones too. My whole world was that small fishing village."

Again he drives in silence and Robyn waits. She enjoys hearing his kiwi twang and that he is telling her about himself.

Without looking at her, he continues, "I'm the youngest of the three Reilly boys and the earliest I can remember is when I was about four and at that time, Paul was… let me see… ten, and Greg would have been… eight. All of us had to prepare the baits each night for the next day's fishing." He glances at her again, wondering if she is bored.

As if reading his mind she smiles at him urging him to go on, "At least I didn't have to help stack the heavy boxes with the hooks and baits, but I did hold the pressure lamp when they were loaded into the back of our old Holden ute." He holds up a hand and wiggles his fingers, "You know, my fingers used to sting for hours after baiting the sharp hooks, but it was the smells that I remember the most. The smell of mud at low tide, old squid and trevally, the spirit lamp and the diesel fumes from the old engine in the boat."

With a grimace he rubs his hand over his face and then drives in silence again. Suppressed memories stab at his heart.

The soul filled wailing of Johnny Cash starts to annoy, so he turns off the CD, "Dad was forever pulling that old Fordson-Major engine apart and then putting it back together again." His knuckles, gripping the wheel turn white as he continues, "He used to come home swearing and shouting as if it was our fault! We learned to dodge his whacks and kicks and hide until he either calmed down or left for the pub." He looks over at her to see if she understands.

She does and can see and sense his hurt. "What about your mother, didn't she protect you?"

He shakes his head. "Not really, she must have been afraid of him as well." He glances at her again, "I don't know all the reasons why she left, but I do know the cottage was too small for our family. The fish company owned it. I suppose they never thought that a family of five would live there. You couldn't call it a house, even a cottage, it was really a shack."

Robyn squeezes his hand again as his mind returns to the small dwelling that was once called home, "The lino on the floor was loose and chipped and the floor boards creaked. Our shack was the furthest from the wharf at the end of a row of shacks." He shakes his head, "Dad didn't earn much." He shakes his head again, "Sometimes he didn't even catch enough to pay the rent! If there was any money left over he spent it at the pub or on the horses!" Again he glances at her, "That was the start of the trouble between mum and dad, she used to send me and my brothers to bring him home. The drinking was the problem, but I used to enjoy going there because it was fun. We would listen to the band playing party songs and climb up on the bar stools and be given fizzy drinks. I can still remember some of the old songs," He starts to sing in a quiet, crooning voice, *"Don't know why, there's no sun up in the sky... stormy weather...."* He stops and looks at Robyn who is surprised at his pleasant voice, "I suppose you haven't heard that song before, really old."

 "I know it, my mother used to play the piano and she had a thick book of old party songs, I guess it kept her amused. Stormy Weather was one of those songs. I loved sitting beside her listening to her sing.... Sing it again Gary." This time she joins in at the end of the chorus.... *"Since my man and I ain't together.... keeps raining all the time......."* Their voices blend nicely and the togetherness means more than they can say.

They sit in silence for a few minutes not wanting to disconnect. Eventually Gary turns to her. "There is another song that the band used to play. It stuck in my mind because I thought it funny that someone would be singing in the rain!" Robyn nods as he starts to sing, *"Just singing in the rain... just singing in the rain....."*

 Robyn continues the song. *"What a won-der-ful feeling I'm happy again...."*

 Neither know the following lyrics, so they end the song abruptly and start to laugh.

Robyn looks at Gary. "You know, Canada and New Zealand aren't that much different."

 Gary frowns. "Isn't it pretty cold up there?"

 "Oh sure, but what I'm talking about is how we started. You know, Colonials and all that! Part of the British Empire and France. We fought together in both World Wars." Gary nods, still not convinced and they drive in silence for some time.

The memories of Pahi are still strong and he glances at her. "I'd like to tell you about the old Pahi pub." She nods, fascinated that he is prepared to talk about his childhood, knowing that it is painful. Again he is silent, staring out the windscreen at the tar seal on the country road.

She breaks the silence. "You were going to tell me about the old pub."

Without looking at her, he nods then continues. "At night a band played on a small stage. A real country band, you know, honky-tonk piano, guitar, drums, accordion and a big double bass. We thought the band was the best. The more drunk they became the louder they played and the leader told jokes that I never understood. Everyone laughed, except me." Again he drives in silence for some time.

Again Robyn waits.

Eventually he sighs and the pained look returns to his face, "It was after one of those nights that mum and dad had a terrible row. I remember we had trouble getting him home, he was very drunk. They started shouting at each other and then mum pulled him into the bedroom and shut the door. It didn't matter because they were still shouting at each other. Dad was swearing, mum was telling him that he was a drunken bastard and that he didn't care for her, or for us, it was terrible!" Robyn's hand is being squeezed so tight that it is beginning to hurt, so she taps him gently on the knuckles. Releasing his grip, the haunted look goes and he stares down at their clasped hands, "I'm sorry, did I hurt you Robyn?... I'm so sorry, I haven't talked about those times to anyone, ever, it chews me up!"

"It can help to talk about it Gary."

He looks at her again, nods, then takes a deep breath. "My brothers and I were in our bunks but none of us were asleep. I mean how could we, with all that shouting? We lay there listening, the shouting got louder and then there was a slap followed a moment later by a crunching sound. Mum cried out in pain, it was a terrible sound and I hid my head under the pillow."

Staring intently at the road ahead the hurt that was evident before, disappears, but she knows he is still suffering inside.

He withdraws his hand from hers and places them both on the steering wheel and drives in silence.

Again Robyn waits.

After a few minutes, without looking at her, he continues, "There was no sound for a while coming from their bedroom so I lifted my head and tried to hear what was happening. Their bedroom door opened and then slammed shut and I heard mum running. Our bedroom door was open and I looked up to see her run past, holding her nose, there was blood between her fingers. Flinging open the front door she ran outside slamming it so hard that the light bulb swung backwards and forwards.

Dad came into the living room and shouted at the closed door, "Get back here bitch!... get the fuck back here!" He must have sensed our frightened eyes because he stopped yelling, spun around and shouted, 'Get back to sleep you lot!'…. As if we could after all that!"

Again Gary is silent for a few seconds, "We never saw mum again and she has never tried to contact us, ever, I don't understand that?"

Frowning, she shakes her head. "Neither do I. Yes, that IS strange, have you tried to find her?"

"Yeah, every time I go to a new town I look up 'Reilly' in the phone book, but there are lots of Reillys and mum may have changed her name, I would have if I was her!"

Robyn taps him on the leg. "I'll help you find her if you like?"

He turns and smiles at her. "That would be great, thanks, hey, sorry for dumping on you like that!"

"I don't mind, sharing hurts is not dumping."

Gary reaches forward and powers up the CD and Johnny Cash's deep soulful voice fills the car once more.

Robyn waits until the end of a song and then turns the music down, "So what happened next? Three young boys and a drunken dad sounds like trouble!"

Gary frowns. "You know, I don't remember it being that bad. Oh we really missed mum and somehow felt guilty, as if we were to blame. It must have shocked dad though because he stopped going to the pub on week days, but still got roaring drunk on Saturday nights and slept in on Sunday mornings. That gave us a chance to escape. He spent more and more time out on his boat and we had to cook for ourselves. I'm a pretty good cook. I can even cook cakes and biscuits."

Sensing his mood change, she decides to tease him. "I would never have guessed, you cooking cakes, a macho man like you? Well at least some good came out of your mum leaving."

"Yeah, I never thought about it that way. I even tried to make some of mum's favourites, like peanut brownies or anzac biscuits." He laughs, "We ate a lot of failures! It was lucky that we lived by the sea because there was always fish and mussels, or pipis and cockles from the beach." This time Gary reaches forward and turns up the volume as Johnny starts singing the song, *'I walk the Line.'* At the end of the song he winds the sound down, "Aunty Pat, our next door neighbor…… she wasn't really our auntie, but that's we called her, came over with leftovers and treats like golden dumpling pudding. Her real name was Missus Hohepa and she was a big happy lady who made us feel good. She said everything with a laugh. It was the only happiness we ever had. We knew dad was scared of her because she would fold her arms and get stuck into him for 'Not looking after us proper'". He smiles, "Boy did we love that! Dad never remarried, probably hard when you have three young boys in tow."

In the silence that follows, Johnny Cash can faintly be heard singing the song, *'God's Gonna Cut You Down'.* Gary turns up the volume and both of them listen until it ends. He looks at her again, "Things carried on the same for a few years. Paul left school when he was sixteen to help dad on the boat. That lasted only two years before he suddenly left to work for a fishing company at Leigh. Dad tried to talk him out of it, but of course Paul knew he could earn more money and he was tired of sleeping in a shared bedroom. We hoped he'd stay and Greg and I missed him. In a way he was our protector and mum's replacement... I guess he tired of that as well." Unknowingly, Gary clenches and unclenches his fingers on the steering wheel.

Robyn nods. "I'd like to meet Paul someday, I'm sure we would get on just fine, he sounds like an okay guy."

"He is. Yeah you'd like him. We'll try and do that before you go."

Robyn nods, but the mention of leaving makes her sad. Gary continues, "Soon after Paul left, the Government cut quotas on the number of schnapper that dad could catch. Something to do with over fishing. It might have been the right thing, but it killed his business. The Government paid him some compensation to help him relocate, which he did, taking us to Waipu where he became a share milker." He looks at her, "That's a dairy farmer, you know...... cows, milk, butter."

She nods. "And ice cream. Sounds better than trying to catch fish."

"It was a better life all around. We lived in a three bedroom farm house and there was plenty of food. I had to round up and help milk the cows in the morning before school, and then again at night. It sounds like a hard job, but it wasn't. The dogs did most of the work. The cows seemed to know where to go, I don't know how they did it, but they always lined up the same way!" He smiles at her for the first time, "I mean how do they know? Do they talk to each other? Weird! I know there was a boss cow that always went into the shed first."

Reaching forward, he turns up the CD as it is playing *A Beautiful Day*. Talking over the music, he continues, "We had chickens and pigs and bobby calves. Greg and I learned a lot about farming, most of it is pretty yucky, like the birth of a calf or the trick of snapping a chooks neck then plucking and cleaning it. Or freeing a cow from bloat," He looks at her with a teasing grin, "Do you want to know how that's done?"

She shakes her head vigorously. "No thanks, whatever you did, I'm sure it was messy, but it must have been better living on a farm than in a fisherman's cottage?"

"Yeah, everything was much better. Dad was milking three hundred cows which is quite a lot and was earning good money. I took to farming like a duck to water. You know I could run a dairy farm myself if I wanted too."

Robyn's thoughts about being a farmer's wife are interrupted when his reminiscences continue. "Life was busy, but that was good for dad, he even hugged us sometimes. I met Tane at that time, we were both in the same class at school and loved playing rugby.

I left school after scraping through my School Cert exam. Greg was helping dad on the farm, so I decided to become a builder's labourer working for a man who played rugby at the Waipu Club. It suited me fine because I love working out-doors and I enjoy hard work. Learning a new trade was not a problem and the best thing was the freedom of having my own money and happy that I could pay dad some board."

Robyn smiles at him knowing that their communication is bonding them closer together, making it harder for her to leave.

By now, the car has arrived at the Veterinary Clinic at Waimauku and Gary parks alongside the Jeeps. Pulling on the handbrake he switches off and turns to her, this time holding her hand with both of his, "Not long after that, Tane moved to Karekare, so I followed, getting a job as a builder's labourer. So that's it, nothing more." Somehow he feels refreshed inside.

Robyn strokes his arm. "Thanks for telling me all that Gary, I think you have had a very interesting life and I'd love to see the old pub at Pahi and to meet your brothers and your dad sometime and I won't forget about trying to find your mum."

Gary nods as Lady's barking can be heard coming from inside the clinic. Smiling at each other, hand in hand they run to join the happy reunion.

Inside, the love between a dog and its master is quantified by the noise. Lady in Tane's arms is showing her joy by licking and barking and whimpering. Mike, Wendy and Julia take turns stroking and whispering sweet nothings that she totally understands. She sees Gary and Robyn and includes them in her welcoming barks.

Emma, watching the reunion, is content. She eats, sleeps and breathes for the care of animals and is glad to be an important part of the happiness. When the noise subsides, she instructs Tane on how to dress the wound and how to administer the antibiotic. All of them are grateful for her skills and after thanks and paying the bill, he carries Lady to his car. Although two soft blankets are ready on the back seat, she refuses to lie down preferring instead to stand with her head as close to his neck as possible. His familiar smell is far better than the sanitised smell of an animal hospital that also smells of cats!

In high spirits, Robyn and Gary return to the Fairlady and when the motor rumbles into life Johnny begins to sing *'Ring of Fire'.* Listening to the music, Gary hands Robyn a list of the songs in his stacker. "Your choice. Most of it's Country, but there is some Blue Grass and lots of oldies from the sixties and seventies. There's a bit of Kiwi Country as well."

She is quiet for a moment scanning down the list of songs, "Oh look, you have my favourite, Tim McGraw." As the Nissan accelerates down the road, she selects, *'Memory Lane'* and soon a strumming guitar sets the familiar railroad rhythm before the clean picked sound of Tim's electric guitar starts the melody line.

Gary turns up the volume so that when Tim starts to sing, they are surrounded by his voice. Having enjoyed their brief duet earlier they join in the chorus... *"I'm walking down memory lane, because I know I will be running into you."* Laughing, Robyn squeezes his hand and leans over and kisses him lightly on the cheek.

At the Waimauku and Highway 16 intersection, the three cars turn left and pass by a Caltex Petrol Station where two Satan's Sons members are standing next to their bikes. They recognise the two Jeeps and their occupants.

Mike and Wendy are pre-occupied in conversation, while Tane and Julia are trying to dodge the nudges and licks from Lady. Also distracted, Robyn and Gary are away in their own 'togetherness' world.

As the cars pass, the gang members look at each other and nod. Removing his helmet, one flicks open his cell phone and makes a call. "Hi Butch, it's Karl.... Rubes and I are at the Waimauku Caltex. Those shits we were chasing last night just passed us on Highway Sixteen heading towards Huapai, do you want us to follow them?"

At gang headquarters, Butch Gueber, with the phone to his ear, turns to a group of Controllers seated at two picnic tables. "Hey guys, shut-the fuck-up, I'm talking to Karl and Rubes, they have just spotted the two fuckin' Jeeps from last night." Turning back to his phone, he nods, "Yeah follow them Karl, but for Christ's sake don't spook em, keep your distance, I'll go and tell Johnny. Shit he'll be pleased. Stay with them and find out where they are going, call me later."

"Sure boss, I'll call you later." Pocketing his phone, he puts on his helmet and signals to Rueben to give chase.

Inside the Nissan, the music and the romance continues. There is love in the air and at each repetitive chorus of *'Memory Lane'*, Robyn and Gary join in the chorus.

The three cars turn right at the Kumeu shops, cross over the railway tracks and then veer left toward the Show Grounds. They are now on a minor road that skirts the foot hills of the Waitakere Ranges and a short cut to Karekare beach.

Three hundred metres behind, Karl and Reuben follow, but lose sight every time the road bends. They are now on the straight in the heart of the shopping centre and the cars have disappeared. Thinking they must be still ahead, around the next bend, they pass by the turnoff without a sideways glance. Accelerating, they are half a kilometer past the turn off before they realise that somehow they have lost their prey. Pulling over, Karl calls Butch with the bad news. Holding the phone at arm's length he waits for the loud abuse to end before placing the phone back to his ear. "Sorry boss!"

Meanwhile, the three cars, a few kilometers to the West, are blissfully unaware of the drama and are enjoying a Sunday drive on a warm summer's day. The countryside is a picture postcard. The fields are cropped short and golden brown with an even scattering of plastic green or blue wheels of hay. The dry rolling pastures are often interrupted by high neatly pruned, green shelter belts, shielding rows of grape vines and kiwifruit. It is the height of the growing season and the narrow road has a bevy of small wayside stalls with honesty boxes. On offer are bags of freshly dug potatoes, scarlet runner beans, peas, avocados, all sorts of berries, watermelon, tomatoes and sweet corn.

Robin spots the sweet corn and excitedly turns to Gary. "Stop the car and go back! They're selling corn. Fancy that! I forgot that we are now in the growing season. Wow the girls will be pleased. Fresh corn is worth the airfare alone."

Pulling over to the side of the road, he reverses back to the stall. Opening a small chiller between the seats, he pulls out a ten dollar note squeezed between two cans of beer. "Here y'are, cold cash, my treat."

Soon Robyn returns with a bag of corn in one hand and a bag of beans in the other. Dropping them onto the back seat, she exclaims "Yummy, we're going to pig out on corn and beans tonight, I'll give them to Jean. Y'know corn to Canadians is like kiwifruit to Kiwis!"

Gary smiles, liking the sound of her words and starts the car. Soon, Tim McGraw's twangy guitar starts to play again and they lose themselves in his music.

After ten minutes, Gary turns off the CD. "Okay Robyn Petheridge, it's your turn, tell me your story." She looks at him in surprise. "Fancy you knowing my name!"

"I sneaked a look at your credit card when you paid for drinks."

"That is sneaky!",

"No.... interested!" Robyn chuckles and then lapses into silence as she wonders where to start.

While he waits, Gary selects another CD, "You might like this one. Suzanne Prentice is kind of New Zealand's Shania Twain. Have you heard of Suzanne Prentice? She's very good."

Robyn shakes her head. "Fancy you knowing Shania is Canadian."

He smiles at her. "I'm full of surprises."

"Nice!"

"I think you'll like Suzanne, she was famous in New Zealand back in the eighties. If you like Shania or Celine Dion, you'll like Suzanne. Here's a song you will know." Selecting track 3, he presses 'play' and Suzanne sings a magical rendition of *I'm your lady, and you are my man.*"

Robyn smiles at the inference and shutting her eyes, floats with the sweet sounds. While she listens, she thinks how romantic that

Gary should select a song so right for the moment. She knows that beneath his macho exterior there is a softness that surprises.

Gary looks at her lying there with her eyes closed and notices how attractive her lips are, with just the faintest upward curl at the edges, lips that beg to be kissed.

At the end of the song, she opens her eyes and smiles at him as if she can read his mind.

Reaching forward he selects track 2 and Suzanne starts to sing... *'The Story of my Life'*. At the second verse he turns the volume down, "Now, how about the story of your life Robyn?"

She nods. "I'm two years older than you, I'm thirty, does that bother you?"

Surprised, he shakes his head. "Hell no, why should it?"

"Well some men are funny about that sort of thing, they prefer younger women."

He gently strokes her cheek. "Not me."

They drive in silence for a few minutes trapped in their own thoughts, then Robyn turns to Gary again. "I might as well start where you started. I was born in Toronto the youngest of two children. My brother Brian was eight years older. We lived in the ritzy suburb of Lawrence Park, twenty minutes north of down town Toronto. Our neighbours were either wealthy Jews, or of English descent and more English than the English, if you know what I mean."

He nods. "Here, we call them snobs."

She nods. "Dad was high up in the insurance world and he was away most of the week, travelling all over Canada. He pampered us by spending money, compensating for his time away. Mum was one of the few stay-at-homes, but we still had a live-in cook and house keeper. Mum filled in her days by attending charity committees and organising our transport to and from school, most of the time it was by taxi. We wanted for nothing but needed a real mum and dad...... In a way I was like you, except my mum and dad were not separated." She looks at Gary to see if he understands. He nods again and she continues, "Our house on Mount Pleasant Road was a five bedroom two story brick house, covered with ivy. It was an imposing house, but not noteworthy as on either side were much larger mansions." She shrugs, "Nothing of consequence happened in my youngest years until I was fifteen. That's when the financial market collapsed and billions of dollars was lost. Dad was one of the casualties, and so were we."

Gary glances at her and then back to the road.

"Yeah, as quick as that! One moment we had everything and the next nothing. Mum hit the sherry bottle and my brother raped me!"

Startled, Gary stares at her and nearly runs off the road. Correcting the swaying car he slows, pulls over to the side and stops. "You were raped by your brother!?"

Flushed by her emotions, Robyn nods. "Like you, I have skeletons in the closet and I try to forget those terrible times." She pauses for a moment trying to slow her pounding heart. Eventually she sighs and is able to continue, "Brian was eighteen and I suppose the trauma of dad's bankruptcy changed him. Whatever the reasons, he forced himself onto me without provocation and wouldn't stop no matter how hard I struggled." She glances at him and then back to her clasped hands in her lap, "Mum and dad were out and my screams were smothered by his hand over my mouth. He was very strong and no matter how hard I tried to stop him, he forced himself into me!" She rubs her hands together as if trying to rub away the memory. Turning her head towards the side window, she watches the foliage flash past.

After a moment, she looks at him with tears of hurt and rage in her eyes, "You know the worst thing was that nobody believed me!" She shakes her head, "Dad was walking around like a zombie and mum said I must have encouraged my brother, can you believe that? I encouraged my brother to commit rape!! She didn't want to believe me her own daughter. Why would I lie?"

As tears flow down her cheeks, Gary gently takes her in his arms and with the tip of his thumb, flicks them off her cheeks. Leaning forward, he kisses her on each watery eye, trying to console her. "As you said to me, it's healing to talk about it. You may feel…. I don't know…. somehow dirty, but it makes no difference to me. You are still the most perfect thing in my life and I promise you, while you are with me, nobody will ever hurt you like that, ever again!"

Robyn wipes her cheeks with the back of her hand. She is

annoyed with herself for telling him as much as she has, but is comforted and surprised by his strength and compassion.

Sitting up, she blows her nose on a tissue, takes a deep breath and wraps her arms around his neck. "Thanks Gary, I have locked those memories away for so long, just like you. I have not told anyone else about the rape." She shakes her head, "Even Julia and Wendy." She releases her arms and turns to stare sightlessly out of the window again.

Gary places a reassuring hand on her leg. "Robyn, that is a shared secret between us. In a way it is a precious secret binding us closer together." Gently he strokes her hair as he tries to imagine living with someone who is a rapist, "It must have been difficult living with your brother after that?"

"Very! The first time we were alone in the house, I told him that if he ever tried to touch me again I would wait for him to go to sleep and then I'd kill him with a baseball bat. I showed him the bat and swung it hard a few times smashing it into a sofa. He knew I wasn't kidding. I didn't speak to him again, ever and he kept his distance, to me he was a nobody, a headless person!"

Knowing she is hurting, Gary starts the car and drives in silence. After a few minutes, she sighs, turning towards him again, "Not long after that we moved to a cheap rental house just off Dundas Street. Dad never did recover, all he did was watch hockey in winter and baseball in summer. Mum was forced to get a job as a secretary at a small goods warehouse. In her younger days she had learned basic computer skills and book keeping, so she kept food on the table and rationed dad's beer. In hind sight, the crash probably saved her. She accepted the sudden responsibility as the money earner and grew from strength to strength." She looks at Gary, "She was now the strong one of the family, but the secret we shared kept a barrier between us. I tried to talk to her about it, a few years later when I thought time may have changed her mind but she hushed me away and told me never to talk about it again, ever, so I never did! Life carried on as if nothing had ever happened and after graduating from High School, I was given a job with a local insurance company. The manager remembered dad and I think he gave me the job out of sympathy." She looks at Gary,

"So that's it, not much more to tell." She continues to study him trying to gauge his thoughts, "See, now it's my turn to be sorry for dumping on you."

"Hey, Robyn, I asked you for your story and I'm sure you would have told me about the rape at some time anyway, now there are no secrets between us." He places his hand under her chin, "Chin up, life's good!"

She places both of her hands over Gary's hand that is resting on the T shift and tenderly squeezes as they accelerate down the road towards the Karekare Beach turn off.

Revenge

At the Satan's Sons Headquarters, Johnny Ray Schmidt has been too busy reorganizing his gang to check on the number plate of the Jeep. Now at his desk, he looks again at the number on his palm. His thoughts return to the unexpected happenings of the previous night and he clamps down harder on the soggy end of his cigar. Pulling the keyboard towards him he ferociously stabs each of the plate numbers into a vehicle tracing website and then hits 'enter'. Information ripples onto the screen, the year of manufacture, transmission, CC, VIN, fuel type, the number of owners, but not the name or address of the owner. Against 'Owner' is a disclaimer. *'We are unable to provide ownership details owing to changes in the Privacy Act, May 2011.'*

Closing his fist, he punches the key board and the iMac squawks. Sitting back in his chair, he consoles himself that at least Karl is tracking them right now.

Hearing the heavy tread of boots in the hallway, he swivels around just as Butch enters. He can tell by the look on his face that there is bad news. "What's up?"

"Karl and Rubes lost them somewhere around Kumeu, sorry boss."

Johnny's blood pressure jumps and he considers how he is going

to punish them. Reaching down he picks up his baseball bat and taps it against his open palm. In the back of his mind is the knowledge that they are reliable soldiers who bring in hundreds of thousands of dollars a month.

Butch is relieved when Johnny places the bat against his desk. "Stupid bastards, hit them with a thousand dollar fine and tell them Carla and Kylie are off limits!" Glaring at Butch as if he is the perpetrator, he snarls, "They'd better stay out of my fuckin' sight!"

Butch nods. "Yeah, I've already kicked their arses boss, but I'll tell them you're pissed!"

Johnny points to the sofa.

Butch sits down pulling out a packet of Marlboro cigarettes and a gasoline lighter from his shirt pocket and flicks on the flint. Smoke billows into the room causing Joey to move from behind his desk and place a tall silver ashtray next to the couch. Returning to his desk, he opens a window stifling a cough, as the acrid smoke assaults his lungs. The strong nicotine smell reminds him of his dad.

Johnny and Butch get a sadistic pleasure out of watching him suffer and laugh at his lame excuses when he is forced to leave the room. This time however, he decides to stay, as he is interested in how Johnny is going to solve the problem of finding the people that harmed his gang. He is fascinated that so few could do the damage they did. Not a competing gang but a bunch of ordinary guys and an especially good female pool player. *'A Yankee bitch that is going to be fucked'*, according to Johnny. Joey is intrigued and he wants to know more.

Earlier in the day he had listened to the furor as Johnny and Butch restructured their gang. They were forced to replace two Controllers who managed the supply and manufacture of P. One of those being his brother, and to temporarily promote eight members into the hierarchy pending the release of those in hospital. He knows that recruiting new members is not a problem as there is an ever increasing waiting list. 'Waiting' is the key word as most of his new recruits are waiting to be released from jail. The sudden loss of man power has caused major disruption to the flow of drug money from the Primary and High Schools, the Technical Colleges and the Universities. The sellers are still there, even as young as eight, but some of the gang collectors are now either reassigned or injured.

Time is the problem for Butch and Johnny. It takes time and effort to first evaluate and then train new recruits. Loyalty is the aspiration, its foundation is not love, but fear, and it takes time to subjugate a new recruit to the required level of fear.

The ideal recruit is not only a person that is afraid, but is desperately wanting to belong. From early childhood they have been seeking love and affection and need to give it in return. The ideal recruit has been denied this and for all their bluff and bluster, their natural God given happiness is crippled by loneliness.

When new recruits come begging, Johnny and Butch manipulate their psyche until they will do anything to please their masters, including to maim or kill.

So the hunt for new members takes time, skill and effort and Johnny and Butch know that they are also competing with the military.

While Johnny and Butch discuss the promotion of some of their gang, a miniature blue ray recorder, taped against the back of one of the two paintings on the wall is recording every word. With the use of his cell phone, Joey can control the recorder from his desk. He knows that Johnny has installed a hidden CCTV camera in his office. It's his job to check the recordings daily, register the coming and goings, then reset the timer. So it was easy, a few weeks ago to install the listening device when Johnny and Butch were absent. Now, with these unexpected happenings, he is glad that he did, although it puts him at great risk. If discovered it would start a witch hunt that would probably point to him! But Max is pushing and it could be the evidence that will secure his financial future, a clean slate, and a new life in Australia.

Earlier that day, when Butch entered the room, Joey reached forward and touched the screen on his iPhone to activate the recorder. He was glad that he did, as the ensuing conversation surely will be hard evidence. Now, sitting back in his chair, his mind returns to the Parakai pub. It was by chance that he was there to have a meeting with the new manager and the pool game is still etched in his mind. It was memorable seeing a beautiful girl thrash his boss, in his own pub, at his own pool table using his own cue stick! He didn't pay much attention to her friends, seated on stools near the pool table. If he had known then what he knows now, he would have studied them with a great deal more interest!

As he was not involved in the previous night's chase, it is only now that he is aware of the deaths and injuries. Secretly he is pleased that Johnny is suffering and watches him tap the ash off his cigar into an ashtray and then turn to Butch. "So how are you going to find those fuckers?"

Butch shuffles his crossed legs, exposing more of his cowboy boots. "Well it's a bit of a fuckin' stretch but Karl is sure he saw you hit that dog with your last shot. It yelped and then disappeared below the seat... When Karl spotted them at Waimauku today, the dog was standing up in the back seat and there was a big fuckin' patch on its hind leg."

Johnny takes a long pull on his cigar as he tries to figure the connection, and then slowly exhales, watching the smoke drift up toward the ceiling.

Butch continues, "As I was saying, it's a bit of a fuckin' long shot boss, but there is a new Vet in Waimauku and I'm guessing that's where they would've gone."

Johnny screws up his eyes and then runs his hands through his thinning grey hair. "So you think the Vet will have the dog's ownership details on her fuckin' files?"

Butch nods as Johnny taps his cigar, "I think you're right, it's worth a fuckin' shot!" He takes another puff on his cigar and then turns and gestures to Joey, "Come here a moment."

Joey gets up and moves to the sofa, "Sit down by Butch, I want your help."

Once he is seated, Johnny continues, "You're doing a bloody good job on the books, but this time I want you to do a fuckin' break and enter for me."

Joey looks surprised,

"I know that I said that you wouldn't have to be involved in my side of the business, but now I need your fuckin' help and I'll pay you an extra fuckin' K."

Joey scratches behind his ear. "So you want me to break into the Vet's office and get the ownership details of the dog... I guess the Vet wouldn't treat too many dogs with bullet wounds over the last coupla days!"

Johnny's eyes bore into Joey's and he begins to squirm, confused by the intense stare, "What? Wasn't I supposed to be listening or somethin'?... Is there a fuckin' problem?"

"Nah, I just reminded myself that sometimes I forget you're over there. Anyway it'll be a night job and you'll have Butch as your watch, should be a piece of piss for a fuckin' pick pocket like you, so what-do-ya-say?"

Joey hadn't told Johnny about his skill as a locksmith only that he had done time after a cannabis bust. The fact that Johnny knows more about him than he realises, leaves him uncomfortable. Trying to hide his fear, he agrees. "No problem Johnny when do you want me to do it?"

"Tonight!"

Joey nods and walks back to his desk troubled by the sudden decision.

Johnny stands and beckons Butch to follow him outside so that he can talk about the syndicate of gangs meeting that afternoon and also to talk about Dan Henare being locked up in the Rarotonga jail, he's about to be told that Dan is dead.

CHAPTER 16

The Puhoi Pub

What does the land of Bohemia have in common with the small farming village of Puhoi? Apart from the fact that both make cheese and drink beer, there is little else! Bohemia conjures up thoughts of middle Europe with ancient castles on mountain peaks, freezing winters, people of alternative life styles and even more fanciful, vampires and werewolves! Puhoi is almost the antithesis of Bohemia, but there is a connection. If you visit the small sleepy town, at the head waters of the slow river, you will find a museum that tells of the arrival of eighty-six settlers from Bohemia in eighteen sixty-three.

At that time, their home town of Staab was like a pinball being bounced around by the surrounding military and political powers. For centuries Bohemia was part of the Austria-Hungary Empire, in the German Confederation and part of Czechoslovakia. In eighteen sixty, a populous campaign was started in Prague by the politicians to change the official language from German to Czechoslovakian. Enraged by this demand and economically squeezed, some of the families of Staab opted to start a new life somewhere else.

By one of those quirks of fate, one of the families had a relative, Captain Martin Krippner who was an adventurer and he told them about free farm land in New Zealand. But there were conditions. The free land was restricted to forty acres per married man, twenty acres for the wife, and twenty acres for each dependent child. Being good Catholics with large families, some were able to claim large acreage, an impossible dream in Bohemia.

What they didn't know was that the gifted land was owned by the Maori who sold portions of it to the Government for their new immigration scheme and that it was classified on the official maps as 'waste land'.

The Bohemians were told that they would be welcomed and transported to their new farms beside a small river, very much like their own in Staab, and that they would be provided with food and accommodation.

The expedition of fifty families was officially blessed by the Archbishop of Prague and they departed with high expectations.

With God on their side, and free land for the taking, what could possibly go wrong?

After one hundred and six days in transit, they disembarked off a cutter at the mouth of the Puhoi river and were met by Chief Te Hemera Tauhia. It is not known how they felt about being transported up a river in small wakas, but you could imagine their concern when all they could see of their promised land was tall mangroves and steep, dense, bush clad hills.

There was no flat land other than at the mouth of the river.

They were accustomed to farming the lower slopes of mountains and in the valleys, but those had been cleared and populated many centuries before, this was raw, unfamiliar land.

With trained eyes, the men and woman seated in the canoes, would have been under no illusions as to how hard their life was going to be! They would have comforted themselves with the knowledge that food and accommodation was waiting for them at the river's end.

Only the children and adolescents with their youthful exuberance would have been excited, chattering and laughing and trailing their hands in the moving water and pointing to the large sea birds perched on the mangrove branches. The youngest would have watched wide eyed and a little afraid of the tattooed faces and the large brown backs of the paddlers as they dipped their strange oars rhythmically into the water.

After a long, boring, sea sick confinement on board the sailing boat, this was freedom, the start of a great adventure. The adults' growing anxiety would have culminated into disbelief when they found their accommodation to be two nikau huts and their food, cooked in a pit in the ground! With horror and fear they would have known that they had made a terrible mistake! There would have been soul searching, incriminations, accusations and a whole lot of tears and prayers.

The promise from Captain Krippner and Governor Gray, was a new start in a new land, flowing with milk and honey. They were a hundred years too soon, as there was sparse milk and even less honey in their new land. They starved but survived, thanks to the Maori, their own fortitude, belief in a benevolent God and their skills.

Acres of hilly bush and valleys were cleared and there was no shortage of timber for new buildings. Soon they had their own church, a school house and a community hall, where they danced their polkas and waltzes, accompanied by an accordion, piano and fiddle. So with hard work and fortitude they carved out their new life at the head of the slow river.

At that time, Cobb & Co., an Auckland based stage coach company, started a service from the wharf at Silverdale to the hot pools at Waiwera. Passengers boarded a sailing barge at Devonport, Auckland and disembarked at the Wade Hotel. From there it was a winding, four horse coach ride, to the pools. The route proved popular and when a new wooden bridge, spanning the Waiwera river, was built in eighteen eighty-one, they extended their route northward to Warkworth. After a difficult and dangerous ride up and over the Waiwera hills, Puhoi was a morning stop for the passengers, helping to prosper John Schollum's 'Baby Saloon' and Vincent Schishka's boarding house beside it.

Within a few years, faster transport and a new road by-passed Puhoi, but the back-woods settlement survived and different owners bought and sold the pub. Today, it's antiquity is enjoyed by curious tourists and motor cyclists looking for an afternoon ride out of town.

So it is an interesting venue for the leaders of the syndicated gangs to talk about their loss of two million dollars in Rarotonga.

Earlier in the day, Joey Moser, organiser of the meeting, reserved two huge picnic benches under a twin peaked Tui tent near the entrance to the pub.

Later that afternoon, the tranquil settlement is shattered by the arrival of the first two, of fourteen, chromed, high handle barred Harleys.

Johnny and Butch wanted to be there first, not to welcome the others, but to show that this is their patch. As agreed, they wear their chain studded black leather jackets devoid of gang patches.

Andrew, the Bar Manager and owner, stops wiping the moisture off the sweating beer taps and watches the two black helmeted men ride up to the car park beside the tent. He is skilled at identifying a gang member's rank by how wide his knees extend outwards. It is as if the wider the spread, the more he owns, not only the road, but every part of the landscape he passes! He notes that these two have legs spread so wide that they must be exerting pressure on parts that are very sensitive to pressure of any kind! He knows that these two must be gang royalty and as they swing their legs off their bikes and remove their helmets, he sees that they have no patches on their backs. *'That is strange!'*

Placing his wet towel on the counter, he turns to Fay and points, "What do you make of that?"

Fay, his bar maid, wife and confidante, frowns, shaking her head. "Dunno?... Gang men. No patches. Strange! Do you think they are part of the booking?" She looks over at an old grandfather clock

that only loses a few minutes a day, "They're a bit early aren't they?"

"Yeah, could be. There's twelve more coming, keep your eyes open, could be trouble!"

She nods and then continues to angle fill a jug of Speight's Dark Ale.

Andrew walks around the bar and out the front door. Johnny is already seated when he arrives and shakes his hand, "Hi I'm Andrew are you part of the fourteen that have booked the tent?"

Johnny releases his hand and reaches over and picks up a 're-served' sign and points it towards him. "Yeah this is for us, the others will be here soon, Andrew."

Andrew nods. "Call me Andy."

"Okay, Andrew-call-me-Andy, keep a fuckin' tab!" He unzips a pocket and pulls out a roll of red one hundred dollar bills and peels off four.

Andrew drops them into his apron pouch wondering if they are counterfeit.

Reading his mind, Johnny smirks, "They're fuckin' real man!... Just let me know when you need more." He waves his hand around to include the tented area, "We don't want to be fuckin' disturbed, okay?" Andrew nods as Johnny continues, "Just keep the food and booze coming, enough for fourteen…. No fuck it, enough for twenty!"

Andrew waits a moment in case there are further instructions then asks. "Do you want to see a menu?"

"Nah man, just keep the food comin! If you see the fuckin' food is gone, bring some MORE!" To emphasis this, he peels off two more red bills from his roll and hands them to Andrew, "The others won't be here until two, have the food and jugs of Lion ready, get me four now!" He studies Andrew for a moment, "By-the-way I'm Johnny and this is Butch."Andrew shakes Butch's huge hand and is surprised at his light squeeze and then retreats to the safety of the bar.

Walking over to Fay he holds open the pouch.

She raises her eyes in surprise. "I hope they are real!"

"Me too, I guess we'll just have to take the risk! They're the booking all right, they want food for twenty, by two, I'll look after the booze, can you warn the kitchen."

"What do they want?"

"They didn't say!"

She raises her eyebrows and then frowns, so he adds, "Make sausages and chips, hamburgers, chicken, fish, battered mussels and oysters… What the hell, cook up a bit of everything that's on the menu!" He taps his pouch, "The more we cook the more we make"

Fay scurries off to the kitchen to pressure their slow moving chef as Andrew pours the jugs and loads mugs onto a tray.

Soon the air is crackling with the arrival of the other six syndicate gang leaders and their Sergeants. The Pit Bulls. The Reapers. The Katapos. The Rattlers. The Highway 69ers and the Sharks. The Mean Maori Mean gang, sworn enemy of the Pit Bulls are not included, they rely on their own drug supply from Bali and Sydney.

If it wasn't for the fact that it is an unholy gathering, it would be an auspicious occasion, being the first time that most of the leading gangs of Auckland have gathered together to discuss business. The catalyst of course is the fact that they have to work out what to do about the loss of their two million dollars. It could be a meeting of a high profile business consortium, the CEOs being relaxed and convivial while their henchmen nervous and sticking to them like shadows with their eyes darting left and right, even when they are eating and drinking. But the format for this meeting is very different. There is no structure, no formal procedure, no Chairman, Secretary or Treasurer, no long winded platitudes or multitudes of drafts-of-agreement or clauses or sub-clauses or parts of sub-clauses.

The Pit Bull's boss, Ozzy Clem, sucks the chicken fat off his fingers, takes a swallow of beer and then wraps on the table with his bulldog ring to get attention. "So Johnny you lost the fuckin' money, what do you fuckin' suggest?"

There is immediate silence. Johnny looks from one leader to the other then shrugs. "We send another two mill, split eight ways."

Ozzy Clem frowns, counts heads and then turns back to Johnny.

"How come eight fuckin' ways, there's only seven of us!"

"What about the fuckin' Chinese?"

Clem, who seems to be the self-appointed M.C., shakes his head and looks at the others to see if they agree. Satisfied he turns back to Johnny. "Nah Johnny, it's too fuckin' complicated, leave the chinks out of it! I say split it seven ways, okay?" Again he looks for support and there is, "So Johnny, we'll split it seven ways and this time I'll arrange the fucking delivery."

Johnny shrugs again. "Sure... okay, you'll have my share tomorrow."

As each of the leaders nod, Johnny is relieved as he expected to pay more, so he turns his attention back to the food and beer.

With business over, Clem walks around the table, slaps Johnny on the back and refills his mug.

Johnny leans close to his ear so that his words can't be heard by others, "What do you know about my man Dan Henare?"

Clem straightens, his forced smile disappears and he holds up his hands with fingers spread, facing forward. "Nothin' Johnny, wasn't me, don't know nothin' about it!"

"Don't know nothin' about fuckin' what?"

"The Raro Chinaman sent me a message, that's all."

Johnny continues to frown, his face growing red with anger. "Why didn't he send it to me? Dan Henare is my man, not fuckin' yours!"

Again Clem holds up his hands. "Don't fuckin' know Johnny.... For-fucks-sake, I can't figure those bastards out at the best of times. Shit knows why he didn't tell you!" Handing him his beer, he puts his arm around his shoulders, "Don't worry Johnny, you're just having some fuckin' back luck at the moment. It'll all work out!"

Not convinced, Johnny pops a battered mussel into his mouth and tries to figure out who killed Dan.

During the afternoon, at opportune times, Ozzy Clem slips a card to each of the leaders. It reads, 'Meet me at the Wade.' No card is handed to Johnny. What he is concealing is that a discussion between himself and Ah Chung the previous day, decided the fate of

Dan Henare. It also decided that the syndicate would be reduced to six, more profits for all! For his part, using his Triad connections, Ah Chung would arrange for the elimination of the Satan's Son gang and be paid four million US dollars for his troubles. Chan Chemicals would also be granted the exclusive rights of supply of ephedrine and pseudo-ephedrine and methamphetamine to New Zealand.

Right now, Johnny and his gang are dead men walking.

CHAPTER 17

Roast Lamb and Castle Howard

The dress code for Sunday dinner at Jean's is clean casual, but this evening Mike, Tane and Gary have decided on smart casual.

Gary at his cottage, has found the iron and with a blanket on the table has already pressed his best party shirt and slim-fit jeans. Standing in front of the mirror, he enjoys the silky feel of the shirt and the tight jeans. Rotating left and right, he admires his rugged good looks. As he spikes his hair with goo, he is not concerned that a few droplets splash onto an old dressing table.

A hundred years ago, it would have been one of the few treasures of a bushman's wife. Now beer stained and chipped, drawers that stick, a scratched mirror and one short leg, its youthful elegance has long since gone. So different for Robyn, Wendy and Julia, who in their prime of life are enjoying preparing to meet their men. It is fun and they want to make an impression. The hair curlers have been working overtime and makeup carefully applied.

Robyn is paying particular attention to her skin, eyes and lips and is glowing with anticipation.

Gary, sitting at his kitchen table, bends down and pulls the legs of his jeans over the tops of his new tan cowboy boots then calls

Tane on his phone. "Are you guys leaving soon?"

"Yeah, I'm just tarting up Lady, I think she misses the Canadian girls already!"

"Me too!"

"Jean said six, so we'd better be on time!"

At the Homestay, Jean, wearing her forget-me-not apron is flushed as she bustles around the kitchen. Usually she wouldn't have started preparing the meal as early as this, but she is determined to cook the best lamb roast for her special guests. The fact that there is blossoming romances has elevated it from just a meal to an important occasion!

Humming a happy tune, she checks the roast vegies under the grill and is satisfied that she isn't cooking the kumara, pumpkin and onions too soon. The pre-boiled Pukekohe potatoes and Ruawai kumaras are golden and crisp and the pumpkin and onions, still firm.

Pulling the roasting dish out a little further, she brushes the pumpkin and onion with avocado oil. Closing the door she turns the heat down to medium and then opens the main oven to check the slow turning leg of Canterbury lamb. It is doing exactly what it is supposed to do, cracking and popping and squirting jets of lamb fat over the salted, golden brown skin. With the door open, the kitchen is filled with the delicious aroma of roast lamb, garlic, rosemary and thyme.

Adding water to a pot of peeled and cut potatoes, she places it on one of her six gas hobs. Exiting through the rear screen door, she walks down the back steps to a raised herb garden where she cuts handfuls of mint and chives. The chives, cut finely, will be mashed into the potatoes with butter and cream. The mint is for homemade hot mint sauce.

Preparing her sauce, in a small pot, she adds malt vinegar, sugar and salt, with a little water, then strips the mint leaves off the stalks and chops them fine. Bringing the mixture to a boil, she tastes, adjusting the ingredients until it is the right blend of sweet and sour and mint flavouring.

Opening the large fridge, she removes the runner beans, bought by Robyn and snap tests one for freshness. Satisfied, she tops and tails, then with a double edged peeler removes the stringy sides. Bunching the beans together, she angle cuts them into bite sized pieces, scoops them into a pot and adds salt.

Glancing up at the clock, she sees it is five, ample time to make a chocolate steam pudding, topped with her own strawberry jam, cook the beans, mash the potatoes, whip the cream and have a shower before dressing for dinner. For her it is more than a-piece-of-cake, it's a pavlova!

Aware of Jean's demand for punctuality, the boys arrive ten minutes early and are now seated at the main dining room table behind their handmade place names. Jean has made sure that the romancing couples are facing each other and not side by side.

Lady, outside the back door, is wearing a pink ribbon and her nose is pushed so hard up against the mesh that it is causing an indentation. Her shaved leg, with a large adhesive pad, doesn't seem to be causing any discomfort, as she tries to keep an eye on the activities inside.

With the meat resting and the vegetables in the warming tray, Jean is sitting at the end of the table drinking a chilled pinot gris. For the first time since the girls' arrival, she is wearing a touch of make-up and a frothy dress decorated with light blue flowers.

The boys have opted for beer and showing that they are on their best behaviour, stand as the girls enter. Immediately the predominant smell of the roast is replaced by wafts of expensive perfume, skin lotion and hair spray.

Wendy leads the way and sits down opposite Mike, before he has a chance to escort her to her chair.

Julia and Robyn follow suit.

Wendy says, with an imperious wave of her hand and in the most English of accents. "Thank you gentlemen, you may be seated!"

Mike sweeps an arm forward, with just the slightest suggestion of a bow. "Well thank you ma-am we are honoured by your presence, and you too, sweet ladies! "

Julia says. "So gal-lant!" Everyone laughs.

Jean suggests a pre meal drink. "We have a Hasting's pinot gris. A Nelson sauvignon blanc. A Marlborough reisling.... or if you prefer, chilled Karekare H2O."

Tane whispers quietly to Julia, but loud enough for all to hear. "I recommend the Karekare H2O, fresh off the roof with a subtle taste of possum."

Again there is laughter, except for Jean, who, caught sipping, splutters into her wine.

Wendy says. "I've never tasted pinot gris, so I'll try that thanks."

"Me too." Says Julia and Robyn.

Jean stands and moves toward the kitchen. "Boys, serve the girls, the bottle's in the ice chiller and the glasses are below in the cupboard." She pauses by the kitchen, "I'm going to get the hors-d'oeuvres. Sorry, but there's only one choice, fresh Kerikeri avocados stuffed with Canadian salmon and New Zealand shrimp in mayonnaise, I thought it appropriate, does everyone want one?"

Everyone nods.

The girls have never tasted stuffed avocados before. They know it is the main ingredient of guacamole, but have never before eaten the fresh fruit stuffed with seafood. It sounded rather good.

The boys serve them the wine as Jean opens the fridge and removes a tray of half cut avocados and then fills the circular cavity with a mixture of fine sliced red salmon, cooked shrimps and mayonnaise, then squeezes fresh lime juice over the top.

Sipping the wine, they are delighted at its soft, slightly sweet, peach flavour.

Swirling the wine in her glass, Robyn asks. "Jean, you mentioned this is a Hasting's pinot gris, is that the name of a winery or the place it comes from?" Jean looks up from her preparations. "It's a place. Hastings is on the East Coast of the North Island, about five hundred kilometres South of here. It is very sunny and dry and ideal for growing the pinot gris grapes, or so I'm told, anyway, I'm a believer!" She takes a sip from her glass before placing the avocados on large paua shells, with wedges of lime and sprigs of mint as a decoration.

After serving, she notices that everyone is waiting, so she raises her glass and proposes a toast. "To health, wealth, happiness and...,"

She pauses looking at each of the couples...., "Romance!" Clinking glasses, they take a drink, then dig into the avocados with their forks. The combination of the wine, fresh avocado and creamy seafood is a delight. Robyn, scraping the last mouthful out of the empty shell, turns to Jean. "That was delicious, thanks!"

"You are welcome, sorry about the corn on the cob, we can have that as a main tomorrow, if that's okay?"

"You're the cook, no worries!"

The silver setting, the bone china plates and the cut crystal wine glasses, could belong in the most elegant Parisian restaurant, instead of at an old Homestay by a New Zealand beach.

At the end of the main course, the girls are charmed knowing that they have just been treated to a once in a life time eating sensation. For the first time they have tasted lamb as it should be cooked. Tender, with just a hint of herbs and garlic, crisp brown skin and sweet golden kumara. The green beans were earthy sweet, not over cooked and the creamy mashed potato light and fluffy and topped with dobs of butter. The roast potatoes were crunchy crisp and the pumpkin, brown, but sweet, like the onions.

They are used to cold mint jelly served with lamb, but never before tasted the sweet acidic tang of the hot mint sauce, or the rich brown gravy that is homemade, not from a box.

One by one, knives and forks are placed on empty plates accompanied by contented sighs.

Julia raises her glass. "I propose a toast to an amazing chef."

Mike stands holding up his glass. "I think this calls for a standing ovation!"

Now, all standing, Julia says. "To Jean!"

Jean is flattered more than she shows. "Oh go on with you, it's just a roast. Now I suggest you boys get some beers and fill the girls' glasses and then adjourn to the veranda while I prepare the dessert."

As they take their leave, the girls are thinking. '*I don't think I can eat anymore, but how can I get out of this gracefully?*' While the boys are thinking. '*Terrific, dessert!*'

Out on the veranda wall lamps beam downwards onto the wood decking. It is not a dark night as a huge moon illuminates everything with a silver glow. A warm sea breeze sways the branches of the pohutukawa and the ponga and constrains the pesky mosquitoes. It is an uplifting, contented night and the call of the morepork belongs.

Robyn and Gary move a two seater swing chair next to the other and seat themselves beside Julia and Wendy. While Tane and Mike move their deck chairs to face them.

Lady waits until her family have decided where to sit, then ambles over and stretches out in front of Tane, close enough to feel his shoe against her back. She shuts her eyes leaving only her nose and ears alert.

Mike decides to tease Wendy. "You must be royalty the way you spoke to us at the table."

"I am!"

He smiles at her. "You're joshing?"

"No..., really!"

Julia had been sworn to secrecy about the little she knew about Wendy's family, now that Wendy has revealed her royal connections, she decides it is time to know more. "It is true. Wendy has a title, it's Lady Howard."

Gary says. "You're having us on, right?" He turns to Robyn knowing that she wouldn't lie. She shakes her head,

"Well I'll be, what-do-you-know, we're in the presence of royalty.... I mean that just doesn't happen here at the beach. Kings and queens and all that stuff!" He frowns turning towards Wendy, "But aren't you living in Canada? That's a long way from a castle in pommy land."

"It's ACTUALLY a castle in Yorkshire, which is not POMMY land. Prisoner of Mother England refers to convicts sent to Australia, not from our castle."

Robyn, uncomfortable that Gary is being corrected, interjects. "You wouldn't know it Gary, but the people from Yorkshire are very proud people, you have to be careful if you step on their toes."

Julia nods. "I know, that's how I met Wendy, six years ago." She turns and looks at Wendy before rocking the swing chair back and forwards, "I was at a summer course at Leeds University, one afternoon while having drinks with a bunch of students, what was supposed to be a fun conversation suddenly turned nasty. They were teasing me about English Canada selling out to the French. I joked that most of the criminals shipped to Australia were from Yorkshire. I didn't know if it was true or not? I was just, as you say." She looks across at Tane, "Taking the piss!" The men smile, liking the impromptu joke as Julia continues, "One of the drunken females, sitting opposite me, shouted, 'You know nothing about Yorkshire people, shut your mouth Yankee bitch!' If that wasn't enough, she reached across the table and slapped me hard on the side of the face. My first thought was to tell her that I was NOT from the United States, and secondly that I didn't consider myself a bitch! I was feeling dizzy and almost collapsed, except Wens grabbed me by the arm." She smiles at Wendy, "Fancy that! Little Wens holding me up!... I didn't know who she was, but I was sure grateful for her help. I vaguely remember being pulled away and Wendy giving them hell for attacking me. From then on we have been best friends and I love her heaps."

Wendy turns and gives her a hug. "Aahh I love you too Jules!"

Mike, watching them gently swinging is intrigued by Wendy's royal connection. It adds to his growing fascination. "So Lady Wendy Howard you must have one hell of a story to tell?"

Five years before, Julia and Robyn had asked the same question, but were told very little. Now with expectant ears, the conversation stops. All that can be heard is the 'chirrup', 'chirrup' of the crickets and the occasional 'morepork' from somewhere in the bush.

Julia continues to push the swing backwards and forwards, waiting for Wendy to continue.

Just at that moment, Jean arrives and noticing the silence, enquires. "Did I interrupt something?"

Gary says. "Hey Jean, you'll never guess, Wendy here is actually Lady Howard!" As if that is not enough, he adds, "That's English royalty you know!"

Jean looks at Wendy and smiles. "Well I'll be, how exciting! Anyway the dessert is ready for kings and queens and commoners alike." She moves over to Wendy and offers her arm, "Your majesty, after dessert do you mind telling us more? This is really exciting!"

"Sure my pleasure but I'd just like to say that I'm only slightly connected to the House of Windsor."

Jean disengages her arm and takes a step backwards. "I wonder if I can remember how to curtsey? The last time was when I was in a school dance, oh well here goes." Elegantly placing one leg behind the other, and holding the sides of her apron outward, she dips down and up in a perfect curtsey.

Wendy acknowledges with a nod of her head, then gets off the swing. "Jean, that was the most elegant curtsey I have ever seen, fancy you knowing how to do that!" Placing her arm around Jean's wide waist, they move along the veranda towards the front door.

Lady, not allowed in the house, makes her way around to the back door where she has been smelling delicious smells all afternoon.

In the kitchen, Jean carefully lifts a bowl of steamed pudding from the double boiler, removes the string from the grease-proof paper lid and turns the pudding upside down onto a silver platter. It keeps its shape although still steaming and moist and the hot strawberry jam glistens as it slides down the sides.

Wendy, helping Jean to serve, is impressed by the elegant and colourful presentation. The gilt edged white porcelain bowls contrast with the chocolate pudding. The crimson red of the strawberry jam accentuates the whiteness of the whipped cream on top and the green of the mint leaves, evenly spaced. It is as royal a dessert as served at Buckingham Palace!

Although Wendy and Jean can't see her, they can hear Lady quietly whining behind the screen door.

Jean cuts slices of meat off the bone into a pie dish, and pushes open the door.

Lady backs away and snatches a mouthful out of the dish before it makes contact with the porch. Her frantically waving tail indicates her hunger and three snapping bites clean the plate. There is no savouring the flavour, although she does lick the dish clean. Now satisfied, she becomes aware of her injured leg and lying down listens to the sounds of the night.

Apart from the usual bush noises, she can hear a possum tearing leaves off the top of a puriri tree. She hates possums as they tease her from the safety of high branches.

Suddenly the 'crack' of a bending branch makes her lift her head, knowing that the possum is climbing down, she is on full alert and her ears twist in the direction of the sound. Standing, she peers into the darkness as it drops onto the hard dirt of the track. Pressing her body down low she ignores the pain and slinks down the stairs. She can tell it is a large possum by the noise it made as it descended and also by the 'thump' as it hit the ground. By luck she is down wind, and her excitement grows the closer she gets.

The possum, having eaten its fill, is now preening itself in the middle of the track.

Lady stops within springing distance and ever so slowly tucks her hind legs under her body. The sharp sting in her leg is ignored by her growing excitement.

The possum, sensing danger, stops licking and looks around, but Lady is hidden by a hump in the track and the crickets have not stopped their noise, so it returns to its grooming with grunts and hisses.

With adrenaline driving her legs, Lady springs forward and snaps onto the end of its bushy tail.

Fighting for its life, it screams and jumps upward and then twists, crashing backward onto Lady's head. Now it has something to scratch, bite and rake with its sharp hind claws.

Lady has a firm grip on its tail, so again and again it rakes searching for her soft under belly. Its frantic scratching makes contact with the plaster covering her incision and penetrates deep into the wound. The sudden searing pain makes Lady release the tail from her mouth and immediately the possum springs to the closest tree and is gone in a flash.

Lady watches it disappear and tries to move, but collapses back onto the track.

Lying on her side, she twists backwards trying to lick the wound. Blood is flowing down her leg and dripping off her hind claws. The wound is deep, a large vein has been severed. Again she tries to stand but her injured leg folds under her and she collapses back onto her side again with a whimper and a moan.

Unaware that lady is bleeding to death, fifty metres away, the men clear the table, while Jean rummages around in her liquor cabinet. "Yes, I've found it, Cointreau! Anyone for an aperitif. I suppose you all want coffee?"

They all nod,

"You know, this is the first time I have ever offered a liqueur to my guests, but this is a royal occasion!" She points to a large gurgling percolator, "Help yourself to the coffee, there's trim milk as well as coffee cream." Arranging seven shot glasses on a tray, she pours the orange flavoured liqueur, "Help yourself."

Once everyone is seated, Jean holds up her glass, "To Lady Wendy Howard!"

The strong liqueur burns Robyn's throat and she catches her breath causing a few droplets to enter her lungs. Turning pink, she begins to cough.

Tane, sitting beside her, forcefully taps her on the back. The jolting works and her face returns to its usual pallor although the tears continue run down her cheeks. Smiling, she turns and gives him a hug. "Thanks Tane, you can tell I'm not used to strong liquor." Looking up the table at Wendy, she apologises, "Sorry for spoiling your toast Wens…Now let's hear what it was like growing up in a castle?"

With all eyes on her, she slowly slides her finger around the rim of her coffee cup as her mind returns to the castle where she was born. "You know, my home, Castle Howard, is not really a castle because it was not built to protect against invaders but to accommodate gentry in the most opulent style possible. At that time, the rich and powerful made huge amounts of money from world trade of sugar, spice, silk, cotton, metal, clay products and slaves… Just about everything. You name it, we owned it, because the Royal Navy ruled the waves."

As Wendy pauses, Jean asks. "When was that? I mean do you know when the castle was built?"

She nods, "Sure do, for three years I was a tour guide so I know a lot about the castle. The build started in sixteen ninety-nine," She nods, "A long time ago, but it wasn't finished until eighteen eleven, so it took one hundred and twelve years from start to finish."

Gary, who finds it uncomfortable being part of group discussions, often contributes an outrageous comment. He doesn't mean to say crazy things, but something happens in his brain that mangles his thoughts. Something to do with wanting to contribute without real knowledge and also acute shyness.

Aware of his often strange interjections, Tane and Mike are not surprised when he says. "Heck, we can build a house in six months!... I bet if kiwis had the contract they would have had it built in, say, twenty years!"

The girls think he is trying to be funny and are ready to laugh, but he is not! Because his comments are farcical there is an uncomfortable silence.

Jean comes to his rescue. "Gary, Captain Cook didn't arrive in New Zealand until well after the castle was started and it was finished before the Treaty of Waitangi was signed. I don't think there would have been many New Zealand construction companies building castles in England around that time!"

Everyone laughs, except Gary who still thinks he is right, he mumbles. "Well, anyway we would have done it quicker!"

Wendy smiles and nods at him. "I'm sure you are right Gary. If New Zealanders can win the America's Cup, I'm sure you can build a castle."

Robyn thinks. *Thanks Wendy, he is sure going to be a work in progress, but it will be fun!*

'Mike is curious. "So Wendy, what is your connection to royalty and all that?"

She turns to him and nods her head. "I've also been asked that many times. I'm a fifteenth generation Howard. Charles Howard, who built the castle, was the Third Earl of Carlisle." She turns to look at Jean, seated at the head of the table, "You may not have known it but you were looking at my home in Brideshead Revisited, you know, the movie."

The men hadn't, but Jean had, and she remembers it well. In her mind she can see the castle, a huge three story stone building, with wide central steps leading to a domed entrance. In front of the building, is a massive fountain surrounded by sculptured gardens. Looking at Wendy, she wonders what her life must have been like and more importantly why she is staying in her little place on the western shores of Auckland, a Homestay that wilts in comparison. She smiles, thinking about the irony of having just bought king sized beds!

The men look at Wendy with renewed interest, particularly Mike, who thought he had her figured out!

Wendy knows that everyone is interested, so she continues, "Of course Brideshead Revisited, is fictional, but the castle and the gardens are just as I remember them. You know it was weird sitting in a theatre in Canada watching actors walk across the tiled floors where I used to play hopscotch with my brothers and sisters." Picking up her liqueur, she sips it, with a far-away look in her eyes, "Of course I was very homesick, right through the movie, and for days after!... I had never been homesick before! Life in a new country is so exciting and different that thoughts of home are forgotten, but when they do emerge they crowd out your mind and you become quite depressed. I know that I became light headed and dysfunctional for a few days." Looking towards Robyn and Julia, she continues, "I know you kept asking me if I was okay, but I didn't want to talk about it.... it would have been like stabbing a wound. Now you know why I never talked much about myself, also, part of it was that I thought you might treat me differently...... I know now that I should have trusted you." She raises her glass to her friends, who in turn raise theirs, "England is far more class conscious than Canada."

There is silence for a moment, as everyone decides to drink either their liqueur or their coffee, or in Gary's case, both.

Jean decides to ask the obvious question. "Do you mind telling us why you left the castle, or is that too private? I'm sorry for asking, but I know we are all curious.... I mean, living in a castle sounds a lot better than……..." She shrugs, "living anywhere else."

Wendy picks up her glass and sips, enjoying the sharp citric syrup. "It's hard to explain, but I'll try. It really was like living in a fairy tale and it was just as you can imagine. Best of everything and not wanting for anything as long as you stayed within the ancient rules of being a Howard. You are not allowed the freedom of being yourself. My brothers and sisters accepted this, but for me, I was suffocating! We were all expected to help run the family business, without the income, Castle Howard would not survive, so we all became part of Castle Howard Tourism and I didn't like it one little bit! My interests were in theatre and film! I wanted to make worthwhile productions, not to shepherd tourists through a castle!" She shakes her head, "Can you imagine how boring it was to say the same thing over and over again, day after day?

Mum and Dad did allow me time off to study for a degree in communication that kept me sane."

She pauses long enough to take another sip, then looks around and can see they are all staring at her intently, "There was not one single event that made me leave, it was an accumulation of many small things. The opportunity happened quite unexpectedly. A friend of mine at the university got a job in Toronto and she said there was a Production Assistant being advertised, so, without telling my parents, I applied and was accepted, subject to a work permit and all that immigration stuff. It wasn't that easy of course I had to become a Landed Immigrant and to do that, you answer a questionnaire that awards points. If you get enough points, then you're in! I can speak French and that helped. Anyway, I was accepted and I used my own email address at the castle and a private postal box down in the village. No one knew what I was up to." Wendy closes her eyes briefly, and then opens them again, "I was really afraid to tell my parents and yet when I did Dad was only annoyed that I hadn't told him sooner. Mum made me feel guilty, as if I had done something terribly wrong! But that all changed on the day of my departure. She asked me to join her in her drawing room and gave me a cheque. It was a very generous amount of money, far more than I'd ever need."

With thoughts of her mother, she can feel the tears filling her eyes then sliding down her cheeks in an unstoppable flow.

Picking up up her napkin, she wipes her eyes and then stumbles on, "Mum told me that she was happy for me and that she wished she had had the same courage when she was young. We hugged and cried and cried." Hiding her face in her napkin, she tries to stifle her sobs.

The men are uncomfortable, not sure what to say or do.

The ladies move on mass to Wendy and surround her with empathic tears and hugs.

Jean decides they all need a refill of liqueur and returns with the bottle and starts to top up the glasses.

Robyn and Julia decline.

Gary asks if it's okay to have another beer.

Jean nods. "Of course, it's yours anyway!"

Recovered from her emotions, Wendy sits up and wipes her eyes. "Heavens, what a spoil sport. Here we are, having a brilliant time, and then I go and spoil it with my tears, sorry everyone." She looks at Mike. "I won't let that happen again!"

He is not concerned and shrugs, then asks. "How did you and Julia keep in contact after the pub thing?"

"It was easy with the internet. I was able to become good friends with Robyn as well." She looks at Julia and then Robyn again, "We must have messengered and twittered at least twice a week and sent text messages at all hours of the day and night. Time zones were a bit of a problem."

The girls nod, and she continues, "It was a bit tricky arranging set days, and times, to meet on the internet, but we seemed to manage it okay, even though we were five hours apart.... I don't know how people keep in touch these days using snail mail and phone calls, how difficult and slow! It was fun keeping in contact, and when I told them I'd got the job with the TV station, they were just as excited as I was."

Julia and Robyn nod again, then Robyn adds. "Julia and I shared a two bedroom apartment in Toronto, so when Wendy said she was coming, I rented another, closer to my job. It worked out fine. So here we are now, nine thousand miles away at the bottom of the globe, what next?"

Every one laughs.

Jean stands. "I'm starting to feel tired. You young folk can stay as long as you like of course, but I'm going to do the dishes and then off to bed. What with gang chases, Lady getting shot and then meeting royalty, I'm all tuckered out!"

The girls offer to help with the clean-up and Jean accepts.

The guys start to move towards the kitchen, but are stopped by Julia. "It's okay guys, we want some girl time in the kitchen."

Tane looks at Gary then Mike. "Shall we call it a night?" When they nod, he turns to Jean, "Thanks for a tremendous meal and you too ladies, for your company."

Mike smiles affectionately at Wendy. "You already were a princess to me and now I find you are a grown up Lady, amazing!" He bends down and kisses her on the lips, not feeling at all intimidated, "Can I see you tomorrow? We'll plan another great day."

Wendy gives him a departing hug. "The earlier the better!"

Robyn goes over to Gary and reaching up pulls his face to hers and gives him a lingering kiss. "See you tomorrow, Gary, it has been a terrific day, thanks for everything."

Tane and Julia's body come together as if drawn by a magnet. They kiss briefly and then struggle to pull apart. Hand in hand, the three couples make their way to the back door where they each have a quick kiss before the screen door closes with its customary bang!

With Tane in the lead, the men walk in single file down the moon-lit track. A short distance later, he hears Lady whimpering, which quickens his step. In the faint light of the moon, he sees her lying on her side in a glistening pool of blood and she greets him with an apologetic *'woof'*.

Standing over her, he can see her injured leg is oozing fresh blood over the darker congealed blood and the adhesive pad has gone. Removing his belt, he loops it around her leg, as high up as possible, fastens it, then pulls it tight. Lady moans and he strokes her head. "Sorry girl but I have to stop the bleeding." He looks up at his friends. "She's lost a lot of blood and will need a transfusion pretty soon!"

Mike nods. "We'll have to get her back to the Vet."

Tane reaches into his pocket, and hands him his phone. "Emma's number is under 'E', give her a call!" Checking the tourniquet, he is satisfied that the blood flow has stopped.

Gary removes his shirt, then gently lifting her, pushes the shirt tail under her head, then works it along the length of her body, until it protrudes beyond her hind legs. Made of silk, it is strong and also large enough to be a makeshift stretcher.

Tane knows how much Gary prizes his shirt and smiles up at him. "Thanks!"

He shrugs, "It's only a bloody shirt!"

Tane nods, "And getting bloodier!"

Mike hands him the phone. "Emma lives at the clinic and she'll be waiting for us when we arrive."

Gary and Mike get into position behind lady and hold a corner of the shirt, while Tane ties the sleeves together, above Lady's head. "Ready, up!"

She is easily lifted and they soon arrive at the back of the cottage and stop beside the Jeep. With his free hand, Tane opens the passenger door and climbs up onto the front seat. lifting Lady up and over, she is lowered onto the back seat. The blanket, rejected just a day ago, is now tucked loosely over her. Tane runs into the cottage, grabs his wallet, car keys and a T shirt for Gary. Handing the shirt to Gary and the keys to Mike, he instructs. "You drive I'll stay with Lady." As he settles beside her, he can feel her shivering.

Gary gets in the front with Mike, and as they bump down the driveway to the road, Tane cradles her head in his lap.

CHAPTER 18

Break-In at Waimauku and the Missed Call

The moon is high overhead by the time Joey and Butch arrive at the Waimauku Veterinary Clinic. They drive past slowly, checking for movement inside. There is an illuminated sign out front, and a small entrance light, all else is dark and still.

Joey is glad, it will be a quick job.

Twice they drive past, checking, before parking behind a factory a block away.

Butch opens the glove compartment and hands Joey one of two black balaclavas, then a headset with an ear piece and a small mic. Next, he checks the magazine of his Baikal pistol, tucking it into the back of his black track pants.

Joey, also dressed in black, opens the boot of the car and takes out a folded bag of tools, then switches on a small modem. Muting his phone he talks quietly into his mic., reminding Butch to do the same. Gently lowering the boot, he checks to see if they are being watched before moving briskly up the street towards the Clinic.

Waimauku is a small rural town and most of the houses are set back from the road with large lawns, flowering shrubs and high hedges. The lights are out in the houses and the night belongs to the flying insects buzzing around a small number of street lamps.

At the Clinic, they crouch to the same height as a side fence and follow it to the rear, stopping beside a small garage.

Night lights in a hallway, shine out through two windows on either side of a glass paneled back door. It is not until they move towards the Clinic that they see a bedroom at the rear.

Seeing a TV flickering behind a venetian blind, Joey signals to Butch to return to the garage so they can discuss a change of plans.

In the bedroom, Emma is in bed reading a book with the TV on and the sound turned off. A phone rings in her reception room, and she looks at her bedside clock, noting that it is just before the 10.30 News. Sighing, she places the book beside her, then pushing back the sheet, walks to the closet and puts on a dressing gown. Frowning, she knows it is unusual to have a call this late and decides it is either a wrong number or an emergency, so she flip flops in her jandals, down the hallway.

Outside, Joey and Butch heard the phone ring and now watch as she passes by the first window, then the backdoor, then the second window, before turning into the reception room and switching on the lights.

Moving to the closest window, they see her disable the alarm and pick up the phone at the desk.

With the light streaming out of the window, Joey ducks underneath and peels back his balaclava so that he can hear.

"Good evening, Waimauku Veterinary Clinic, Emma speaking." There is a pause, "No problem Mike, bring her in as soon as you can, sounds like she needs some blood. How long before you get here?"

Again a pause,

"Twenty minutes? Okay, see you soon." Hanging up, she looks up at the clock on the wall, before moving briskly down the hallway back to her bedroom.

Staying just outside the light from the windows, Joey and Butch are forced to move quickly to keep up. Now close to the bedroom window, the view through the blinds is restricted, but they see her take off her dressing gown, then her nightie and turn towards them stark naked. She is tall, tanned, blonde and beautiful. Moving to a chest of drawers she pulls out black panties and a bra. Stepping into her panties, she bends down and pulls them up to her waist. Pushing her arms through the straps of her bra, she fastens them at the back. Returning to the chest of drawers, she shimmies into a black satin slip, then covers all of her under garments with a green surgical gown, fastening it at the side.

Like Peeping Toms, Joey and Butch watch all her movements, but their reactions differ.

Joey is aroused, while Butch feels no desire at all, being sexually stimulated only when he is inflicting pain.

Lifting each foot in turn, Emma puts on sterile slippers, then shuffles down the hallway and enters the Surgery. Turning on the light, she pumps disinfectant onto her hand and then rubs both hands together. Using a nail brush, she scrubs her nails and fingers, then pumps more disinfectant into her palm and spreads it on each arm up to her elbows. Drying her hands and arms under an air dryer on the wall, she pulls on surgical gloves. Now sterilised, she sets up an I.V. pole beside the operating table, then rolls over a stainless steel cabinet and places a luer needle and a catheter on a tray, on top. Bending, she pulls out a bag of wet antiseptic swabs placing them also on the tray. After a final check, she removes her gloves and returns to the reception room.

On the desk is a computer. Turning it on, she enters her password and clicks on a *'Vettec'* app. A software programme loads and once the cursor appears, she clicks on *'Clients'.* and scrolls down to 'Lady'. Then clicks again to open the file. After a brief read, she gets off the chair and moves to a large filing cabinet. Pulling open the second drawer, labeled J – L, she removes Lady's file. A picture of a black and white Collie is stapled to the front. Opening the file, she removes a number of x-ray photos then returns to the Surgery, clipping them onto a viewing window. Turning on the background light, she studies the photos for a few minutes before turning off the light.

Returning to her bedroom, she looks at the TV, hoping to catch the end of the News on TVONE.

By moving from window to window, Joey and Butch have been watching her, and at last, Joey sees his chance. He knows from the phone call that he has about ten minutes before someone arrives. Luckily the computer is on, the alarm disabled and the Vet in her bedroom, but he has to hurry. Speaking quietly into his mic., he asks Butch to keep watch and then moves silently up the steps to the back door.

Switching on a small directional light, strapped to his head, he shines it on the lock, inserting a small L shaped key. After a few twists and turns, the door opens to the length of a security chain. Expecting this, he removes a small bolt cutter from his tool bag and inserting it into the gap, snips the chain. This creates some noise, so he switches off his head light and steps back into the darkness.

Again he whispers into his mic., "Has she moved?"

"No."

Stealthily moving to the back door again, he slowly pushes it open until it is wide enough for him to enter into the hallway. Pausing for a moment, he looks towards Emma's room. There are no untoward sounds, other than the News on the TV.

Tip-toeing down the hallway to the reception room, he enters and looks out the front window checking for passing cars or late night joggers. No movement, so he closes the slats on the venetian blinds. Walking over to the desk, he looks down at the computer. The file for Lady is still on display, but it means nothing. Clicking on *'Calendar'*, the previous day's activities appear in rows of fifteen minute intervals. He is surprised at how busy she is. Starting at 7.00am, she checks the animals in the recovery room…… four cats, two dogs and a rooster. In a separate column, against each animal, are her comments.

Skipping over a report on a Red Setter that has an infected paw, he reads more carefully about a Collie dog named Lady. *'Lady, recovering from a shot gun wound. She is alert and calm and no suppuration. Two shot gun pellets removed from the right rear leg @ 23.00. Phoned owner 7.45am. advised discharge @ 16.00'.*

Unfortunately there are no details about the owner, so he scrolls down to 15.30, where he reads, *'Lady, Border Collie, 7yrs, bitch, released to owner. No signs of infection. Betadine prescribed. Bill paid, $150.00.'* There is more about medication and instructions for her care, but again, nothing about the owner.

Seating himself, he contemplates what he has learned. *'The dog is a Border Collie, shot in the hind leg and its name is Lady.'* His eyes stray to the folder on the desk in front of him. Jolting forward and pulling it closer, he opens it and there neatly typed are the words, *'Lady's owner, Tane Lendic, 15 Beach Road, Karekare.'* There is a mobile number and an email address.

Clicking open his cell phone, he copies the details onto his *'Messenger'* screen and sends it, just as Butch's urgent voice explodes in his ear. "Hey Joey, she's on the fuckin move! She's coming down the hallway!"

Jumping out of the chair, he knows he is trapped, so he races around to the front of the counter and crouches down in the corner, close to the wall.

Emma, thinking about Lady's injury, knows the tetanus vaccine will still be active, but she can't remember which antibiotic ointment she prescribed. Now seated at the computer, she is surprised to see the previous day's calendar open. Frowning, she shakes her head and then notices that the folder is not where she left it, something is wrong!

Glancing over the counter towards the front windows she sees that the venetian blinds are closed. She never closes the blinds! There are too many things wrong with the room! Feeling uneasy, her heart starts to beat faster.

Standing, she looks around the room, but sees nothing untoward. Frowning and shaking her head again, she walks to the front window and opens the blind slats with a twist of a nob. Turning, she starts to walk back towards her chair, when out of the corner of her eye, she sees movement. Jerking her head to the left, she sees a man wearing a balaclava staring up at her from the corner of the counter! Jumping with fright, she lets out a shriek that is stifled by a huge hand clamping hard over her mouth. A large muscular arm wraps around her arms, pinning them to her sides and she is lifted, so that she is suspended above the ground.

Thrashing her head backwards and forwards, she tries to dislodge the suffocating hand, but it presses even harder over her mouth, bruising her lips.

A voice snarls close to her ear. "Relax lady, you'll not be hurt. Just close your fuckin' eyes and shut your fuckin' mouth."

This makes Emma even more frantic and she throws herself backwards and forwards trying to break his hold, but he holds her even tighter!

"Stop it bitch! Relax! Don't fuckin' move!. Keep your eyes shut! You've seen nothin'. If anyone asks you, keep your fuckin mouth shut!. Nothin' happened, do you understand?... Nod your head if you understand!"

Emma can hardly move, let alone nod, but she does her best and the voice continues, "Do not call the cops...." He doesn't finish, because the headlights of a vehicle, turning into the driveway, blaze between the blind slats, streaking the room with strips of bright white light.

Butch and Joey can only see the car lights, but Gary, Mike and Tane can see a robbery in progress and Emma being held!

Jumping out of the Wrangler while it is still moving, Gary tries the front door, but it is locked so he smashes it open with two powerful kicks of his cowboy boots. The locks remain fully extended but the catches are now splinters of wood. Rushing into the Reception Room he is closely followed by Mike and they see two men running down the hallway, the front man dragging Emma who is kicking and struggling.

The other man can't get past, so Gary sprints down the hallway and hits him with a bone crunching tackle, just below the ribs, picks him up and then dumps him head first onto the floor. Up ahead, Butch is distracted and releases the pressure on Emma's mouth allowing her to bite down hard on his fingers.

Swearing, he swings her hard against the wall, banging her head and knocking the wind out of her lungs.

Reaching behind, he grabs the handle of his pistol but only manages to pull it out of his track pants before a crowbar hits him on the back of the head and he topples forward and the pistol flips out of his senseless fingers.

Tane, who has come through the back door, kicks the pistol down the hallway towards the bedroom and then lifts Butch's arms off Emma who is pinned to the floor.

Helping her to stand, he holds onto her until she is steady on her feet. Her head and chest ache and her lips are bleeding. Some of the blood is from Butch's hand! Looking up, she sees the concern in Tane's eyes. "Are you Tane, Lady's owner?"

"Yes I am, looks like we came in the nick of time!"

"You sure did, thanks... I think you saved my life."

"No problem!" He frowns, "Maybe you shouldn't stand?"

Looking into the Surgery, he points, "I'll get you a chair."

Shaking her head she pulls away, brushing her surgical gown with her hand as if to wipe away the memory of the assault. "No, I'm all right, just a bump on the head." Carefully she fingers her head, then looks at her hand to see if there is blood, there is no blood.

Next she checks herself for concussion by bringing the tips of her fingers together with hands held horizontal, "See I'm not concussed!" Looking down at the unconscious Butch, she kneels beside him and pulling up his balaclava to expose his neck, feels for a pulse. Looking up, she says, "He's alive! ...You hit him pretty hard!" Standing, she turns and studies Gary, sitting on Joey, "Hi Gary, we meet again!"

He nods. "Hi Emma, do you know these guys?"

"Don't think so, they look like burglars."

Reaching down, he pulls the balaclava off Joey's head who is still trying to breathe. "Recognise him now?"

She shakes her head. "Never seen him before, do you think they are after drugs?"

"I guess, we'll find out soon enough."

"Good thing you guys were bringing Lady back to the Clinic, eh!"

Tane looks toward the shattered front door. "Hell, I've forgotten about Lady!" He turns back to Emma, "You okay to fix her? She's pretty sick, lost a lot of blood."

Emma nods, then points to the doorway beside her. "Bring her into the Surgery."

As Tane hurries out through the front door, Mike, who is standing over Butch, turns toward Emma. "I need to secure these guys, do you have any wide bandages or sticky tape?"

"Will duct tape do?"

"Perfect!"

Passing through the Surgery and into the Recovery Room, she returns with a roll of tape.

Mike wraps it tightly around Butch's ankles. After doing the same to his wrists, he throws the roll to Gary.

Meanwhile, Joey, who at last is able to speak, shakes his head towards Gary. "Hey mate, you don't have to do that, I'm not going to run away."

Gary laughs. "I know you won't, mate! Roll over and put your hands behind your back!"

Joey thinks about escaping, using his judo skills, but reason prevails, *'Why bother, I'll be released soon, anyway.'* Shrugging, he rolls over, placing his hands behind his back.

With wrists taped together he is effortlessly pulled over to the wall and propped up in a sitting position. Joey looks across at Butch, making sure that he is still unconscious, then up at Gary. "I work for the Police."

Gary snorts, "Sure you do, and I work for Mother Teresa!"

"No, really, I do! …Call Superintendent Max Henderson at Police Headquarters… You can use my phone if you like… It's in my pocket! Tell him you are holding Joey Moser… Did you get that? Joey Moser." Turning his head, he looks again at Butch, then back up to Gary, "You don't know who you are dealing with, that's Butch Gueber he's one of the bosses of the Satan's Sons gang. Tell that to Max as well."

Mike walks over and looks down at Butch then back at Joey. "Tell your story to the cops, they'll be here soon." He looks at Emma, "I'll call them, okay?"

"Yes thanks!"

Dialling 111 he bends down to check that Butch is still breathing.

At the Police Communications Centre, Constable Mary Clarke looks at the clock on the wall and is relieved that her ten day shift is going to end in an hour. She is tired but happy, with the thought of four days off.

The 111 call lights up her screen and she positions her mic., noting that the call is coming from a Veterinary Clinic in Waimauku. Clicking an 'answer' button on her screen, a prerecorded message informs the caller that they have reached the emergency section and that they are being recorded.

She clicks a 'go' button. "I'm Constable Mary Clarke of the New Zealand Police, how can I help?"

"Oh hi Mary, I'm Mike Robinson calling from the Waimauku Veterinary Clinic where there has been a break in. We've caught two burglars and have them tied up. They roughed up the Vet. a bit, she's standing beside me." He turns and looks at her, "She seems okay, but I don't know for sure." Next, he turns to look at Joey, propped up against the wall, "One of the burglars told us his name is Joey Moser and that he works for you guys. He says the other is Butch somebody and he's a Satan's Sons gang member. I'm not sure what's going on, but we'd like you to be here as soon as pos. Oh,.. and can you tell the ambulance guys to come, Butch got a whack on the head and is still unconscious."

Mary shakes off fatigue and changes screens checking for available patrol cars. "Mike, I'm dispatching two cars from Kumeu, they should be with you soon."

"Thanks."

"Stay on the line." Scrolling down a list of on-duty patrol cars, she presses a button on her desk, "Cars 57 and 58 please report."

Mike hears the two replies. "Car 57."…. "Car 58."

"Proceed to the Waimauku Vet. Clinic where a break and enter has been reported. Two intruders are being restrained, possibly gang related. More details to follow." As she speaks, she raises her hand and beckons Inspector Ronnie Vaiili who is seated in an office not far from her desk.

When he arrives, the strain of the weekend is evident in his red rimmed eyes. "What's up Mary?"

She holds up a finger, then points to her screen, "Thanks for holding, Michael, can I have your full name, home address and mobile number please?" As he answers, Mary types the details onto her screen and the Inspector reads over her shoulder. When she is finished, she asks Mike to hold again. With phone on mute, she turns to the Inspector, "Two burglars are being restrained by locals at the Waimauku Vet. Clinic, she points to the name 'Joey Moser', then swivels around, looking up at him.

He nods and she turns back to the screen, "Michael, are you the Vet?"

"No, we are here at the Clinic by chance, our dog is injured. When we arrived we saw two men attacking Emma."

"Is Emma the Vet?"

"Yes. Do you want to talk to her?"

"Please, put her on."

"This is Emma Swift."

"Hi Emma, I'm Constable Mary Clarke of the New Zealand Police. Can you give me your full name and date of birth please." Emma gives the information, then adds quickly, as she sees Tane carrying Lady, coming through the front door. "I have to go Mary, I have a sick dog to attend to, I'll hand you back to Michael."

"Sure."

As Emma gives the phone to Michael, Mary adds the Vet's details onto the screen, then asks, "Are you there Michael?"

"Yes."

"Is it just you and the Vet. at the clinic?"

"No, I have two buddies with me, Tane Lendic and Gary Reilly."

Again there is a pause, as she types, then asks. "Does Lendic have an "H" on the end?"

"No, it ends with a 'C'. It's a Dally name." He can hear her tapping away and then stop.

"You said Emma was roughed up a bit, she sounded quite calm."

"She's a gutsy lady. As I said, she appears to be okay, but I saw her being dragged and thrown against a wall. There's blood around her mouth, but she's doctoring our dog right now, amazing!"

As Emma walks alongside Lady, she strokes the dog's head then checks the leg wound.

Lady opens her eyes and whimpers, then looks up at Emma, remembering her smell.

Emma is glad to see the movement and gently strokes her again.

Meanwhile, Mike turns back to the phone and can hear Mary still clicking on her keyboard, writing her report. "Is there anything else Mary?"

"No, that will do for now. Police Officers Mark Richardson and Andrew Mulligan will be with you soon, call back if you need further assistance."

"Okay Mary, thanks." Mike hangs up and nods to Gary, who has been listening while keeping a close watch on the two burglars on the floor.

Now in the Surgery, Emma becomes detached, composed and focused on what she has been trained to do. She asks Tane to place Lady on the operating table with the injured leg facing up.

Lady is too weak to complain, or even move, but lies on her side, panting. Her tongue is hanging out the side of her mouth and her eyes are dull. Emma moves to the sink to prepare herself for surgery. Looking in the mirror, she sees the dried blood around her puffed lips and washes it away. After sanitizing herself and now wearing surgical gloves, she examines Lady's wounds under the glare of the surgery lights. There is extensive damage to the weeping wound with most of her stitches either torn, or completely missing. It is obvious that her first requirement is to seal the wound once again, before administering a blood transfusion.

Injecting an anaesthetic around the wound, she quickly removes the damaged sutures then dexterously re-applies them once again. Covering the stitched area with a large antiseptic pad, she bandages it tightly, then removes Tane's blood splattered belt, placing it in a plastic bag.

Handing it to him, she manages a smile. "Smart move!"

He nods, as she swabs, then disinfects, numerous scratches and teeth punctures on Lady's back and sides. None are serious. Again she looks up at Tane, "The next thing is to determine how much blood she has lost, that is the priority." He doesn't realise, neither does she, that she is quoting, verbatim, her University Lecturer's instructions.

Not knowing why he is being informed, he nods anyway.

Lady's front leg is already shaved, so she swabs and inserts a luer needle, taping it in position. Extracting a vial of blood, she checks the PCV. The count is very low. Bought blood is expensive so she decides to use what she has on hand and that is in the Red Setter in her Recovery Room. Pulling the side rails up to secure Lady, she gestures for Tane to follow.

As they enter the Recovery Room, next to the Surgery, he marvels at her calm authority and can't help being attracted by her obvious inner strength.

A variety of animal noises greet them as they walk around the cages. There are clucks, meows, oinks and polite barks. Emma smiles down at a Red Setter in a large cage. "This is Eric the Red and he is going to give Lady some of his blood, aren't you big boy!" Eric wags his tail, not understanding a word other than 'Eric' and the possibility he might get a reward.

Opening the cage, she clips a short lead to his collar, lifting him down she leads him to an examination table which she pats, "Up!" Obliging, he stretches out, when she says, "Down!"

Rubbing his neck, she rewards him with a small dog biscuit then hands the lead to Tane, "Keep him still while I take some blood." He is uneasy about, 'Take some blood', but is surprised how quickly she inserts a needle into his front leg then fills two large syringes. As she removes the needle he questions. "That seems like an awful lot of blood, doesn't that harm him somehow?"

She shakes her head. "Nah, he's a big healthy dog and can replace blood quickly."

Now holding the lead, she returns him to his cage and rewards him again with a hug and another biscuit.

Back at the Police Coms Centre, Inspector Vaiili, in his office, finishes reading Mary's report and thinks about Joey Moser. He looks at the clock on the wall and sees it is 23.30 then picks up the phone.

Max Henderson shakes off sleep and answers. "Hi Ronnie, more news on the Satan's gang?"

"Yes... umm..... Max, but it's weird. We just had a one, one, one call from a Waimauku Vet Clinic, a break in. Two people are being held, one is Joey Moser the other, believe it or not, is Butch Gueber!"

Max is now wide awake. "Why the hell are those two involved in something like that? That's crazy, that's small time stuff, it doesn't make sense." He pauses for a moment deep in thought, "It's got to do with Lone Kauri Road and Woodhill Forest, maybe even the shooting in Rarotonga. It's bloody confusing, something's going on! Bring them into Central in separate cars, got to keep Joey away from Butch until we can hear his story. Thanks for the call Ronnie, see you soon."

Ronnie sits back in his chair and thinks again about Joey Moser, Butch Gueber, Johnny Ray Schmidt and his Satan's Sons gang. As the head of Gang Control in Auckland, it's his job to know what is going on and at the moment he feels uncomfortable. There have been some strange happenings over the past few days!

Taking a deep breath, he stands, tightens his tie, then swings his jacket over his shoulder and walks into the Operations Room towards Mary. "Tell Mark and Andrew to deliver Joey Moser and Butch Gueber to Auckland Central in separate cars." He sighs, "Do you mind texting Saolo, tell her I'll be home later in the morning."

She nods, knowing her boss has already done nine hours and will probably work many more. "No problem Inspector. Don't leave till I get you a fresh coffee, you'll need it!"

"Thanks Mary." Slumping into a chair, in an empty Call Station, he waits for her to return with his coffee.

Relaxing, he drinks it slowly. When finished, he touches her gently on the shoulder, "You've done a good job tonight, Mary, see you next week." Exhaling loudly, he wipes his hand across his tightly closed eyes before departing.

Emma and Tane are now in the surgery. Emma reaches up and clips the bag of blood onto the IV pole, opens the valve then gives the tube a few 'flicks' with her finger. Crimson blood flows downward to Lady's front leg. Turning towards him, she says. "It will take about twenty minutes." Removing her gloves, she brushes a few strands of loose hair off her face, feeling very tired, "I'll keep her overnight and then tomorrow I'll check the sutures again.... We'd better keep her at least another night after that."

He can see her exhaustion. "You are an amazing lady Emma."

She smiles a wry smile. "Just doing my job."

Reaching down, he gently strokes Lady's head. "You know she is part of me, when she hurts, I hurt, when she is happy, I'm happy!"

She nods, knowing that is why she chose to become a Vet. Turning toward the doorway she points with her head. "We'd better see what's happening out there."

In the hallway, Butch moans and tries to sit up, but Mike pushes him down with his foot, then pulls his half removed balaclava off his head, causing fresh blood to flow from a gash on his head.

Butch looks at his bound feet, then up at Mike. His head is hurting and it is hard to think, but he recognises Mike as one of the men in the pub and more importantly one of the Jeep drivers they chased! *'What the fuck!... It's them again!... It's crazy. Why them? It's not supposed to happen this way.'* He studies Mike, looking for a weakness, searching for a way to get free, *'Shit any other time I could make him disappear with the snap of my fingers..... Fuckin' hell, here I am the most feared fuckin' enforcer in New Zealand and I'm lying here tied up like a fuckin' lamb on a spit!'* He is angry now and shakes his head, which makes it ache even harder. Panting he suppresses his rage as he tries to figure out a way to escape, *'This guy, standing over me, looks fuckin' strong but is probably soft, like all the city guys. They think they're tough, but I know how to make them cry like babies!'*

Changing his thoughts, he speaks to Mike as politely as he can, "Look mate, whoever you are, this is all a big fuckin' mistake, we weren't trying to harm anyone. If you hadn't come bargin' in, we would've been out of here and there would've been no fuckin' trouble." He smiles a conspiratorial smile, "Hey, how about I give you a thousand bucks and we'll call it quits?"

Mike shakes his head.

"How about two thousand?" Butch doesn't miss seeing the contempt in Mike's eyes and his composure snaps,"Listen you little fuck-shit if you don't untie me now I'll hunt you down and kill you very, very fuckin' slowly."

Mike says quietly. "Shut up Butch!"

At the mention of his name, Butch looks startled and then glares at Joey, who quickly looks away.

Senior Sergeant Mark Richardson arrives first at the clinic, then waits until he is joined by Senior Constable Andrew Mulligan. Donning flak jackets, they check their Tasers before entering the building through the shattered front door. They both have body cams., that record, not only vision and sound, but time and date and GPS location. This is a new innovation and it is appreciated by the Police whose investigations were previously hampered by keeping hand written notes. Now unencumbered, they can concentrate on the job at hand.

When they return to their desks, it's a simple matter of connecting the camera to their PC where a voice recognition programme transcribes the audio, prints, then forwards the pictures and sound to their Supervisors.

The immediacy of the report is appreciated by the Senior Staff, also by the front line who find report writing difficult and time consuming.

From her desk at Northern Dispatch, Mary has already sent pictures of Joey and Butch to Mark and Andrew and informed them of what to expect, so they are not surprised when they see two men dressed in black, bound and guarded by two young men.

One of the prisoners is smaller than the other and is propped up against the wall.

Under instruction from Inspector Vaiili, Mary has also told them not to reveal to Butch or Joey that they know they are members of the Satan's Sons gang and that Butch is its Sergeant and enforcer. They are told to take a statement from Butch, but not from Joey as he will be questioned at Central, later.

Mark, first through the doorway, immediately identifies the one called Butch and can see dried blood caked on his head. He looks at Andrew, then points toward Joey.

As he walks past the open door of the surgery he sees a man and a Vet. beside a dog on an operating table. Deciding not to interfere, he approaches Butch noting his size, facial rings, tattoos and black military boots.

Like all Auckland Police, he knows quite a lot about Butch, so he is curious, *'So this is Butch Gueber. Look at him now, tied up and helpless on the floor with his fat white belly pushing out at the top of his track pants, he doesn't look that dangerous!'* Instinctively, Mark touches the handle of his Taser as he reminds himself that Butch is a known killer and one of the Controllers of the P trade.

Police protocol demands that he has to inform Butch that he is being recorded, but he doesn't. "Hi, I'm Senior Sergeant Mark Richardson and I want to check your injuries before you tell me what happened here." Keeping his distance, he assesses Butch's physical condition.

Butch studies Mark in return.

Receiving no reply, Mark asks, "What's your name, are you able to speak?"

Butch grunts. "Talk to my fuckin' Lawyer."

"I can't talk to your Lawyer unless I know your name."

He mulls this over. "Butch Gueber, call Keiran O'Nally QC."

"Thank you Butch." At the mention of a lawyer, he decides to add, "I'm recording this conversation."

Butch laughs. "Fiddly-fuckin'-dee!"

"As I said before, I just want to check your injuries."

"Don't bother."

"Well it's not a matter of *'bother'*, it's a matter of doing my job! The medics will be here soon, they can make a call on your condition. What I can see is that your hands are swollen from being tied with the tape, I'll free them."

Butch holds up his hands towards Mark. "As I said before, call my fucking Lawyer."

Mark calls out to Andrew who has taken Joey and Gary into the reception room. "Andrew, see if you can find some scissors." He looks down at Butch. "I have a Taser and I will use it, do you understand?"

Butch again says nothing but there is hatred in his eyes.

Andrew soon arrives with surgical scissors. "I have removed the tape from the other one and I'll take him to my car."

Mark nods. "Cut the tape on Butch's hands." He is aware that Butch has been darting his eyes around the hallway, looking to escape and is thankful that three fit looking young men are also on hand to help. The tape is cut without incident and Mark forces Butch to roll over onto his stomach and pulls his arms behind his back. With Andrew covering him with his Taser, Mark secures Butch with a plastic restraining tie around his arms. Rolling him over, with difficulty, he pulls him into a sitting position against the wall.

Andrew hands the Taser to Mark, then cuts the tape around Butch's ankles.

Just then two Paramedics arrive and immediately approach the Senior Sergeant.

Megan Farley, attractive and seemingly too young to be a Senior Medic with Saint John, can see the dark patch of congealed blood on Butch's head. She squats down so that her eyes are level with Butch's. "Hi, I'm Senior Paramedic Megan Farley, do you mind giving me your name?"

Butch stares at her, then deliberately shifts his eyes downward to her breasts.

Mark answers for him. "His name is Butch Gueber and he was hit on the head with a crow bar!" He points toward a crowbar lying on the floor by the wall.

Megan turns her head to look, then back up at Mark, raising her eyebrows. "A crowbar?"

Mark nods. "He was unconscious for about fifteen minutes."

Frowning, she turns back to Butch. "Butch, I want to check if you're concussed, then check your blood pressure and also have a look at your wound, is that okay?"

This time he nods without comment, with his eyes still fixed on her breasts.

Megan is handed a small torch by her partner, Ross, and shines it into each of Butch's eyes, noting that the pupils dilate, "Well you're not concussed, which is a surprise."

Handing the torch back to Ross, he gives her a stethoscope and a blood pressure bladder. Wrapping the bladder around Butch's large tattooed arm, she pumps it, then slowly releases the pressure, "One hundred and eighty over ninety, not surprising!"

Ross taps the information into his iPhone.

She listens to Butch's heart through the stethoscope, using her watch to count the beats for 30 seconds, "Eighty per minute."

Again Ross records the details.

Pulling on surgical gloves, she takes wet antiseptic swabs from a bag and parting his hair, cleans around the deep gash on top of his head.

Butch winches, but is closed lipped, making no sound.

The cleaning has caused the wound to bleed again, so she presses a large dressing against the wound winding a bandage under his chin and over his head a few times securing it with a clip. The large dressing, strapped by the bandage, looks like a bonnet, but nobody is smiling. Depositing her gloves and bloody swabs in a rubbish bag held by Ross, she straightens and then turns to the Senior Sergeant. "Butch is not concussed, his blood pressure is high, but he will need stitches in his head and I recommend that we take him to Henderson Emergency."

Mark knows that Inspector Vailli has asked for Joey and Butch to be taken to Police Central. "Would it be okay if the wound is treated by a Doctor at the city cells?"

Remembering Butch's profile on her MDT screen in the ambulance, she studies the gang man at her feet. "Okay I'll give you a medical release form."

Mark nods his thanks as Megan completes the paper work and Butch is lifted then pushed towards the police cars.

Mike and Gary, released from guard duty, hurry into the surgery and are relieved to see that Lady is alert and sitting up on the operating table.

Welcoming them with a faint "woof", she flicks the tip of her tail backwards and forwards.

The transfusion finished, Emma has removed the luer and the catheter and they move out of the way as she pushes the I.V. stand to the corner of the room. Megan enters the surgery and walks towards Emma.

The two women appraise each other, instinctively knowing that they are of kindred spirits.

Megan sees a young, beautiful Vet, who is courageously doctoring under extreme conditions.

Emma sees an equally young and attractive medic, whose eyes radiate calm intelligence and humour and wonders about the horrors she must see every day. Their smiles speak of unexpected professional friendship.

Megan holds out her hand, which Emma shakes. "You must be Emma Swift. Our Coms sent me a report about what has happened here, seems like you've had a pretty rough time of it?"

"I've had better days!"

Releasing hands, the conversation turns official. "I'm Megan Farley, Senior Paramedic. I believe you were injured, do you mind if I have a quick examination?"

Emma looks over at the operating table and knows that the love and attention Lady is receiving is more healing than anything she can administer, so she turns back to Megan. "Thanks Megan but I feel okay, very tired, but okay."

"Coms say you were physically assaulted, so I have to prepare a report. It won't take long. I'll check the usual, you know, signs of shock, blood pressure, contusions, bruising, disorientation, but you probably know more about that than me." She continues with a laugh, "You know, you're the first Vet. I've had to treat, fancy that!"

Emma smiles, then sighs, as fatigue sets in. "Okay, come to my office."

As they leave the room, they are stopped by the Sergeant. "Are you Emma Swift, the Vet?"

Emma nods.

"I believe you were hurt?" Before Emma can reply, he turns to Megan, "How is she?"

"She can probably do a self-assessment better than I can, but I'm checking her anyway." She points into the Surgery, "Go and have a chat with the boys, we'll be back soon."

Earlier in the evening, Johnny Schmidt's mobile phone, sitting on his desk, barked its bulldog bark, telling him that a new text message had arrived. It was what he had been waiting for, but he was snoring in a drug and alcohol induced sleep. The barking did not belong in the warmth and comfort of his utopia.

Now, hours later, his mouth is open and his head is slumped against his shoulder. Saliva dribbles out of the corner of his mouth and his face has an angelic glow. This is not the first time he has slept at his desk. Whenever he becomes anxious he always seeks the solace of P.

Earlier in the evening, while he waited to hear from Joey and Butch, his head had started the same familiar throb, escalating to painful and continuous pounding. Drinking bottle after bottle of beer, with swigs of bourbon, his only relief was urinating in the toilet, that's when he filled his syringe and at last escaped into the comfort and warmth of his fantasy world.

Now underneath a dangling arm and a pointing finger is a long thin rubber tourniquet on top of an empty syringe.

It will not be for another twelve hours, when the drug wears off, that he will stumble into his bedroom and fall onto his bed.

His sleep will not be curative, but fitful, and agitated and his mobile phone with Joey's message will remain unanswered on his office desk.

CHAPTER 19

Police Headquaters – The Karekare Falls

At the turn of the century, it was expected that a police officer's ranking matched the opulence of his or her office. The higher the ranking, the higher up the building and the size of the room. Times have changed and all spending is now under scrutiny. That is why Superintendent Max Henderson's office is modest. The only luxuries are a stocked bar, hidden behind cupboard doors, and on the floor, red, deep pile carpet. It could have been royal blue or green, but it amused him to select the colour of his political leaning. Not that politics is ever mentioned, but they all know that the Minister of Justice changes with the change of Government and that many directives are politically motivated.

It's the second time that Joey has sat at Max's conference table, but it is the first that he has met Inspector Ronnie Vaiili, Head of Gang Control. He has phoned him and sent text messages, but now he sees him face to face and senses, just like Max, that he is one smart and powerful man.

Being early morning before sun rise, everyone is tired except Max. His eyes are bright and he radiates energy.

Once everyone is seated, he presses a 'record' button under his desk. Looking directly at Joey he asks. "What's going on Joey?"

Joey had earlier declined whiskey and opted for a cup of coffee knowing that he would have to be on his guard. He noticed that Max and Ronnie had also stayed clear of alcohol and were watching him closely. Feeling uncomfortable, he looks down at his coffee, buying time. He knows that he must come clean and comforts himself that he has twenty thousand dollars in a plastic bag under the spare tyre in the BMW.

He wonders how much they know about his illegal dealings and also how much they know about the gang, so he asks a question. "Are you talking about tonight or the whole picture?"

Max snaps back. "Joey, don't answer me with a question, I always think someone is hiding something when they do that!"

Ronnie sees Joey stiffen and decides to intervene. "Joey, we're all tired, so the sooner we hear your report the better, I'm sure that's what the Superintendent is saying." He nods towards Max. "Yeah sorry Joey, we're all in this together, it's just that we haven't heard from you for a few days and some very strange things have been happening with your gang! I guess you know that Dan Henare was caught with two million dollars and then was shot?"

Joey nods, then relaxes back into his chair, causing his ribs to ache. They notice his discomfort, but say nothing, waiting for him to answer.

Deciding where to begin, he drinks his coffee, then looks up at Max. "Johnny and Butch keep me in the dark about their side of the business, but I'd have to be deaf and dumb not to know about the shooting in Rarotonga. Kylie, Johnny's girl told me it was something to do with him losing the money." He shrugs, "That's all I know, look, I know you want me to find evidence about P, but that's fucking hard! I'm in charge of the legit business and it is as clean as, everything is accounted for. The books balance and the IRD get their money." He shakes his head, "But I'm given hundreds of thousands of dollars to spend, that does not come out of my books!" He shakes his head again, "Whether that's enough evidence, I don't know? That amount of cash must be from drugs. Prostitution being legal, passes through me, that's not where it comes from."

Max looks at him for a moment, then scrolls through his files until 'Waimauku Vetinary Clinic - Break and Enter', appears. He has read the reports and watched the videos supplied by his Sergeants, but nothing makes sense. Refreshing his memory, he skims through the reports again until he comes to the information from Saint John about Lone Kauri Road, and then at Woodhill Forest.

Joey tries to stifle a yawn, which annoys Max, "Look, I know you are tired and I won't keep you any longer than I have to, but I need more information. What do you know about the incidents at Lone Kauri Road and Woodhill Forest? The Saint John report says two deaths and ten injured, some of them serious, what the hell is that all about?" He glares at Joey and shakes his head, "What the fuck were you and Butch Gueber doing at the Waimauku Vets?... For Christ's sake give me some answers." Red faced, he turns back to his computer.

Joey looks from Ronnie and then back to Max. "Do you want to know about the Vet thing?"

Max glares at Joey. "Of course I do, and what happened at the Parakai Pub?"

Joey shrugs. "Believe me sir, I don't know anything about the deaths and injuries, I was at the pub and saw Johnny being cleaned up at pool by a pretty American girl. I knew there was going to be trouble, so I left. It wasn't until yesterday that I heard that there had been major fuckin' trouble. Johnny and Butch talked about finding the girl and the two Jeeps. Butch said he was sure a dog in one of the jeeps was shot and the same dog, with a patch on its leg, was seen by one of his gang the following day. There is only one Vet in the area so Johnny figured the dog must have been taken there. He asked me to break into the Clinic last night with Butch keeping watch, I was supposed to find the address of the owner." Joey shrugs, "As you know we got caught… That's all I know."

Max shakes his head. "You must know more than that…What about Dan Henare? Tell me about the two million dollars."

Joey looks directly into Max's angry eyes. "You're right, there has been some crazy shit happening over the past few days." Picking his words carefully, he tells them about the pool game and the resulting chase and the deaths and injuries and how Johnny was then forced to restructure his gang, he tells them that he has been secretly recording the discussions between Johnny and Butch and that it will be useful evidence. That information is a surprise and Joey can feel their concentrated stares, so he adds more, "Johnny keeps a record of everything in a small black book in his pocket, that would be the most damning evidence of all, if I could get hold of it." He nods his head. "Yeah that book would sink Johnny."

Joey leans back in his chair and looks from Max to Ronnie, "So that's it, not much else I can tell you."

Max nods and smiles for the first time. "What about the break-in at the Vets?"

Joey is feeling very tired and struggles to keep his eyes open, but he does his best to tell them as much as he can remember about the guys that tied them up. Also about Emma and the injured dog.

Ronnie leans forward and asks quietly, "Did you find the address of the dog's owner?"

"Yeah, his name is Tane Lendic and I sent his details to Johnny in a text message, he shakes his head, "I wish I hadn't, but I wasn't sure what would happen next and I had to cover my arse!"

"It's on your phone?"

Joey nods and pulls the phone from his track pants pocket, selects 'sent messages', and hands the phone to Ronnie, who scribbles Tane's name and address on a small pad and then hands it to Max.

He recognises the Karekare postal address as the same as on the report of Tane's friend, Mike Robinson.

Handing the phone back to Joey, Ronnie turns to Max, "This guy, Tane Lendic is in danger and we'll have to do something about that real smart, it may be too late already?"

Max looks at his watch noting that it is now 4am, then looks up at Joey. "What time was the message sent?"

"Ten thirty."

Max shakes his head. "No, there's no urgency yet!... Johnny will be waiting for you to return before he does anything. We have

taken Butch's phone and I have made sure that he can't contact anyone.

Surprised, Ronnie raises his eyebrows at Max, then looks at Joey, as Max continues,

"Joey, you'll need to get that recorder and a copy of that black book, so you'll have to go back, we haven't got enough to prosecute… Well, let's say we haven't got enough hard evidence that Johnny and his gang are manufacturing and selling P. I want to clean out the gang and put them away for a long time. Max stares intently at Joey, but is actually deep in thought, planning his next moves, "If Butch is convicted of aggravated robbery, that will lock him up for five years. Good behaviour will have him out in three." He shakes his head, "We have to have him convicted with Johnny for the manufacture and supply of methamphetamine, heroin and cannabinoids, we don't want him or Johnny, locked up on lesser charges!"

He turns to Ronnie, "Lessen the charge on Joey and Butch to unlawful entry, I'll put that in writing if you want."

The Inspector shakes his head. "You don't have to do that boss!… and I mean boss! Max makes me uncomfortable."

Max shrugs. "Whatever, it's not a biggy. So I'll lessen the charge and this conversation never happened."

He turns to Joey, "Okay Joey?"

He nods. "Sure, this conversation never happened, you have my word!"

"Actually, it will be your head! You and Butch will only have an unlawful entry charge against your names. If I don't charge you and Butch, then that mealy mouthed Keiran O'Nally will wonder why. Once this is over, I will have the charges dropped."

He looks across at Ronnie, "What have I missed?"

Ronnie thinks for a moment. "Only the Ambus report, but no one will dig that deep."

Max nods, then looks at Joey. "Joey I'm going to put you in the same cell as Butch while waiting for the bail. That should make him less suspicious, but for God's sake be careful, watch what you say."

Joey nods, not liking the thought of being locked up with Butch. He was hoping that his assignment may have been over, but he understands that Max still needs him inside the gang. He decides to tell Max about the six properties that he has purchased on behalf of JS Holdings. "I think I can give you six addresses that I'm sure are P labs."

Max immediately gets up and goes over to his desk, opens a drawer and removes a pad handing it to Joey. "Now that is what I want to hear, do you have the addresses with you?"

"Yeah they're on my phone." Using his touch screen, he shows him the addresses, "You can copy them straight to your computer if you like."

Max shakes his head. "Don't know how."

"That's okay, I can send them to you as an email."

This time Max nods. "Send them to me now."

Soon, a tell-tale 'ping' advises it has arrived, and Max prints three copies.

Everyone remains silent, as Max and Ronnie study the addresses.

Deep in thought, Max taps his fingers a few times on the side of his coffee cup and then stops when Joey continues. "Oh, one other thing, yesterday there was a meeting of the Auckland gangs at the Puhoi pub. I made the booking for fourteen and heard enough to guess it was a meeting of the syndicated gang leaders."

Max frowns, thinking about the two million dollars held by the Rarotonga police and wonders if the meeting had something to do with the money. "That is exactly the sort of information we would like to hear about, before it happens, Joey, not a bloody day later!"

"I thought about giving you a call, but wasn't sure if it was important enough."

Max's face turns pink again. "A meeting of the syndicated gangs of Auckland is not important?" His anger makes him throw words like spears, "What's the matter with you, of course it is important!"

Ronnie intercedes again. "Maybe he was waiting to get more information Max?"

Safely behind the lie, Joey nods.

Max sips his coffee as he regains his composure. After a moment, he turns his interrogative eyes back on Joey. "What do you know

about the two million dollars sent to Rarotonga?"

He shakes his head. "Only as I said before, Dan Henare lost it and then was shot, it was a surprise to Johnny, so he didn't order the shooting."

Max nods, pushes back his chair and stands. For the second time he allows himself a smile and he walks toward Joey with his hand extended.

Knowing that the meeting is over, both Joey and Ronnie stand. If Max's eyes were bright before, they are now positively glowing. Shaking Joey's hand, he places the other hand on Joey's shoulder. "I'm sorry that I'm sometimes rough with you Joey, you are doing a great job, but it's not over yet, we haven't wiped out the gang… Don't go soft on me now!" He gives him a final squeeze and then releases his grip.

Joey was thinking of quitting, but in the quiet of the moment, he thinks back to when he accepted the assignment. Then, it was a dangerous business deal, with a great financial outcome, now it is personal. He despises Johnny and Butch as they are a reincarnation of his father and that stirs up painful memories. So part of him is scared, while another part burns, deep inside. Mentally bracing himself, he knows that he has committed himself too far to back out. Remembering the pitiful pleading look in Kylie's eyes, he knows that she is part of the unfinished business. An image of Kylie's sad, beautiful face, flashes before him and he remembers how Johnny had offered her to him, on many occasions. At their first meeting he treated her with respect, not as a sexual object to be used. Some of that was because he desperately needed a friend. Mostly, it was because he could see past what she had become, and sensed that there was a very different Kylie deep inside.

As an outback Aboriginal, Joey walked her walk and understood not being allowed to develop self-belief and confidence. From an early age, people whom Kylie trusted, took advantage of her, sexually and otherwise. She was never loved or had close relationships and now she was an emotional cripple, knowing this, he gently offered his friendship and trust.

Kylie at first was confused and rejected his advances. '*Maybe it's a trick so that he can tell Johnny?*' Withdrawn at their first few contacts, like a frightened doe, she slowly responded, until now she talks to him about the love she has for her two children, Wiremu eight and Caitlin four. As her only real friend in the gang, she tells him how she is planning to start a new life, once she has enough money. He remembers seeing the love and desperation in her eyes when she showed him photos of her children, telling him how they are living with her sister in Ranui, a small town, not far from Henderson Valley. He sensed her anguish that most of the money she sends is not going for their up-keep. He knows that she is oppressed and suffocating but the love for her children and a once a week visit, keeps her going.

Now that Max is showing his softer side, he decides to tell him about his growing relationship with Kylie. Figuring that he is owed a favour, he asks if he can help her somehow?

Max is already aware of the gang's two prostitutes, but until now did not know how he could use them. With this new information he decides to trade the black book for a new start for her and her family.

As plans race through his mind, he is conscious that he cannot directly involve Joey as it is far too dangerous for his cover. He taps him on the shoulder. "Joey, we'll do our best."

Getting up, he goes behind his desk and removes a hotel room key from his drawer and slides it across the desk, "This is for the Regent across the road, go and have a good sleep and a meal, put it on the room tab, then report back to me at ten and bring the key with you, we have an arrangement with the hotel." He holds out his hand, "Do you mind giving me your cell phone please? We already have Butch's. I'll get I.T. to copy your sim card and then remove anything that may be traceable. I'll give it back to you once released, that's when you can call Johnny, okay?"

Joey nods and hands Max his phone.

Max shakes his hand again, "Joey, we've been trying to bust the Satan's Sons gang for four years. I just want you to know that what you are doing is of huge importance to New Zealand, stay safe and good luck."

He turns to Ronnie, "Tomorrow you and I will pay a visit to the Vet, and also to Tane Lendic and his friends, they might be able to direct us to those Canadian girls. One of them sounds like she is a pretty good pool player! Mostly, I want to keep this under wraps, a personal visit may help. I'd hate her story to come back and haunt us via the international press or worse, the internet."

Ronnie nods. Compared to Max's energy, he is beginning to feel very weary.

Max walks beside Joey as they leave the room, "I'll see you to the front door, in your burglar clothes, you don't look like a policeman!"

Joey smiles and is suddenly aware of his own fatigue, and struggles to walk in a straight line.

Pushing the *'Down'* button at the lifts, Max turns to him again, "One last thing, do you know if Kylie has a regular day that she visits her children?"

Joey is surprised. "Yes, Sundays, why?"

"Not a biggy, it just might be handy to know her movements."

Too soon the clock alarm beeps on Emma's bedside table. Usually she is awake before six-thirty and eager to start her day, but this morning she is lethargic. With eyes closed, she thinks about the horrific events of the night. Touching the sore spot on her head, she is relieved that the bump has diminished. Her mind continues to dwell on the night, remembering Megan Farley's compassion and the unexpected empathy she shared with the handsome Tane. Thoughts of Lady motivate her and she dresses quickly, covering her inner garments with a surgical gown.

Walking down the hallway, she sees the chair jammed against the knob of the smashed front door and reminds herself to send a letter of thanks to Tane, Mike and Gary, and to call her Insurance Company.

As she enters the recovery room, she is pleased to hear Lady's welcoming bark. A quick appraisal confirms that the transfusion has worked. Using her iPad to record progress, she inspects the other animals, then carries Lady to the operating table. Pulling up the restraining rails, she sterilises her hands and arms at the sink, then pulls on surgical gloves. Returning to Lady, she inspects her previous night's work and silently compliments herself on the neat stitching she managed under trying conditions. The wound is already healing, so she replaces the bandages and then carries Lady back to her cage. Just as she is rewarding her with a biscuit and a drink, the phone on the wall rings. The call is from the police, which reminds her, unwillingly, of the terrors of the night.

Twenty kilometres South at the Homestay, the same early morning sun brightens the dining room table where Jean and her three Canadian guests are eating breakfast.

The night before, while helping with the dishes, they told Jean that her big breakfasts were incredibly good, but more than they could eat.

She reluctantly agreed to provide them with a continental breakfast. Not being able to restrain herself, this morning she has cooked a small helping of cheesed silver beet on toast, topped with a poached egg.

The girls look at each other, shrug, then start to eat. They taste the sprinkle of nutmeg on the mustard and cheese sauce; the bright orange runny egg yolks and the astringency of the silver-beet.

Julia finishes first. "That was delicious Jean, thanks, sure beats a continental breakfast, what is the green vegetable? It looks like spinach, but tastes stronger."

"It's called silver-beet, don't you have it in Canada?"

"No, but I'm sure it is very good for you."

"It's full of iron."

Julia laughs. "Now you're doctoring us, Jean!"

One after the other, the empty plates are pushed forward with contented sighs and Jean refills their coffee cups. "So what's on today?"

Robyn answers. "The guys are taking us on a hike to the Karekare falls, they say we can swim in the pool. Is it safe, no crocodiles or snakes?"

Jean laughs, shaking her head. "Heavens no, there are no snakes or crocodiles in New Zealand. I suppose sharks are the deadliest, but there are very few attacks, I guess there are a few nasty insects, but nothing lethal. I've never heard of anyone dying from a spider bite." She smiles at Robyn, then continues, "It's great you are going to the falls, you will be impressed. Very pretty and you can cool off in the pool at the bottom. The Karekare falls are quite famous you know!"

Wendy nods. "Yes we looked them up on Google.... There's quite a few photos. One shows a picnic bench, is that still there?"

Jean nods. "Sure is, would you like me to pack a picnic basket?"

Wendy claps her hands. "I love picnics, it reminds me of home. Thanks Jean!... I'll pay for two bottles of sparkling wine, if that's okay?"

Jean enjoys her spontaneity. "Of course it's okay. I'll pack a chilled white and a rosé."

Standing, she moves around the table collecting the plates.

Wendy tries to help but Jean shakes her head. "Don't do that, you're wasting your holiday.... Go get yourself ready for the hike. Do you have good thick socks?"

They shake their heads,

"No problem, I have enough wooly ones."

Carrying the dishes into the kitchen, she adds, "I'll get you three large beach towels. Go visit the boys and tell them about the picnic basket, I'll prepare enough for you all. Pick it up on your way back." She nods with her head facing the front widows, "The falls are that way, down the road by the car park."

Not long after, the girls in T shirts, shorts and loose fitting socks approach the back door of Tane's cottage. They are surprised that all is quiet and Lady is not there to greet them.

Robyn who is the closest to the door turns to the others. "I wonder where Lady is? Maybe she's down at the beach with the guys?"

Julia and Wendy shrug.

Looking at her watch, Robyn sees that it is nine, then knocks loudly on the door.

Julia and Wendy look through the kitchen window but there is no one inside.

Robyn knocks again, then waits, "They must have gone for a run."

Julia ever pragmatic, shakes her head. "No, they know we are going to the falls, maybe they left a note?"

This time, Julia moves to the door and is about to knock when it is opened by Mike, rubbing his eyes. He smiles a welcome then yawns. Stretching his arms above his head, he vigorously massages his scalp with his fingertips. Yawning again he tries to shake off sleep. "Good morning ladies.... Sorry, but we were up late last night."

Tane, also looking sleepy, emerges through the doorway and stands alongside Mike. He smiles at Julia. "Guess what, we caught two of the Satan's Sons gang last night and handed them over to the police! One of them was at the pool table the other night."

Julia puts her hand to her mouth. "Say what! Was it Johnny the boss?" Tane shakes his head. "Nah, it was one of his leaders, Butch somebody."

Julia frowns. "Damn, I was hoping we had finished with that lot!" She shakes her head, "You know it's strange that there hasn't been any news about that gang, I checked this morning's paper and did a search on my iPad... Nothing!... Don't you think that is strange?... It is as if it didn't happen, but I saw bikes falling on top of other bikes! There had to be injuries, even deaths! It's really strange."

Tane nods. "Yeah it's too quiet, even a bit spooky."

There is silence for a moment, until Robyn remembers Lady. "Where's Lady?".

"She's back at the Vets, something attacked her last night and tore her injured leg open again. Might have been an opossum or a feral cat? We found her bleeding on the track and took her back to Emma at Waimauku.... But wait, there's more, when we arrived Emma was being attacked by two of the same gang members, that were at the Parakai pub. Gary grabbed one of them and I clobbered the other with a crowbar!"

The girls stare at Tane wide-eyed.

Mike, knowing there is going to be a lot of questions, changes the subject by pointing at Gary's cottage. "Do you mind waking up Gary?"

Robyn is quick to agree. "Don't mind if I do, come on let's go, we can hear the rest when we get back."

This time Wendy leads the way, then remembers the picnic basket and nearly causes a collision when she stops abruptly.

Turning, she calls out. "Are we still going to the falls?"

Mike looks at Tane who nods, so he answers. "Why not, the exercise and the cold water will wake us up." He looks at Robyn, "I know Gary will be a starter!"

Wendy laughs and then adds. "Jean said to tell you that she is packing a picnic basket for us all!"

Tane shouts back. "Just love Jean's picnic baskets!"

Robyn shouts in return. "We're treating you to some bubbly!"

Mike mumbles. "I'll bring a few tinnies!"

Julia, walking behind Wendy, is not at all excited about the picnic. She is beginning to wonder, not only about her own safety, but the safety of all of them, in this remote wild bushland. Maybe it is time to put the guys and the gangs behind them and to move on?

Later that morning, after picking up their picnic basket, socks and towels, the group quicken their steps as they hear the roar of the falls out-of-sight behind a screen of dense bush.

The men deliberately lag behind allowing the girls the first sight.

Rounding a bend, the narrow track suddenly widens to reveal a large canopied glade and the sun, directly overhead, highlights the falls and its jade lake below.

The falling water, smashing on rocks, looks like a sixty metre bridal veil. The clear water plunges downward, then fans out, turning white, before curling over three rocky outcrops and disappearing into the mist above the dark waters of the lake.

As it is a working day, the glade is not blemished by the loud excited chatter of locals and tourists. The idyllic vista stops the ladies and they silently absorb the moment, storing the view to memory. They each have the same thought.

Opening their back packs, they search for their cameras. This is as close to a Garden of Eden as they could ever imagine.

Mike places an arm around Wendy's waist, interrupting her photo snapping. She cuddles against him. "This is heavenly, do you think the water is too cold for a swim?"

"I've brought my togs.... I'll let you know in a minute." He releases her and walks quickly towards a sprawling trunk of a puriri tree, at the rear of the glade.

Gary moves behind Robyn, wrapping his arms around her and rocking her gently from side to side.

She frees his arms and turns to face him, reaching up and placing her arms around his neck. "Gary this place is going to be special to me!" Turning again, she pulls his arms around her, so that her fragrant hair is close to his nose and they begin to rock again.

Julia, crouching to get a better shot of the falls is unaware that Tane is standing close behind. When she stands, she backs into him and he hugs her close from behind. Frowning, she turns and removes his arms. "Tane I want to take more photos." With a puzzled look, he watches her move along the track towards the falling water. Without looking back, she stops every so often to snap another picture.

Mike comes out from behind the puriri tree dressed in skimpy togs with a towel wrapped around his shoulders. He drops his backpack on a large wooden picnic bench that offers an unobstructed view of the lake and the plunging water.

Robyn and Wendy remove their bikinis and towels from their backpacks and head off into the bush, in the opposite direction to the puriri tree. By the time they emerge, the men are splashing around in the chilly water, pretending that it's warm!

Dropping their towels onto a large warm rock beside the pool, the ladies cautiously wade into the dark waters of the lake. Complaining, they make it up to their knees before they decide to turn and go back.

Anticipating this, Mike and Gary grab hold of their arms and pull them under the water.

Apart from the initial ear splitting shrieks, it works, for their bodies soon adjust to the cold and they join in the fun of splashing their new found boyfriends.

Tane, left on his own, swims across the lake to Julia, who is now lying on her back on a grassy mound, pointing her camera upwards at the white, cascading water.

Climbing onto a large smooth rock close to the falls, Tane is sprayed by the falling water, glistening his brown muscular body. She stops clicking, wipes her lens for the umpteenth time and rolls over on the wet grass to look at him.

His faultless body is bathed by the overhead sun and she wonders about her decision to end the relationship. Shaking her head, she reminds herself about the real dangers of staying. *Oh what a handsome man and what a setting'*. Pointing the camera at him sitting on the rock with his arms locked around his knees, she clicks, adjusts the lens, then clicks again.

He stands and waves. "Come on in Julia, it is really refreshing!"

She decides to tell a lie. "Ummm... I can't.... You know...., woman thing!"

"Ohhh, sorry for asking, see you back at the picnic table." He turns and dives into the water. With powerful strokes and leg kicks, he is soon out in the middle of the lake.

Julia watches his broad back and athleticism and reminds herself again, *'You've made up your mind girl, now stick to it!'*

The group exit the water together and stand around the large rock, drying themselves, enjoying the warmth of the sun.

Julia arrives soon after and dries her hair, as the girls change into tramping clothes. Moving to the picnic bench, they discover that there is just enough room for them all to sit at the table.

Julia lifts the lid on the wicker picnic basket and unstraps six plastic plates, hands them around and then opens the first plastic container. Inside are six slices of cold bacon and egg pie. The girls have never seen pie like this before. The cold wedges, surrounded by flaky pastry, contain chunks of pink bacon, yellow and white egg, a layer of thinly sliced potato and onion, and a sprinkle of green peas throughout. Even though there is no ketchup, the wedges are quickly consumed. Needing a drink, Julia finds plastic wine glasses tucked in a sleeve and hands a chilled bottle of pink bubbly for Tane to open.

Handing it back, he reaches under the seat and unzips a small chilly bin containing cans of cold Lager beer.

It's Wendy's turn to see what other surprises are in the basket. This time it is six, thin sandwiches, filled with sliced cucumber, coated in mayonnaise, just what you want on a hot day in the bush!

After eating the sandwiches, Robyn pulls the basket towards her and finds six large squares of sweet, dark Christmas cake, wrapped in foil. The cake and bubbly complement each other, but not the beer. No one is complaining.

The meal over, Tane becomes more and more confused at Julia's continued rejection. Turning to her, he asks quietly. "What's the matter Julia, is something wrong?"

She stands and gestures for him to follow.

He looks at Robyn, then Wendy, who shake their heads shrugging, so he follows her to the large rock by the edge of the lake.

By the time he catches up, she is already seated and pats a place beside her. "Tane, this is very difficult for me to explain, but I'll try.... All of my life I have been forced to respond to my instincts. When I was a child, mum and dad moved me from place to place and quite often I found myself in uncomfortable, even dangerous, situations. I have learned to be aware of those instincts and I trust them implicitly. Those feelings are with me now and I must obey them. I know I caused you and Lady and your friends, problems, but I can't change what happened and now I'm scared!" She reaches over and holds onto his hands, "You are the most wonderful and gifted man I have ever known and I can feel myself falling in love with you! I also know that would be a mistake. The visit of the Police, telling us that they would protect us, did the opposite! It freaked me out! I came to New Zealand for sunshine and to escape the pressures of my job and thanks to you, I've had a really great time.... except for the gang thing of course, which was my fault!"

She pauses and turns towards the falls, listening to the roar of the water, then continues with tears in her eyes, "This is truly a magical place. Thank you for allowing me a brief insight into your life, here at the beach, I will never forget you." She knows she has hurt him, but he refuses to show any emotions.

There is an uncomfortable silence between them, then he coughs to clear his throat, pulls his hands out of hers and turns to watch the falling waters.

After a moment, he looks at her and holds onto both of her hands again. His serious look turns to a smile. "You don't know it, but you have just made it harder for me to let you go.... I love the way you are so forthright, and yes, I believe I am in love with you, but I will respect your decision." He shrugs his shoulders, "What else can I do?"

Squeezing his hands, she feels tears swelling in her eyes again. "I'm so sorry Tane, I never meant for our friendship to go this far, or to hurt you in any way, please forgive me."

He smiles at her again and slowly shakes his head. "Nothing to forgive!"

The silence is less uncomfortable this time, and he releases her hands and stands looking down, "You've still got a couple of weeks of holidays left, what are you going to do?"

"I'd like to see the Bay of Islands and then come back here to say good bye, if that is okay?"

Looking over at the group still seated on the large bench, he turns back to her. "Of course it is, but what about Robyn and Wendy, what's happening there?"

"I haven't talked to them yet, I thought it only right to talk to you first." He nods as she continues, "They may want to stay here, who knows?... If they do, then I'll go to the Bay of Islands on my own, but it would be more fun with my friends!"

Getting up, they walk back towards the picnic bench.

Watching them, the others know that something is wrong. Julia sits by Robyn and Tane sits beside Mike. Robyn, only just finishing her share of the Christmas cake, wipes her hands on a paper serviette and turns to Julia. "Something the matter, or do you want to tell us later?"

"No, now's good.... I've just told Tane that I would like to leave tomorrow to go and see the Bay of Islands... I would like you and Wendy to come with me, but I can understand why you may want to stay here at the beach." She looks at Tane for the first time, "I've already apologised to Tane for wanting to leave and promised that I would return to say goodbye. You can make up your own minds of course, but it would be more fun with you two."

The group are silent for a moment making them all more aware of the roar of the falls and the 'cheep', 'cheep', 'cheep' of the fantails. Wendy suggests a solution. "Maybe the guys could come with us?" As Mike and Gary nod in agreement, Tane looks at them and then speaks on behalf of Julia, hoping that it will make it easier for her. "Julia thinks it is better that she and the girls have a couple of weeks break away from the beach." He gestures towards himself and then at Gary and Mike, "From all of us, that way it will be easier to say goodbye!"

Again there is an awkward silence. Robyn looks at Gary and Wendy and Mike exchange looks.

Julia gets up from the seat and turns to face her two friends. "You don't have to make a decision right now, we could talk about it later, if you like?"

Robyn shakes her head. "No, we decided to come together on this holiday and together we should stay." She turns and strokes Gary's arm, "We definitely will be coming back before we leave. Maybe it will be good for us all to have the break."

Wendy stands and hugs Julia. "I agree with Wendy, the three of us will go to the Bay of Islands, that place sounds fabulous with whales and dolphins and lots of islands to explore."

Julia, relieved, hugs her friends and then turns to the men. "I'm really sorry Mike and Gary for dragging them away, but who knows for the future? You know the old saying, 'absence makes the heart grow fonder!'"

Unknown to the others, Mike has been making special plans for the Saturday before they leave, he decides that this is the right time to see if they would like to take part. Turning to Wendy, he says "Before you return home, there's a fun dance happening on the Saturday night. That will still give you a day to pack. Are you interested in going to a dance?"

Wendy looks at the others who nod. "Shouldn't be a problem, we can sleep on the plane. What sort of dance is it anyway?"

"It's a fancy dress, buccaneers and pirates. There's usually rock'n'roll, jive, line dancing and disco, but it's the location that is different.... The dance is in a cave, not far from here." He points southward, "At Whatipu beach."

Everyone is interested. Wendy says. "A cave dance, how quaint, how different... It must be a big cave!"

"It's huge."

Robyn looks at Gary and nods her head. "Sounds like fun. I'm a starter, great planning Mike!"

"Well it's not my idea, it's a one-off fund raiser for the Huia Settlers Club. We run a small museum... It's not the first time they have had a dance inside the cave, they used to have them way back in the twenties, then again in the sixties, this will be the first one since then." He points, "Whatipu is the next beach down that way. It's a bit of a walk, but it's flat all the way. You follow an old train track that runs along the beach... As you say, it should be fun, something to remember, shall I make a booking?"

The girls look at each other and nod again. After packing up their lunch, and with mixed emotions, they depart the glade.

Later that morning, Johnny Schmidt abruptly awakes from an escalating nightmare. As always, after a needle, his lips are chapped, mouth dry and tongue swollen. The good news is that his headache has gone but his brain feels like cotton wool. Somewhere deep in his subconscious he is warned that he is in danger and that he has to survive. The adrenalin kick gets him moving and he staggers to the toilet where he urinates loudly while supporting himself with one hand on the wall. He doesn't notice that some of the urine splashes on his boots.

Trying to clear his mind he remembers that there is something important that he is supposed to do! Entering the office, he bends and picks up the syringe off the floor and throws it in the bin, the tourniquet, he returns to a drawer under his desk.

On his desk is his cell phone and then he remembers about Butch and Joey, he frowns. *'Strange that Joey has not returned to the office?'* Switching on the surveillance system he does his usual morning check. Butch and Joey are nowhere to be seen and his BMW is not in the garage, *'They should be back by now, their assignment was simple, something must have gone wrong!'*

Like any good leader, Johnny relies on information and will not make decisions until he is fully informed. Neither will he start to worry, not yet, but he is perplexed that they have not been in contact. Frowning, he realises that they may have done exactly that. Cursing his drug addiction for leaving him exposed and vulnerable, he snatches up his cell phone and checks for missed calls. Nothing there, then he checks messaging and it shows *'1 new message'*. He presses 'view', then reads.

Leaning back in his chair, deep in thought, his blood pressure rises, causes his forehead veins to swell and pulse, and his face to turn red. Looking again at the message, he sees it was sent at 10.30pm. Placing his wet boots on the desk, he dials Joey. It rings and rings and then goes to voice mail. When he hears the 'beep' he grunts a message, "Call me!"

Next he selects and dials Butch with the same result. Dangling his arms over the sides of his chair he shuts his eyes and thinks about the girl who humiliated him at pool, then the disastrous chase and his whole body aches for revenge. *'So, Tane Lendic you live at 15 Beach Road Karekare. That's helpful, but where the hell are Joey and Butch?'*

Getting out of his chair, he paces backwards and forwards, then stops, turns toward the hallway and shouts, "Carla, Kylie, get me some coffee…. Now, not in half-a-fuckin hour but now!... Do you hear me bitches?.... Answer me!"

Kylie responds from the kitchen. "Coming up boss."

Johnny stops pacing, returns to his chair and continues to stare, unseeing at his cell phone.

Joey Moser, after a long dream filled sleep and a late breakfast at the hotel, arrives at Max's office and makes the long awaited call to Johnny, who is still at his desk. "Hi Johnny, it's Joey."

"Where the fuck are you?... Where's Butch?... Why haven't you called me sooner?"

Joey looks up at Max and winks. They are recording the call and Ronnie and Max are listening. "This is the first call I have been allowed to make…. Butch and I are at Police Central because the job went bad… We're being held on an unlawful entry charge."

Johnny sits up straight in his chair. "Shit, you screw-up arse-holes!" He taps the phone on the top of his desk and wonders, 'Why the hell are they at Police Central, not Henderson?"

Returning the phone to his ear, he continues "Listen, you fuckwit, don't say anything more, we're probably being recorded!"

Max smiles, as Johnny continues, "Keep your fuckin' mouth shut and I'll have our fuckin' legal eagle bail you out, we'll talk later." He slams the phone back on its holder and then paces the floor shouting, "Fuck!… Fuck!… Fuck!" With the occasional, "Son-of-a-bitch!"

Kylie hears the commotion and comes in to remove the coffee urn. Johnny stops pacing and looks at her dressed in a tight blouse, miniskirt and black boots up to her knees. When she bends with her back facing him, her skirt rides up and he becomes aroused. Sensing his stare, she tries to hasten out of the room with the urn and his coffee mug. She knows, from past experience, that when Johnny is upset, he demands sex and she knows how painful that can be. In her haste, she drops the mug and the hesitation is her undoing.

Johnny beckons with his finger. "Leave the mug, come here!" Reluctantly she walks towards him pleading with her eyes, "Put the coffee maker on the desk."

She does so.

"Take off your blouse and pull up your skirt!"

This time she openly pleads. "Please Johnny, does it have to be now, can't it wait until tonight?… It's so much better in bed. Hey, I'll dress up, anything you want!… How about a school girl?… You like that!"

He stands grabbing the front of her bra in both hands and roughly pulls downwards exposing her large brown breasts and dark brown nipples.

Letting out a loud frightened shriek that annoys Johnny, he slaps her hard on the side of the face with the back of his hand. Her head jolts violently sideways and she starts to faint then he hits her on the other side of her face with an open palm. As she collapses, he stops her fall by grabbing her around the waist. Reaching under her skirt, he pulls down her panties and they drop onto the tops of her boots. "Kick them off Kylie!"

She steps out of them, then tries to reason with him again. "Please Johnny, you hurt me when you're like this, it's much better when you are not so angry. Please stop!" Her pleading arouses him even more.

Grabbing her arms, he spins her around and pushes her face down over the top of the desk with her buttocks facing towards him. Lifting her miniskirt, her bottom mounds are exposed, with a large tuft of black pubic hair hanging down between.

Instead of unzipping his fly, he reaches over and grabs his black baseball bat and reversing it, jams the handle hard up between her legs, again and again.

Kylie screams, first in surprise and then in pain.

CHAPTER 20

Rarotonga – The Rifle and the Banquet

It is late morning in Rarotonga and the police station at Avarua is at its busiest issuing drivers' licenses to the next plane load of tourists. Senior Detective Albert Maana, sitting at his desk receives an email from Inspector Ronnie Vaiili in Auckland. Albert knows Ronnie very well, as they grew up together and he's the younger brother of his boss, Carlos Vaiili, the Commissioner of Police.

The message reads.

'Our Forensic Division has just sent me the following attachment.'

Albert opens the attachment.

'With reference to exhibit 2044, the bullet is 8.5ml. and most likely fired from a sniper's rifle of recent British manufacture. It is showing clear barrel markings consistent with markings fired from an L115A3 sniper rifle, manufactured by Accuracy International. Without a forensic study of the weapon that fired the bullet, this information is guess work. We strongly recommend that we do an on-sight analysis of the weapon, the impact zone and the victim, to determine the firing distance and direction of the missile.'

Forwarding the attachment to Carlos, he also sends it to a shared printer outside the Commissioner's office. Picking up the printout, he taps politely on his boss's open door.

Carlos looks up and gestures him in, then points to a chair. "So we have a possible match with the Chinaman's rifle?"

"Looks like it, it's going to be tricky getting that rifle!"

"Yeah you're right, it's trickier than it seems! A search warrant is easy, but if there's no rifle we'll have to answer some pretty awkward questions from Caucus, Ah Chung has a lot of friends…. I guess you know he's the Honorary Chinese Ambassador?"

Albert nods and Carlos continues, "He's the direct link to Chinese aid…. I don't think Tusi would be amused!" Sitting back in his chair he rests his chin on his clasped hands deep in thought. Swiveling left and right, he suddenly stops, then bangs his open palms down on the desk, "We'll do it another way, pick one of your brightest female officers to masquerade as a Health Official. Get her an outfit and a photo ID, a clip board with letterhead and one of the Health Department cars, that shouldn't be too hard to organise. Who do you have in mind?"

Caught by the sudden request, Albert pauses as he thinks about his new recruits. Saolo George jumps into mind. "Saolo, the youngest of the George family, you know, she starred in all her school plays. I believe she always wanted to be an actress, or at least a movie star."

"Oh yeah she's the pretty one, is she smart enough?"

Albert nods. "Smart as, she came top of her induction class."

"Okay set it up, can it be done tomorrow?"

Albert grimaces. "Ouch, yeah, I guess, all going well!"

The Commissioner nods and as Albert hurries out of the office he adds. "Give my regards to your dad and George Henare."

Albert raises an arm in acknowledgment without stopping.

Inland, at Ah Chung's mansion, Miriama Maana is feeling strangely lethargic. She has felt this way for a few days now. Even though it is mid-morning she is still dressed in her red silk dressing gown. Seated on the edge of her bed, she tries to decide what she will wear for the day and then in the evening.

It is a special occasion. Chan Chemicals is hosting a delegation of Chinese Government officials from the Department of Fisheries and Foreign Affairs, as well as the Prime Minister of Rarotonga and his wife. The Minister of Foreign Affairs and his wife and two other Chinese who are representatives of Chan Chemicals. But that is far from the truth! The gathering is important, not only for Ah's business, but also for his promotion within the company. It is also a chance to have an intimate conversation with two of the most powerful leaders of the Hong Kong Triad organisation.

In the mix is Ah's status as an Honorary Ambassador. That elevated position did not happen by chance, as it opens doors, usually closed to illegal drug dealers! Of no lesser interest than the movement of chemicals and drugs is the chance to discuss financial assistance for the struggling Cook Island Government. Behind the smiles, the handshakes, the food and the drink will be an attempt to trade the Cook Island's Exclusive Economic Zone for grants and interest free loans. But what is two million square kilometres of maritime resource worth? How desperate is the Cook Island Government to sell? How big is China's need?

The phone rings in the office beside Miriama's bedroom interrupting her thoughts. Knowing that Ah has left early to meet his guests at the airport, she walks quickly into the office and picks up the phone. The call is from her cousin who is on duty at the front gate. "Hi Miriama, this is Pita…. Saolo George from the Health Department wants to do a check on our kitchen, is that okay?"

"Sure Pita, send her around to the back door, I guess it will be good to see if Wah Lee is keeping everything clean!" They both laugh. Miriama hangs up then moves back into the bedroom to a clothes closet that fills the length of a wall. Most of the space is for her clothes, but two sliding doors conceal her shoes. Being barefoot as a child, she now has a hobby, almost a passion to own the most elegant and casual designer shoes available.

Sliding open the clothes closet door, she pulls and pushes the hangers one-by-one with their suspended elegant trappings.

Even though it has been five years since she moved in with Ah Chung, she still finds it hard to adjust to her affluence, preferring instead the practical and colourful clothing of her people. Of the fifty sarongs in the cupboard, she chooses her favourite, a happy and elegant combination of pink and orange hibiscus flowers. All the designs are either of sea life or tropical flowers and palms. Today she feels like she should be part of the beauty of the land. Throwing the sarong on the bed, she opens the shoe closet and selects a pair of thongs that are decorated with plastic pink and orange hibiscus flowers attached to the top.

With thoughts of evening attire, she returns to the closet and removes Ah's favourite, a crimson, dragon embossed, high necked silk dress with slits from her ankles up to the middle of her thigh on either side. She knows that the dress accentuates her tall lithe body and her firm uplifted breasts and it also allows her long, elegant legs to be on display. That is why Ah Chung chose her in the first place over hundreds of applicants. He instantly recognised that this olive skinned beauty was a wonderful mix of Polynesian and European bloods.

Removing the dress from its plastic covered hanger, she lays it alongside the sarong on the bed. Already she knows which pair of Jimmy Choo shoes she'll wear, they are red, silk covered stilettos, matching the colour of her dress.

Moving to the shower, she luxuriates in the warm water and the silky feel and smell of the jasmine shower gel. Facing away from the jetting water, she closes her eyes and rubs the gel through her hair, her face, her arms, around and over each breast causing her nipples to swell. Turning, she rinses then opens her eyes and squeezes more gel onto her hands and lathers the triangle of fine black pubic hair between her legs. Directing the jets of water onto the slight mound of her belly, she gently runs her fingers over her stomach and wonders, not for the first time, if she is pregnant.

It is just over a month since her last period, and she reminds herself that she must go and have a test. A warm glow fills her body. How wonderful to have a baby, but she will have to be certain before she tells Ah. Her smile disappears. Ah can be strange and unpredictable at times and she worries how he will react. Turning off the water, she dries herself, puts on her undergarments, then wraps the sarong around her waist and up over her chest, tying it behind her neck.

On the dressing table is Ah's guest list. Picking it up, she reminds herself of the names and numbers and the seating arrangements, *'Thank God for Wah Lee, what a terrific cook!'*

At first she was shocked at the amount of US dollars Ah instructed her to transfer regularly to Wah's bank account at Western Union, but now she understands why. Again she checks that she has done everything for today's events; organising the transport from the airport to the Rarotongan Beach Resort; paying extra for beer and wine and a sea food lunch, a spa, a massage and transport to the house for the important evening banquet. Shaking her head, she remembers Ah's unexpected curt reply when she asked him about two numbers, not names on the guest list. "Friends from Chan Chemicals!"

In the kitchen, Leilani Henare, mopping the floor, is interrupted by a sharp knock on the fly screen at the back door. Moving into the hallway she is surprised to see her friend Saolo George dressed in a Health Department's uniform with a clipboard in her hand. They are of the same age and have known each other for many years.

"Hi Saolo, what a surprise, nice to see you again, what brings you here?"

"Health Department business."

"Really?" She beckons, "Come on in."

Saolo pulls the screen open and enters the hallway while Leilani places her rope mop between two rollers on top of her bucket and withdraws it, squeezing out the water. Placing it on the floor with its handle leaning up against the bench, she turns to hug her friend.

Saolo returns the welcoming smile. "How've you been girl? It's been a while."

"Yeah, too long, good to see you Saolo!" Leilani looks at the badge on the pocket of her blouse and frowns, "Do you work for the Health Department? I thought you joined the police."

Saolo uncomfortable in telling a lie, is under orders not to let Leilani know the truth, for her own safety. "Nah, this is a better job, who would want to work for the police?"

They both laugh, "Hey, the Health Department is doing a check on all premises that serve food to overseas guests. Is it okay if I take a few bacteria swabs? It's to show if there are any dangerous bugs in your kitchen, is that okay with you?"

"Sure!" She frowns, "I hope everything is all right cause I might get into trouble with Wah Lee, I do most of the cleaning."

Saolo places the clipboard and satchel on the bench, then drapes an arm around Leilani's shoulders. "I bet this is the cleanest kitchen on the island, don't you worry girl, this won't take long." Picking up her satchel, she unzips it, removing rubber gloves, some small capped containers and a box of swabs. Pulling on the gloves, she systematically swabs different areas of the kitchen, labeling each container with location and date and trying to make it appear as if she has done it before! Eventually she returns to Leilani, "Do you have a food storage room? That needs to be swabbed as well."

Leilani nods and leads her into the room across the hallway.

Swabbing the handles on the lids of a large bin, Saolo asks if it can be moved so that she can check behind.

Leilani nods and starts pulling on one end. It is heavy, so Saolo gives a hand. When the bin is in the middle of the room, she moves behind and crouches down.

Leilani, knowing that is where the rifle is hiding, peers over the top. The pouch with the rifle is no-longer there!

Saolo straightens and turns to her with a smile, "Well everything is clean down here, no need for more swabs!"

Together, they push the bin back into place and then spin around in fright when a voice barks. "What are you two doing?".

Tattoo Chung's large frame fills the doorway. He looks from one to the other with suspicion.

Leilani timidly introduces her friend. "Oh, hi Tattoo, this is Saolo George from the Health Department doing a check on our kitchen."

As Saolo bows her head, Tattoo looks at the badge on her blouse and the dangling photo I.D. A frown turns his eyes into slits and he turns towards Leilani. "This is not the kitchen!"

Saolo quickly intervenes. "I told Leilani that food storage had to be checked as well."

Losing his frown, he turns to study Saolo again. After a moment he nods, turns and leaves the room then exits through the back door.

Saolo whispers, "Woooh that is one scary person!"

"You're right!"

Saolo removes her gloves. "Look, I'm sure everything will be fine here.... I'll catch you later."

They hug and she walks out the back door to her car.

Driving around to the front gate, she waves at Pita in the guard hut, then turns right and heads down the hill towards Ariki village. Moments later she catches her breath when she realises that if the rifle had been where Leilani said it would be, then both of them would have been caught red handed! Saolo's instincts and her police training tell her that Tattoo Chung is capable of murder!

Two hours later, dressed in her police uniform, she timidly knocks on the Commissioner's door.

Turning away from his computer, he motions her inside, then points to an empty chair beside Albert. She seats herself with head bowed.

Being in the presence of the two most important policemen in Rarotonga she is respectful and shy.

The Commissioner is used to this, and stands extending his hand, which she shakes without looking up. Smiling he soothes her with his rich bass voice that seems to emanate from deep within his huge frame. "Thanks for coming Saolo, I have just finished reading your report, it is very helpful. I know you didn't find the rifle, but that of course is not your fault. What I would like to know is something about your friend Leilani.... I believe you have known each other for many years, is that true?"

She nods, not making eye contact with the Commissioner. Remaining silent, she stares at her clasped hands, resting on her lap.

Losing patience, he continues, "Don't be nervous Saolo, this is not about you and it would help us if you could tell us as much as you know about Leilani.... I mean, is it possible that she could make up a story about the rifle? Is she that sort of person?"

This time, she looks at him directly. "Oh no, she's not like that at all, she would never do that, she's a very honest person Commissioner."

Again he calms her. "Okay, what about Tattoo Chung, what were your impressions of him?"

"I didn't write it in my report, but I believe that Tattoo is a trained military man. I've met a few Chinese soldiers before and he is the same." She shakes her head, "I wouldn't want to cross him."

"So you wouldn't be surprised to know that it was Tattoo Chung that Leilani saw hiding the rifle?"

"No I wouldn't!"

"Well, again, thanks for your excellent report, take the rest of the day off." Standing, to indicate that the meeting is over, it prompts Albert and Saolo to do the same. He congratulates her again with a handshake before she leaves the room.

Carlos is silent for a moment staring at his hands pressed hard against the desk top, then looks up, "You okay for a luncheon meeting today at the Tamarind?"

Albert nods. "Sure, what time?"

"One o'clock. It's to do with the Dan Henare murder and I'd like you with me because I've asked the Minister of Justice, Leo Pasi, his Legal Counsel Ray Gandhi, and the Minister of Foreign Affairs Robert Afaai if they would attend as well.... With Robert there the Prime Minister will be informed but will not be directly involved."

Albert thinks about that for a moment and the Commissioner notices his hesitation, "You think it's too early to talk to Robert Afaai?"

Albert nods, so the Commissioner explains, "In these sort of cases, it's politically expedient to inform all of the parties at the earliest." Sitting back in his chair, he gestures with hands, "Already there are rumors within Parliament and I don't want misinformation leaking to the press. Also, and I suppose this is the big one, it protects me!"

Albert shrugs still not convinced, preferring to find the missing rifle before the politicians become involved. It is understandable, as he thinks, as he should, like a policeman.

The Commissioner is silent for a moment staring at his hands again spread open on the desk in front of him, then looks up, "We need a motive for the shooting. Why would Tattoo Chung want to kill Dan Henare? Better still, why would his boss, Ah Chung want Dan shot, what is the connection?" With his elbows resting on the desk and his hands clasped together in front of his face, he opens and closes them with a silent clapping movement. After a moment he looks at Albert, "Dan is caught with two million New Zealand dollars at the airport, my brother in Auckland tells me he is a member of the Satan's Sons gang who deal mainly in drugs and sex, that sort of money is not paid out in the sex trade, so it must be drugs. Ah Chung must have wanted Dan silenced, meaning he knows something that Ah Chung doesn't want out in the public. That means Ah Chung is involved with the gangs and is involved with drugs, what do you think of that as a supposition?"

As if the effort of staying still in his chair is too restrictive, Albert stands, nodding. "I came to the same conclusion Commissioner. I looked at the facts from every angle and challenged my own assumptions and instincts, but I kept coming back to the same conclusions, I believe you are right!"

With effort the Commissioner levers himself out of his oversized chair and turns to look out of the grey tinted windows down onto the stone courtyard below and then beyond to the busy main street of Avarua. Everywhere there are bikes and scooters and tourists seeking shade under the coconut trees and overhanging verandas. Raising his eyes, he looks out into the bay to the narrow entrance where two dragon boats are racing. Studying a large Chinese merchant boat moored against the wharf, he sees a sling load of pallets being unloaded. Swiveling the back of the chair around until he is facing Albert again, he continues. "You know, you are right, it is too early for our meeting with the Ministers. I'll postpone our luncheon, but I'll still have a chat with Ray Gandhi and see what he thinks of our legal position, in the mean-time talk to some of the workers at the wharf and also at the warehouses of Chan Chemicals and Chung's Coffee Company. Hey, be very careful, send only your most experienced people, keep it low key." He lowers himself into his chair and the leather and the springs complain, "We'll still have that luncheon but after you've found something, okay?"

"Sure boss!" They shake hands across the desk and Albert stands and moves to the door and opens it, pausing to inquire if he wants it left open, the Commissioner nods.

That evening at Ah Chung's house, the Right Honourable Tusi Pisi, Prime Minister of the Cook Islands, is very pleased with himself and a little intoxicated as he pushes away from the edge of the table. At last his midriff is free!

Miriama has taken the women to the lounge, leaving the men to talk and the servants have cleared away the last of the many exotic dishes. The wine steward, pushing a trolley, offers a selection of the world's most expensive liqueurs. Why shouldn't Tusi feel expansive, he has been elegantly wined and dined and has been treated with the utmost respect by the Chinese delegation.

A cigar is offered then lit and the pungent odour drifts up towards the air-conditioner, joining numerous tendrils of cigar and cigarette smoke. How pleasant that he can smoke at the dining table and personally rues that his Parliament has passed anti-smoking laws in restaurants. With eyes closed and head resting on the red silk embroidery of the high backed chair, he revisits the many hints and innuendos that have come his way over the past two hours. He re-evaluates and reflects on his own indirect comments, requiring all of his political guile, intimating that he would welcome an approach by the Chinese Government to share in the Cook's under used maritime resources. This has already been agreed to by his Caucus, who are expecting him to return with some form of monetary offer.

Opening his eyes, he takes another puff on his cigar and then turns his attention to the far end of the table where Ah Chung is engrossed in a conversation with two business partners from Hong Kong. A list of who was attending the meeting was given to him yesterday morning, but he gave it only a cursory glance and then left it on his desk. Tusi incorrectly surmises that they are from the Chan Chemical Company, he would be very concerned if he knew that Shan Chu, the thin elderly man on Ah Chung's right, is known in the Triad world as number 489, or 'Dragon Head' or 'Mountain Master'. Any three of those titles would advise that he was the supreme boss of the nine regions of gangs in Hong Kong and China.

To Ah Chung's left is number 426, 'The Red Pole', the military commander. Little does Tusi know that those two men are the most powerful in the room and that Shan Chu controls a budget a million times larger than that of the Cook Islands.

His deliberations are interrupted by the halting, but precise English of the Chinese Minister of Fisheries sitting opposite. "Excuse me Mister Prime Minister."

Tusi removes his cigar and places it on a cigarette stand beside his chair. "Call me Tusi, please."

"Yes Mister Prime Minister... Tusi please…Thank you. As we have intimated, my Government would like to share in your fisheries and to help it expand. We know that it brings you ten million dollars in exports a year. Having studied your fisheries, we believe you should be processing your catch here, not at Pago Pago. Your fleet is twenty boats in the North and seven here at Aratui."

Tusi nods and the official continues, "With the help of the People of China, we would like to increase that fleet to a hundred and also to provide naval security patrols."

Reaching down beside him he opens a black leather satchel that has been resting conveniently against the leg of his chair. Extracting two stapled documents he places them on the table before handing the top copy to Tusi, "I would like you to look at our plans for a co-operative venture." He taps his copy, "The last page looks at the potential growth of your fisheries, I think you will be surprised at the numbers! Please take these documents back to your Caucus for consideration." Opening the document in front of him, he turns to the last page, "If you turn to the last page, you will see that we are predicting that your revenue will increase, after two years of operation, to eighty million Cook Island dollars, a fourfold increase per year!"

While Tusi turns the pages as indifferently as he can, the Fisheries Minister reaches down and extracts another document from his satchel, "I have taken the liberty of drafting up an agreement between our two countries for the exclusive rights to fish in your territorial waters and for naval protection of those resources."

Flipping through a duplicate copy of the agreement, he waits for Tusi to hand the first document to his Minister of Foreign Affairs, Robert Afaai, seated beside him, before he hands the agreement to the Prime Minister.

Tapping the agreement, he continues, "This is an identical copy to the one you now have in your hands. Please go to the second to last page, that is page six."

The Prime Minister flips through and then creases page six, so that it stays open.

The Minister continues his monologue with perfect grammar, delivered imperfectly, "You will see that we agree that you should continue with all contracts already in place except the agreement for tuna fishing with the United States of America. We want that terminated. Of course we will compensate you for the loss of the one million US dollars paid to you annually." He looks across at the Minister of Foreign Affairs, Robert Afaai, "Our Government would like to become partners so that your under resourced fisheries can expand. The People's Republic of China will grant to the people of the Cook Islands sufficient monies and expertise to build a new factory to process all your catch. Please note that we are gifting you that cost and that we will share the profits equally."

Sitting back in his chair, he knocks the ash off his cigarette and then smiles across at Tusi, "Don't you think that is very generous Mister Prime Minister... Tusi please?"

Because the offer is so sudden and far better than he could have expected, Tusi is stunned into unusual silence.

Robert uses that moment to inform his leader of the international consequences of the signing. Coughing gently into his hand, he gains the attention of the Chinese Minister of Fisheries. "As you no doubt know, Minister, we have constitutional ties with New Zealand which includes the defence of our islands. We also have an active Development Co-operation programme with Australia and New Zealand totaling more than seventeen million dollars. The Royal New Zealand Air Force and The French Maritime Forces fly surveillance missions over our waters, and our patrol boat Te Kukupa is funded by Australia and New Zealand, so with all due respect it may be a generous offer but it is not a simple matter."

He turns towards his Prime Minister, who is frowning and then continues, "I'm afraid both New Zealand and Australia will have to be informed of your offer, if that is okay?"

This time it is the Chinese Minister of Foreign Affairs who speaks for the first time. His tone is authoritative and correctly gives the impression that he is the senior minister. "Yes we know of all of your agreements and as comrade Chow said before, the Chinese Government has no concerns about you continuing with those agreements with the exception of the United States of America, they must be excluded. It will be up to you how you inform Australia and New Zealand and the U.S. of our offer. I'm sure you are aware that the defence agreement between yourselves and New Zealand can only be activated by a direct request from your Government. No request and New Zealand cannot interfere. The aerial surveillance by France is an arrangement between New Zealand and France and has not been officially sanctioned by your Government." He pauses for a moment to allow the words to sink in before continuing, "Not written into the agreement, but subject to your Government's signature, China will fund all future Pan Pacific Games."

Again the two Chinese officials sit back in their chairs and puff contentedly on their cigarettes with unblinking eyes.

While these negotiations have been taking place, at the other end of the table, Ah Chung, speaking in the old Cantonese language, addresses the Triad leader seated to his right. "Honourable Mountain Master, I hope you are enjoying our simple attempts at hospitality?"

Shan Chu turns toward him, causing his long straggly beard to swish across his black silk jacket and his smile displays gold filled teeth.

Ah Chung touches him gently on the sleeve, "Is there anything else I can get you?"

The leader shakes his head. "No Ah Chung I'm very pleased with the meal." He taps his stomach, "Unfortunately I can't eat like a young man anymore!" He studies Ah for a moment, "I have been hearing good reports about your work here in Rarotonga, your father must be very proud."

Ah closes his eyes and bows his head. "Thank you Honourable Mountain Master for your kind words."

The leader dismisses his reply with a wave of his hand. "Straw Sandal tells me that you have something to discuss other than the Chinese Government's offer to the Cook Island Fisheries?"

"Yes Honourable Master, it concerns a gang in New Zealand that needs to be eliminated to ensure a more efficient management of our resources in the South Pacific. This has been requested by a syndicate of Auckland gangs. They have asked for your involvement as they are under close scrutiny by the New Zealand Police."

Shan Chu studies Ah Chung for a moment, amazed at his brashness. He knows that it comes from youthful enthusiasm and from his years in an English University. The decision to eliminate a small gang in New Zealand is not worthy of his attention, it is an insult that usually would be punished. Tempering his anger is the knowledge that Ah Chung may have a future in his Triad movement and he desperately needs new blood. That does not mean he will forget the disrespect. Not allowing his irritation to show, he asks. "Apart from more efficient management, what other benefits would we receive by removing this gang? Convince me why we should get involved!"

Ah Chung noticed the sharp look from the leader and realises that he has been too direct. Gently touching him on the arm he tries to placate him. "Honourable Head of the Dragon, the syndicated Auckland gangs will guarantee that Chan Chemicals will have the exclusive rights for the supply of drugs to all of New Zealand. That will mean a huge increase in profits for Chan Chemicals and of course to you. Also at the completion of the mission, I personally will transfer a million US dollars to your bank account in Hong Kong."

These words cause pain in the elderly man's abdomen. A mere one million dollars does not buy or influence his decisions. To conceal his annoyance he removes his small black rimmed glasses and cleans them with a serviette.

Close associates of Shan Chu dread that simple action because it means that he is deciding their fate.

Ah Chung, in his ignorance is spared that fear.

Decision made, Shan Chu reaches forward and picks up a jade cigarette filter from off a gold ashtray, inserts a thin reefer in one end and then turns his head towards Ah for a light. A flame is offered and he sucks deeply waiting for the smoke to anaesthetise his aching teeth, his abdomen, and his annoyance that this young pup should offer him such a paltry sum!

Ah Chung is now breathing the grassy smoke, so he reaches forward and opens his own silver box embossed with mother-of-pearl and filled with orderly rows of white, twist ended reefers. He extracts one, lights it, and then sits back in his chair to await the powerful man's decision.

489 with his eyes shut, continues to draw deeply on the smouldering marijuana as he thinks about Ah Chung and his own reasons for visiting Rarotonga. The first was to have a holiday in this beautiful island and the second, to study Ah Chung at close quarters. His organisation is aging. White Paper Fan in charge of Administration is showing signs of forgetfulness and uncharacteristic sloppy decision making. Like himself he is getting too old for the job. A frown crosses his brow as he thinks about the ages of all his 483 administrators. The Operations Officer, the Deputy Mountain Master and the Ceremonies Officer. Yes, new blood is required. He didn't know why Ah Chung had asked for his attendance at the meeting and now that he has discovered that it is only a trifling matter, he is disappointed.

As the marijuana dulls the incessant ache in his jaw, he is able to plan more carefully. Yes, maybe his organisation could use the same strategy in Australia and get the same exclusive rights, that would really be a significant increase in the flow of money into his coffers! Let New Zealand be the tester!

By now the reefer is only ash and he opens his eyes and removes the filter from his mouth, tapping it into the ash tray.

Sitting up, he turns to Ah Chung. "Alright, you have my permission to proceed with our help, do not talk to me again about the matter. Motioning with his hand towards Ah Chung's left, he continues, "Talk to Feng Tai-Lung about what you need.... I suppose you have information about the New Zealand gang?"

Ah Chung nods. "Thank you Shan Chu, you honour me with

your decision!" He turns to his left and looks at the Triad enforcer who has been listening. He has known Feng for many years and is aware that he is the son of Lee Tai-Lung a deceased enforcer with a pedigree going back to the earliest days of the fighting Monks. Feng is a big man, short and wide with no neck, causing problems with his black bow tie and white collar. He is not a pretty man, belonging more in the sumo ring than in a fashion parade.

Ah Chung pushes back his chair, stands and walks over to a large black lacquered cabinet that stretches the length of the wall and pulls open a drawer. Extracting a slim leather satchel, he returns to his chair and places it in front of the enforcer. "This has been sent to me by the Pit Bull gang in Auckland, it is a comprehensive dossier on the Satan's Sons. Let me know if you want any further information, I can get that almost instantly."

Feng opens the satchel, exposing a bundle of stapled pages that he flicks through with his fat thumb before clicking the satchel shut and placing it beside his chair. He turns and looks briefly at Ah Chung before lifting his beer mug. All his skills are in martial arts; how to inflict pain, quickly or slowly; how to extract confessions; how to out maneuver an enemy and then to silently kill, but he has never learned the delicate art of cut and thrust of polite conversation.

Usually the early morning roosters would not have woken Robert Afaai, but his sleep, after the banquet, was troubled. Not from the rich food or the alcohol as he was disciplined on both, but owing to the document in a brown leather briefcase by his bed. Made from tanned kangaroo hide, the briefcase is a reminder of his friendship with his ministerial counterpart in Australia.

Sitting up he reaches down and extracts the six page fisheries agreement between China and the Cook Islands. Robert is not your usual politician, as he is deeply religious, being an elder in the big, white, Uniting Church at Titikaveka. He is in Parliament for the right reasons. Not for financial gain or self aggrandisement, but because he wants to help his people. There are a number of reasons why he feels that the pending agreement threatens his islands. He feels uncomfortable about modifying agreements with friends in

New Zealand and Australia and also terminating the agreements with the United States, they have all been powerful allies when his small country has needed them. His main concern is that the short term financial gain offered by the Chinese will probably mean the loss of their Cook Island identity. Preservation instincts warn him that the Cook Islands will be suffocated by the Chinese colossus! He is also aware that the existing international arrangements, while doing little to ease the island's financial difficulties, do allow them total autonomy. He reasons that there is more than just money involved in the signing of the agreement and that it has something to do with the closeness of Pago Pago and Guam, strategic US naval bases in the South Pacific!

Whenever he feels that a decision is greater than his own limited abilities, he does what he always does and that is to close his eyes and pray.

Now in the calmness of his beliefs, he knows exactly what he has to do.

His wife enters the room with a cup of tea and he stops his electric shaver to explain that he has to visit Leo Maana about some urgent Government business.

Although curious, she doesn't ask, but helps him to wrap his best lava lava around his waist; hands him a newly ironed white shirt and kneeling, ties his best leather sandals around his large ankles. She stands and he places his hands on each side of her face and kisses her gently on the lips.

Following him out onto the veranda, she waves as he drives away in their rusting eight seater van.

Three hours later, after a lengthy discussion with the Paramount Chief, it is decided that the details of the agreement should be send to their international partners, prior to its signing.

Both Robert and Leo are aware that this precipitous disclosure will initiate a flood of concerned international communication and they are not wrong. From Roberts office in the Government buildings at Avarua he sends the following e-mail to the Ministers of Foreign Affairs of the United States of America, New Zealand and Australia.

Please be advised that the Government of the Monarchy of the Cook Islands has been approached by The Peoples Republic of China to be partners in an exclusive co-operative venture in fisheries in our economic zone. The agreement has yet to be ratified by Parliament. There are financial implications as well as conditions. Please see the details in the unsigned document attached.

Yours Sincerely.
Rt. Honourable Robert Afaai,
Minister of Foreign Affairs,
Government of the Cook Islands.

Received at 1.00pm Washington DC time, it was referred upwards fifteen minutes later and stamped *'Urgent'*. The Secretary of State asks the question, 'When is the agreement due to be signed?' That question bounces back down the chain and pops up on Robert's computer.

The Minister of Foreign Affairs in Wellington, opens his e-mail three hours later, at 8:00am and the Australian Minister of Foreign Affairs, two hours after that. Both Prime Ministers have been briefed before morning tea. The President of the United States has yet to be informed. Clearly the ramifications of a Chinese resource agreement with the Cook Islands is of general concern, however Robert's reply to the Minister of U.S. Foreign Affairs, negates immediate action.

The Cabinet of the Democratic Party of the Cook Islands has approved in principle the signing of the agreement. However, the first reading of the bill has yet to be scheduled. The required three readings, even if presented under urgency, usually take three months. Please refer all return correspondence through my office.

Rt. Honourable Robert Afaai.
Minister of Foreign Affairs,
Parliament House, P.O. Box 13, Rarotonga, Cook Islands.
rafaai@Parliament.gov.ck

Two days later the New Zealand Embassy in Washington receives a locked State Department bag, hand delivered by an agent. The Ambassador signs the receipt and her signature is verified by a small scanning device. She wonders what would happen if the scanner rejected her signature, aware that the very polite but powerfully built agent is armed.

Relieved when he leaves, she pulls the bag towards her noting the push button lock. The unlocking code changes weekly, so she goes online and activates a website that gives free weekly Sudoku puzzles. The numbers in the first square are the code. She wonders what would happen if she was to make a mistake, would the bag self-destruct? She shakes her head, reminding herself to stop watching spy movies.

The code works and she clicks open the bag. Inside are two envelopes, the largest is addressed to the New Zealand Minister of Foreign Affairs, Wellington and the other to her, stamped, 'For Your Eyes Only!'

This is only the second time that she has received direct correspondence from the Secretary of State, the first being a welcome letter when she was posted to Washington two years previously.

Pulling open a drawer, she removes a greenstone letter opener, gifted to her by her parents. Slitting open the letter, she reads the instructions to forward the other envelope, by Embassy Secure Mail, to her department in Wellington. Attached to her letter is a copy of that document. Being aware of the pending agreement between the Cook Islands and China she is fascinated by the American reply.

There is a suggested counter agreement to be presented to the Cook Islands via the Government of New Zealand. The document reads.

'Please initiate negotiations with the Cook Island's Government for a shared partnership in the development of their economic zone. The partnership will be funded by the United States of America from a dormant ANZUS Treaty fund.

The United States of America will offer expertise to expand the Fisheries of the Cook Islands as well as providing ten new vessels a year over the next five years. It is believed that the fifty additional boats meet the capabilities of the Cook Islands to service and man the fleet. A modern processing plant will be designed and built at a site selected by the Monarchy at nil cost.

New Zealand will be reinstated as an 'Ally' in the ANZUS Treaty, up grading it from its current, 'Friend' status.

The United States of America applauds New Zealand's contribution of four hundred thousand U.S. dollars towards the cost of surveillance of nuclear production in South East Asia. The people of the United States of America stand alongside all New Zealanders at their sad loss of military personnel in the Middle East.'

Kylie's Kids – Crucified

It is mid-morning when Joey Moser, inside an unmarked police car, is dropped off beside his BMW near Emma's clinic. The dark clouds and rain match his mood, as he drives to the gang's headquarters at the end of Henderson Valley Road. Stopping beside the back door, he hurries into the hallway and hears sobbing behind Kylie's and Carla's bedroom door. He was heading for the office, but stops to listen. The sobbing is pitiful. Briefly checking that the office is empty, he returns to the bedroom door. With his hand poised to knock, he leans closer, listening. Convinced it is Kylie, he gently knocks, the sobbing stops. "Kylie is that you? It's Joey, are you alright?" He waits a moment and hears footsteps, then the door is partly opened, restrained by a chain. In the gap he sees a frightened, tear streaked, eye. "Are you alone Joey?"

"Yes, let me in."

The chain is removed and she shuffles over to the bed and lies down facing away from him. There is congealed blood on the sheets.

Gently seating himself behind her, he strokes her shoulder and arm, "You poor thing, what have they done to you Kylie?"

Lifting her head, she half turns, so that she can see him out of the corner of her eye. "Johnny hurt me Joey, with the baseball bat, you know," She points towards her crotch, "Down there."

Moving around the bed, he reaches down and gently strokes her hair until her sobbing stops. Pulling a tissue out of a box beside the bed, he hands it to her and she sits up, blowing her nose. Discarding it, she reaches forward and grabs hold of his hand, looking up with pleading eyes, "I don't know what to do Joey, I have to get out of here, what should I do, I'm scared."

Still holding her hand, he seats himself on the edge of the bed. "I know what to do Kylie, trust me, we'll have you fixed in no time."

She shakes her head. "I can't stay here Joey, I'm too afraid."

"Don't you worry about Johnny. I have plans for that bastard! Can you walk?"

"Yes, but it hurts!"

He studies her for a moment. "We can't call an ambulance so I'll take you to emergency, my car is by the back door."

She nods. "Thanks Joey!"

"Do you have a coat?"

She points towards an old cupboard with a sliding door. The door jams in its track as he tries to open it, so he rocks it backwards and forwards until it is wide enough to look inside. Removing a black leather overcoat with a fur collar, he holds it open towards her.

Grimacing, she stands and he wraps it over her hunched shoulders, tying the belt around her waist. Supporting her, they make it to the back door and down the steps to the car. The rain soaks her hair and coat, as he opens the car door and helps her onto the passenger seat.

Across the compound, inside the barn, with the doors closed, Butch is telling Johnny and a number of the gang's Controllers, about the events at the Vet's clinic and also being locked up at the Police Station. They are too preoccupied to notice Kylie's departure.

The Accident & Emergency Department at the Henderson Hospital is only moderately busy as it is the start of the week, mid-morning, and wet.

In the waiting room are mostly Polynesian and Asian mothers

with bored sniffly children, fidgeting on their seats. Keeping their distance, is a sprinkling of elderly men and women of all races with breathing and limb problems.

It is too early for work injuries, and the road and other drink and drug related problems of the night before have been departmentalised so efficiently that the hurt and pain has been distributed evenly around the wards. Most have been diagnosed then discharged. Fathers, mothers, grandparents and flat mates are asked to be doctors and nurses and aren't sure what they are supposed to do. 'How many pills was that? How often? What were the danger signs?

Joey helps Kylie into a chair and approaches the receptionist a middle aged lady with smiling lips but clinical eyes. "How can we help?"

"My friend Kylie over there." He cocks a thumb over his shoulder, "Has just been raped and needs urgent medical attention."

The receptionist studies Kylie for a moment before deciding it is not life threatening. "Has she been here before?"

"I don't know."

"Do you know her name?"

Yes. "Kylie Temata... T-e-m-a-t-a."

The computer shows that Kylie has been admitted a number of times before. "Does Kylie still live at six hundred and twenty Luanda Drive, Ranui?"

Joey nods, remembering she told him where her children lived.

"You say you are her friend?'

Joey nods again.

"As you are the person admitting her, I need to know your name and phone number,"

Joey thinks about that for a moment but cannot see a problem. "Joseph Moser... M-o-s-e-r"

"Can you be a point of contact?"

"Sure, no problem." He gives her his mobile number.

"I have one final question, is Kylie a resident or a New Zealand citizen?"

Joey's temper flares. "She's a Maori for God's sake, she's more Kiwi than you are!"

The forced smile disappears. "It's policy, I have to ask." Still angry, he cocks his thumb over his shoulder again. "Kylie's in pain, I've already told you that she has been raped! I don't understand you people, she needs help right now not a whole lot of bloody questions!"

The receptionist stiffens. "I'm sorry, but it's my job to ask those questions, anyway all the doctors are busy attending other people at the moment, some of those have critical injuries." She looks over at the distraught Kylie and for the first time allows compassion to intrude, something she has conditioned herself not to allow. If she did, she would not survive her job. "Look, I do understand, there won't be much of a wait, please return to your seat and I'll call for a wheelchair."

Joey nods, returns to Kylie and comforts her by gently holding her hand.

Soon a young Fijian nurse's aide arrives at the front desk pushing a wheel chair and is directed over to Kylie and Joey. With a Bachelor of Medicine from the Fiji School of Medicine, he is quite capable of assisting Kylie into the chair, then out of it and onto a bed in a nearby examination room. As he leaves, he pulls the plastic curtains closed with the usual clatter.

Kylie points to a chair and as she does so pain stabs in her crotch.

Joey hearing her moan, strokes her hair, not knowing what else to do.

For a few minutes he stays close beside her without talking, when suddenly the curtain rattles open again, this time by a young female doctor of Asian descent. She is carrying a clip board in one hand, a pen in the other and a stethoscope draped around her neck. She looks at the information on the board and then up at Joey. "Hi I'm Doctor Emily Chou, are you Joseph?"

"Yeah, that's me." He studies her ID tag and wonders about her name, *'Emily? Why do they do that? Why not Ming, Ling or Fang-Hua?'*

Annoyed at his lack of eye contact, she interrupts his thoughts. "You're a friend of Kylie Temata?" Turning towards Kylie, she looks for confirmation, wondering if he is the rapist. He looks like a gang member.

Kylie opens her eyes and nods, as if she can read her mind. "He's my friend."

Emily turns back to Joey, "Thank you for helping Kylie, do you mind returning to the waiting room while I examine Kylie?"

Joey is relieved. "Sure, give me a call when you're done!"

She stares at him for a moment. "Of course I will!"

In the waiting room he selects an out of date motor magazine and thumbs through the pages. Although his eyes register the pictures of last year's motor cars, his mind is thinking about Kylie and what has happened to her. Eventually he returns the magazine to its rack and walks outside to make a phone call. The rain has stopped so he moves away from a group of hospital workers on a smoke-o break and calls Max. It is answered almost immediately. "Hi Joey, you okay?"

"Sure mister Henderson, I'm at the Henderson Accident and Emergency with Kylie Temata, you know, one of the gang prostitutes I told you about?"

"Yes, you kind of like her don't you?"

"Yes sir."

"What's the matter with Kylie?"

"She's been raped by Johnny, the bastard used the end of a baseball bat! She's bleeding and all that, what a fucking animal!... Jeez I'm ready to deal with that guy! When are you going to do something Max? I mean Mister Henderson."

There is a moments silence as Max carefully prepares his words. "Joey listen to me, no matter how angry you get, or whatever the provocation, please promise me you won't try something on your own. I know you are angry right now, but there is more than just a rape happening here, leave the rough stuff to us. If you don't you will get hurt! We have the resources to deal with the gang, not you!... Do you hear me Joey, don't do anything silly, okay?"

Joey takes a deep breath, letting it out slowly before he replies. "Sure boss, I'll be careful, but what about Kylie? If she stays in a hospital ward she'll need protection, Johnny will come looking for her for sure!"

"Yes I'll do that. Tell Kylie that I'll look after her safety and that means around the clock protection. How's she looking? I mean how soon can I talk to her?"

"Well she can talk, she's not unconscious or anything like that, but I guess you'd better ask the docs."

"Sure, sure, but tell her that I would like to talk to her when she is feeling better, or when the hospital says I can.... is that okay?"

"Sure, but then she will know that I'm working for you, what about that?"

"That's okay, I don't want Kylie to go back to the gang anyway. Tell her that we will move her and her kids to a safe house as soon as she can be released."

"She'll like that... How much should I tell her about my job?"

"How much do you trust her?"

"She won't talk and yes I do trust her."

"Good, tell her only what you need to. Tell her that Johnny will be stopped. Stay with her and I'll meet you at the hospital in an hour."

"Okay Mister Henderson thanks, are you close to grabbing Johnny?"

"Yes! I'll be in touch soon."

Joey pockets his phone and moves back to the waiting room and seats himself as far away as possible from the crying babies and the asthmatic elders with red rimmed, watery eyes.

Having paged through all the car, boat and fishing magazines once again, he is contemplating reading an Australian Woman's Weekly, when Doctor Emily beckons him with her finger. Standing, he follows her back to the examination room.

Kylie has been sedated and is sleeping with a bag of plasma suspended above her head. The doctor closes the curtain. "I suppose you know what happened to Kylie?"

"Yes, how is she?"

"Internally there is tearing and bleeding, that will heal. She has lost quite a lot of blood, but that will be replaced." She points to the bag of plasma, "What I'm mostly concerned about is her mental state. Rape, particularly a brutal rape, causes deep emotional scarring that takes years to heal, if ever! She is traumatised and in shock and I'll place her in Intensive Care for a couple of days."

She turns to look at Kylie, then back to Joey, "The Police are to be notified and that means you will be involved."

Joey nods, wondering if he should tell her that they are already involved, as she continues, "Do you know if Kylie has parents or brothers or sisters in Auckland?"

This time Joey shakes his head, not wishing to tell her about Kylie's sister as it involves the children.

"Too bad, support like that is helpful. Are you willing to be Kylie's support person?"

"Sure, whatever I can do to help her, as she said, I'm her friend."

His sympathy forces a re-evaluation. Smiling at him for the first time she wonders about the nice guy beneath his tough-guy facade, "I'm sorry but it might mean you're going to have to fill in a few forms and all that."

Joey winces but nods.

She turns to look at Kylie, sleeping peacefully on the bed, *'Kylie must have a girlfriend?'* Her thoughts are interrupted by Joey.

"I have to tell you that the police have been informed and that Superintendent Max Henderson will be here shortly. He is going to provide protection for Kylie at the Hospital." He studies her for a moment wondering how she will react to his next words, "This is gang related Doctor Chou and she is in real danger, the person who hurt Kylie will want her out of here."

Emily studies Joey, aware that there is more going on than she wants to know and decides to focus on Kylie's medical condition. That is her expertise, not gang related complications.

Moving to the end of the bed, she unhooks a clip board, removes a pen from her top pocket and starts to write. Without looking up she checks her writing, "The policeman's name is Superintendent Max Henderson?"

"That's right."

The plastic curtain rattles open again and a greying, bespectacled man in a white shirt and tie enters with a file labelled, 'Kylie Temata'.

"Is it okay if I interrupt a moment?"

Emily nods and then turns to Joey. "This is our Administration Officer, Barry Jones."

He shakes hands with Joey. "I've just spoken with Superintendent Max Henderson and he said to come and have a talk with you about Kylie." He looks over at Kylie, "I suppose that is Kylie?"

Joey nods and the Administrator continues, "Do you mind coming with me to my office?... I'll only take a few minutes of your time?" He sees Joey frown so he continues quickly, "All I need is a signed statement about where you found her; at what time, and what she told you about her injuries."

Joey doesn't like the request, but agrees, knowing Max will soon take over the paper work anyway. As they leave the room, he pauses by the curtain and looks down at Kylie with her long black hair framing her face. He marvels at how pretty she looks even though she has experienced such awful humiliating pain. Anger knots his chest, and for the first time since killing his dad, he is determined to hit back at all that is wrong with his world.

At four in the afternoon, an unmarked police car turns off Swanson Road, West Auckland, onto Luanda Drive. Not far away a Telco van has been parked across the road from Kylie's sister's house. Inside the van are two policemen dressed in phone company uniforms. They have the house under surveillance and are recording all phone calls.

A voice on the RT, on the dashboard, breaks the silence. "Surveillance vehicle ten, this is car fifty-four, Constable Rene Ranger. I'm turning off Swanson Road onto Luanda Drive, ETA two minutes, over."

The handset is removed and the answer button pressed. "This is Telco surveillance vehicle ten, car fifty-four. Suspect is still in the house; no suspicious movements; caution, a pit-bull terrier is on the property behind a fence, over."

"Copied Telco ten."

The police car drives past the van and stops outside the house. Constable Ranger and another constable get out from the front seat, and behind them, two female Detectives in civilian clothes.

On the other side of the footpath, behind a high, red stained fence, a pit-bull terrier is rushing backwards and forwards, barking and snarling.

The Detectives are about to call Dog Control when Hailey pokes her head out of the front door and shouts obscenities at the dog.

Instead of obeying her, it becomes even more frenzied, jumping and twisting its body in the air and snapping its teeth. When his master is away, he's the boss, not her!

Hailey rushes down the pathway and whacks him with a lead before clipping it onto his collar and dragging him behind the house.

With the dog secure, Constable Ranger lifts the latch on the gate and they enter the property.

Hailey returns wondering why they have come. *'Maybe a complaint about the dog?'* She puts on her best smile. "Hi yous guys, sorry about that, he's usually not that bad." She looks from one to the other, "I suppose you have come about the bloody dog?" Caroline shakes her head. "Are you Hailey Temata?"

"That's me, who are you?"

"I'm Detective Sergeant Caroline Fatialofa and this is Detective Ngaire Adams, we've come about your sister Kylie. Is it okay if we go inside for a chat?"

"Sure, but I don't know too much about my sister." She frowns, "Is she okay?"

"Well as a matter of fact, she is not, and that is why we have to talk to you."

Hailey beckons with her hand, turns and leads the way, stopping beside the open front door. Turning to face them she points towards the two Constables. "Do those pigs have to come in too? There's only me and the kids inside."

Detective Fatialofa turns and looks at the two Constables and raises her eyes. Turning back to Hailey, she decides to ignore the insult. "I'm sorry Hailey but we are on police business and the Constables must accompany us at all times."

Hailey shrugs then turns and enters the house.

Wiremu and Caitlin, Kylie's two children stick their heads around the edge of the living room door and look wide eyed at the policemen and wonder what they are doing inside their house. They have never seen policemen this close and Wiremu wonders, with the mind of a five year old, *'Why do they call them pigs? They don't look like pigs!'*

Hailey snaps at them. "Get to your bedroom and shut the bloody door!"

They scurry down the hallway stopping to take a last look before giggling and slamming the door behind them.

The Detectives follow Hailey into the living room while a Constable stays at the front door and the other by the bedroom. He pretends not to notice that the kids are trying to involve him in a game of peak-a-boo.

Hailey stops in the middle of the small living room and turns around to face the Detectives, "So what's the matter with Kylie?"

Caroline asks. "Okay if we sit down?"

Hailey motions toward a fraying two seater couch and sits down on an equally grubby single seater beside them.

Caroline opens a folded clip board removing a document from the sleeve and reads it for a moment before writing Hailey's name, address, date and the time. Still holding the pen, she looks across at her. "Just for the record, you are Hailey Temata, sister of Kylie, and you live at six hundred and twenty Luanda Drive, Ranui."

Hailey nods and Caroline continues, "You have been living in a de-facto relationship with Karl Toa for five years?" She nods, "You have no children of your own, but provide food and lodging for Kylie's children, Wiremu and Caitlin."

Annoyed, she sits up straight and glares defiantly at Caroline. "Where did you get that shit, it must have been from Kylie. Why would she tell you all that shit? Anyway, so what, it's not against the law to look after someone's kids."

Caroline holds up her hand and waits for her to stop. She can see and hear that she is becoming agitated. "Kylie has been sexually attacked by one of the Satan's Sons gang, we know that's your partner's gang."

The aggressive look leaves Hailey's face to be replaced by a worried frown. "What's it to do with Karl, is he in trouble?" Her face flushes, "I'll kill the bastard if he's touched her, tell me it wasn't Karl?"

"No, this is not about Karl, it's about Kylie's two children. They are in danger from the gang and maybe even you are in danger!"

Turning, she looks through the doorway into the hallway, "Is that Wiremu and Caitlin in the bedroom?"

Hailey is feeling stressed. "You don't mind if I smoke do you?"

Caroline snaps back. "Yes I do, you can smoke after we leave." The reply is so forceful and unexpected that Hailey immediately stops pulling a cigarette from a box and thinks about what she has just heard. Shaking her head, she removes the cigarette, shutting the box with a snap. With it unlit between her fingers she glares defiantly at Caroline. "This is my house and you can't tell me jack!... If I want to fucking smoke, I will fucking smoke!" Red faced and angry, she jumps out of her chair and points her finger, "Shit on you girl, try and stop me bitch!" She looks at Ngaire, "All of you, try and fucking stop me, this is my fucking house!"

Expecting the outburst, Caroline surprises her by reaching over and tapping her on the leg. Her voice is gentle and sympathetic, "I know this must be tough for you, try to be calm Hailey, getting angry will only add to your troubles," She shakes her head, "We are here to protect you and Kylie's kids. Please sit down and I'll tell you what this is all about." She points to the typed document in the sleeve of the folder, "This is a Court Order that gives the New Zealand Police the right to remove Wiremu and Caitlin from your house and to place them under the protection of Child, Health and Welfare."

Deflated, Hailey sits down, the cigarette forgotten, unlit between her fingers.

Seeing the wild look fade from Hailey's eyes, Caroline continues, "You know Johnny Schmidt, of course?" Hailey nods, "We believe that he will try and use the children to silence Kylie."

The words have their effect and Hailey slumps deeper into her chair, all her anger gone replaced by a haunted scared look, the look of a frightened child.

Caroline reaches over again, this time gently stroking her arm, "If you have any feelings for the children, or your sister, you will not interfere with our duties."

Tears swell in Hailey's eyes. "Okay, do what you have to fuckin do... can I smoke now?"

Caroline doesn't answer, but stands and holds out her hand,

which Hailey limply shakes, still slumped in the chair. Turning, Caroline nods to Ngaire who stands, and together they exit the room. She knows that her next job is to win the trust of the two bewildered children.

At the hospital, Joey, having answered as many of the questions as he can, is relieved when Max knocks on the Administrator's door. Nodding towards Joey, Max enters and shows his I.D. to Barry. "Sorry to interrupt. I'm Superintendent Max Henderson of the New Zealand Police, we spoke earlier."

Barry stands and shakes his hand, then points towards a vacant chair beside Joey. "Take a seat, Joey has been most helpful, how can I help the New Zealand Police?"

"I'd like to talk to Joey in private for a few minutes, out in the hallway is okay."

The Administrator stands. "No, use my office. Give me a call when you're done." He hands Max a card off his desk and Max sits down beside Joey. "How's Kylie?"

"She was asleep when I left. They've drugged her up with pain killers. This is the best place for her… I've agreed to be her support person."

Max taps him on the shoulder. "Good on you, rape is a terrible thing… I just wanted to let you know that we have removed her two kids from her sister's house and right now they are eating ice cream at the Regent Hotel. Before you return to the gang, you can tell her that they are safe."

Joey nods, but doesn't like the thought of confronting Johnny again. Instinct tells him that his protected status at the gang may have changed. Someone must have seen him come and go and Johnny would have viewed the security tapes. He is wary of Johnny, having seen his increased madness and violent outbursts and his most recent crazed attack on Kylie.

Departing the hospital, he drives to the West City Shopping Centre, parks behind the Post Bank and rents a Post Box for a year. Copying the number of the box and its security code onto his iPhone he returns to the car, opens the boot and removes a brown paper bag containing twenty thousand dollars. After depositing it in the box, he locks it then drives out of the car park feeling more secure.

It is late afternoon when he steps his way past the newly formed puddles next to the security gate key pad at gang headquarters and punches in the code. The corrugated iron gate, topped with razor wire, swings open and he drives up the gravel road and wonders if Johnny is watching. As it is still drizzling, he parks as close to the back steps as possible.

Johnny and Butch are watching and are facing the doorway when he enters the room. Sensing Johnny's eyes boring into his back, he removes his raincoat and hangs it on a coat rack then moves towards his desk.

Johnny's harsh voice stops him in mid stride. "Joey, come here!"

Turning slowly, he is not surprised to see a maniacal look on his face and can sense Butch's dark presence on the sofa. Joey has seen that mean look many times before, but this time it is directed at him! It is the look he gets when he is high on P and he knows that is when he is the most dangerous!

Johnny barks a question, "Where did you take Kylie?"

"To the hospital."

"Which hospital?"

"Henderson Emergency."

"Why?"

"She was bleeding.".

"How do you know?".

"I heard her crying in her bedroom and went to check." To break the intensity of Johnny's searching eyes, he looks toward the bedroom and then back again, "There was blood on the sheets and she was in pain.... I did what I had to do."

Johnny stands and moves around his desk until he is inches away from Joey's face, with their eyes locked. "What did she tell you?"

Joey hopes his calm exterior conceals his inner turmoil and he answers as nonchalantly as he can. "Nothing, just that the gang had been rough with her!"

"I don't believe you!"

Joey shrugs without flinching. "Why don't you believe me, that's what she said, 'The gang roughed me up!'"

Johnny turns and walks back to his chair, sits down and picks up the black baseball bat and starts tapping it onto his open palm. After a moment, he stops, but continues to swivel his chair backwards and forwards, still keeping his eyes locked on Joey's like a lion stalking its prey. He knows Joey and Kylie are friends and he is curious about Joey's reaction to his next words. "It was me that rammed this handle up her cunt!" Pointing the handle at Joey, he raises his eyebrows, waiting for Joey's reaction. That will tell him everything!

Pushed to the extreme, Joey's initial fear is now replaced with anger, the same cold, calculated anger that made him kill his father and his hands begin to shake, but he remembers Max's warning!

Both Johnny and Butch see the trembling and mistake it for fear. They snigger at his submissive reply. "Your business boss, nothin' to do with me!"

Johnny relaxes and places the bat down beside his chair then stabs with his finger, as if thrusting a sword. "Now this is what I want you to do, go to the hospital and bring Kylie back here."

Joey shakes his head. "I don't think that is possible boss."

Johnny springs up out of his chair shouting. "Why not Joey? Why the fuck not? Just do what I tell you as quick as you can, you little Aussie fucker!" Red faced, he points towards the door, waiting for him to leave.

"She's under Police protection."

His eyes open wide with surprise and he drops his pointing finger. "She's fucking what?....... How?"

Pacing backwards and forwards with increasing agitation, he stops abruptly when Joey says. "The doctor told me that Kylie had been sexually violated and that the police would be guarding her. They told me to stay away from her, even though I told them I was her friend."

Johnny stares at him, deep in thought, before moving over to the window and seeing, but not heeding, the dusk filled valley below. P has sharpened his brain and he is able to plan without moral discomfort.

After a moment, he swings around to face Joey again. "Go get Karl from the barn, you and him can pick up Kylie's kids from his house, bring them back here, don't come back without them."

"Yes boss." He is happy to leave the room not knowing how long he could have controlled his anger and also thankful that the kids have been taken to a safe place.

It is dark by the time he returns with Karl, parking his car in the barn between Johnny's ute and Butch's Harley. The barn is quiet and only partially lit by a thin strip of light coming from beneath the closed door of the monitoring room. Joey knows that the bright lights and the security camera at the front gates have already revealed to Johnny and Butch that they have returned empty handed! Delaying the unpleasant as long as possible, he shuts his eyes and gathers his energy trying to blot out the violent confrontation between Karl and Hailey when they arrived at his house. The bruise on his forearm throbs, as a reminder of his intervention when Karl tried to hit her for the second time. That was when Joey made his move and it was unexpected, sudden and violent.

Eleven years before, when he first arrived at the boarding school in Queensland and being a small Aboriginal Jew he was picked on, humiliated and sometimes beaten. A caring P.E. teacher took the time to instruct him in Judo. From the very beginning he enjoyed his lessons and became so proficient that it only took a few punishing encounters before the bullying stopped. He progressed so swiftly that the teacher was able to organise a scholarship with a club in Brisbane. Eventually his black belt status guaranteed him a high ranking in the pecking order at the school and he became a minor celebrity within his peer group.

Much later, while in prison, he sharpened his skills, so it was easy for him to parry Karl's punch with his forearm, lock onto his arm, step over it, so that it was twisted and threatening to dislocate.

At that instance of agonising pain, Karl looked up into Joey's cold eyes and knew that he could and would break his arm. Gritting his teeth he wheezed. "Don't do it Joey… Please, you're killing me, don't do it!" To his relief the pressure was released and he slid to the floor holding his injured shoulder.

Looking down, Joey reasoned with him. "Hurting Hailey will not bring the kids back, Karl!"

Submissively he looked up at Hailey and nodded his head.

Joey turned to Hailey, who was looking at him with admiration, "Do you know where the cops have taken the kids?"

She shook her head. "Nah, something about Child Health and Welfare."

Relieved that she did not know, he offered a helping hand to Karl.

Just for a moment, Karl contemplated continuing the fight, but thought better of it, and allowed himself to be pulled to his feet.

Now in the dark of the barn, Karl opens the front passenger door, turning on the interior light, which jolts Joey back to the present. Karl turns to Joey. "We'd better go tell Johnny, he's gonna be pissed!" He shakes his head, "Fuck me, I wish Hailey had kept the kids!"

There is just enough light in the barn, for Johnny and Butch to watch their movements on the monitor in the office, as Joey and Karl walk towards the house.

Johnny reaches across his desk and grabs the neck of a half empty bottle of bourbon. Lifting it, he takes a long swig and then hands it to Butch. Not only are they both high on P they are both very drunk.

Johnny is feeling the pressure and doesn't like it, he knows that too many things have been going wrong and deep down, is aware that he is losing control of his gang. He is also aware that he is becoming more and more dependent on P, but he is not going to stop, not right now when there is new evidence that tells him that Joey is not all that he seems to be. Up to now, he hasn't been able to trip Joey up on anything! Also, there's that thing between him and Kylie, *what's going on there, a fucking prostitute and a fucking Aussie.... I guess that works!'* He smiles, enjoying his own twisted humour, then becomes serious again, *'I wonder what those two are up to?... I've seen them with their heads together, yep, they're up to something!'* Lifting his boots onto the desk, he leans back in his chair with his arms behind his head and closes his eyes.

That is how Joey and Karl find him when they enter the office. They remain awkwardly silent beside his desk, not sure if he knows they are there.

Opening his eyes, he swivels around and then startles them by smiling affably from one to the other. The smile renews their fear.

Karl is the first to break the silence. "Boss......" That is as far as he gets, as Johnny holds up his hand. "I can see that you don't have the fuckin' kids!"

Karl stammers. "Yeah, sorry boss, we went to get them but....."

Again the hand is raised, stopping him in mid-sentence. "Piss off to the barn, I'll call you when I want you." He flicks his fingers towards the door, "Go! Go! Get the fuck out of here!" He backs toward the door then looks down at Butch, his controller, but Butch deliberately looks away. Feeling alone and rejected, he opens then closes the back door and wanders out into the dark of the courtyard.

Johnny, hearing the door close, fixes his eyes on Joey, "What's going on Joey?"

"What do you mean Johnny, nothin's going on. The kids got picked up by the cops, that's all!" He shrugs his shoulders, "Kylie probably asked for them, who knows?"

Johnny swings his legs off the desk and pulls open the top drawer removing a mini disc recorder and holds it out towards him, slowly swinging it from side to side. "I wasn't asking about the kids, I'm asking about this fuckin' recorder. I had a security sweep yesterday and look what was behind that painting!" He points above Butch's head, then studies Joey again, looking for even the faintest glimmer of fear, or surprise, or both, but Joey remains poker faced. Johnny looks at the swinging recorder between his fingers, "The IT man says it is operated by a cell phone with blue tooth connectivity, whatever the fuck that means." He holds out his hand, "Let me see your phone Joey."

As calmly as possible Joey reaches inside his suit jacket and hands him his phone.

Johnny puts down the recorder and swipes the screen turning it on. He faces the phone towards Joey, "This has blue tooth!" He tosses it back to Joey, "Play the recorder Joey!"

"I can't, I don't know how?" He decides to follow up with a half-truth, "That's not my recorder, it must belong to someone else?" He shakes his head, "It's not mine!"

Butch gets off the couch, moves past Joey and picks up the recorder. "Doesn't matter Joey, I can play it from here!" He presses the 'Play' button, and puts the recorder back on Johnny's desk. A loud conversation between Johnny and Butch fills the room. Johnny reaches forward and presses the 'stop' button then looks up at Joey, "You know something, every fucking recording on this machine happened when you were in this fucking room." He smiles up at Joey and then reaches down and lifts up his baseball bat and starts to tap it gently against the palm of his hand. He stops, then smashes the bat down hard on top of his desk in front of Joey.

Butch, standing beside Joey, has been watching him closely and as the bat descends he wraps his massive arms around Joey's body pinning his arms to his sides.

Joey reacts instinctively pushing backwards into Butch which half breaks the hold, then forward, before pushing backwards again and they topple to the floor on their backs.

Johnny is instantly on his feet and races around his desk lifting the bat ready to strike.

Butch, facing upwards, with Joey on top, rolls his huge frame sideways throwing Joey towards Johnny and his swinging bat. As it descends, Joey tries to protect his head with his arm. The bat smashes into his forearm knocking it to one side and it dangles beside him at a crazy angle. He knows that the bone is broken.

Instead of striking him again, Johnny drops the bat, reaches down grabbing him by the lapels of his suit jacket and hauls him to his feet, pulling him close to his face. "You want to know my secrets, Aussie spy? I'll show you my secrets, you fucking little snitch!"

With his arm dangling beside him, he is shoved down the hallway towards Johnny's bedroom.

When they are standing beside his bed, Johnny moves in front of Joey and back hands him hard across the mouth and as he sags, grabs him by the lapels again to stop him falling, "Do you want to see my stash? Do you want to see how rich I am? Hold him Butch!"

With Joey held upright by Butch, Johnny stoops then lifts the overhanging bed covers to reveal two locked drawers under the mattress. Kneeling, he rotates the tumblers on the right hand drawer, then pulls it open. Inside is a large canvas sports bag. Unzipping it, he exposes bundles and bundles of neatly tied red one hundred dollar bills! Removing a bundle he waves it backwards and forwards under Joey's bleeding nose, "Do you know how much this is? …Come on, you're a fucking smart arse money man, have a guess."

Joey looks at the waving notes and then back into Johnny's eyes. His eyes say it all. He has been in the same situation before and he is past being afraid.

Johnny is aware of it. This stops his bullying and he studies Joey for a moment, "So you don't want to play my game, eh? Well I'll give you the answer, it is fifty thousand fucking dollars!" Grabbing hold of Joey's hair, he pushes his head backwards, stepping up close to his face, "There is a jackpot question, how many bundles of fifty thousand dollars are in the fucking bag?"

Joey, unflinching, looks him straight in the eyes again without fear. "I don't care!"

"That is not the right answer Joey!" Releasing the hold on his hair, he backhands him again, hard across the mouth. His rings cut tracks across his cheek and lips.

Joey's head swirls and he feels blood running out of the corners of his mouth, but he straightens and continues to stare directly into Johnny's eyes. Joey has been bullied many times before. By his father, and then in his early school days, he knows how to survive. The most important thing is not to panic and show fear.

Johnny is still close to his face, "Well I care, little shit!... I care about my money and there are forty of these in that bag, that mister accountant, is two million dollars and no little fucker like you is going to take it from me!" His anger makes him slow and he telegraphs the next slap.

Joey ducks and Johnny's hand hits empty space.

Reacting, Butch holds him firmly around his chest so that Johnny's punch into the stomach knocks the wind from his lungs and he gasps for breath.

Butch flings him to the ground and them kicks him hard in the ribs.

Johnny, looks down at Joey's face, contorted with pain, "I have more secrets for you, snitch!"

Butch reaches down and pulls Joey up to a sitting position, "I won't play another game, because you are such a fucking spoil sport, so I'll tell you what's in the other drawer!"

Squatting down beside him, he touches the tumbler locks on the drawer, "If this drawer is opened, he throws his arms up into the air, BOOOM! There's enough explosive in here to start another fuckin' Christchurch earthquake!" His face is red and he is short of breath, making him pause, "Why am I telling you all this? Because when it goes off, you are going to be tucked up in bed sound asleep never to wake up again, bye, bye, black bird!" Stepping up to Joey he kicks him hard in the head, knocking him unconscious.

The sustained aggression, the alcohol and the adrenalin kick of methamphetamine effects the rhythm of Johnny's heart and he starts to pant. Perspiration beads form above his lips and on his brow. Shutting his eyes he leans against the wall until his heart stops pounding. Opening his eyes and still breathing hard he looks down at Joey and then back up to Butch, "We'll have to find out how much he knows and what he is up to. Is he working for himself, the fucking cops, or for fucking Ozzie Clem?" Removing the recorder and Joey's cell phone from his shirt pocket he studies them for a moment before handing them to Butch, "Check them out with the IT man, see if the phone works the recorder. Maybe the little shit didn't plant the bloody machine but my guess is that he did, fucking Aussies!" Again he boots Joey hard in the ribs, but Joey doesn't feel any pain, until much later, "Go get Karl and Hemi and chain this bastard to the back of the barn." As Butch leaves, Johnny returns to his office and reaches for the almost empty bottle of bourbon.

Twenty minutes later, Joey regains consciousness, but not for long. Crucified, each arm is stretched out above his head taking the full weight of his body. His wrists are bound by leather straps connected to chains, anchored to the back wall of the barn. His broken arm is stretched straight and pain seers through his brain. He vomits and the contraction of his cracked ribs sends him, thankfully, back to the sanctuary of oblivion.

Not long after, Hailey is in bed but not asleep, when Karl enters the room and she immediately turns on her side away from him.

He notices her rejection and undresses to his under pants, lifts the covers and slips into bed.

Still with her back to him, she grasps his hand that is sliding towards her breast and pushes it away, pulling the covers high up under her chin.

Karl rolls onto his back and stares up at the ceiling frowning, then he turns his head toward her and mumbles a half apology. "Sorry for hitting you Hailes, I just got mad because Johnny wanted the fuckin kids and I didn't know what to say to him? He told me and Joey not to come back without them! Shit, I didn't know what to do, I was just," He shrugs, "fuckin confused!" He stares at her rigid back waiting for a reply, but she says nothing. Reaching over he touches her gently on the head, "Shit Hailey, I've said I'm sorry!"

With her face turned away there is anger and hurt in her voice. "Don't you ever hit me again Karl else I'm fuckin' out of here!"

He strokes her back.

Again she shows her displeasure by aggressively wriggling her shoulders, so he flops back onto his back and stares up at the ceiling again. Hearing her muffled sobs, he searches in his mind for something that will distract her, then he remembers Joey, "You know that guy, Joey."

Hearing his name she reaches behind her and turns on the light, then sits up cradling her arms around her knees. "Yeah what about him? If it wasn't for him, you would have hurt me more!"

He can see her bruised, tear streaked face and it makes him uncomfortable. Shutting his eyes, he rubs his hands up and down his face, as if that will somehow blot out what he has done.

After a moment he sighs and pushes his fingers through his long straggly hair and she waits until he opens his eyes and looks at her again, "He was a real good guy to stop you Karl, anyway, what about Joey?"

"Johnny thinks he's a snitch working for the other gangs, or the cops. He got beaten up pretty bad by Johnny and Butch before we chained him to the wall at the back of the barn. He's still alive cos I heard him moaning." He shrugs, "I don't know why they think he's a snitch? Shit he was a mess! Johnny beat him with his fuckin' baseball bat!"

Hailey looks at him silently for some time. "Karl you got to get the shit out of there, those two bastards will do you in next!"

He shakes his head. "Nah, I bring them too much money, they won't fuckin' touch me!"

Getting out of bed, she grabs her cigarettes and lighter from off the bedside table and then turns off the light before leaving the room.

The news about Joey has upset her, there was something about him that she liked, not only because he protected her, but she sensed that he was an all-right guy. Thinking about him, she remembers Kylie telling her that he was the only friend she had in the gang. Kylie had never talked about men friends before so she knew he was someone special.

Comforted by her cigarette, the sofa and the dark, she remains curled up in the sitting room until the cigarette begins to burn her fingers. Stubbing it out, she stands and turns on the light before returning to the bedroom where she can hear Karl's loud snores. Quietly she lifts her handbag off the dressing table, closes the door behind her and returns to the sofa. Unzipping a side pocket she removes her phone and dials Kylie. She waits as it rings and rings and is sure Kylie has either turned her phone off, or she is on the phone, when a slightly apprehensive, sleepy voice, answers...... "Hello?"

"Hi Kyles, it's me Hailes, the cops came and took the kids and said that you had been hurt by Johnny, is that right?"

"Yeah that's right sis!... Listen, I have to whisper because I'm in a hospital ward, there's a fuckin' cop sitting out in the hallway protecting me so I'll keep it quiet. Hey, I've got my own private room, fancy that! TV and all."

"You're still in hospital, are you okay? Are you hurting much? The cops said you were sexually assaulted or something like that! What happened sis?"

"Johnny was drunk and on P and he pushed the handle of his baseball bat up my crack... I didn't know what he was doing, because I had my back to him and he was holding me down... I wasn't expecting it and it hurt real bad."

She is silent for a moment, as her mind tries to block the memory, "The Doc. says that there is some damage but that it will get better. So that's good!" She shakes her head, "I'm not going back to the fucking gang Hailey, that's it for me, you should get away too!... Hey, if Karl won't go you should shoot through on your fuckin own!... Listen, things are packing up at the gang, there's rumours on the street that the doggies are going to wipe out Butch and Johnny pretty soon, good fucking riddance I say! Hey, thanks for handing over Caitlin and Wiremu to the cops! I spoke to the kids about an hour ago and they are safe, all they could talk about was having smoothies at McDonalds. They don't know anything about what's happened to me, hell if they did, I might have started blubbering!... Hey, enough about me sis, what's up with you?"

"I'm okay, Karl came with a guy called Joey to pick up the kids, Johnny's orders, but I'd given them to the cops already! I guess that's what you would've wanted me to do?"

"Shit yeah! Johnny would have used the kids to blackmail me. That's why I'm afraid for you Hailes, he'll come after you next!"

"Don't worry about me hon, big sis can look after herself.... Well kind of... That Aussie fella you talked about, Joey, he stopped Karl from hitting me when I told him the kids had gone... He's only a short arse but he nearly broke Karl's arm, shit it was fast! Karl had to beg him to stop! I can see why you like him, something special about Joey!"

"Shit Hailes you don't know the half of it, I think we've got something going there, he's a real honey, we've got plans, I'll tell you soon."

There is a long silence on Kylie's phone and she wonders if they have lost connection, "You still there sis?"

"Yeah. I hate to tell you this Kyles, but Johnny and Butch think Joey's a snitch and have him chained up at the back of the barn." This time Hailey wonders about the disconnect, "You there sis?"

Kylie's stomach is churning and her head feels woozy, she nearly faints, but Hailey's voice penetrates the fog, "You still there Kyles?"

She shakes her head, trying to rid herself of the nausea and the swirling darkness. "Yeah, sorry Hailes... Joey's pretty special to me, that's all, is he all right?.... I mean he's still alive?"

She tries to soften the truth. "Karl said he was still moving after they chained him up, I don't know any more than that.... Look I'll come and visit you tomorrow at the hospital, if that's okay?"

"No, don't do that sis, the gang might follow you! Hell, I really need you right now. I'd love to see you! Hey, I'll be alright, you know us Tematas', we're pretty tough, just look after yourself, I love you heaps!"

"Me too sis, things will work out, say hi to the kids for me and tell them that we'll all be together soon!"

"Thanks Hailes. I'd better get some sleep, kiss! kiss! Love you!"

"Love you too, see you soon, bye."

They both switch off.

Hailey goes back to bed while Kylie turns on her overhead lamp and picks up Max Henderson's card with his cell phone number and starts to dial.

CHAPTER 22

The Raids – Free Joey

At Police Headquarters, it takes only two hours to assemble fifty Armed Offenders Squad members in support of the Special Tactics Group. To gather that many AOS, most have been released from their regular duties and a few from off duty. There is healthy competition within the force to serve with the AOS and even greater, to be a permanent member of the STG. So when the call came from Max, they were quick to respond.

All of them have spent time together training at military camps and have already supported the STG on life threatening call outs. As a combat group they are more than friends they are brothers-and-sisters-in-arms, a bond that makes them unique members of a tightly knit police family.

In a large conference room there is an excited buzz. All the components of a big op are present. Eight canine handlers; two helicopter pilots; eight drivers for the Nissan Patrols and two Senior Paramedics from the Special Emergency Response Teams of Saint John Ambulance. The added presence of two Senior Fire Brigade Officers suggests raids on P labs.

The chatter subsides when the Superintendent and the Inspector enter the room and stand on each side of a screen facing their semi-circle of chairs.

The gathering respects the two Senior Officers for differing reasons. They respect Max's forty years of service and his hard nose, straight talking. Many have felt his bite but no one holds a grudge.

The soft spoken Ronnie Vaiili is known for his calm accurate decision making and an encyclopaedic knowledge of New Zealand gangs.

Max surveys the gathering of eager faces knowing their capabilities and their short comings. They look to him for direction and discipline and he treats them like his surrogate family, something his wife was never able to understand or accept, divorcing him soon after the birth of their daughter. Deeply hurt he never re married.

Picking up a microphone, he blows into it to check if it is working and to get attention. "Thanks everyone for responding so quickly, Ronnie and I would have liked to give you more notice but unexpected events have made that impossible. As you can see, this is going to be big. Tonight we will make a huge dent in the manufacture and distribution of methamphetamine in Auckland and that involves the Satan's Sons Gang."

He takes a drink of water as an appreciative murmur swells around the room. Once the noise subsides he continues, "At O three hundred hours we will attack and destroy six P labs out West, as well as the gang's headquarters at Henderson Valley." Turning to the screen, he clicks a remote and an aerial shot of a house and its surroundings appears. "Starting from the North at Muriwai, this is the first P house we will close." He continues to click, pausing between each photo until all the remaining five P houses and their locations have been shown. The seventh click reveals a wide shot of the gang's headquarters on the side of the Waitakere Ranges. He allows the graphic to stay long enough for them to memorise the various buildings before changing to a close-up of Joey Moser, "Some of you will know this guy, his name is Joey Moser and is on our files as a petty thief and a convicted drug dealer. That however was in the past, Joey is now working for us. He is a dedicated undercover agent planted by me a year ago in the Satan's Sons gang."

Max looks up at the large smiling picture of a young black haired, olive skinned man, "Unfortunately, Joey is not smiling right now, he was severely beaten by the leaders of the gang and then dragged unconscious to the barn." He points with his mic to a large building at the back of the section, "This barn and the other buildings have been under surveillance since this afternoon, that's how we know what is happening. Another source informed me that Joey is chained to the back wall of the barn and is still alive."

Again the group murmur and he waits until there is silence, "The release of Joey is critical, not only will you be saving the life of a fellow policeman, but also saving our main witness. He is the reason why Ronnie and I have decided to clean out the gang tonight!"

Clicking his remote, he points it at a composite picture of two gang members, "On the left is Johnny Schmidt, the leader, on the right, Butch Gueber his Enforcer and Sergeant. Right now they are asleep in the house. Carla their prostitute should also be in the house. Johnny and Butch must have discovered Joey's secret and will want him silenced. His release must be swift and clinical. Those of you assigned to his release will be given photos of Joey and Johnny and Butch to help with identification, please memorise those faces. Intel have told me that there are three un-patched gang members sleeping in the barn, there is also another manning the surveillance cameras in the lean-to beside the barn."

Turning, he points above the screen to a large LED clock, "Please set your watches to this time."

Heads are raised and lowered, as he continues, "The briefings should take about an hour and then a further half hour to collect your kit, protective clothing and armaments from Senior Sergeant Brian Franklin in the Armoury." He points his remote to a tall elderly Sergeant standing to one side of the group.

Brian waves his hand as heads turn towards him, "Brian will also assign transportation. All vehicles will depart the garage at 0 one thirty sharp."

A few questioning hands are raised and he shakes his head, "I suggest you keep your questions for your team briefings." He turns to Ronnie, "Inspector Vaiili will announce the teams and their leaders and also the strategy of the entire operation. At the conclusion of the overview, those selected for the attack on the headquarters will re-assemble in conference room B, I will be in charge of that operation. Ronnie will be looking after the raids on the P labs. Two choppers will be the command centres, one for me and one for Ronnie.

He pauses for a moment and looks around at the attentive men and women, "Neutralise and secure all targets, apprehend all suspects, stay alert and safe, minimise collateral damage and above all, protect each other!"

He turns to his Inspector, "Ronnie it's all yours!" Handing him the mic he leaves the room.

In contrast to Max's rasping, brittle voice, Ronnie's is subdued and almost melodic, but none-the-less effective. "At O three hundred hours we will commence the operation with strikes against the headquarters in Henderson and as you have heard, the most northerly of the P labs at Muriwai." He turns to the screen, clicking his remote and a list of names appear, "This is the team selected for the attack on the gang headquarters. Please stand and reassemble in conference room B."

There is shuffling of chairs and movement as the selected thirty officers leave the room. The remainder, reposition themselves closer to the screen.

Once the hubbub ends, Ronnie clicks the remote again and the screen changes. "Starting with Muriwai, this is a picture of the first lab, its location and the assigned team and its leader."

There is movement again as the group scramble to find pen and paper. The activity is stopped by Ronnie, "No need to write anything down, you will all receive hard copy specific to your team and your assignment at the conclusion of the briefing."

The officers settle back into their chairs, "As Max has already said, I will be leading the attacks on the P labs. So that I can be overhead at each of them, they will occur sequentially from North to South." He turns to the screen and repeatedly clicks and pauses, until all six teams and their targets have been displayed, "As you would expect, all targets are still under surveillance so here are the most recent intel reports, starting at Muriwai."

Clicking through each short report, he pauses long enough to

accommodate the slowest reader, then clicks for the final time, "These are the three staging points and their locations. The first is at Glen Eden, the second at Henderson and the third at Kumeu." He turns and points towards the wall behind the officers, "Hard copy, with your name attached is provided on the table behind you. They are in alphabetical order of surname. After collection, join your Team Leader who will discuss how you are going to execute your mission and then return to me with any questions."

Leaving the screen area, he walks toward a large coffee urn, as chairs are pushed back and officers make their way to the rear table.

As instructed, allowing for coffee and pee breaks, the briefings in the conference rooms conclude at O one hundred hours. Thirty minutes later, the roller door at the bottom of the ramp on Hobson Street rattles upward and an impressive convoy of marked and unmarked police vehicles turn left up the one-way road that leads to the North-Western Motorway. Operation 'Free Joey' has begun.

The targeted P labs are spread throughout the Waitakere Ranges from Little Huia, the back blocks of Glen Eden, Henderson, Oratia, Piha and Muriwai. Joey supplied the list of the six locations to Max, but there is one more, used as a safe house at Huia Beach. He has kept that information to himself for a very good reason.

A small group of police vehicles peel off at Point Chevalier. A larger group at Te Atatu and the few remaining continue on to the end of the motorway towards the turn off to Muriwai beach at Waimauku.

Ten minutes later two New Zealand Airforce helicopters lift off from the pad on the top of Police Headquarters. One, with Ronnie, heads North-West, while the other, with Max, heads South-West towards the gang at the end of Henderson Valley Road.

Inside the police vehicles the officers with their earphones switched on in their helmets, and some with ear pieces, can hear the increasing flow of information coming from the surveillance teams already in position. Only the STG, Team Leaders in AOS, and Ronnie and Max have mics, so the chatter is limited to reports and questions.

By the time all the vehicles are in place, at their designated assembly points, they have an accurate picture of what to expect.

All the reports are positive, with little or no activity at any of the P labs. Some security lights are on at the gang's headquarters, illuminating the courtyard and the gate. The lights are out in the barn and at the house. The only bright light is coming from the monitoring room.

Earlier in the evening, just after Kylie's call, Max had ordered a scout to check on Joey's condition and anything else out of the ordinary. By the coming and goings at the barn, the scout thought that Joey was still alive, but he couldn't be sure. At least no body was removed!

At a much earlier meeting than their last, Joey gave Max the layout of the house and the barn, he also told him about the three Doberman dogs in wire cages at the perimeter of the compound. Max has also been informed that it is the job of one of the un-patched members, living in the barn, to look after, then release them at midnight, after bolting and padlocking the front gate. He discussed the problem of the dogs, with a Vet, who organised the injecting of a tranquilizing fluid mixed with pig's blood, into four rabbit carcasses. These were thrown over the fence by the Scout, well below the house near the front gate.

Neither the Vet nor Max were certain the Doberman Pinschers would eat the tainted meat, so Max arranged a backup of three marksmen with dart rifles.

There should be little resistance from the three in the house, as the lights are out, but Max knows that gang members come and go at all times through the night, he is prepared to take that risk.

Ronnie's chopper slowly circles over the Kaipara Harbour while Max's circles at low altitude three kilometres off shore from the Manukau Heads, well below the flight path of incoming international planes and far enough away from the gang, that the 'chop', 'chop', 'chop' of the blades, cannot be heard.

Fifteen minutes before three, Max makes the call to take positions and then asks for the latest surveillance reports. Again they are positive. The planning for the attacks on the P labs differs from the planning for Joey's release. The P labs are to be hit hard and fast, while Joey's release will be by stealth.

At a P lab, the strongest AOS agent will batter down the front door and then step aside as an STG point man lobs in a percussion grenade. Immediately after the explosion, six squad members in close single file will storm the building each taking position and control of a specified area of a room. Shouting orders to the occupants to lie face down on the floor with arms and legs spread, their surefire flashlights, attached to semi-automatic rifles will light up the room.

Once the house is secure, the occupants will be restrained with plastic ties, read their rights, and then man handled out to a waiting paddy wagon.

The noise and aggression of the squads will be so traumatising that only the stupid, drugged or drunk will not be affected.

Many of the apprehended will be foreign students studying chemistry at local learning institutions and there will be no resistance, in fact, they will be so afraid, that they will either defecate or urinate into their shorts or pyjamas, or in some cases, both. So there will be offensive smell rather than resistance for the police and the supporting paramedics, but anything can go wrong in a raid!

Just before three, Ronnie's helicopter on full throttle, with a directional searchlight circling the ground, skims over the gently rolling farm lands North-East of Muriwai beach, then heads downward following the seaward slope of the Waitakere Ranges. Rushing over the tops of a pine forest, the pilot corrects the downward flight as it speeds above the empty Muriwai Golf Course. Only the rabbits scuttle for cover. Changing direction southward, he zooms along the sand and grass of the fourth fairway like a well hit golf ball! To Ronnie's right, the white rollers and surf are just visible in the gloom of the night.

Hovering over the water out in the bay, exactly at three o'clock, the pilot swings the nose inland and heads back towards the edge of the pine forest. The noise of the engine wakes tourists in their cabins and camper vans as well as the permanent residents in their prestigious houses overlooking the beach.

The lights come on in the motel units, at the intersection of Motutara and Coast Road as the patrons hear the angry 'chop' 'chop' of the helicopter and the high revving engines of the fast approaching AOS Nissan Patrols. The vehicles turn off Motutara Road and race down a long driveway to a secluded cottage next to the pine forest fence.

Everything is going to plan, and Ronnie has a bird's eye view as the directional search light illuminates the P house and the activity below. A few minutes later he gets the all clear from the team leader and instructs the SERT paramedic to enter the building.

It is a good night for Ronnie and his teams, as P lab after P lab are secured with little injury to the police or the occupants, other than trauma, bruising and superficial cuts from flying glass and glass on the floor. But nothing is ever perfect and at two of the labs the percussion explosives shatter flasks of volatile methamphetamine, starting fires in the kitchens which are soon extinguished by firemen wearing protective clothing and carrying breathing apparatus on their backs. At those locations, Ronnie orders the construction of decontamination tents and all those affected, including the restrained prisoners, are subjected to washing from high pressure shower heads.

The preparations for the attack on the gang headquarters, started well before Joey was brutalised.

The circumference fence with its vertical sheets of corrugated iron topped with spirals of razor wire, looks impregnable, but closer inspection proves otherwise. The sheets have been fastened by a nail gun from the outside. With the use of a long crow bar they have been levered away from the vertical and horizontal posts. The camouflaged police, quietly working the bar, out of sight behind the fence, and the barn, create very little noise. Only the dogs, in their cages suspect something, but tire of being yelled at by their dumb masters, and stop barking.

It's an ideal day job for the police, as their activity is hidden by the loud comings and goings of the gang, with revving bike engines and even louder rap music. There is just enough room to stand between the barn and the fence and the fence and the clay bank. This allows easy concealment for the forcing of the corrugated sheets. The surveillance team hide in the thick bush, further up the bank, above the barn.

Just after midnight, Max is informed that the dogs have stopped their usual circling of the compound and are nowhere to be seen! The three marksmen with their dart rifles, continue to scan the compound just in case. At three a.m. on a warm cloudy night, where the moon comes and goes, the security lights do not detect the silent approach of twelve policemen of the STG behind the fence, dressed in black flak jackets and helmets with night vision. Each armed not with rifles or shot guns, but Tasers and automatic pistols.

The team leader lowers himself down the narrow gap to the fence and pulls open an edge of the corrugated iron. One by one, in close single file, they move through it and form a line behind the barn. Advancing around the corner, they crouch even lower as they pass under the brightly lit window of the monitoring room. The closer they move toward the wide open window, the louder the television noise from inside. Any sound they make is concealed by the excited commentary and roar of the spectators at a live rugby league game being played in Hull, on the other side of the world.

Tau Henare, younger brother of Dan, deciding that the game is more interesting than watching the pictures from the security cameras, reasons with himself that it is keeping him awake! His other choice, the Playboy Channel has lost its appeal after five hours of titillating viewing.

Because it is a hot night, the barn doors and the single door to the monitoring room are wide open. There is no light coming from the barn, but the monitoring room is brightly lit. The light from the side window diffuses into the darkness while the doorway casts a rectangle onto the hard packed gravel of the court yard.

The team leader halts, holds up a hand, then removes a small black cell phone from his leg pouch, presses a button and watches as a thin telescopic wand extends until it reaches its maximum one metre length. At its tip is a tiny camera and he slowly pushes the wand forward at the bottom of the door until he can see a clear picture of what is inside.

Six metres away, is a side view of Tau in a swivel chair, with arms behind his head, and legs resting on the desk top. The team leader freezes the picture then retracts the wand and hands the screen to his team to view.

Gesturing for the four behind to push up their night glasses, he waits for their eyes to adjust, then beckons with his hand and they advance past him, strapping their automatic pistols to their backs. Taking a Taser out of its holster, he waves his hand forward. His team leap into the room and in three strides have a gloved hand over Tau's open mouth, stifling any noise. One pins his arms to his sides, while the another grabs his legs, lifting them upwards, forcing him deeper into his chair. The fourth officer ties his legs together with a plastic tie, then bends him forward and ties his hands behind his back. The officer with his hand over Tau's mouth, whispers in his ear to remain still and silent else he will be zapped by a Taser.

Tau is too much in shock to do anything else, but the threat of the Taser is not forgotten. All the gangs fear the weapon. Many horrific stories have been embellished to such an extent that they fear the Taser as much as a bullet!

When the restraining team rushed into the room, the team leader signaled for the remainder to take up position in the barn.

Entering the monitoring room, he pulls the door closed behind him, then quickly wraps duct tape around Tau's head and mouth.

Lowered to the ground, he is guarded by an officer, while the other three follow their leader out of the room and into the barn, clicking down their night vision glasses.

All is quiet except for snoring and heavy breathing coming from the fold-a-way beds at the opposite end of the barn.

The leader looks past the Holden, the BMW and four motorbikes to Joey's body hanging on the back wall. He is sagging forward with eyes closed and head resting on his suit jacket. Holding him up are leather straps around his wrists attached to chains secured to the wall. His arms are spread above his head stopping his fall.

The leader signals his men towards the sleeping youths while he stands guard at the doorway.

The nine officers stealthily approach each of the sleeping gang, splitting into predetermined groups of three, and stand above them waiting for the order.

The leader scans the court yard. All is quiet, so he whispers. "Go!"

Instead of a hand over mouth, as in Tau's case, three officers each grab a head and turn it, pushing it hard into a pillow. They hold the head firmly in both hands while a second officer pulls the prisoners' arms behind their backs and the third officer applies the plastic ties. Next the legs are secured and then duct tape is wrapped around the head and mouth. Two are silenced but the third manages a shout.

The shout wakes Carla, as her bedroom is the closest to the barn. Scrambling out of bed, she turns on the light and looks out the window.

Seeing Carla in the window, the team leader breaks RT silence and calls Max.

"Joey team leader to Max, over" The reply comes back immediately. "Yes Joey team leader, this is Max, over."

"We have secured the barn, four prisoners… Joey located but not released… A light has come on in the house following noise from a prisoner, over."

"Joey team leader, good work, we will commence the attack on the house. Attend to Joey as soon as you can, I want to know his condition, over."

"Roger Max, out."

Max orders the attack on the compound. There is no need for further stealth and the front gate is smashed open by the bull bars of a Nissan Patrol. The black Patrols with fully armed troops, holding onto the sides and at the back, roar up the driveway and come to a sliding halt in the middle of the courtyard. The troops jump off and race towards the house simultaneously smashing the front and the side doors.

Starting at the office, they search from room to room. The house seems deserted until they get to Johnny's bedroom!

Back in the barn, the team leader supervises Joey's release. He is semi-conscious and not aware of what is happening around him, or that his horrific pain will stop.

The police relieve the pressure on his shoulders by supporting him on either side as the straps around his wrists are untied. His eyes are open and he moans, rocking his head from side to side. Lowered to the ground, the concrete seems a blessing, after his hours of torture. He sighs loud and long. His shoulders are numb, so he feels nothing, but his ribs and broken arm send shock waves of pain to his brain. Slowly the sympathetic voices, penetrate his fevered brain and he starts his journey back to sanity.

Soon after, the SERT paramedic arrives and does a quick check of his condition and immediately calls for an ambulance.

After the scream, Carla woke Butch, who then woke Johnny. Looking out of her bedroom window, nothing seemed amiss but Johnny orders Butch to go and check, that is when they heard the front gate being smashed.

They are well prepared for a fast escape, often rehearsing their moves knowing that at some-time they would be attacked. Johnny paid for the construction of a very expensive escape route under his bedroom. First came a concrete bunker, then a concrete culvert that extends outwards under the fence. Now galvanises into action, they race towards the bedroom with a bewildered Carla following. She stands in the doorway, confused, scared and still fogged up from the night's drinking and cocaine.

Johnny has had only a few hours of sleep himself, but the dopamine is still active in his brain and he reaches under his pillow withdraws a pistol with a silencer and shoots her three times in the chest. There is a look of disbelief on her face as she flops forward onto the bed.

Flinging back the duvet, he turns to Butch. "Hurry, cover her with the blanket." As Butch pushes her limp body into the middle of the bed, Johnny spins the coded lock on the right hand drawer, opens it and pulls out the large canvas bag. Unzipping one corner, he exposes the red one hundred dollar bills and inserts the still warm pistol.

Butch hurries to a walk-in closet, opens the louvered doors and bends down lifting up a rectangle section of wooden flooring covered in carpet.

As the front and the back doors of the house shatter, Butch clambers down the iron ladder to the concrete bunker beneath and turns on the light.

Johnny drops the bag onto the bunker floor and then standing on the rungs of the ladder pulls the closet doors shut, then lifts and lowers the flooring back into place.

The bunker is an arsenal. Clipped to the wall is a row of new Kalashnikov AK 12 assault rifles, sawn-off shot guns and beneath them boxes of ammunition. Dressed only in underpants, they hurriedly make their choice of weapons.

Butch removes a shot gun and drapes a belt of cartridges around his neck and down over his bare chest.

Johnny takes a Kalashnikov and slings it over his shoulder, then grabs a handle at one end of a box of ammunition. He nods to Butch who grabs the other. In single file, they scurry towards a bolted side door that opens to the start of the long concrete culvert.

Four years have passed since it's construction and the telltale excavation is now covered with flax and ti-tree. The original scar is hidden, stretching outwards from the fence for a hundred metres before ending in dense bush close to a creek.

They are hunched over, moving along the culvert when Carla's body is discovered under a blanket on a bed. It is at that moment, that Max orders an unexpected and surprising withdrawal of all troops from the house!

Soon after the police stormed the house, an ambulance with Senior Paramedic Megan Farley and her partner Ross, raced into the compound. Usually paramedics are not permitted into a danger zone until it is secure, but tonight with Joey injured rules have changed.

The gang members have been removed from the barn and the lights turned on so that Joey's injuries can be better assessed.

He is now fully alert lying on his back covered by a blanket up to his chin and hurting everywhere.

Megan recognises him from their encounter at the Waimauku Clinic, she smiles. "Hello Joey, we seem to bump into each other in strange places, do you remember me? I'm Megan the paramedic."

Turning his head slowly towards her, a brief smile stretches his lips. Although it hurts, he forces air through his vocal chords. "Sure I do, you are my guardian angel sent by Saint John. I've been hanging around waiting for you to come, what kept you?"

Reaching forward, she gently brushes a few black strands of hair off his face, admiring his courage. "You're safe now Joey."

He nods, then winches in pain, for the first time he is aware of police activity around him. It is then that he remembers the explosives in the drawer in Johnny's bedroom. Trying to sit up, he flops back down in pain, but continues to stare at her with anxious eyes. With effort he forces words through clenched teeth. "Listen to me Megan, there are explosives in the house, tell the police!" He turns his head toward the protective cordon at the entrance to the barn, then back to her, "Tell them that there are booby traps in the house!"

Ross, who has been kneeling beside Joey, gets up and runs over to the team leader.

The warning relayed, Max orders the unexpected and immediate withdrawal from the house and calls up the bomb squad from the assembly point at Glen Eden.

Joey, still in acute pain and with memory of his terrible ordeal becomes agitated and beads of sweat form on his brow.

Megan wipes them away with a tissue, handing them to Ross to discard and then gently places her hand on his head stopping any movement. "Don't move your head Joey, you may have a neck injury. Ross and I will secure your neck with a cervical collar. We'll be as quick and as gentle as we can, but it will help to keep your neck protected, okay about that? Just say yes or no, don't nod your head."

Joey was about to nod but stops. "Yes, pretty blue eyes."

Megan who has pretty blue eyes and knows it, looks up at Ross. "How come you don't talk to me like that?"

"Company policy!"

She smiles. "Good answer mate!"

The collar is fastened, then Ross returns from the back of the ambulance with two separated sides of a curved stretcher and places one half alongside Joey.

Megan looks down at him again, "Joey, we have a scoop stretcher to put under you. I'm afraid it will be painful, I'm sorry about that, but it is the safest way of getting you onto a stretcher. Ross and I will roll you onto your side, then place one side of the stretcher under you, then we'll do the same on the other."

This time Joey gives a small nod even though his neck is restrained. He frowns, steeling himself for the pain that he knows will come.

As Megan pulls back his blanket, in preparation to roll him on to his side, she notices his left arm inside his suit jacket is at a strange angle, so she stops immediately.

Concerned, she looks up at Ross, "Get the large surgical scissors as quick as you can, I'm sure Joey has a broken arm."

As Ross hurries to the back of the ambulance, Megan is now aware of the extent of his injuries and suffering, "Joey, your arm is broken! Before moving you onto the scoop I'm going to slit your jacket so that I can have a look. I will also give you a pain killer that will help you heaps."

Joey can hear her, but he doesn't answer as he fights to stay conscious.

Taking the large scissors from Ross she cuts open the sleeve up to the shoulder, peels it open and then does the same with his shirt sleeve. It is a clean fracture and there is no external exposure of the bone. Before securing it with a brace and a sling, she injects a strong pain killer into his upper arm and waits for it to take effect. She watches as his previously tightly closed lips relax back to a smile.

He looks at her again and lets out a long sigh. "Whew, that's better!... Thanks Megan."

"Do you hurt anywhere else?"

"I think my ribs are broken, it hurts to breath!"

She unbuttons his shirt, exposing his brown hairless chest and lightly runs her experienced fingers over his rib cage. "They may be cracked, but not broken. Your ribs will probably hurt more than your broken arm. The pain will go in about a week."

"So short a time, eh! I'm not feeling anything at the moment!"

"That was a strong dose I gave you."

"Thanks, can you stay with me and be my nurse?"

"I'll be your nurse until we reach the hospital, sorry, but there are other Joey's waiting for me!"

"You sound like a hooker!" She laughs and playfully taps him on the cheek.

"We'll get you onto the scoop. Are you ready to be rolled onto your side?"

"Sure!"

The scoop is re-positioned and with only a few moans at each turning he is carried to the back of the ambulance and then pushed inside. Megan is about to climb up beside him, when the team leader approaches with a mobile phone. "Megan is it okay if the Superintendent talks to Joey?" She looks at Joey for a moment, and then back to the officer. "I've sedated him quite heavily so he may fall asleep during the call."

The officer will not be put off. "It's about the explosives."

Nodding, she takes the phone and places it next to her ear and can hear the distinctive chopper noises in the background. "Hello Mister Henderson, this is Senior Paramedic Megan Farley. Joey has a neck brace, a broken arm and cracked ribs, so I'd prefer if he didn't move. I'll hold the phone close to his ear. He is heavily sedated and may slur his words."

Max shouts above the noise of the engine. "Poor bastard, look I'll be as quick as I can, thanks Megan."

Climbing up inside the ambulance she looks down at Joey who is floating in the comfort and warmth of the pain killer. "Superintendent Max Henderson would like to talk to you about the explosives, is that okay with you?"

"Yes!" Joey smiles, knowing that Max for all his gruffness is

more like a father to him than his real father ever was, "Hi Mister Henderson I'm lying down on the job again!"

Max smiles for the first time that night. "No you're not Joey, you're a very brave young man and I'm sorry that I have had to place you in danger." He says something that Joey has never heard before, "I'm proud of you son!" Then after a pause.... "Are you alright Joey, I mean how's your pain?"

"I'm okay boss, I'm on a pain killer so the world's rosy!"

"That's great! I won't keep you long, what do you know about the explosives and the booby traps?"

"Not much, all I know is that Johnny says there is a pile of them in the left drawer under his bed, don't open that drawer! Johnny's bedroom is the last on the left in the hallway."

"He's one sweetheart, anything else you can tell us?"

"Only that he found the recorder behind the painting, so I guess that evidence is gone!"

"Don't worry about that we've got him for murder!"

"Who?"

"I'd say it's Carla, dead on a bed, probably Johnny's, above the explosives, we haven't moved her yet, as I wasn't sure what you meant by booby trap. I guess she was supposed to go up with the explosives as well as us! Strange that Johnny and Butch have disappeared but we haven't done a full search yet. Well I better let you go, thanks again for a terrific job, by-the-way, Kylie tipped us off about you being chained in the barn, she's a nice kid, eh! Have fun in Hospital, get well soon, see you later Joey!"

Max hangs up and Megan looks down at Joey, smiling. "Who's Kylie, friend of yours?"

A policeman climbs up into the ambulance and Ross closes the doors and soon they are racing out of the compound with lights flashing and siren blasting.

Dressed only in their underwear, Johnny and Butch curse and slap as they are attacked by mosquitoes and sand flies. They slip and slide down the narrow track to the creek, wade across it and then use the overhanging flax leaves to pull themselves up the other side. Clambering up the steep slope with the ammunition box and the canvas bag of cash between them they often lose their footing, stubbing their toes on roots and stones. The serrated edges of the cutty grass slashes at their arms and legs, leaving long thin strips of blood.

Their escape through the bush is painful and difficult, but they are driven on by fear and greed and the ever present noise of the helicopter circling overhead.

They are not concerned about being seen, as the track, cut two years previously, is now concealed by dense regrowth.

With little or no moonlight, depending on the coming and going of the thick clouds, they have trouble following the kilometre long track as it winds its way up the valley. Often losing their way, they are forced to back track. What drives them on is the knowledge that not far away is their means of escape, a new Toyota Land Cruiser, fully fueled inside a locked windowless garage beside the Scenic Drive.

At last the terrain levels off as they emerge out of the bush and Johnny spins the numbers on the lock until it reads 6666 and the padlock springs open.

It is still the early hours of the morning and only the kiwis, possums, hedgehogs, moreporks and trillions of insects are awake as the Toyota leaves the garage and turns left towards a safe house at Huia Bay.

Sitting between Johnny and Butch is the shot gun and the Kalashnikov, on the back seat is the belt of cartridges, the ammunition box and a Baikal pistol on top of two million dollars in the canvas bag.

CHAPTER 23

Miriama Learns the Truth. Utu

It is midmorning and Miriama answers the phone in her office at the chemical company. She is surprised to hear the voice of her grandfather and Ariki, Leo Maana, speaking to her in Cook Island Maori. She is not surprised that he is speaking in their own language, but that he has never called the office before! A frown creases her brow as they exchange pleasantries and then deepens when he asks her to meet him at the Marae.

She pokes her head into Ah's office. "I'm going out for an hour."

He looks up without smiling, annoyed that she has interrupted his research of the Satan's Sons gang. He dismisses her with a nod and then returns to the documents spread on his desk.

Ever hopeful for a happy loving smile, she seeks the solace of music and turns up the volume of the CD player in her gold BMW coupe.

As she drives South along the old inland road, she wraps herself in the island songs of Tere, George and Arbs. It's her security blanket. Being a happy person, the words and music of 'Topu Ikonei Rarotonga' soon have her feeling good and she has forgotten about Ah and his moods when she turns off the main road towards the old Marae.

As the granddaughter of the Paramount Chief, Miriama has been schooled in the history and culture of her ancestors, her whakapapa. From an early age she has been instructed on Maori tangata and her place in the iwi, hapu and whanau and the deep spiritual understanding of aroha, mana, tapu and utu. Mostly, she respects and fears the ancient Gods. She is comfortable that the old Gods somehow morphed into the new Christian God, after all, if the Christian God can be three persons in one, why not add a few more?

Approaching the car park, she is surprised to see two other cars and a scooter parked out front. She recognizes her grandfather's shiny red Holden and her great uncle, George Henare's old Corolla and also the beat up Vespa belonging to her school friend and kitchen help, Leilani Henare. Curiosity aroused, she walks through the entrance of the au, a rectangular fence made of stone that surrounds the marae and with reverend steps, makes her way across the open ground stopping in front of the largest building, the whare runanga.

Stepping up onto the porch, she is consumed, once again, by superstitious anxieties. Her belief is that her tribe's recent and ancient dead reside in this building. To her, it is not a structure but a living body containing all their parts. From the carved head, the tekoteko, high above the entrance where it rests on downward sloping arms, to where she is standing, the roro, the brains. Inside, its backbone, the tahuhu is supported by ribs that rest on legs called poupou. Intricately carved, with protruding genitalia, they tell the story of the six tribes of Rarotonga. Tempering her fear, as she stoops to enter through the low opening of the doorway, is the knowledge that she is protected by Rongo, the God of Peace who is always present in the wharenui.

Now standing, she pauses to allow her eyes to adjust to the subdued lighting of the huge hall. At the other end she is able to see her grandfather and great uncle sitting on a wooden bench on the stage. As she moves forward, two women who are sitting crossed legged on woven mats facing the stage, stand and turn towards her.

Miriama recognises her grandmother and Leilani Henare. With smiles and tightly shut eyes, she touches noses three times, then climbs up the steps and does the same with the Chiefs.

Returning to the mat, she wonders why she has been summoned by such important people and in her ancestral home.

Looking down at Miriama's anxious upturned face, Leo knows that his favourite granddaughter should not be afraid in this house of peace, but at the same time knows that he is about to enter into a very intimidating and challenging discussion.

Speaking in Rarotongan he starts as gently as he can. "Thank you for coming Miriama, you look as beautiful as ever and I'm proud that you are my granddaughter."

Smiling, she enjoys the warmth of his welcome but turns her eyes downward to show that his words do not fill her with arrogant pride.

Leo becomes more serious, "I've asked your grandmother to come along to be your tatao so that you will not feel alone."

Her grandmother stretches an arm around Miriama and gives her a hug. She always enjoys being pulled into the soft warmth of her grandmother's body, but it makes her even more confused about what is going on?

Leo continues, "I'm sure you are wondering what this is all about?"

Miriama looks up and nods.

"It's about the shooting of your cousin in the jail."

She is surprised and raises her eyebrows wondering what that has to do with her.

The Chiefs notice the surprise and questioning look, an indication that she knows very little, if anything, about the murder.

Leo makes a decision, "Miriama, Leilani has something to tell you, it will explain why you are here." He looks at Leilani, "Leilani dear, tell Miriama about Tattoo Chung and the rifle you found."

Surprised at the sudden request, she looks at the floor in front of her as she thinks about what she should say. Still with her eyes lowered, she turns toward Miriama and places a hand on her leg in a gesture of respect and friendship, then looks up shyly into her eyes. "On the morning that Dan was shot I saw Tattoo Chung hide a rifle in the storage room next to the kitchen. He seemed kind of sneaky, that is why I remember it so clearly." She shakes her head, "I didn't know about the shooting until that night and it bothered me so much that I went to work early the next morning and found the rifle and copied its make and number onto a pad and gave it to granddad George…. That's all I know." She looks up at George, who nods.

He rises from the bench and moves a few paces to the front of the stage. Sitting down, his legs dangle over the edge. "Miriama, you know that Dan was a very special grandson to me and that his death hurt me terribly." Taking a deep breath, he slowly exhales before continuing, his words catching in his throat, "Leo's son, at the Police Station, matched the bullet that killed Dan with the rifle that Tattoo Chung hid in the storage room!" Pausing, tears stream down his face and overcome with grief, he is unable to continue.

Leo clears his throat as a polite way of catching Miriama's attention. "The bullet was not **exactly** matched to the rifle, because the rifle has disappeared from the storage room. The bullet is the same type used for that rifle, but an exact match can only be done by comparing the rifling in the barrel to the rifling on the bullet…. Rifling is the grooving inside the barrel. Every rifle is slightly different, do you understand what I'm saying?"

Miriama nods, still wondering how that information has something to do with her!

Leo continues, "Until Albert has recovered that rifle there is no evidence that Tattoo Chung is the shooter or even if it is the murder weapon at all. What I **can** tell you, is that the rifle is a special type, and it would be unlikely to find another anywhere in the islands." He shakes his head, "Even in the whole of the South Pacific!" He pauses for a moment allowing his words to sink in, then decides to dispense with pleasantries, "Miriama dearest, do you know anything about the rifle or the shooting?"

She is shocked at the suggestion and feels tears welling up in her eyes.

Her grandmother stands, moves behind her, gently stroking her lowered head. She fully understands Miriama's turmoil, the disbelief that her boss and lover would have anything to do with a murder and the acceptance that her grandfather and great uncle are telling the truth.

Leo waits, and then asks gently, "Do you know anything Miriama?"

With tears running down her cheeks, she shakes her lowered head slowly from side to side.

Her grandmother offers a tissue from a box and she wipes her eyes and blows her nose then looks up directly at her grandfather again, shaking her head.

Leo and George know that she would not lie to them, particularly in the ancestral Marae, where there are too many listening ears.

Miriama shrugs her shoulders slowly, "I don't know why Tattoo Chung would want to kill Dan"

After the shock of the question, her mind had frozen with hurt. Now she is able to think more clearly. *'Is it possible that Ah, is a criminal?'* She has never questioned where Ah's wealth was coming from. She knew the coffee and chemical businesses were profitable, because she did the bookkeeping, but she never asked herself if that was Ah's only source of income.

Shifting uneasily on her crossed legs, the first doubts enter her mind, *'Maybe that is why he has such unexplainable mood swings and the feeling that he is keeping something from me?'* She shakes her head at a new thought, *'As a lover, he is caring and gentle and the passion between us is genuine and fulfilling, but why the reluctance to continue that intimacy in everyday life?'* As if to remind her of their sexual intimacies, for the first time she feels movement in her womb, this abruptly brings her mind back to the present.

She turns towards her grandmother beside her, then looks at Leilani, then up to the stage at George her Rangatira and finally at the most important person in her life, her grandfather. "What do you want me to do grandfather?"

Her grandmother, acknowledging the decision, begins to massage Miriama's neck muscles, gently stroking downwards from under her ears. It is one of Miriama's greatest pleasures and with eyes closed she begins to relax.

Leo stands and moves down the stairs, then squats directly in front of her. When he places his hands on her shoulders she opens her eyes. "Find the rifle Miriama, but be very careful… Do you know that Ah Chung is connected with the dangerous Triad gangs of Hong Kong?"

She shakes her head,

"That is why I'm asking you to be very careful. If you are scared at any time, call me, I will protect you!"

She wipes her eyes with the back of her hand. "Thankyou granddad. I know you will!"

The Supervisor's office at the Chung Coffee Company at Avarua, stands on cross braced metal legs, high above the floor of the warehouse, allowing a clear view of the workers below. Access is gained by two flights of metal stairs so Tatto Chung and Ah Ting are not surprised by the polite knock on their office door.

The island born factory foreman, with cap in hand, enters, followed by two fit looking island men. Respectfully averting his eyes, he says. "Ah, bosses, this is Simote Henare and Selwyn George, they're filling in for Pita and Sonny for a week, if that's okay with yous guys?"

Tattoo studies the newcomers, checking their strength. He stands, then moves close to Simote, inserts his fingers between his lips then pulls them open to expose his teeth. Satisfied that they are straight, white and strong, he does the same to Selwyn. Nodding towards the foreman, he wipes his fingers on his shirt. "Are they good workers?"

"Yes boss, very hard workers."

"They will start on time and keep working even though it gets hot?"

The foreman nods.

"What's the matter with Pita and Sonny?"

"They've gone to a funeral at Aitutaki."

Tattoo looks at Ah Ting, who shrugs. "Okay, same pay." He points towards the warehouse next door, "Go and talk to Miriama in the office." He dismisses them with a wave of his hand.

Outside, Simote and Selwyn spit on the ground trying to remove the insult and the taste of Tattoo Chung's fingers from their mouths. As constables of the Rarotonga Police Force they know that their undercover mission is not going to be easy, they also have a burning hatred for the Triad Chinamen.

Tattoo Chung and Ah Ting don't know it, but the same worker exchange is happening next door in the Chan Chemical building. The Rarotonga foremen don't know why they have been instructed to make the changes by the Paramount Chief, but they do know that the substitute workers are from the police. They wonder why but don't ask as their loyalties are always with their tribe, not the foreigners who pay their wages.

The call to make the changes, came that morning after Leo had talked to his son at the police station. It is the beginning of the utu and once it starts it will not end until honour is restored.

It takes two days for the undercover policemen to find the evidence.

It is late afternoon and Simote, Selwyn and their boss, Albert Maana are seated at the Commissioner's desk.

Cradled in Carlos's palms are two white sachets made of perforated cloth and printed with the words, 'Silica Gel-Desiccant'. Comparing their weight, he notices the one in his left hand feels slightly lighter, so he discards the other and looks up at Simote and then to Selwyn. "So the lighter one contains silica-gel and ephedrine?"

They nod.

He looks down at the other sachet, "And this one, only silica-gel?"

They nod again.

Studying each of the sachets, he continues, "They certainly look the same." Gripping two corners of the sachet containing the ephedrine he swings it backwards and forwards then places it on the desk squeezing it with both hands, "You can't tell that there is a separate sleeve and it would be pretty hard to spot on an x-ray."

He looks up at Albert, "Are the crystals similar in appearance?" Albert nods.

Carlos pushes the sachet beside the other then continues

thoughtfully, "A puncture test, unless it penetrates right through to the middle, would only reveal the drying agent, very clever!" He looks at his two constables, "So tell me, how did you figure out the difference?"

Simote looks at Selwyn, who remains silent, so he answers. "We were looking for something that was out of place, you know, something odd! Our foreman had to show us what to do in the warehouse. He told us to put the packages from the red bin in the sacks of coffee beans with "Export Quality Coffee Beans" printed in red across the top. The packages printed in blue were to be placed in the sacks printed in blue! It seemed important to put the same coloured packages in the same coloured sacks!" Pointing to the sachet containing the ephedrine, he continues, "That one was always in the sack with the red printing."

Selwyn speaks for the first time. "There was something else that was strange, we were told to push the red silica-gel deep into the coffee beans but to leave the blue ones on top. It was easy to slip a package from the red bin under the top of my shorts and to cover it with my T shirt. Simote did the same with a blue one. When the midday hooter went we met outside and transferred them to our lunch boxes. Mister Vaiili told us to take them to forensics, they found the inner sleeve of ephedrine."

The Commissioner picks up the forensic report from his desk and studies it for a moment. "One hundred grams of ephedrine will make a lot of P." Looking up, he smiles at his men, "Terrific job, I will make sure it is mentioned on your files, take the rest of the day off, you've earned it!" With a push of his legs he propels his chair backwards away from his desk, stands, and then moving around to the front, shakes their hands.

After they have gone, Albert, anticipating the request, shuts the door before returning to his seat and waits for the Commissioner to speak.

Carlos returns to the rear of his chair and standing, looks out the window. Rubbing his palms up and down the sides of his face he thinks about the new evidence. Sighing, he moves to his desk and sinks down into the chair. Grasping the edge of his desk, he pulls himself closer and then looks across at Albert, tapping the sachet in front of him, "So we have the motive for Dan's killing, but still no murder weapon, I think we should have that luncheon tomorrow and this time I'll invite the Prime Minister, what do you reckon?"

This time Albert agrees.

The Tamarind Restaurant, like its name, is shaded by the spreading branches of a tamarind tree with its distinctive dangling pods and feather like leaves. It's a great name for a restaurant as the tree provides edible seeds that can be used, not only to add a sweet-sour flavour to fish masalas and other Asian foods, but it is also used in every day sauces like Worcestershire and HP. The restaurant, likewise, caters for Western and Asian tastes. *Tamarindus indica*, is an ancient tropical tree and it derives its name from the Arabic *tamr-hindi*, meaning 'Date of India'. In contrast, the building that it shades is a relative new comer, being built in nineteen ten to house the manager of the fledgling Union Steamship Company.

Now it is the favoured meeting place for tourists and the rich and powerful of Rarotonga.

Small, polite, Philippino waitresses and waiters hover near a large table closest to the beach.

Seated at the table are distinguished guests, the Prime Minister of the Cook Islands, Tusi Pisi; his Foreign Affairs Minister, Robert Afaai; the Minister of Justice, Leo Pasi, and opposite them, the Commissioner of Police, Carlos Vaiili; his Senior Detective, Albert Maana and the Justice Department Counsel, Ray Gandhi QC.

Albert's presence seems out of place, but being the son and spokesperson for the Paramount Chief, he is treated with the utmost respect.

So everyone is on their best behaviour as they tip-toe around the vexatious shooting of Dan Henare and the more recent discovery that Rarotonga is being used as the Pacific Rim distribution centre for contraband drugs.

The Commissioner is pushing for the immediate arrest of Ah Chung and his Chinese workers.

The Prime Minister however, buoyed by his caucuses agreement, in principle, of the Chinese offer, is determined to delay the prosecutions as long as possible. His rationale is that the death of a gang member and the trafficking of illegal drugs is insignificant to the financial security of his country. It galls him, that a lack of money binds his country, although tenuously, to New Zealand. At last there is a glimmer that the Chinese yuan will help his country. That is his official position, but his real beliefs are quite the opposite. He is playing a cagey game and only two others know it!

So much is at stake in the polite discussions that are about to take place, but first he might as well enjoy the superb cooking of the Philippine chefs without a second thought that it is being paid for by the people of Rarotonga, where twenty eight percent of the population live below the international poverty line.

From the outset, formal introductions are not necessary, as everyone knows everything about everyone else, including their secret agendas and their character flaws.

As they near the end of their meal they are reminded of their island's bi-lateral trade with New Zealand. Deep fried Cook Island banana topped with New Zealand ice cream, and the final course, platters of New Zealand cheeses and cups of Atiu coffee.

As a signal that pleasantries are over, Prime Minister Tusi pushes his chair away from the table, wipes his mouth with a napkin folding it neatly into a square, then places it on top of his empty plate. He looks directly across at his Commissioner of Police, Carlos Vaiili who called the meeting. He knows that Carlos wants to change, or influence him on some important matter. That makes him wary. He moves his gaze from Carlos and briefly scans the others at the table, searching for a common link. It doesn't take him long to realise that this meeting is something to do with Dan Henare's murder and maybe the recent discovery of ephedrine in the shipments of green coffee beans to New Zealand.

Two of his Ministers, Leo Pasi for Justice and Robert Afaai of Foreign Affairs have already politely challenged his verbal directive to slow down the investigation and now here they are with the obvious support of the Commissioner of Police and his legal advisor, Ray Ghandi QC, this is going to be difficult!

Sighing, he interlocks his fingers and then rests them on his immense belly. Turning his head he looks briefly at each of them, then sweeps a hand around in an encompassing circle, "So Carlos, what's this all about?"

"Tusi I'd like to talk to you as a friend, not as Prime Minister, is that okay with you?"

Tusi has heard those words before and it gives him a chill. His smile disappears. "Sure, but this meeting is off the record, okay?"

They nod, as he looks at each of them.

Satisfied, he turns back to Carlos, "Does this have anything to do with Dan Henare and the Chinese involvement in smuggling drugs?"

"Yes!"

Tusi pauses for a moment, wondering how much Carlos knows about the negotiations with the Chinese and then guesses that he probably knows everything...... Well, almost everything! What Carlos won't know, is that there is another very good reason why he is hoping to stall the prosecutions and that reason is a confidence known only to one other person who is not at the table, "Look, I'm not asking for you to stop your investigation, I'm just asking you to delay any prosecutions until after the contract with the Chinese has been signed.... I don't want to impede the natural course of Justice, I'm asking for you to deliberate a little longer, is that too much to ask?" He looks at Ray Ghandi, Parliament's and the constabularies' legal advisor who remains non-committal.

Searching for support, he turns his attention to his Minister of Justice and is annoyed that he gets the same reaction. Not deterred, he presses on, "The contract with the Chinese means financial stability for us all! I'm asking you to put that into your decision making."

There is awkward silence as no-one wants to be the first to challenge what is a ministerial directive, even though they have agreed to speak only as friends.

As Commissioner of Police, Carlos is in a squeeze between his duty as a policeman and his duty to the Prime Minister.

Ray Ghandi, who is steeped in the traditions of Westminster law, is extremely uncomfortable, but no-one has asked him for his legal advice, so he remains silent.

Robert Afaai, Minister of Foreign Affairs is the only one present who knows the intricacies of the Prime Minister's mind, so he also stays silent.

Carlos decides to check if Tusi is fully conversant with the recent happenings at Chang Chemicals. "Just in case you have not been fully briefed on all the recent events, I'd like to give you a quick over view, will that be okay?"

"Sure, fire away."

"Dan Henare, a member of the Satan's Sons gang in New Zealand is caught with an undeclared two million dollars of cash at the airport and then is subsequently murdered. The bullet that killed Dan is found and forensics in Auckland say that it has been fired from a recently made British sniper rifle. That same rifle with markings," He looks at his palm, "L115A3 was accidentally discovered at Ah Chung's house a day after the shootings."

He pauses and looks around at the attentive group, "We had no motive for the murder until our investigations discovered that the Ah Chung's Coffee Company is exporting contraband drugs to New Zealand. The distributor of those drugs is the Satan's Sons gang, so we have more than sufficient evidence to win a prosecution."

Turning, he looks at Ray Ghandi for confirmation.

Ray nods, so he continues, "So we don't really care about the other thing with the Chinese Government."

Tusi folds his hands and rests them on his stomach. "But you don't have the rifle!"

Carlos is silent for a moment, wondering how the Prime Minister knows about the missing rifle. "No, but we are working on that, anyway, Ray and I believe there is enough evidence to press for an immediate prosecution of Ah Chung and all his Chinese workers."

Tusi slowly shakes his head.

Carlos is angry, but doesn't show it, instead he pushes his large frame out of his chair and beckons, then directs with his finger, that the Prime Minister should follow him outside.

Walking side by side on the fine white sand of Muri beach, they hold their sandals in their hands and the gentle trade wind flaps their black lava lavas against the sides of their legs.

It is the height of the tourist season and they are forced to make detours around two wedding groups close to the water's edge. They don't mind the distractions, as they are aware of the importance of the tourist dollar. Both are also aware of the incongruity of a Pakeha bride in all her pristine white fluffery being paddled towards the beach in a narrow, rough cut vaka.

Carlos suppresses a smile when he looks at the waiting, red faced bridegroom, stuffed into his black tuxedo and nearly fainting from the heat.

They stop and turn to watch, wondering if the canoe will capsize as the bride stands waiting to be carried up the beach, no such luck!

The semi-nude warrior lifts, then carries her effortlessly towards the tipsy bridesmaids who can't stop giggling.

With the wedding groups behind them, Carlos and Tusi are joined by two, wet, long haired dogs with driftwood in their mouths. This is their playground with an ever changing retinue of tourists who are so lonesome for their own pets that they are showered with excessive affection. Spoilt for choice, the dogs are selective whom they approach and these two large men with the right smell are big enough to throw their sticks out into the shallow, clear waters of the lagoon.

Tusi and Carlos become boys again trying to out-throw each other. As they watch the dogs racing towards the water, Carlos turns to Tusi. "I'm still talking to you as a friend, and yes, it is off the record.... I doubt that you know that an utu has been placed on Ah Chung and his Chinese workers, I nor you can change that.... As you know Albert is in charge of our investigation and being the son of the Chief is keeping me informed of what is happening at tribal meetings. George, the grandfather of Dan has succeeded in convincing the tribes that the balance must be restored."

Tusi nods, as Carlos continues, "On your behalf, I will try and slow the utu, but I can't promise anything! What I can say is that when it happens there will be no prosecutions! Of course there will be an investigation but no prosecutions! We will make sure there is no evidence, do you understand?"

Tusi touches him on the arm, nodding.

Carlos in turn slaps him gently on the back, "Come on, let's go and have a couple of cold beers with the others." They turn and head back towards the restaurant with the dogs trotting behind.

As they pass the beachside bars, Tusi, ever the politician, acknowledges the loud greetings with a smile and a wave of his hand.

After the meeting at the Marae, Miriama Maana is troubled. It is not in her nature, or Christian beliefs to harbour doubts about anyone, particularly against the man she loves! Part of her doesn't want to believe that Ah is a criminal, but deep down there are gnawing uncertaincies. She always accepted his mood swings and secrecy as part of being Ah Chung. For the first time she questions her own unconditional love and is insecure and afraid.

Having promised her grandfather that she would try and find the rifle, she sits on the edge of the bed and wonders where she should begin. Kicking off her slippers, she flops backwards, closes her eyes and twists strands of long black hair between her fingers as she decides what to do.

Decision made, she swings her legs over the edge and walks into a small office next to the bathroom. Seating herself, she looks at her watch and sees that it is 6 pm, not a good time to call Leilani in the kitchen, but she is desperate to seek her help. Pressing an intercom button on her desk, Leilani answers. "Kia orana, this is Leilani."

"Kia orana Leilani, this is Miriama, are you busy right now?"

"Oh hi Miriama, yes, I'm preparing the vegetables for tonight's meal, it's prawn and Chinese vegetables.... If you want to change the menu you'll have to to talk to Wah Lee, shall I put him on?"

"No, it's about something else, it's really important, can I talk to you alone up here in my bedroom?"

The request surprises her because she can't image what her boss would want to talk about. Not allowing her answer to sound curious she replies brightly. "Sure thing, Wah takes over in about fifteen minutes, is that too late?"

"No problem, thanks, see you soon."

Leilani frowns, the only times she has been in Miriama's bedroom is delivering a meal when she is sick. This is different, this is a personal invitation. She shakes her head, *I wonder if she wants me to help find the rifle?'* Wiping the steel counter with a cloth, she shakes her head, *'Nah, she's so capable, she doesn't need me!'*

Fifteen minutes later, ill at ease and seated on a soft chair in the bedroom she soon learns that it is about the rifle and she becomes even more uncomfortable.

Miriama can tell that she has withdrawn into herself and tries to reassure her by placing a hand gently on her leg. "Leilani, we are akatua, we are whanau, don't be afraid, nothing will happen to you. As you heard at the Marae, I've been asked to find the rifle that killed Dan. It is difficult for me too, because I have to keep the search a secret from Ah Chung and I don't like hiding things from him.... Do you have any ideas where the rifle might be?"

Leilani is silent for some time as she searches in her mind for a likely hiding place. It could be anywhere on the property. *Maybe Tatto has buried it somewhere and it will never be found, or dumped at sea?'* Eventually she looks at Miriama and shakes her head.

Miriama stands and looks around the room and then down at Leilani, "Maybe the Chinese have sent it away from the island or even buried it in the forest?" She ponders that for a moment, then shakes her head, "But I don't think so, Ah and Tattoo are always laughing at the stupidity of our police. They are so sure of themselves that I doubt that they would get rid of such a useful weapon." She comforts herself again by twisting strands of hair between her fingers, "But where?"

Leilani wanting desperately to help, offers a suggestion. "It's not in the storage room because I keep checking." She looks around the large bedroom and then back at Miriama, "If I was them I would hide it in an unlikely place like somewhere here in your room!" She points across the room to the walk-in closets, "Maybe in the closets under your clothes?"

Miriama shakes her head. "I thought of that already and had a real good look," She turns towards the closets and shakes her head, "No, not there!"

Leilani stands and looks toward the bathroom. "How about the bathroom?"

Again Miriama shakes her head. "There is only the hand basin. No room in the toilet or the shower and the spa bath is covered in tiles." Pausing for a moment she remembers seeing a small hinged door at the rear, "You know, there's a small cupboard door at the rear, where the pumps are, I'd forgotten about that!"

Leilani follows her into the bathroom and watches as Miriama kneels down and pulls on a knob attached to a small tiled door. With it open, she looks inside and there, beside the plumbing and a pump is a long canvas bag! Still on her hands and knees she looks up at Leilani with fear in her eyes. If it is the murder weapon then her world is about to come tumbling down. With a beating heart, she scrambles to her feet and steps away from the open cupboard, "I think it is the rifle, you have a look. Oh God, I hope it is not the rifle!"

Leilani kneels and allows her eyes to adjust to the half-light before reaching in and pulling the bag out through the doorway. As she stands she lifts up the heavy bag with one hand and then holds it with two, placing it on the narrow top of the spa with the strapped flap closest to her. Turning to Miriama, she nods. "This is the same bag that was down in the storeroom, shall I open it?"

Miriama nods, holding the bag, as Leilani unbuckles the leather straps.

The folded butt of the rifle is exposed. Looking up at Miriama, she grimaces then nods, "I'm sorry Miriama, but it **is** the same rifle!"

"Are you sure Leilani, how can you be so sure?"

"I'm sure!" Pulling on the butt, the small Union Jack and the manufacturer name are visible. Again she looks up at Miriama, "That's the rifle that killed Dan!"

Miriama with her hand over her mouth steps backwards and then grabs the towel rack for support as the room starts to spin. A chill passes through her body and perspiration beads form on her forehead. Controlling her nausea, she remains standing.

Leilani quickly moves beside her and touches her on the arm. "What are you going to do with the rifle?"

Miriama stares at it for a moment. "I'll need a hand carrying it into the bedroom."

Leilani nods.

With Miriama leading they walk to her bed. Lifting the covers, she pushes the bag underneath, then turns to Leilani, "You'd better

hurry back to the kitchen, Wah Lee will be wondering where you are." Reaching over, she clasps her arm, "Do you mind coming back after dinner to help me carry the rifle to my car?"

Leilani nods, "Yes of course."

Hurrying away she stops at the doorway looking back at her distressed mistress, "See you at the dinner table Miriama." Then quickly decends down the back stairs.

Still dazed Miriama moves to the clothes closet and shuffles through her colourful silk dresses. Usually dressing for dinner is a joy but tonight she is crying inside. She still doesn't want to believe that Ah would be involved in Dan's murder. Absently shuffling through her clothes, she chooses a sleeveless, floor length, azure blue gown that accentuates her tall slender body.

Seated at her dressing table, she has difficulty fastening a silver neckless studded with aquamarine stones when the contrary clasp is taken out of her fingers and fastened dextrously by Ah Chung. Closing her eyes, she feels his lips gently kiss the nape of her neck. With tears in her eyes she stands and wraps her arms around his neck and then kisses him long and passionately on the lips. His tender caresses were always there at the beginning, but for the past two years have become less and less frequent. She knew it was not her fault that he had withdrawn into himself, and become detached. Time and again she would cajole and tease him, even try and reason with him, but the harder she tried the more he rejected her.

After another lingering kiss, he smiles down at her. "You look beautiful my dear." He frowns, "Why the tears?" His tender words cause even more tears to flow and he reaches down and removes a tissue from a box on the dressing table and gently wipes her face, "What on earth is the matter Miriama?"

Shutting her eyes, she shakes her head unable to speak. Eventually she looks up and suppressed words flow in quick succession. "I-found-the-rifle-that-killed-Dan-Henare. It-was-in-my-bathroom." Her eyes are now pleading, "Tell me that you had nothing to do with the shooting, Ah!..... Please tell me you didn't do it!"

He stares at her without expression or emotion.

Reaching up, she grabs hold of the lapels of his dinner jacket, "I love you so much, tell me you didn't do it!"

Carefully, but forcefully he removes her hands off his jacket. His handsome face hardens. "What rifle?"

She turns and points. "It's under the bed."

Abruptly turning he strides over to the bed, bends down and lifts the cover. Slowly straightening, he glares at her.

Once again she sees that cold guarded look in his eyes and for the first time is afraid.

Walking towards her, he quietly asks. "Who told you about the rifle?" Grabbing both of her arms he shakes her, "Why do you have the rifle?"

"Please stop Ah, you're hurting me!"

Instead of stopping, he shakes her even harder, so that her head snaps backwards and forwards and his face is now twisted with rage. "What do you know about the shooting?" Throwing her hard onto the ground, he stands over her, "What's going on Miriama?... I thought I could trust you!"

Sobbing, she cradles her knees in her arms and looks up at him. "You don't understand island ways Ah... I'm loyal to you, but also to my Chief, my grandfather... I was asked to find the rifle and I have, just tell me you had nothing to do with the murder of Dan."

A sneer crosses his face. "I don't have to tell you anything! That is my business and you have no part in it, I can't let you keep the rifle, you know that!"

She shakes her head. "No, I don't!... If you are innocent, then you have nothing to hide."

"I can't let you have the rifle Miriama." Methodically he removes his black silk tie until it is dangling in his hand, "Get up!"

"Please don't hurt me Ah, if you hurt me you will hurt our baby."

He stiffens and studies her abdomen as she stands. His angry face drains of all expression and his eyes become steely cold.

Moving close to him she gently strokes downward over her stomach, "I've been meaning to tell you Ah, but there just hasn't been the right moment.... are you pleased?"

"No!" The word is like a sword stabbing her heart and she puts a hand to her mouth as he wraps the ends of the tie around his wrists. "Turn around!"

"Please Ah, don't hurt me." He takes a step towards her and raises his fists wrapped in the tie, as if to strike her.

As she cowers, he pushes the tie over her head and then pulls it tight, twisting it against the back of her neck. Using all his strength he maintains the pressure and she struggles to breathe.

She is very strong, but he is stronger and when her thrashing body is threatening to loosen his hold, he pushes forward so that she falls face down into the carpet with him on top, his knees pressing into her back. After only a few seconds, she becomes limp and still and he keeps the pressure on for a further minute until he is sure that she is dead.

Breathing hard, he gets up and closes the door to the bedroom and then drags her into the bathroom, lifting her up and over the top of the spa. A final heave and she slides like a floppy doll, face down to the bottom. Turning on the tap, at the hand basin, he washes his hands and his face and looking in the mirror, combs the parting back into his long jet black hair.

Retrieving the tie from the bedroom floor, he snaps it straight, lifts up his collar and then ties a perfect knot. Before leaving the room, he removes the rifle and bag from under the bed with a promise to himself that it will never be found, ever again.

Leilani, serving dinner that night to Ah and Tattoo and the three warehouse supervisors, stops beside Ah and asks if Miriama is coming down to dinner.

Without answering, he lifts his bowl and shovels prawns and vegetables into his mouth.

She waits expectantly behind him until he has emptied the bowl and then asks again. "Sir, is madam dining with you tonight?"

This time he turns and dismisses her with a wave of his hand. "Miriama is visiting her family and won't be with us for a few days."

Leilani nods her head. "Thank you Mister Chung I will remove her place setting."

Back in the kitchen, she hurries up the stairs to the bedroom. The door is closed so she knocks politely, "Miriama, are you there?"

There is no reply, so she knocks again, still no reply. Opening the door she looks inside and quietly calls out, "Miriama it's Leilani, are you there, are you okay?"

Looking around the room, she sees a broken necklace on the floor. Moving quickly forward she bends down and picks it up, *'That is strange!'* With the necklace dangling from her hand she looks into the office and sees that it is empty. Turning she notices that the door to the bathroom is closed with a sliver of light underneath. *'Maybe she's in there and didn't hear me call?'*

Knocking politely on the door she waits, but again there is no reply, so she knocks more loudly. Fearfully she gently opens the door and looks inside and sees the back of Miriama's head resting against the bottom of the spa. Taking a step forward she freezes when she realises that she is looking at a corpse. Shocked words explode from her mouth, **"OH MY GOD!"**

Rushing forward she pulls on one of Miriama's lifeless arms and her head flops around towards her and she stares upward with bulging eyes. Leilani shrieks again, repeating over and over, **"Oh my God!.... Oh my God!"** Taking a deep breath, she reaches forward and feels for a pulse, but there is none. A final anguished cry erupts from deep inside her as the enormity of what she is seeing sinks in.

It takes only a moment before she regains control. Rushing out of the bathroom through the bedroom she descends the stairs two at a time. Her rapid downward movement is checked only to make the turn into the kitchen. All her instincts tell her to leave the building and run, but intellect tells her to continue her kitchen work as if nothing has happened.

Wah Lee has just finished preparing desserts of hokey pokey ice-cream and lychees, Ah's favourite, and summoning all her strength and courage, she places them on a tray and takes them out to a serving shelf beside the table. As if in a dream she removes the empty champagne bottles from the chiller stands, opens new bottles and pushes them down into the iced water.

Once the main course plates and the left-over food has been removed she serves the desserts and returns to the kitchen. Faking a severe stomach ache she asks to be excused.

Wah Lee can see that she is not well, so he sends her home with a wave of his hand.

As quickly as she can she takes off her apron, walks out the back door, kick starts her scooter and waves at Pita who opens the front gate.

Once out on the road heading down the hill toward the airport with the cool wind whipping through her hair, her heart beats subside and she opens the throttle wide as she races to tell her grandfather about Miriama's death.

An hour later Pita Henare still on security duty at the gate, at Ah Chung's house, receives a call on his cell phone and is surprised to hear the voice of his Ariki.

"Hi Pita, this is Leo Maana, are you well?"

"Yes thank you Mister Maana, are you well?"

"Yes Pita, thank you for asking, listen carefully because I have some terrible news and the tribe needs your help."

He answers tentatively. "Yes Chief but I'm on duty here until morning, can I help you then?"

"The help we want is right where you are at the Chinaman's house, right now."

Pita frowns. "Okay, no problem, what is the bad news Mister Maana?"

"I'll get to that in a moment, first I have to tell you that the Council of Tribes have decided to terminate the lives of your Chinese bosses."

The blood drains from Pita's face and he suddenly feels light headed, the information is too abrupt and too confusing and he is silent for a few seconds.

"Are you still there Pita, did you hear what I just said?"

He swallows hard. "Yes Chief, how can I help?" He frowns, "Do you want me to kill them or something?"

"I'll get to that, but first I have to tell you the bad news." He speaks quickly because he is not sure he can say the words without choking, "Miriama was murdered inside the house earlier this evening."

Pita almost drops the phone as his legs sag and he falls against the window frame of the security shed. His forearm stops his fall but he feels nothing and is not aware that he is bleeding.

Hearing the crashing noise, Leo becomes concerned, "Are you there Pita?"

Shaking his head in an attempt to make some sense of what he has just heard, Pita straightens, then returns the phone to his ear. "Yeah, sorry sir, I mean the news about Miriama, is, terrible. It's hard to believe! Miriama, dead?" He shakes his head again. Not Miriama, she's so……. alive!"

"Yes it is terrible that is why we want utu for my beautiful grand-daughter." He pauses for a moment, trying to regain control of his voice, "You know, I promised to look after her, that I would protect her!" Unable to continue he starts to sob.

Pita has tears streaming down his face and like his Ariki is wracked with sorrow. Unabashed, his sobs grow louder and join the sobs coming from his phone.

Eventually Leo sighs, clears his throat and with difficulty contin-ues, "Pita… we're seeking utu not only for Miriama but also for your brother, do you understand?"

Pita's sorrow quickly changes to anger and he nods towards his phone. Realising that he has to answer, he struggles to control his voice, "Yes sir, what do you want me to do?"

"Use this number if you see anyone leaving the house. Already it is surrounded by warriors so there is no escape. Go and open the front and rear gates as quickly as you can, later I will want you to identify Ah Chung and Tattoo Chung. Right now go and open the gates then return to your shed, do you understand everything I have told you?"

"Yes Chief, I'm watching the house and opening the gates and then waiting for you to arrive. Do you want me to turn off the lights?"

"No, I'll tell you when that will happen."

Again burning rage threatens to choke Pita's voice. He had heard the rumours about the death of Dan, but wasn't sure if it was just a few making trouble for the Chinese, "Chief, can I be part of the utu, please?"

"By helping us you are part of the utu.... Miriama and Dan will be honoured. See you soon, don't do anything on your own, okay?"

"Yes sir." He hears the 'click' as Leo disconnects.

A hundred metres above the house on the road to the hospital, Carlos Vaiili and his Senior Detective, Albert Maana stand behind two tripods supporting their night glasses.

Two hours before, Albert had been phoned by his grandmother and told about the death of his daughter and also that his father was going to Ah Chung's house with warriors seeking utu. Wisely, Carlos restrained Albert from joining his father knowing that it crossed the line between duty and revenge.

Now, below them, the lights illuminating the compound are suddenly extinguished. Adjusting their night glasses they watch as warriors flit through the open gate at the rear of the compound and advance toward the house. Bare chested they are streaked with white paint and a few have bird of paradise feathers bobbing on their heads. The same scene was repeated hundreds of years ago, but this time, they have cell phones, in pouches, dangling from their necks. Some carry ancient war clubs, but most have machetes, pistols and rifles.

Carlos swings his glasses towards the front gate where another stream of warriors is rushing through and taking positions around the main building. He spots Leo Maana's large frame hurrying towards the house, with Pita beside him.

Leo is also bare chested with a cell phone swinging freely around his neck. His body glistens in the moonlight and he has a large headdress of ceremonial feathers. Albert has seen him wear it before at important tribal gatherings, but never before into battle. Although a policeman, restrained by modern protocols, he feels a satisfying glow deep inside. Retribution for his daughter's death is happening island style.

Turning towards Carlos, he points. "My dad has arrived."

Carlos swings his glasses towards the front gate and nods.

They lose sight of Leo and Pita when they enter the building by the back door with warriors following close behind.

So swift is the capture and gagging of Wah Lee in the kitchen that he is too surprised and frightened to call out. His mouth, arms and legs are taped and his slight frame is easily carried out onto the parking lot beside the back door.

Unaware of the violent activity all around, Ah Chung and his warehouse foremen have just finished consuming numerous liqueurs and for the past half hour have been passing around an opium pipe. Their brains are befuddled and they find it difficult to comprehend why the dining room is now full of island warriors with weapons, painted faces and wearing funny head dresses.

Ah Chung finds it particularly amusing and starts to laugh, but Tattoo, with his Red Army training, is the first to react. Without a weapon, he grabs two empty champagne bottles by the neck and smashes them against the edge of the table. Jumping to his feet, his chair clatters backwards as he thrusts the sharp edged bottles towards the intruders. He is quickly surrounded and when he thrusts to his left a spiked wooden club smacks into the back of his head and he topples sideways over his chair. The sharpened bottles fall from his hands smashing on the tiled floor below.

As if on cue the three remaining warehouse supervisors jump to their feet but are roughly pushed back into their chairs.

Ah Chung puts down the opium pipe, looks around at the warriors and then brazenly gestures for them to join him at the table but nobody moves.

The huge frame of Leo Maana enters the room with Pita beside him, he turns to Pita, "Which one is Ah Chung?"

Before Pita can reply, Ah Chung speaks up. "Hey mister warrior king, I'm Ah Chung, what do you want?"

Leo slowly walks over to him and stares into his eyes without speaking.

Challenging him, Ah stares back.

The Chief grunts, straightens and then speaks very clearly and slowly. "My name is Leo Maana.... I'm the Paramount Chief of the tribes of the Cook Islands. More importantly I'm the grandfather of Miriama Maana." Again he stares silently at Ah Chung waiting for a reaction. When it doesn't occur, he turns to Pita, "Which one is Tattoo Chung?"

Pita points to the unconscious Tattoo, draped over the chair. "That's him Chief."

Leo turns to his men, "Tape him up and take him to the car park then come back here." He points to the other three Chinese who are sitting very still and now very afraid, "Tape them up as well and take them outside, I'll deal with them later." He points at Ah Chung who still has a silly grin on his face, "Tape his arms and keep a close watch on him." He turns to Pita, "Show me Miriama's bedroom."

At these words, Ah Chung jumps out of his chair but is immediately punched in the head and his face is banged hard onto the table, smashing his small elegant nose.

Leo turns and selects three of his largest and most trusted warriors, gesturing with an upward movement of his head, "Take him up to the bedroom."

Pita leads the way through the kitchen out into the hallway and then up the stairs, followed by Leo and Ah Chung, who is pushed, punched and dragged when refusing to move.

Pita opens the bedroom door and they enter.

Heading straight to the bathroom, Leo stops abruptly in the doorway when he sees Miriama's crumpled body in the bottom of the spa. His usually expressionless face turns to anguish. Unable to contain his pain he opens his mouth and the quiet of the night is shattered by a roar, that changes to a howl that ends in a sob.

For some time he is frozen with grief before he slowly moves forward and wraps her lifeless head in his arms, kissing her long black hair. Now on his knees, with her body in his arms, he rocks backwards and forwards in agony until all his sorrow is spent. Eventually he turns his tear filled eyes toward Ah Chung in the bedroom and gestures for him to be brought into the bathroom.

With his arms held tightly by his sides and his head forced downward by a fist in his hair, he is now close to Leo but his eyes remain unblinking and expressionless.

Leo releases Miriama, stands and pushes past Ah Chung without looking at him and then turns and gestures that they should all follow him back down the stairs.

Outside he opens his cell phone pouch and calls George Henare. "Hi George, I have them, bring the ute to the back of the house. The gates are open." He clicks off his phone and returns it to its pouch.

Unseen above him, Carlos and Albert watch with increasing apprehension as the bound Chinese are brought out to the car park. They are hoping that they will not witness a mass execution, knowing that will not properly remove the utu. There are ceremonies that must come first. They recognise the small frame of the cook Wah Lee and the much larger frame of Tattoo Chung who is dragged out by his feet and Ah Chung, who is sitting defiantly with his head up against the wall. They watch Leo as he paces backwards and forwards stopping every so often to talk to one of his warriors as if he is trying to make up his mind. Being far away, they are unable to hear what he is saying but they clearly see him stop beside Pita and point to his leather holster strapped to his waist.

"Is your pistol loaded Pita?"

"Yes Chief, but the safety's on."

Leo holds out his hand. "Give it to me!"

Pita unclips the flap on the holster and removes a Chinese TT33 and hands it to Leo, who then moves immediately over to the cook.

Carlos slaps Albert on the arm and shakes his head. "He shouldn't shoot Wah Lee, he's only the cook."

Robert quickly removes his cell phone from his shirt pocket and calls his father.

Leo, still burning with revenge looks down at the little cook whose eyes are wide with fright and he starts to raise the pistol when the phone rings in his pouch. With the pistol pointing directly at Wah Lee he answers with a distracted. "Yes?"

"Don't do it dad!"

The words jolt him and he turns, looking around in the darkness.

"Is that you Albert?"

"Yes."

"Where are you?"

"Up on the road above you."

Leo looks upward but can only make out the dark silhouette of the trees.

Wah Lee is whimpering and Leo returns his gaze to the cook and knows that it would be a mistake to kill him, or the other three supervisors. His overwhelming desire is to lash out and hurt anyone involved in his granddaughter's death, but reason prevails, and he shuts his eyes, placing his hand on his forehead and slowly moving it downward over his face.

He remains still for a moment with eyes closed, then opens them and places the phone against his ear, "Thanks son, you are right, Miriama would not have wanted that. I'll call you later from the Marae." He disconnects, then directs the warriors to remove the tape off the supervisors' and Wah Lee's mouth and legs and arms. Helping them to stand, he orders them to follow him back into the house.

Carlos and Albert swing their night glasses to the right of the building, as they watch a fast approaching ute that stops in the parking lot beside the back door. They zoom in and recognise the elderly figure of George Henare climbing down.

Inside the house, Leo has taken the three prisoners up to the spa bath and they are now looking down at Miriama's body. For the first time they realise their predicament and wonder about their fate.

Leo kneels and once again gently strokes her hair. Fighting to control his emotions, he looks up at the Chinese, "Ah Chung did this, this is my beautiful granddaughter! In remembrance of her I'm going to spare you! Remember her and this moment for the rest of your lives." He looks from one to the other, "Do you understand English?"

They nod, so he continues, "You are to pick her up gently and carry her to the bed, after that, you will go to your rooms where you will pack a suitcase, as quickly as you can. You have been spared only because Miriama would have wanted it. The police will take you to a prison cell where you will wait until the next plane to Hong Kong, do you understand all of that?" They nod as their fear subsides, "You will be escorted to your rooms by my warriors, that is for your own safety!" He pauses so that his words are clearly understood, "My tribe want you dead, right now! Even I want you dead! Do not try to escape as there is no place to hide on this island. If you try to escape you will be dead by the morning!" Leo looks down at his granddaughter and then with tears once again blurring his eyes he looks up and issues a chilling warning, "When you get to Hong Kong tell your Triad bosses that if any of you ever return to the Cook Islands you will not leave here alive. Your smuggling of drugs will stop! The police will confiscate your properties, you will never return, understand?"

Again they nod. "Let me hear you say, "Yes!"

All three say. "Yes."

Again he points to Miriama, "Now carry her to the bed!"

Once she is laid out, face upwards, Leo gently pulls her eye lids closed and folds her arms across her body, pulling the duvet over her, he lifts her, and gently carries her down the stairs placing her in the back of the ute.

Ah Chung and Tattoo, with legs tied and now gagged with duct tape are picked up and placed beside her.

As four warriors climb onto the back to keep guard, Leo gathers his men around him, "Eight of you are to stay with these four," He points to the supervisors and the cook, "They are to go to their bedrooms and gather their belongings. They will be spared! Do not harm them!" At these words there is a murmur of dissent, "Miriama would have wanted them to live, it is for her." There are no further challenges, "The police will come shortly to take them to the cells where they will wait before leaving our islands never to return. I have told them that if they do, or any of their Triad friends, they will be killed!"

There is a loud shout of approval and he points to the back of the ute, "We have unfinished business with those two!" Leo dismisses his warriors with a wave of his hand, "I'll see you back at the old Marae."

An elder climbs in beside George and the ute departs.

Leo calls his son on his phone, "I've told the cook and the

warehouse Chinese that they will be spared and that you will come and pick them up soon. I will arrange with Robert Afaai for them to be removed from the island, in the mean-time, can you look after them in your cells at Police Headquarters?"

"Sure dad, no problem, what about Miriama, where are you going to take her?"

"She's on her way to the Marae where she will remain overnight. Send an ambulance in the morning to take her to the morgue. I'll arrange a tangihanga for Dan and Miriama sometime next week...... It's a sad day son, thanks for your help."

"Anything for my Chief and my dad!..... Yes it is a terrible day, we have lost our baby girl!...." He is unable to continue, so Leo clicks off the connection as they both grieve in silence.

After a moment, Albert, overwhelmed by the loss of his daughter, loses his studied policeman control and releases a whispered sigh, a sigh that started as a roar from the deepest pits of his soul, constricted his stomach, throttled his heart and choked his throat, so that the hurt escapes only as a whispered sigh.

CHAPTER 24

Jean Farley's Advice

For the past week, even though Jean had guests coming and going to keep her busy, she pined for her girls. When they left for their northern holiday in the Bay of Islands, she felt empty and listless, but today they are returning and she rises with the sun, invigorated.

Dressed in her burgundy satin nightie, she is seated in front of a mirror with her head to one side, brushing then parting her long, grey streaked hair, preparing to plait.

After years of practice, her nimble fingers have a mind of their own as they separate three strands and tightly plait from the scalp to the end. This allows her to dwell on the girls and their romances with her adopted sons. Like any mother she is intrigued and concerned.

Tying off the first length with a few twists of a rubber band, she shakes her head thinking of Tane and Julia's relationship. Smiling, she is aware of the huge sexual attraction between the two. Her smile turns to a frown when she thinks how dissimilar they are, *'I wonder if it will last?'*

Turning her head to the other side, she starts to brush again, *'Mike and Wendy, now that is a match! Mike is such a gentleman and*

Wendy, what an English rose!... Fancy her being royalty, it's almost like a fairy tale, now that may last.'

Her brushing is so vigorous that a spark 'cracks' between her hair and the brush, reminding her of what she is doing. As she weaves a new plait, she thinks about Gary and Robyn, *'Salt of the earth those two. There is no reason why that shouldn't last. They are so happy together. Look how Gary has come out of himself since Robyn arrived, self-assured, more confident. Yes, it will last! He is trustworthy, strong and reliable and she has the brains.'*

Clipping two ends of hair together, behind her head, she smiles, *'Isn't that always the case!'*

Whenever she is happy she hums a happy tune. It is a subconscious tune with no melody, beginning or end, and like now, she is not aware that she is doing it.

Standing, she moves to her oak tallboy opens it and then tries to decide which outfit would be the most welcoming. She needn't have bothered, because her large wrap around blue forget-me-not apron conceals most of her under garments.

Entering the kitchen, she hears scratching on the door which tells her that Lady has arrived and that the men must be close behind.

Opening the fridge she removes a roll of dog food and waits for Lady to back away from the door. Her tail is wagging so vigorously that her hind legs sway, like a hula dancer, and she looks up at Jean with expectant eyes. "Hullo girl, you must be feeling better if you are that hungry, I bet those boys are still feeding you rubbish!" Reaching down, she rubs behind each of her ears while checking her wound. The shaved leg is almost healed and covered with short new hair, "You know where to come for a good healthy meal, don't you!"

With her foot, she pushes a twin cupped bowl away from the wall and slices a chunk of meat off the roll.

Lady darts forward and snatches the slab, carrying it to the comfort of the grass beside the back door steps.

The guys emerge from the track and Jean waves, then hurries to get the coffee ready.

Now seated around the small kitchen table, she waits until they have consumed six hot scones and jam before she broaches the subject that is on all of their minds.

"So the girls return this afternoon?"

They nod,

"Not long before they fly home!"

Again they nod.

She pauses looking from one to the other, "So how do you feel about that, am I prying too much?" Again there is silence, until Tane decides his situation is easiest to explain. "I guess you saw what was going on between Julia and me?" She nods and he continues, "Well we are splitting."

"Really!"

"Yeah, she was smart enough to know that it wouldn't work out. Believe me I tried to change her mind." He sips his coffee, "Now that I have had time to cool off, I can see that she is right. She doesn't want to live in New Zealand and I don't want to live in Canada."

"Is that right!"

"Well I don't think I'd like to live in Canada, my roots are here."

Jean shrugs, "You could live there for a while, then come home for a while. Be a nomad. It would be fun playing in the snow and you'd like the cheap petrol! You'd sell your pottery for much more." He shrugs. "I guess!"

After a moments silence, he continues, "Julia is more practical than me, I would have let our relationship grow and then waited to see what would happen." He shrugs, "In everyday life Julia is a risk taker. Look what she did to that gang leader, but in relationships, she is cautious, quite the opposite."

"So you'll part friends?"

"Of course, Mike and I and the girls have talked about us having an exhibition in Toronto. Robyn seems to have connections as well as Julia and Wendy. They're going to be our agents and help pay for the trip!" He smiles at the thought, "It's exciting! It means we have to produce new work, it gives us a focus, a direction, something we need!"

Jean is surprised at the news and looks from Tane to Mike and then back to Tane. "How wonderful, an exhibition of your work in a huge city like Toronto." Again she looks from one to the other,

"You know, you are both very talented, I don't think you realise how talented you are. What worries me is that you will become so famous that I won't see you anymore."

Tane gets up from his chair and drapes an arm around her shoulders and gives her a hug. "Jean, if we get that famous, we will fly you over, what would you think about that? Have you seen the Niagara Falls or Banff?"

"Have you?"

"No, only on TV, but it would be neat for us all to be there together don't you think?"

Jean reaches up and squeezes his hand. "You're a dreamer Tane, but a precious dreamer, thanks for the thought." She releases his hand and turns to Mike, "So what about you and Lady Wendy Howard?"

Mike cradling his mug in both hands looks over the rim directly into Jean's searching eyes. She has become so much part of his life that he is not offended by her probing questions. There is a smile on his face and a twinkle in his eye as he places his mug on the table. "There are plans!" Teasing her he lifts his mug again and drinks while Jean's eyebrows remain raised in expectation.

"Plans?"

"I'm going to London to visit the Queen!"

It's the first time Tane and Gary have heard this and wonder how they fit in? 'When? Where?'

Jean has questions of her own. "Before or after your exhibition in Toronto?"

"After."

She nods. "Sensible!"

"We haven't talked with the girls about the dates of the exhibition or to Wendy about going to visit her folks."

Gary twists an imaginary moustache and fakes an English accent, "I say old boy, you'll have to shine up your armour, what, what!" He bumps Tane with his elbow and they laugh. Gary's laughter is brief, as he sees Jean staring at him and his face turns pink. He has always hated being the focus of attention, *'Uh oh, now it's my turn.'*

"So you and Robyn, how's that working out? You both seem pretty happy together!"

He screws up his face and scratches his hair as if that will make it easier for him to explain how much they are in love. Giving up, he simply replies. "Yeah, we're an item!"

Jean nods. "I guess you know Danny Topu is bringing them here at one o'clock, I've invited him to lunch, do you guys want to come to tea tonight?... Or how about Sunday for a farewell dinner?"

Mike looks at Tane, who nods. Mike turns back to Jean. "Plans have changed a little Jean, that is why we have come this morning. The girls arrived in Auckland last night and booked into a hotel. They were going to be picked up by Danny, but my folks have invited them to a barbecue at their apartment in Mission Bay. Sorry for the change of plans, but it will be nice for them to meet Wendy and of course Robyn and Julia, we're going to pick them up shortly."

Jean nods. "Not a problem. Does Danny know?"

The boys nod.

"Are the girls still staying here tonight and over the weekend?"

The boys nod again.

"So no Danny Topu, no lunch but a light supper tonight."

Mike nods. "That's it, except they would like to go to a fancy dress dance in the cave at Whatipu tomorrow night, you know, the pirate dance."

She nods.

"If it's okay with you they would like to eat earlier, say six o'clock?"

"No problem, I don't have any other guests booked so they can eat at any time they like. Why don't you all come, I'd like that."

Tane asks. "Would it be all right if Emma Swift joins us for dinner? Emma is the Vet that operated on Lady when she was shot. She's very pretty, you'll like her a lot."

Surprised again, Jean studies him for a moment, confusing Tane by her silence.

He frowns, "It's just that she's going with me to the dance... I'll pay for her meal if that's a problem?"

Jean scoffs. "No such thing, of course she is welcome here, I was just wondering about Julia, how does she feel about that?"

"She knows, she's fine, Emma and Julia are friends already."

Jean smiles, the news pleases her. "I'd like to meet her, she sounds like a special person." Again she studies him for a moment, "You

know Tane, I'm actually glad you are dating a local lass, at least I won't lose all of you!"

Tane shakes his head. "It's early days Jean!"

Gary has a thought. "Jean why don't you come with us to the dance?"

"Oh I couldn't, it's for young people, also what would I wear?"

"We have rented all sorts of pirate stuff, there's enough for you as well." He laughs, "You'll make a great pirate I know Robin would like you to come."

Mike says. "Come on Jean, when was the last time you had a night out?"

"It's been a while!"

"You know the saying, 'All work and no play makes Jean a dull girl'."

"Here's another smarty pants, 'All play and no work makes Mike a poor man'."

"But we're not talking about me, we're talking about you! The last time you went out…Let me see, we took you to that movie about the Marigold Hotel."

"Yes, but I don't need to have distractions, I enjoy myself staying right here." She shrugs, "Every day is a new adventure, why should I go anywhere else?"

"This is the first dance in the cave since the sixties and it may-be the last. Don't you want to be there, it's historic!" She shrugs again.

Mike continues, "The Huia Historical Society had a bloody hard time getting approval for the dance. In the end the Auckland City Council agreed because the Society needs money for their museum. But the Council agreed to a one off, there won't be another. Think about it Jean, what a hoot of a send-off for the girls and you'll be there too."

She holds up her hands in surrender. "Okay! Okay! I'll go to the dance!"

The men do high fives as Jean continues,

"Do you have any plans for later today? I just want to know when I should prepare a meal?"

Tane nods. "After the barbeque we're taking the girls to the old Huia Store to pick up the dance tickets, that means we'll be back around six, is that alright?

"No problem, I'll make a salmon salad, that will be light and refreshing, you should stop for a coffee at twinkling heaven."

Tane frowns. "Where's that?"

"Titirangi, you should know that!"

"Titirangi, twinkling heaven... I should have guessed"

"While you're there, you might as well show the girls the souvenir shops."

Mike nods. "Good idea Jean."

Standing she collects the empty mugs stopping to smile down at Mike. "I'm always full of good ideas, well I'd better get myself ready for their return, it will be good to see them again." As she moves into the kitchen, she shakes her head, *'Now I'm going to be a pirate at a cave dance, what next?'*

CHAPTER 25

Mission Bay and the Huia Beach Store

Mission Bay, Auckland, gets its name from the mission school built by an Anglican Bishop, George Selwyn in eighteen fifty-eight. Missionary zeal was sweeping the British Colonies and the school was built to educate Melanesian children. Some of the buildings still stand today on the edge of a white sandy beach. It is not surprising that they have lasted, being constructed from the hard igneous rock of Rangitoto Island with its volcanic peaks dominating the horizon, out in the bay.

In Bishop Selwyn's day, the bay was on the outskirts of a young and fast growing Auckland township, today, being only seven kilometres from the CBD it is the most sought after real estate in the land.

4005 Tamaki Drive is right in the middle of the bay, opposite the Sicilian marbled fountain, beside the beach. Its location makes it the most expensive of the expensive and that is where Mike Robinson's parents live.

Owing to height restrictions, their five bedroom apartment is on the top floor of a three story building and the large half circular veranda, out front, provides an uninterrupted view of the fountain, the beach and the harbour beyond. It is an idyllic setting particularly at night when there is an enchanting light display at the fluted stone fountain.

With such luxurious surroundings, you would think that Mike would visit often, but he doesn't, preferring the more natural beauty of the West Coast beaches.

His mother, Raechel, scolds him about his long absences, but Gregory, his father, sees himself in Mike's independence.

Both love him equally and he loves them.

Mike gets his fair hair and green eyes from his father, who is of large build, but his athleticism comes from his mother, who is tall and olive skinned, complimenting her auburn hair. Both in their fifties and because they can afford the luxury of their own daily schedule, Raechel makes sure that she and Greg start the day with exercise. That includes a cycle around the bays, then a swim the length of the beach, before walking their bikes across the road and down the ramp to their underground car park.

But not today, Raechel begging off exercising as there is too much to do.

Greg knows this is not true, but decides to keep the peace.

She misses her son more than her husband, simply because she would quite happily tie her only child to her apron strings.

Gregory however recognises the same single minded drive that he had as a young man, which made him his fortune in the property market. It still confuses him why that same energy is concentrated on painting landscapes and not on money. So he doesn't love Michael any the less but is prepared for him to live his own life, without dwelling on the reasons why he should choose to live in comparative poverty.

Mike both likes and objects to his mother's attempts to tie him down and respects but regrets that his father doesn't understand why he wishes not to join him in the family business.

The difference is in the make-up of the two Robinsons. Gregory John strives for the accumulation of wealth while Mike strives for the perfect painting. Mike is also aware that his parents' wealth has made it easy for him to focus on his artistic talent.

Today's impending visit excites both parents, but they handle it in their own ways. Raechel is consumed with anxiety, while Gregory is simply curious.

Since maturity, Michael has never brought a lady friend home and Raechel is reading everything into the visit and discussing the reasons repeatedly with her husband, who tries to appear interested. He is more relieved than she, when a bright, hot, morning sun appears over the Saint Heliers hills. Already the six burner stainless steel BBQ has had its cover removed and the grill scrubbed clean. Four large black umbrellas with silver ferns have been raised and firmly anchored in the centre of teak tables and the cushions on the deck chairs plumped and repositioned each time Raechel passes by.

On the half circle seat attached to the front wall of the veranda, the long curved cushions have been reversed and then turned upside down to hide the fading.

The outdoor fridge is stocked to over flowing and bottles of red wine, spirits and liqueurs festoon the top of a moveable bar.

A stack of CDs are ready beside the player with music for all tastes.

Thick T-bone steaks and Canterbury lamb chops, as well as king prawns are on a shelf in the kitchen fridge, above two kinds of salad, Caesar and Greek.

Only the nibbles need attending too, but Raechel is worried that she has forgotten something and scurries around wiping and cleaning and making small adjustments. She even checks that Mike's huge painting of Karekare beach is hanging straight.

She shouldn't have been so worried, because when first introduced to Wendy, she is captivated by her open smile and a suntan that cannot hide a perfect peaches and cream complexion. Her first thoughts say it all, *'What a beautiful young lady, full of grace and charm. Look at those tight black curls! Michael you beach bum, how did you snare this one? She's so British, I love her already!'*

Wendy, not sure what to expect is instantly at ease, enjoying Raechel's friendly welcome. Instinctively she knows that they will become close and will be able to share the love for the same man.

Greg's first impression is Wendy's elegant but relaxed sensuality and can understand why his son would be attracted to her.

Michael is fully aware of the impact Wendy is having on his parents and delays introducing, casually into the conversation that she is Lady Wendy Howard of Castle Howard!

Taken by surprise, Raechel can't stop a plethora of words. "Really?... I mean, how wonderful!... But what are you doing here in New Zealand?.. Of course you are very welcome!,..... Oh my, what a surprise!... How wonderful!... You'll have to tell me all about being Lady Howard!.... How amazing!"

Placing her hand under Wendy's elbow, she guides her out onto the veranda to one of the deck chairs. Seating herself, she asks if she would like something to drink.

Wendy nods. "Do you have a pinot gris? I had a glass the other day and really liked it."

"Sure do, that is my favourite afternoon drink, what a coincidence, you and I are going to get on just fine!" She turns towards Michael and Greg who are drinking beer from a bottle in the kitchen. "Hey you two how about a drink!" Turning back to Wendy, she gives her a wink. "Bums, they never change!"

Unfazed, Mike ambles over to the two most important girls in his life and enjoys their mutual possessiveness. "Sorry we were talking about the Black Caps, the All Blacks and the America's Cup." With that excuse he knows that he will be forgiven, "What would you like?"

Raechel answers. "There's a cold pinot gris in the fridge, two of those please."

Mike turns and calls out to his dad holding up two fingers. "Two pinot gris please dad!"

Door-bell chimes clash with Greg's favourite music, Kenny G's soothing sax.

Mike looks down at his mother, "That will be the rest of the gang. You haven't met Gary, he's a really good friend and lives next to us at the Beach." He looks at Wendy, "Wens, do you mind telling mum about Julia and Robyn?"

She nods as he disappears through the folded doorway towards the front door.

Later that day, after a successful barbecue and a stop off at the Titirangi souvenir shops, the two Jeeps turn into the parking lot at the iconic Huia Beach Store. Facing them is an enclosure for outdoor eating. A high wooden fence gives privacy and shelter from the prevailing wind that sweeps up the bay. The fence is painted sky blue with faded wording celebrating the store's one hundred and twenty years of existence, 'The Huia Store, 1886-2006'. Beside the wording is an attempted painting of a godwit. The locals know that their annual visitor arrives every summer, flying non-stop from its breeding grounds in Alaska, an amazing eight day flight of eleven and a half thousand miles to feed on the abundant food available on New Zealand's marshes and swamp lands.

The girls walk past the painting without a second glance not knowing that their fellow North Americans, feeding on the mud flats have just flown the same route as themselves without the help of two huge Rolls-Royce engines.

After all those years, the Huia Store is still the centre of the community. A place where locals gossip; post letters; stick notices on the ever crowded notice board; sell home grown produce and find out who's catching what. When the chit-chat stops they buy a coffee to read with the free newspaper and then depart with what they came for in the first place, a jug of milk and a loaf of bread.

Tip-Top ice cream's contribution to the celebrations was to provide three purple and gold beach umbrellas emblazoned with their red white and blue logo to shade the three picnic tables. Now, years later, the sun, wind and sea spray, have faded their tip-top condition. Seated under one of them, are our three couples, licking double scooped ice creams.

Under Tane's table, Lady licks an ice-cream that is resting on an open pizza box.

The girls have never tasted hokey pokey before. A delicious kiwi invention of vanilla ice cream impregnated with small chunks of honeycomb. There is little chatter, as it is a race against the fast melting mountain of frozen cream. So preoccupied are they, that they don't notice the arrival of Butch Gueber.

Butch and Johnny have been hiding out in their safe house, on the beach, not far from the store. The group do not recognize him as he is now clean shaven wearing smart casual clothes that conceal his tattoos. On his head is a stylish, white straw hat with a black band. Covering most of his face, is a pair of gold embossed black Gucci sunglasses.

Glancing in their direction, seated out in the patio, he recognises them instantly! Paying for a coffee, he picks up a newspaper and seats himself at a picnic bench behind them. With his back to the group he can hear every word.

Wendy asks, "So where is the cave from here?"

Gary changes his ice cream to his left hand and turns pointing over the fence to a peak in the ranges at the entrance to the harbour. "That's Jackie's Peak."

Tane and Mike, also seated with their backs to the bay, turn and look, just above Butch's white straw hat,

"The road winds over the hills to the right of the peak ending at Whatipu beach."

Mike turns to face the girls. "The road is really narrow and windy, because it used to be an old bullock track that followed the contours of the land. At the turn of the century the bullock teams use to haul huge kauri logs to the mill, down here by the beach." He turns his head back to the ranges, raises his arm on an angle to match the steep slope of the hill and then turns back to the girls again, "Not only did they have the difficulty of coming down the slope but they had to turn around and pull a load of cut timber back up again, poor bloody cows!" He drops his arm back onto the table, "You know, one of the drivers was a pretty young lady named Charlotte-Anne."

Julia raises her eyebrows. "You had a woman in-charge of a bullock team?"

Mike nods. "The suffragette movement was started in New Zealand, not England!"

Julia frowns. "Are you sure about that?"

"Putting on my Historical Society hat, I'm very sure. I've actually seen a copy of the minutes of a meeting from the wives of a West Coast mining town, that called on the New Zealand Government to give women the vote… I forget the date, but it was way before the turn of the century.”

"I'm impressed.”

"Although isolated, we are still a socially aware country.”

In silence they concentrate on their ice-creams, that's when Wendy remembers her first question. "So how far is the cave from, how do you say it, fffoteepooh?”

Being an exaggeration they all laugh.

Again Gary answers. "Not far, about a ten minute walk.”

Butch turns the page of the newspaper but he is listening,

"For the dance tomorrow, we thought it would be fun to walk along the beach from Karekare to the cave, it's an easy walk, quite flat.”

Robyn asks, "How far is it from the hotel to the cave, if we decide to walk along the beach?”

"I don't know how far it is, but it will take us about an hour-and-a-bit.”

Julia asks. "How much is, 'and-a-bit'?”

"Don't know for sure, depends how fast you walk!”

Robyn thinks that's a pretty smart answer and smiles at him, he smiles back, "Oh yeah, there's a tunnel we have to go through, if we want to take a short cut." He is about to expand, when Tane interrupts. "The weather forecast is for clear and warm and the tides out so it should be fun, we'll take torches.”

Robyn asks. "How long is the tunnel?... I mean, no bats or trains or anything like that?”

The men laugh and then Mike answers. "No, nothing like that, it is quite a small tunnel. It was made for a bush locomotive that pulled cut timber to the wharf at Whatipu.”

The ladies know that he enjoys talking about the history of the ranges and they don't mind, they find it interesting,

"There used to be a train track all along the beach that was raised on wooden trestles." He shakes his head, "It has all gone now, you know, erosion, changes to the shoreline. The train used to go through the tunnel with its funnel down so it wouldn't get knocked off. If you decide to walk to the dance, I'll show you some of the old rusting spikes tomorrow.”

Julia nods. "I think it will be fun, something different.”

Gary has a thought. "Yeah and after the dance there won't be any cops doing breath-a-lisers along the beach!"

They laugh at his unexpected humour but he is not joking.

Mike has a thought of his own. "We'd better buy the tickets." He points towards the store, "The shop keeper said there's not many left. By the look of the traffic going past I'm surprised there's any left at all!" They enter the store, without a backward look at the man sitting behind them who leaves soon after, with tickets of his own.

The cave dance at Whatipu is no small undertaking. All day Thursday and Friday, Huia Road has been busier than it has ever been before. In the early days it would have been bullock teams transporting logs and supplies and later, stage coaches.

Yesterday, there was a convoy of six container trucks accompanied by a variety of trade vehicles.

Today the road is busy with the arrival of officials. The Auckland City Council; Transport Authority; Ministry of Agriculture and Fisheries; Department of Conservation; Department of Health; the Police and last but not least a car from Occupational Safety and Health, even Saint John Ambulance personnel.

In one of the six containers is a huge marquee with the tent poles strapped to the top.

In another, a massive generator with rolls of electrical cabling.

The third has a portable floor for the lighting and sound mixing desks. Also scaffolding, spotlights, floodlights and coloured decorative lights and large speakers.

The fourth is a portable stage for the floor of the cave and a hundred round tables with white table cloths and five hundred plastic chairs with white cloth covers for inside the marquee.

The fifth is refrigerated, with a portable bar, barrels of beer, soft drinks, non-alcoholic drinks, casks of wine, water, plastic jugs, mugs and wine glasses and the sixth, the most necessary of all, port-a-loos!

The huge cave at the bottom of the cliff face is surrounded by marshy wetlands and accessed by a roped, narrow track, lit with solar lamps every ten metres. All the paraphernalia of the dance has to be transported by helicopter. That in itself is a health and safety nightmare and why the Project Foreman wearing ear muffs and a hard hat is red faced and anxious. Anybody would be! What with shouting all day while roasting in a safety jacket; is blasted by black sand and forced to put drops in his red rimmed eyes every half hour. But generally, there is a spirit of adventure, excitement and co-operation within the working group and by afternoon the marquee is erected and butting up to the mouth of the cave.

The years of accumulated sand on the cave floor has been removed by members of the Huia Historical Society and the portable stage is now locked into place over the remnants of the original wooden floor.

By Friday evening the generator is running and most of the lights are in place. The dark cliff face above the cave dwarfs the marquee, but it is still an awe inspiring sight. The pukekos that have had their solitude shattered for the past two days, are too stupid to notice. But the frogs are mesmerised by the brightly lit circus tent and blink their bulgy eyes and every so often puff up their throats and give an occasional croak.

By Saturday the helicopter has gone but there is still a hive of activity at the camp ground and the parking lot is full of trucks and trade vehicles. A long line of private cars is forced to park on the sides of the road. Against all predictions, there has not been an accident on the narrow road that links the world with Whatipu!

At the conception stages, the Transport Authority put up the biggest objection on the grounds that the road was not safe for heavy commercial use. Even though they are right in theory, they are proven wrong in practice, because they didn't factor in the Kiwi 'can-do' attitude.

CHAPTER 26

Apartment by the Sea – Joey's Story – Triads

Early Saturday morning, while it is still dark, Kylie Temata is wakened by Joey's yelp for help. With Caitlin and Wiremu still asleep on either side, she carefully pushes the top sheet off her legs, digs her heels into the mattress and concertinas to the end of the bed.

Opening the door to Joey's bedroom, she flicks on the light. It is the same every night since his discharge from hospital! The doctors warning her to expect trauma.

He is standing in the middle of the room with eyes wide open, but not seeing, as his dream relives his ordeal. She knows he is asleep, but it is unnerving to see someone staring at you with pleading, hurt filled eyes.

With practiced hands, she guides him back to his bed and strokes his head while murmuring soothing words. Almost immediately his eyes close and his breathing becomes deep and rhythmical. Looking down at his sleeping face, she knows she loves him and sends another mental thanks to Max Henderson for bringing them together in this luxurious penthouse on the wharf beside the Ferry Buildings. Sure it solves the problem of keeping his star witnesses

safe, but she sees past those words, sensing that under the stern exterior of the District Superintendent beats an astute heart.

It is confusing for Kylie, as her long held conception of the police is not as a care giver. After a lifetime of living in a world of dog-eat-dog, kindness is a stranger.

Joey stirs and opens his eyes, this time fully conscious. Reaching forward he strokes her leg. "Hello beautiful, what brings you to my bedside? Was I sleep walking again?"

Nodding, she gently pushes strands of his long black hair away from his eyes. "I'm sorry for waking you Joey, you need your sleep."

"Hey, I'm the one that should be saying sorry!"

She taps him on his plastered arm, decorated with colourful tattoos by Caitlin and Wiremu. "You can wake me anytime, I'm always available!"

Smiling, he raises his eyebrows. "Really, anytime?"

Punching him playfully on the arm, he reacts as if it hurt, "Just wait till I'm fuckin' healed, I'll show you some interesting holds of my own.!"

Leaning forward, she kisses him gently on the lips.

When he tries to embrace her with his good arm, she pushes him away. "Wait until you're better, I'll be happy to lock bodies."

"Can't fuckin' wait!" Turning, he looks out the sliding doors towards the clock on the Ferry Building tower, but it is still too dark. "What's the time?"

"Five o'clock, the sun will be up in half an hour."

In the distance, she can see Rangitoto Island with its three peaks silhouetted against the faint glow of the rising sun. Looking down again, she runs her fingers through his long black hair enjoying the feel, "Would you like a cup of coffee?"

"Sure, let's have it out on the balcony."

They stand and he wiggles into his slippers as she wraps his dressing gown around his plastered arm then helps him to insert his good arm into its sleeve. As she ties the belt around his waist he clumsily grabs at her again, but she skips away. "I'll go make the coffee."

Sliding open the glass door he steps out onto the balcony and

is enveloped by the smell of the sea and also bitumen from the sleeping city. Below him, he can just make out the white and grey shapes of seagulls that haven't started their morning challenges.

As Kylie sets down a tray of perked coffee, mugs, milk and sugar onto a table behind him, Joey with his arms resting on the balustrade, looks down at the opposite wharf, deep in thought. After a moment, he turns and seats himself beside her, "Thanks hon."

She smiles, liking his possessiveness. "You're welcome.... hon."

He returns the smile, before relaxing back into the soft patio chair enjoying the smell of the freshly brewed coffee. They also enjoy their silent togetherness, but each have very different thoughts.

She is wondering when the bubble will pop. All her life the good times have ended in disappointment, *'Why shouldn't this end the same way? Am I living in a fuckin' temporary world? It is just too good to be true!'*

His thoughts are on money. Since his discharge he has been pre-occupied with the same thought, *'How do I get my hands on Johnny's fuckin' money?'* Reaching forward, he gently squeezes her arm to catch her attention. "Did you know that Johnny had two million dollars hidden under his bed in a sports bag?"

Her eyes open wide. "That much! I knew he was raking in the dough, there was loads of it coming in." She shakes her head, "But I didn't think that much. I always wondered what he did with his fuckin money." Sipping her coffee, she looks at him again, "I thought you would know... I mean being his money man and all that shit!"

He shakes his head. "I only knew about the legit stuff."

Frowning, she asks. "How do you know about the fuckin' money? Only Carla and myself were allowed into his room, were you snooping?"

"No, he showed it to me."

She is surprised. "He showed you two million fuckin' dollars, why would he do that?"

"Coz he had already made up his mind to shut up shop and shoot through, blowing up the fuckin' house and me in it! I'm sure he thought I would die in the barn."

Involuntarily, her hand shakes, rattling her mug against the top of the table. "So you would be dead and then he'd come after me!"

Pointing upwards, he nods. "All the evidence gone in one big fuckin' bang!" Pausing for a moment, he studies her intently, "Carla was found shot on Johnny's bed."

She hides her shock. "Is she dead?"

"Yeah, she was shot four times in the chest."

Allowing her some privacy he studies his coffee mug before taking a sip.

When he looks up he sees tears, but there is no sorrow in her eyes. She shakes her head. "I never liked Carla very much, mainly, I suppose, because she never was my friend. I tried but for some reason she kept her distance. I mean we were both the same, we lived the same life. Shit Joey I was no better than she was except I think she liked being a prostitute and I didn't! Maybe she resented that, if you know what I mean?"

He nods, feeling uncomfortable, knowing that the memories of being a sex slave must be distasteful. He admires her honesty.

Reaching across, she strokes his arm, "Not like you sweet Joey, you kept me sane in that fuckin' hell hole." She wipes the tears with her hand, "That is so much in the past, even though it was only like, yesterday! Nothing like that should happen to anyone, poor Carla." Tears flow again.

Drinking their coffees in silence they have mixed feelings about Carla.

Kylie regretting that she hadn't helped Carla and Joey thinking, *'Good riddance!'* Then, owing to his Catholic upbringing, immediately feeling guilty.

Kylie suddenly sits upright with a frown on her face, "How did you know about Carla?"

"I found out after Max picked me up yesterday."

"Yeah, I was wondering when you were going to tell me what that was all about."

"Well he filled me in on what happened after your phone call." Leaning over he kisses her on the cheek, "You saved my life."

"Actually, it was Hailey who told me that you were fuckin' chained to the back of the barn, did Max tell you that?"

"No, only that you had called."

"She thinks you're pretty cute."

Joey screws a finger into his cheek. "Oh shucks!"

"And so do I!" Kylie picks up her mug in both hands and thinks about Max, then turns back to Joey placing a hand on his plastered arm, "Tell me what else he had to say?... I mean I want to know all about the fuckin' raid and what happened to the gang? She shrugs her shoulders, "What happened to Johnny and Butch? Were they shot, or locked up?"

When he shakes his head, she sits back into her chair with a frown, "How come?"

"The police found a fuckin underground tunnel in Johnny's bedroom, leading out into the bush." He shakes his head, "I didn't know anything about a tunnel! Max wanted to know if I knew, but I didn't. I'm not sure he believed me. Johnny kept it a secret." He shrugs, "They must have escaped because they weren't in the house. It was surrounded. There were tracker dogs and Max was overhead in a fuckin chopper. It was the only way they could have gotten away!"

"Cunning bastards!"

"Yeah, we should have known that they would be slippery."

"Did the police find the money?"

It's Joey's turn to sit up and turns to look at her. "Good question! I asked him if they had found lots of money. He said there were a few thousand dollars in the safe beside my desk." He nods, "I knew about that, but he didn't mention anything about a bag full of cash under a bed, I'm sure he would have told me! They found lots of drugs, not just P. Max says it would have a street value of millions of dollars." He shakes his head, "But no mention of millions of cash.

"Did you tell him?"

Joey looks down at his coffee mug on the table and rotates it, before answering. "No!"

They sit in silence for a few moments, "I think I know where they are hiding, where they have taken the fuckin' money!"

"Really?"

"Yeah! One of my first jobs was to buy a house at Huia Beach.

Johnny must have seen it on Trade-me. Anyway, he gave me a huge wad of cash to buy the house under your name. It was the first time I'd seen so much fuckin' money."

She raises her eyebrows. "He bought a house under my name?"

"Yeah, your name, Kylie Kiri Temata. The ownership papers gives your sister's address as your place of residence."

She is surprised that he knows her middle name and also why Johnny would have bought the house in her name. "Why would he use my fuckin' name?" She shrugs, "I wasn't that important to him."

"So that the house couldn't be traced back to him."

She raises her eyebrows. "You mean to say that I'm a fuckin' landlord?... I mean." She tilts her head up and repeats the words with more elegance, "I'm a fuckin' landlady?"

He smiles. "Yeah, you've been a fuckin' esquire for two years now and you didn't know it!"

She smiles back, enjoying the moment, then punches him on his good arm. "You could have bloody-well told me!"

He shrugs. "It was just business and if I'd told you, you may have told Carla and then Johnny would have known that I'm telling you his fuckin' business. It would have been a breach of confidence. I guess I was just being careful."

"Thank God for that!"

He points a finger at her. "By the way, you don't have to worry about paying the bills at the house coz I've set up automatic payments on everything."

"You're paying with your own fuckin' money?"

"No from your business account at the Kiwibank, it's called Kylie Investments."

"Really? How much is in my account Santa?"

He laughs. "Ten thousand dollars!"

"You're shitting me!"

He shakes his head.

The information is too much of a surprise. Pushing back her chair, she stands and walks over to the edge of the balcony, after a moment she turns, "Can he take it away from me?"

He shakes his head. "Not easily, because I'm the sole signatory on the account, Johnny doesn't know that. Anyway, it will be the last

thing on his mind at the moment."

"Why do you think he is hiding at the house?..... My house!"

"Johnny never did anything without a fuckin' reason. He had something on his mind to spend that sort of money. I almost forgot about the purchase, because it was so fuckin' quick and I never had to follow up with renovations or improvements. All the other houses that I bought were modified so that he could make P, but not the house at Huia. I'm sure he bought it as a fuckin' hide-away in case of trouble." He rests his chin on his clasped hands, "The more I think about it, the more I'm sure that is where they are hiding." He is silent for a moment, "By the way, Max says all the P labs have been busted."

"Fuckin good job, I've seen what P can do to anyone, it turns them into monsters.... Look at Johnny!" Returning to her seat, she refills their mugs from the thermos jug, "What happens next? I mean, how long do we stay here, how safe are we?"

"Max says to stay put while he rounds up the rest of the fuckin' gang." He shakes his head, "That won't be easy, coz they scattered real quick. Hailey and Karl have disappeared."

"I hope she's alright!"

He nods. "She'll be okay, she's a lot fuckin' smarter than Karl. It must have been her choice to stay with him."

This time, Kylie nods. "Yeah she would! I really think she loves him, why I don't fuckin' know, he's such a prick!"

Joey nods, remembering how Karl punched Kylie in the head. "Max has set up an account for us with New World, down at Victoria Market, they will deliver any food we want and DVDs" He shrugs, "What else are we going to do with our time together?"

She moves her chair closer and whispers. "Maybe we can be creative, I know a few tricks!"

The words sting him, "Don't remind me... I don't like what you had to fuckin' go through, you know what I mean!"

Screwing up her face, she is mad at herself for joking about being a prostitute. She makes a promise to herself never to do it again. "Sorry I won't let that happen again, it was silly of me. I'm still excited about owning a fuckin' beach house." She nods, "Sex will be different with you Joey, I know it will! Everything that I do with you will be different from now on. I'll forget what happened before, it means nothing, believe me, it means nothing!"

He reaches forward and kisses her gently on the lips. "You and me now Kyles, everything else is gone, forgotten."

She returns the kiss with passion. "You and me Joey, a new beginning." Looking towards the bedroom where the children are asleep, she continues. "Being cooped up is going to be bloody hard for the kids, I'll try to make it as much fun as possible. It's amazing how happy they seem! They really are good kids considering what a bloody awful mum I've been to them all these years."

He shakes his head. "Don't beat yourself up Kyles, they know you love them." Nodding, he continues, "I'm slowly winning their trust, I like them a lot."

"Thanks Joey, you're wonderful."

"I enjoy their company more than they enjoy mine, but I'm working on it!"

They sit in silence thinking about Caitlin and Wiremu and their futures together. Kylie speaks first. "I suppose we can take them to the gym and the swimming pool on the ground floor. I guess walks around the wharf would be safe enough."

He nods. "I've asked for my laptop to be given back to me. No doubt Max would have copied the hard drive, not that I care. I'll buy a Play Station for the kids and some games, they'll love that!"

She leans over and kisses him on the cheek. "Joey you are the best thing that has ever fuckin' happened to me, I'm so lucky!"

"Me too!!"

She suddenly has a thought. "Are you okay money wise? I mean, have the cops frozen your accounts or anything, I've got some money if you need."

He laughs. "Money's not a problem but thanks anyway! I can't use the gang's company account any more, but I've salted away a few thousand dollars for something just like this! Don't worry about fuckin' money! Anyway, you're worth marrying with a house by the beach."

She snuggles up close to him and locks her fingers into his. "I hope so Aussie Abo."

With fingers still locked he pulls away in mock indignation. "You know the last time I was called that I put a guy in hospital." He smiles, "But from you, it's sweet!"

She squeezes his hand. "I meant it to be!" She pushes up against him even closer wondering about his talk of marriage.

By now the sun has risen and early morning traffic noises intrude on their conversation. Seagulls scream over the spoils of an overturned garbage bin and at the opposite wharf, a tethered ferry churns the green water into a muddy brown.

The increased sounds of a seaside city stirring awake doesn't disturb their togetherness and they remain content, side by side, absorbing the warmth of the morning sun. The coffee in their mugs is cold, but they don't care, as they enjoy the luxury of allowing time to pass without the nagging guilt that they should be doing something.

In this euphoric state, Joey decides he should tell her what has been on his mind for the past week. "You know Kyles, I can't forget about that bag filled with red one hundred dollar bills! It's there when I go to sleep and it's there when I wake."

Kylie withdraws her hands from his. "What else are you thinking?"

"I would like that money, for both of us, for the kids."

"Aren't you still getting paid by the cops?"

"Yeah, sure, but two million dollars would see us on easy street. Anyway I want to take it from Johnny. I don't want the cops to have it, I want it! We both got hurt for that money, do you understand Kyles, it's pay-back time!"

It is the second time he has used her pet name and she likes it. "Yeah... I guess I do." She shakes her head, "Shit, I hate putting us in danger again!"

"I'll be putting me in danger, not you!"

She shakes her head. "No you won't!" They stare at each other for a moment before she reaches forward and gently strokes his arm, "I won't let you get that money without my help, is that a deal?"

Looking down at his injured arm, he nods. "Okay, but we'll split it fifty, fifty."

She squeezes his arm. "I don't care about the money, you can keep it all, I really don't care."

"No, fifty, fifty."

"Okay!"

"Good, now we have some planning to do. The first thing will be to organise a babysitter for the kids. Max may be able to arrange that if we tell him we need a break. Like flying to Queenstown, or something like that, I think he'll go for it!"

She nods as he continues,

"We won't tell Max about the money, okay?"

"Okay!"

Not far from the Ferry Building is a large marina nestling under the Auckland Harbour Bridge. Amongst the rows of neatly tethered boats is a large launch and inside, asleep, is a Triad hit man, Feng Tai-Lung. In his organization, he is also known as The Red Pole or Master Executioner.

He opens his eyes and feels the rocking and hears the slopping of water against the hull. In the comfort of the familiar movement and sound, he almost drifts back to sleep, except the smells are wrong.

As a young man there never was perfume on the pillows of his father's drug smuggling sampan, only the smell of dried fish, diesel and sweat!

Responding to years of army training, his mind is now alert and the smile disappears. He sits up and turns to look at the naked back of a young Thai prostitute gifted to him by Ozzie Clem, owner of the launch and leader of the Pit Bull gang. She is still asleep and not aware of the pending soreness of her bruised body, her dreams are troubled.

Feng, being three times her size and many times stronger, was demanding all night with an insatiable sex drive. At last he had fallen asleep, stiff inside her and crushing her with his sweaty body, she used all her strength to wriggle out from under him, and soon escaped into her own exhausted sleep.

After a quick check for any danger he sinks back into his pillow and looks down at the sleeping girl's faultless skin. She is beautiful and he wonders why white men always think that Chinese only like to fuck Asians? His own preference being tall, blonde, blue eyed Scandinavians. Something of a treat when asked to deal with European drug cheats. He shakes his head. *'Why are Europeans so predictable?'*

Looking around the master bedroom of the fifty foot launch, he admires the precision and opulence of its finish. For some time now, he has been wanting to buy a new boat for cruising around Macau Harbour and he likes the feel, the size and the trim of this one.

The previous day, Google told him that a 'Salthouse Sovereign', the name attached to the stern cabin, was built in New Zealand. He looks at the mahogany and walnut finish of the master bedroom and nods. *'Yes I'm going to buy one of these. Too risky right now. I'll wait until I return to Hong Kong and use a fuckin' ship broker.'* With these thoughts, he wonders how quickly the syndicate of Auckland gangs will be in finding Johnny and Butch. He remembers again the unfortunate coincidence that on the same night they were going to break into the gang's headquarters they had been forced to pull over to the side of the country road while a large number of police vehicles rushed past. It was obvious where they were going and the three assassins couldn't risk being stopped and searched, so they turned around and headed back to the marina.

Feng is jolted out of his reverie by heavy footsteps on the deck above and speculates that Clem and his gang have arrived. Pushing the sleeping girl off the bed he scrambles to find his clothing. A moment later, proving him right, Clem's bright blue eyes and flattened nose appear in the hatchway. He laughs at the sight of Feng's rotund nudity. Typical of his outback upbringing, he flings an insult. "Hey mate, I told you I was coming at nine, you Chinese fucker!"

Being the most feared killer in all of Asia, uncouth insults never happen, so he is momentarily stunned. Ice flows through his veins and all movement seems to go into slow motion. It is the prelude to another killing, but he is checked by Clem's friendly advance with a capped cup of coffee. "Didn't know what sort of tea you Chinese drink so brought you a fuckin' coffee instead!... You do drink coffee?"

Feng nods as Clem continues,

"Sorry mate, no sugar, there's some in the galley if you want it"

Feng shakes his head, as the moment passes. *'What strange people these Australians, they offend one moment, then befriend the next!... It must be lack of an ancient culture!'* He decides to ignore the insult this time, but it won't be forgotten. "No, I don't take sugar, you fucking oor-strail-yin!"

Clem laughs, whacks him on the back and then hands him his coffee. "I've got some good news for you!" He points upward, "I'll meet you up on the bridge when you're ready. Take your time, I'm in no fuckin' hurry!" Looking over at the young girl cowering in the corner, he asks, "She look after you last night? I'll get you some-one else if you like, how about a dwarf?" He laughs again.

Feng stops buttoning his island shirt and stares at him in disbelief, then shrugs. "She's okay, her tits are small," He looks up at Clem with a forced smile, "But so is everything else!" He jerks his pelvis forwards, "And that I like!"

Clem laughs and punches him hard on the arm before turning and climbing up the stairs.

Feng scowls, then shakes his head, bending his elbow backwards and forwards to rid himself of the pain.

Once dressed, he opens the door to the crew room and talks to Wi and Po his two soldiers who are armed and watching behind the slats of the door.

The enclosed fly bridge, on top of the boat is spacious with a blue padded couch sweeping around in a half circle facing the bow. A matching four seater faces the stern. Behind it are the boat controls and a Captain's Chair.

Clem is seated in the centre of the half circle facing the stern, with two of his enforcers on either side.

Feng enters and seats himself, facing Clem, also with his men on either side.

Without a preamble, Clem gets straight to the point. "We have located Johnny's fuckin' hideout." He gives his iPad to one of his men and gestures towards Feng.

As Feng studies the street view of a beach house, Clem continues, "Johnny and Butch are in that fuckin' house right now. It's not far from here, about an hour, South West." He points, "It's on the Manukau Harbour, that's the next fuckin' harbour. The house is at the end of Huia Bay, number two thousand one hundred and eleven. Even I can remember a fuckin' house number like that, two one one one."

Looking up from the laptop, Feng wonders if it is a trap, "How did you find them?"

"Johnny took me there once when we had to talk. I thought that might be where he would go after the raid, so he's not such a fuckin' smart arse after all!"

"How do I get to……," He looks down at the screen and has trouble saying the Maori place name, "Huia?"

"No fuckin' problem, I've printed a copy of Google Maps with the directions from here to there. You also have fuckin' GPS in your car." Feng nods, as Clem hands him the print out, "Do you need anything else from me?"

Remembering the earlier insults, Feng stares directly into his eyes and delays answering so that his words will have more effect. "Why would I want any help from you? We are professional killers. We can kill without trace, anyone, anywhere at any-time!"

The inferred threat irritates Clem, but the mission is too important for him and the syndicate, so he pretends he hasn't noticed. Only the pulsing of a vein on his neck indicates that the taunt has hit its mark.

Feng stands and smiles his best smile while handing the iPad to Po, his most trusted soldier and gestures toward Clem, "Thanks for your hospitality and for the use of your car, I'll leave it at an airport hotel. I'll text you where and leave the keys at the front desk."

Clem nods and then waits for Feng and his men to depart.

Once out of ear shot, he turns and whispers to his two enforcers. "Did you hear what that fat fuck said?" They nod, as he continues,

"So help me, one of these days I'll find and kill that fuckin' fat arsed chinky chonk!"

One of his men asks. "Thinking of a trip to Hong Kong boss?"

This time it is Clem's turn to nod.

Max Henderson thinks it's a good idea that Kylie and Joey should get away for a few days and knows that Queenstown is far enough to be safe. He is relieved to hear that they will be paying for the trip themselves, as he is already way over his monthly budget. Also pleasing, Kylie's kids will be staying behind ensuring their return. The baby sitting issue was solved after a quick chat to Correction Services. A new recruit is given the live-in job of feeding and caring for Wiremu and Caitlin. She is fully briefed and is looking forward to her first assignment that has an element of danger.

Soon after the phone call from Max, Joey covers his head with the hood of his jacket and at a rental car shop on Quay Street, pays a deposit with a credit card that is active and matching to a false passport.

It is mid-day by the time the Corrections Services lady arrives and Joey and Kylie emerge from the covered parking concealed behind the grey tinted windows of a new Kia Sorento. It is their first taste of freedom for two weeks! With Kylie driving, Joey relaxes back in the luxury of the soft seat and flips open his cache of CDs extracting his favourite album, Pete Murray's, 'Blue Sky Blue'. Selecting track four, the opening guitar chords of 'Free' starts to play and he is transported back to his surfing days at Byron Bay. Instead of soothing, Pete's familiar mellow voice has the opposite effect and he becomes homesick and melancholy, he misses Australia and he misses his mum.

Kylie turns up the sound, listening to Pete's voice.

Joey nods. "He is my favourite singer, Pete Murray, he's an Aussie, have you heard of him?"

She shakes her head. "No, but I like the sound of his voice."

"He writes his own stuff, good eh!"

They are silent for a few minutes, listening to the words of his song. At the end of a track, he turns towards her again, "Did you know we went to the same college, Saint Joseph's Nudgee? He was there before my time, but I heard a lot about him, he was a bit of a fuckin' legend!"

Joey is silent for quite some time thinking about his teenage years. He decides to tell her about his life in Australia, "One summer I met him surfing at Byron Bay, it was a chance meeting. Because we were from the same school, we hit it off straight away. I guess it was because we had lots in common, I kind-of play the guitar a-bit and sing." He shakes his head, "Not as good as Pete though! It was a blast the best fuckin' summer of my life! We surfed and partied," He looks at her again, "His songs are about his life, you know, the troubles he had. I understand what he is singing about, like he is singing to me…. Listen to him sing, you wouldn't think he was a tough fuckin' rugby player would you?"

Kylie shakes her head intrigued that he is at last telling her about his life in Australia.

Turning off the North-Western Motorway at the Waterview tunnel, Kylie heads West along Old Great North Road.

Joey closes his eyes as he listens to the music. Thinking about the good times at school, he sits up and turns to her again, "You know he would have been a top fuckin' athlete if he hadn't buggered up his knee."

She smiles at him. "You like him a lot don't you Joey?"

"Yeah, he lost his dad when he was eighteen, just like me."

She is aware that he has opened up a chapter in his life that he has avoided in their times together. She has told him about her life, but he has been secretive about his own. She knows he has been hiding something. "Tell me about your dad. When you say you lost your dad does that mean he's dead?"

Nodding, Joey stares out the front window,

"What happened?"

"He was killed!"

Because she loves Joey, she delves deeper sensing that his father's death had a huge influence on his life, "Do you want to talk about it?"

She gets a curt reply. "I'd rather not!

Kylie studies Joey for a moment and he stares back, with

expressionless eyes, *Is this the right time to tell her?* He looks down at his hands and whispers, "I killed him"!

Not sure that she heard him correctly, she asks. "Did you say you killed him"?

He looks at her with torment in his eyes. "Yeah, I killed the son-of-a-bitch!"

Raising her eyebrows, she slowly exhales through pursed lips. "Pheww, that is not good!"

"You said it!"

She studies him for a moment. "Is that why you are in New Zealand, are you on the run? Did you do time?"

Shaking his head he doesn't look at her as he continues, softly. "He was beating my mum, I had to fuckin' stop him!" With the killing of his dad, still etched in his mind, he looks at her with wild eyes. "She took the fuckin' rap, I didn't want her too, but she did! Jeez I owe her heeps!"

She is so engrossed in his story, that she almost misses the bypass at the Avondale Race Course, as they head towards the Waitakere Ranges. Reaching over, she places her hand on his injured arm. "Is your mum still in jail?"

He mumbles. "She's still there, but she says she'll be out soon. Early parole, you know, good behaviour and all that!" Not wishing to discuss his life any further, he turns his head away and looks out the side window.

Both are silent for some time listening to Pete's lyrics, *"... I've seen better days....."* The song continues and when he sings. *"... when I go down on my knees and pray...",* the words invoke a thought in Kylie's mind.

Not sure she should say anything, she looks at Joey and sees that the haunted look has returned. Deep inside her, is a cultural demand that makes a Maori woman protective and loyal to her man. It is this fine trait that compels her to voice her thoughts. "You're a Catholic boy, right?"

He nods,

"Do you go to confession?"

Glancing briefly at her, he turns away again,

"It might help... I mean, I'm the last person to talk about going to Church, but I know the few times I've gone, I've left feeling good. Something happens inside of me that I can't explain. Not as dirty. Not as guilty. Maybe it would help you too."

Joey remains silent for some time with his head still turned toward the window and she is worried that she has gone too far! Reaching over, she strokes the back of his head, "It's just a thought Joey. I only want to help you, sometimes problems are just too fuckin' big!"

This time, he turns back to her, and his face is pale and he lets out a tight throated laugh. "You know what my school motto is?"

She shakes her head,

"Signum Fide. That means you are supposed to be a sign of faith, some bloody sign I've turned out to be eh."

She surprises him with her next words. "Good people kill in war Joey, you were in a fuckin' war zone with your dad!"

Crossing, then uncrossing his legs, he nods. "Yeah you're right, I should go to confession, I'll take mum, yeah the two of us will go to confession, she'll like that!" His mood changes and he smiles at her, "You are an amazing lady Kylie."

She can feel him studying her intently for some time and is not prepared for his next words, "Will you marry me?"

Glancing at him briefly, she frowns. "Don't tease me Joey, that is too serious a question."

He nods. "I meant it to be!"

"Really?"

"Yeah, really, really, really!"

"Well I'd better say yes before you change your fuckin' mind! I do love you Joey!"

"Me too!"

"Does that mean you love yourself or me?"

He laughs. "Both!"

As she drives, Kylie wriggles the fingers of her left hand and wonders what sort of ring he will buy? She feels more content than she has ever felt before and laughs out loud, *Fancy that, I'm going to marry this wonderful man!'*

At Titirangi, they stop to buy binoculars, backpacks, some food and drink, large sunglasses and two floppy hats. Holding hands, they cross the street looking like two backpackers, which is exactly what Joey intended.

Back in the car, they turn South down Huia Road and follow the windy road towards the mouth of the Manukau Harbour.

Kylie smiles at Joey. "So mister super sneak, how are we going to steal the money?"

He shrugs. "Don't know exactly.... I have a kind of a plan that is pretty loose!" He frowns, "Mainly because I don't know for sure if Johnny and Butch will be at the house... I think they will be coz I'm guessing that they will think that I won't remember buying it." The frown goes and he taps the dashboard, "They won't recognise this baby, so it will be safe to drive past a couple of times. I visited the house so I can remember its location and a few of the land marks around it. It's just past the local store and across the road from a boat ramp, should be easy to find." Pushing his head back into the head rest he thinks about a plan that has been evolving over the past few days. Still deep in thought he turns towards her again, "I'm pretty sure the car park to the right of the boat ramp is out of sight of the house, that's where we'll leave the car! As long as we look like backpackers I don't think Johnny or Butch will recognise us. There's a side road that goes up the hill beside the house." He laughs, pointing at her, "Your house! The side road has a bush clad ravine between the house and the road, that's where we can keep watch." He shakes his head, "We won't be able to see the front but they would have parked their car out the back in the garage anyway. If they leave we'll be able to see them." He kooks at her and shakes his head, "We may have to keep watch until it's dark, are you prepared for that?"

Kylie cocks her thumb towards the back seat. "I bought some mosquito spray."

He nods. "I noticed, not just a pretty face eh?" His smile fades as his thoughts return to his plan, "It will be sheer bad luck if they stay in for the night, but I'm picking they will risk going out, seeing it's Saturday. I bet they hate being cooped up." Concentrating hard, his eyes are squeezed to small slits, then he nods, "Yeah, they've both done time." He turns to her, "What's the bet they'll be on fuckin' P and drunk, they'll want some action."

Glancing briefly towards him, she nods. "Yeah, that's what's fuckin' freaking me out. What if we get caught? We both know what sort of animals Johnny and Butch can be. They're worse when they're high. I'm weaker than those two and you with your arm in a fuckin' sling!" She shrugs. "I'm just weighing up the odds."

Reaching forward he opens the glove compartment. "I'll show you something." Removing two items, he shows her a black leather pistol holster and then a belt with a sheath, exposing the handle of a Taser. Placing them beside him on the console, he pops the clasp of the leather holster, withdrawing a small black pistol and waves it backwards and forwards, "This is a police issue Glock seventeen, semi-automatic pistol." He taps it against the dash, "It's made of fuckin' plastic, but it can kill at fifty metres." He returns it to its holster and clips the flap shut. Removing the Taser, he studies it closely, "Yesterday I told Max that I wanted to be armed, he took me down to the armoury and showed me how to use the pistol and this Taser. I'm not supposed to use them unless attacked, I think he said something like, 'Only if it's a matter of life or death!'"

Studying the Taser again, he rotates it left and right and then looks up with a determined look on his face, "Kyles, I'll use these weapons against Johnny and Butch no fuckin' problem, so don't be afraid!.... I don't know too much about Tasers, except they whack you with fifty thousand volts." He points towards the pistol, "I know all about the Glock I was captain of our college shooting team and we were never beaten!" He shakes his head, "Never thought I would have to use one of them outside the fuckin' shooting range!"

Sheathing the Taser he returns it to the glove compartment, shutting it with a bang, "You can have the Taser and I'll have the fuckin' pistol, okay?"

She shakes her head. "I don't know how to use it! I mean, do you have to touch them with it or can you fire it like a pistol? How far away can you be? I've seen it being used on TV, but I can't remember what you have to do."

"When we get to Huia Bay, I'll show you, it's worth taking a risk for two million dollars!"

Still not convinced, she frowns. "I guess, but if it becomes a matter of life or death versus two million bucks, I'd rather choose, life!"

"It won't come to that."

"I fuckin' hope not."

CHAPTER 27

Unexpected Rendezvous – Money! Money! Money!

It is low tide at Huia bay. The half kilometer sweep of muddy sand is spotted with shallow puddles and flocks of sea birds. It is a pretty bay, protected from the prevailing southwesterly by the headlands of the Waitakere Ranges. Always too shallow for modern day commercial use, only flat bottomed sailing barges of yester-year were able to ply their trade bringing supplies to the few settlers at the mill beside the river. Dictated by the tides, the sailors would hasten to unload, and then reload, before returning to Onehunga with a few cans of cream and kauri timber. When the timber ran out there was always a market for the cream and long lengths of kanuka firewood.

The bay was sleepy then and it still is, except for a flurry of activity in eighteen sixty-three when H.M.S. Orpheus ran aground on a sandbar at the mouth of the harbour. The horrific loss of one hundred and eighty-nine sailors is still the greatest loss in New Zealand's maritime history! Making it even more tragic, most of the sailors were trainees between the age of twelve and eighteen. The resulting Admiralty inquiry found everyone else to blame except the Captain and his Senior Officers! No one asked the local

Maori who believed that their God, Rangi was seeking utu for the cutting down of a sacred puriri tree on an island in the Manukau Harbour!

Whatever the reasons, Kylie, driving around the semicircle of the bay is too preoccupied to remember being told about the shipwreck. Even the tranquil beauty of the bay does not register as she counts the beach houses on the inland side of the road. *'One, two, three, four, there it is, as Joey said it' would be, tucked up under the slope of the bush. Can't see anyone inside?'* Slowing, they pass the house, glad that they are hidden by the tinted windows, she looks at Joey. "Is that the house? Did you see anyone?"

"Yeah, no, I didn't see anyone." He shrugs, "We were too fuckin' quick, they could be out the back." He points to the end of the beach, "Carry on down to the reserve there's a turn-around by the toilets."

She nods. "Just what I need, a fuckin' toilet, how'd you guess?... I was going to stop at the store but forgot!"

Driving past the reserve with its cut grass, picnic tables and a playground, Kylie can picture her kids climbing up the ropes and swinging on the swings, "This is a really pretty spot."

Turning at the entrance to the park, she stops beside the toilets, "I'm going to enjoy using my beach house, the kids will love it here!"

Joey nods but is pre-occupied, worried that Kylie's involvement in his plans will cause complications, he always prefers to work alone.

As she disappears around the side of the toilet block, he removes his sling and tests his arm up and down. Yes, even with his arm in plaster he would be better off on his own.

When she returns and starts the motor he decides to speak his mind. "Kyles don't take this the wrong way, but I'd prefer to find the fuckin' money on my own." He continues quickly, seeing her frown, "If all goes well it will be no fuckin' problem, but if it turns to shit, I have to have the freedom to react. There won't be time to tell you what to do, do you understand?"

She studies him for a moment reluctant to let him face danger alone. She also knows that he underestimates her strength and ability to survive. Not being sure of her thoughts, he adds, "I'll show you how to use the fuckin' Taser, you can keep it with you in the car."

Nodding, she turns off the motor then looks around the Reserve to see if they are alone. They are both aware that for some reason there seems to be a continuous flow of cars heading towards the entrance to the harbour. Most pass by without stopping, but one turns towards them. It is moving far too fast for the condition of the road and skids to a halt beside them, propelling loose stones into the flax bushes. To their surprise, two couples dressed as pirates jump out of the car and yahooing, race towards the toilets. Re-appearing a short time later, they smile at Joey's quizzical look jump into their car and race back to join the flow of traffic heading to the dance.

Kylie looks at Joey who shrugs. She points at the glove compartment. "Do you want to show me how it works?"

Nodding he opens the car door and gets out, then checks again to see if they are alone. Leaning into the car he is about to remove the Taser from the glove compartment when another car turns off the main road and drives rapidly towards them.

Again they are surprised to see that the passengers and driver are also dressed as pirates and they also disappear into the toilet block.

On reappearing, Joey calls out. "Gid-day guys, what's with the pirate gear? You're the second lot that have come down here dressed as pirates, what's up?"

One of the pirate answers. "There's a fancy dress dance at Whatipu." He turns, looking at the line of slow moving cars, "We're not the only ones going to the dance, eh!" He raises his hand, "Catch yuh later matey."

Once again Joey reaches into the car and this time removes the Taser and cartridges from the glove compartment and walks around to Kylie's side of the car. With the flax bushes and the toilet block screening them from the road, he opens her door. "We'll have to be quick!"

Holding the Taser up-side down, he inserts a loaded cartridge with the other, "You clip it in like this. When you pull the trigger two electrodes shoot out of the Taser. The maximum distance is ten metres so you need to be quite close to your target. It's just like shooting a pistol, you point and shoot. It's very light so you don't need two hands, do you want to give it a go?" When she nods, he continues, "Shoot it into the flax." Handing it to her, he can see she is nervous, "Just point and pull the fuckin' trigger Kyles."

Swinging it backwards and forwards at full arm's length, she asks. "Does it kick much?"

"A little, and upwards, it's not that bad." He points towards the flax in front of the car, "Go on, shoot the fuckin' flax!"

Taking a step forward, she raises the Taser and with eyes half closed pulls the trigger. There is a sharp 'crack!' and the electrodes thump into the pulp of the flax leaves producing a whiff of smoke. She turns, smiles and hands him the Taser. "Easy as!"

Releasing the spent cartridge he returns it to the glove compartment and then reloads with another, "It's ready to go!"

Nodding, she gets into the car and starts the motor as he places the Taser beside her on the console between their seats.

High above the bay, Ozzie Clem's black Holden Cruz descends around a cliff top bend. Although the three Chinese are hardened killers they are not immune to nature's beauty. Apart from Feng, son of Lee Tai-lung who lived an opulent life on Macau Island, the other two have grown up in crowded high rise apartments.

The unspoiled and unpopulated bay is a treat for Wi and Po who have an unobstructed view through the front window of the car.

Feng, Triad warlord, is seated in the back behind his driver Wi Chun. The Triad soldiers are in their mid twenties and they obey Feng without question. In their world he is number 426 and known as 'The Red Pole' and his word is law.

Feng trusts Po Ling but not Wi Chun who has a tenuous family connection to number 489, 'The Dragon Head', leader of all the Triad gangs. Feng can't understand why the Dragon Head has asked him to come to this small country to kill two insignificant gang leaders. Why him, is it to keep an eye on his grandson? Does he not trust Wi? This worries him as he senses in Wi an unpredictability and the same ruthless, demonic determination as in his grandfather.

As the three look at the sweep of the bay, most of the appeal is the

lack of human habitation. It is a luxury that only the very rich of Hong Kong or Macau can afford. Here it is spread out before them, and theirs to enjoy, without restrictions. Even the cockles, pipis, rock oysters and mussels are free!

They had no trouble finding Huia Road, as their GPS speaks to them in Cantonese. As they follow the winding road downwards the now familiar sing-songy female voice tells them that they are a kilometre from their destination, two thousand, one hundred and eleven Huia Road. The pronunciation of 'Huia' is incorrect, but of no importance to Feng who has Google Maps open on his lap. Still above the bay, he can see a row of houses on the inland side of the road that follows the sweep of the beach. Pointing, he instructs. "That's the target, the last house at the end."

Immediately Wi and Po switch to soldier mode and search for strategic locations around the house. The windows of the Cruz are tinted black so they are not worried about their close scrutiny as they drive slowly past the house. There is nothing particularly outstanding about the two storey, white planked house, except it is tidy and functional. Its main job is to be a beach house and as that it is more than adequate. The upper level houses three dormitory style bedrooms cut into the slope of the red tin roof. Below, on the ground floor, are another two bedrooms. At the rear of the property, against the fence, is a large garage and a mobile home sitting on concrete blocks.

Since the purchase Johnny has created an extra entrance at the side of the property, leading to another road. Between the house and the side road is a small but steep bush clad ravine.

Not detecting any movement inside or out, Feng instructs Wi to turn right up the side road and discover Johnny's second entrance cut through the thick bush. Like its name, Upland Road is steep and windy and there is no convenient place to park, so they turn around at the next driveway and make their way slowly back down again.

At the intersection with the house partially obscured by bush to his left, Wi stops and waits for further instructions. He is surprised by the number of cars passing by and not towards Auckland but towards the uninhabited mouth of the harbour, *'Very strange?'*

Feng also studies the traffic for a moment, then turns his attention towards the boat ramp and the car park across the road. An L shaped row of large macrocarpa trees shade the parking lot on two sides. One row is parallel with the highway and the other at right angles, ends at the beach. A good place to hide, out of sight of traffic and the target house.

After a short wait there is a gap in the traffic and Feng points across the road and Wi accelerates forward.

It is not until they turn into the car park that they notice the rear of a late model silver Kia parked under the trees. Wi drives under the over-hanging branches, swings around and then backs the car until their bumper touches the boundary posts. To their left, twenty metres away, and closer to the beach, is the silver Kia. They watch to see if it is occupied, but its dark tinted windows make it impossible to see inside.

Still seated, they search the surrounding area for the occupants of the car, the beach, the footpath, even the wide expanse of the Reserve behind them, but there is nobody to be seen.

If it wasn't for the increasing flow of vehicles on the road, the area would be deserted.

Feng shrugs. "Don't know where they are? There's no boat trailer and they don't have a tow bar so they are not out in a boat. Anyway the tide's too far out!"

Po points to the orange number plates. "It's a rental, maybe tourists?"

Feng shrugs, he doesn't mind collateral damage but it's untidy and he doesn't want to leave any incriminating evidence no matter how unlikely that might be.

The mystery of the occupants, or occupant is solved, when the driver's door is suddenly opened by an olive skinned, long haired young lady who is looking intently at her cell phone. Without a sideways look towards them she holds it above her head before moving around to the front of the car and then towards the beach.

Stopping on its grassy verge, she presses the key pad with an agile thumb, places the phone up to her ear and listens for the dial tone.

This time she is connected and she turns and signals towards the car for Joey to come and join her. "Hi Charlotte, this is Kylie." She listens, "Yes, I'm well thanks," Again she listens, "Yes a great holiday, thanks to you. I just wanted to know how you're getting on with the kids, are they behaving themselves?" She nods, "That's great, can you put them on please?"

By now, Joey has joined her and they stand side by side facing out into the broad reach of the empty bay, "Hi Caitlin, are you having fun?" Again she smiles, "Charlotte is nice eh! You be a good girl and go to bed when she tells you, okay?" She listens again, "Yeah, we're having fun too." Turning to Joey, she winks.

He holds out his hand for the phone and she reluctantly gives it to him. "Hi Caitlin, this is Joey, I'm looking after your mummy real good!" He wraps his plastered arm around her back and squeezes her with is fingers, "Yeah I'll bring you a present!....... No, it won't be an iPod!" He looks at Kylie and raises his eyebrows, "It will be a surprise, okay?.... Good, here's your mum again."

"Hi Caitlin, be a good girl and give the phone to Wiremu please."

There is a pause and then Caitlin's voice is heard again.

Kylie nods, "You had fish and chips for tea, that sounds yummy, now give the phone to Wiremu please."

Again there is a pause, "Yes we're coming home soon, Caitlin give the phone to Wiremu!"

Standing beside Caitlin, Wiremu has been impatiently rocking from one foot to the other, but now in frustration snatches the phone out of her hand and she storms out of the room slamming the door behind her. He places the phone to his ear. "Hi mum, are you all right?"

"Yes son, Joey and I are fine, we are having a real good time, are you okay?"

"Yes mum!"

"Be a good boy and look after your sister, okay?"

"She's a pain, she wants the Play Station all the time."

"Yeah I know, but you have to be a big boy and share it with her. Maybe you could teach her some easier games, will you do that for me?"

He screws up his face. "Sure mum, when are you coming home? I'm tired of being here at the wharf! Can we go and visit Aunty Hailey soon?"

Kylie sighs. "Not much longer now, you have to be a strong boy for me and look after your sister." She presses the phone harder into her ear as if that will bring him closer, "If we're all really good maybe Joey will take us to Australia for a holiday, wouldn't that be fun?" She looks up at Joey who nods vigorously, "Go to bed when Charlotte says so, okay? We'll be home tomorrow.... Bye son, see you soon."

Wanting to hold onto her a little longer, he asks, "Will you bring me a present too?"

"Of course we will, kiss, kiss, love you, see you tomorrow... bye Wiremu." She hangs up and clutching hold of Joey starts to sob.

Hand in hand they return to the car still oblivious to the other car parked beside them.

Once seated, Joey turns to Kylie. "I'm sure they'll be all-right. The baby sitter is a trained professional, they'll be fine."

Kylie wipes her tears with the tips of her fingers and then sighs. "I guess you're right, we'll be back with them pretty soon anyway."

Feng thought nothing of the pretty Maori girl making a phone call, but he is sure he has seen a picture of Joey before. Opening a file on his computer he scrolls through the gang members until he sees Joey's picture and double clicks to enlarge it. Turning his iPad towards the front seat he shows the photo to Wi and Po who nod. "He is Joey Moser an Australian, Johnny's book keeper.... I wonder what he is doing here in the car park? Why isn't he in the house?"

Po smiles then pumps his hips as if having sex.

Feng and Wi laugh. Then Feng shrugs and the smile disappears, "Maybe, but should we kill them, they are not our targets, only Johnny Schmidt and Butch Gueber. Let's wait and see if they will leave. If they don't then I'll decide whether they are a threat. I don't want anyone to connect this car with the killings."

Further discussion is interrupted when they see the car door open again and Joey gets out wearing dark glasses and a floppy hat. He opens the rear door and pulls out a backpack depositing it on the front seat. They see him bend down but are not able to see him open the glove compartment and remove the pistol and loaded magazines, placing them in his back pack. They are also unable to see Kylie reaching behind her and pulling her backpack over the headrest, unzipping it and removing a can of mosquito spray. She offers the spray with one hand and pulling his T shirt towards her with the other, kisses him on the lips. "Good luck double-o-seven!"

He pulls away with mock indignation. "Well I never Miss fuckin' Moneypenny!" Zipping up his backpack he ambles towards the road and waits for a gap in the traffic before wandering up Upland Road.

Feng frowned then shook his head as he watched Joey walk past their car with just the briefest glance in their direction before crossing over the road. When he didn't head toward the house but up the road beside it, he was even more confused. "*What's he doing?*" He shakes his head again, "That's got to be the book keeper! I've checked the photos again and the girl is one of the gang. I'm sure of it, she's one of Johnny's fucks! But what's she doing with Joey?" He pauses for a moment deep in thought, "Doesn't matter we'll kill them both and leave their bodies on Johnny's doorstep. Better still, we'll remove the Cruz ownership papers from the glove compartment and place them in Joey's pocket. That will be a nice little reminder to Ozzie Clem. I wonder what the cops will make of that?" He laughs, but it's not a pretty laugh. Thinking of Clem he reaches down and pulls out a black leather case from under the driver's seat. Placing it on his lap, he flicks up two spring loaded clasps on the front of the lid. Inside are a variety of weapons supplied by Clem. Three thin wired garrotes, with bone handles, three .40 Smith & Wesson pistols with screw on suppressors and extra magazines. Taking up most of the space are three Chinese Army night glasses. He hands each of them a garrote. "We'll use these, no bullets, no trace!" He is about to issue further orders when a Toyota Landcruiser turns into the driveway at Johnny's place and he knows that this is a game changer!

Joey, hiding beneath the nikau palms and kawakawa creepers

growing in the ravine, gets a partial view of the Toyota as it approaches the garage. He hears the clatter as the roller door opens and sees the top of the Toyota disappearing inside.

A moment later, Johnny and Butch emerge into the late afternoon sun wearing pirate hats, eye patches and knee length black leather boots. They are drunk and jump into the air trying to click their heels together before clumping up the wooden stairs to the back door.

Joey's phone is on 'silent mode' in the side of his backpack, removing it he makes it active and waits until it connects, then dials Kylie.

The Kia is facing away from the house and she doesn't see the arrival of the Landcruiser. She is startled by the phone ringing. Answering, Joey's voice cuts in and out, so she tells him to hold on as she makes her way to the edge of the beach. Once there, Joey's excited whisper can be heard more clearly. "Can you hear me Kyles?"

"Yes Joey, okay now, I had to go to the beach, where are you?"

"I'm hiding in the ravine at the back of the house. Hey thanks for the spray, there's bloody sand flies and mosquitoes every-where! Anyway, did you see Johnny and Butch arrive in their fuckin' Landcruiser?"

She immediately swings around towards the house. "Bugger, no I didn't, are they in the house now?"

"Yeah they are! Hey guess what, they're dressed as pirates just like that other guys we saw at the park! They must be going to the dance tonight... They're pissed out of their fuckin' minds!"

"Maybe they'll leave soon, that would be good!"

"That's what I was thinking, this could be our lucky day!"

There is silence for a while, then his whispering voice becomes more urgent. "They're coming out of the back door and heading for the garage. They've got a bottle of fuckin' booze in each hand."

There is silence again which lasts longer than she would like, which worries her. "You all right Joey, you still there?"

"Yeah no problems, they're leaving now, can you see them?"

As soon as she sees the Toyota she turns her back to the road and involuntarily matches his whisper. "They're coming this way, I'm

going to move slowly back to the car, shit I hope they don't come into the fuckin' car park!" Her heart is pounding as she strolls back toward the Kia as casually as she can without looking up. What she really wants to do is run and hide.

Once inside the car she is able to relax, "It's okay they have gone past, they're heading towards the ranges, they must be going to the fuckin' dance.... I'm in the car now."

The reception is bad again, but she is able to make out his words. "Wait for my call, drive up the side road, I'll be hiding in the bushes just past the bus shelter, okay?"

"Sure Joey. Just be as quick as you can! Good luck finding the money, love you!" Kissing the phone she clicks it shut and sends a silent prayer for his safe return, something she has not done for many years.

The decision to kill Kylie, then Joey, was made by Feng, just before the arrival of Johnny and Butch. Their departure soon after catches Feng in two minds. Should he abandon the killings and follow the Toyota, or stay in the car park and wait for their return? Deciding to do both, he leans out of the window and tells Po to kill the girl, then find and kill Joey then wait for his return.

The window goes up and the car departs, turning left, just in time to see the Toyota two hundred metres ahead, also turning left at the end of the Reserve.

Po with map in hand walks towards Kylie. He is smartly dressed in a suit and an open necked shirt and looks every bit the part of a tourist seeking information.

Kylie doesn't sense danger, although she wonders why the car has gone. The afternoon sun is still scorching hot and Kylie has the air conditioning running at full blast with the windows up as the man approaches.

Bending down his smiling oriental face is close to the window.

She presses a button on the arm rest and the window slides down.

Returning the smile, she is completely off guard. "Can I help you?"

His English is not good but sufficient to indicate that he needs directions. Tapping his map and stepping back from the car door he hopes she will get out, but she stays seated. Still smiling, he approaches the car again and reaches down to open the door, but it is locked.

Kylie immediately knows she is in danger.

Sensing her fear he attacks throwing a short knockout punch through the open window, but she is street wise and instinctively jerks backwards and his fist brushes the side of her chin. There is hardly any contact, but it is sufficient to jostle her brain and for a moment she is dazed.

Reaching behind, he withdraws a garrote from under the flap of his jacket and holding it in both hands pushes it over her head and twists it around her neck.

Kylie knows she is being throttled, but instead of panicking and tearing at the wire with her hands, she feels for the Taser beside her, pulls it out of its sheath and sticks it hard into his face and pulls the trigger.

At point blank range it shoots its two electrodes up inside his nostrils, discharging its fifty thousand volts. The closeness of the explosive charge pushes splinters of nose bone up into his eye sockets and the electrodes embed into the moist upper limits of his nose cavity. His limp hands release their grip on the bone handles and follow his body as it slides down the side of the door. Making contact with the ground, his body folds, causing his head to snap backwards against the hard rocks of the carpark. Unconscious his unseeing eyes look upwards in astonishment, all bodily functions and movement have stopped as his short circuited brain tries to make sense of the massive charge bouncing around inside his skull.

With the release of the noose around her neck, Kylie gasps for air, drops the Taser on top of the garrote in her lap and massages her neck. Feeling the warm, sticky, wetness of blood on her hands, she also feels an unexpected surge of relief that she has survived once again!

Turning off the motor, she opens the door but it stops against the grey suited body. Looking down through the gap she pushes with all her strength and it slowly opens wide enough for her to get out. Once standing the enormity of what has just happened kicks in, and her stomach contracts forcing vomit out of her mouth and onto the body at her feet. Panting and spitting she leans up against the car for support until the shaking stops. Looking towards the road she is thankful that the trees screen her from the passing traffic. Her next thought is to contact Joey so she retraces her steps to the beach and selects his number.

It is answered almost immediately and he is annoyed that after an easy break-in the silent vibrating phone interrupts his search. "Hi Kyles, no luck yet!" As there is silence at the other end he becomes concerned, "You all right hon?"

She takes a deep breath. "No, I'm not all right. I've just killed a man who was trying to strangle me!... I used the Taser. He might be Chinese, I don't know. He tried to kill me with a wire around my fuckin' neck."

The blood drains from his face. "I'm coming as fast as I can Kyles, hang in there, where are you?"

She sobs into the phone and has difficulty speaking. "Still at the car park, come quickly Joey, I'm hurt!"

"I'm on my way Kyles!" Picking up his backpack, he runs out the back door, jumps over the gate at the back of the property and runs up the entrance to Upland Road. As fast as he can, without causing attention, he jogs down the hill, crosses over Huia Road and jumps over the low log barrier that barricades the car park. Under the overhanging branches of the trees he can see Kylie leaning up against the car and beneath her, the body of a grey suited man.

Rushing to her he wraps his arms around her as best he can, hugs her tightly while rocking her from side to side.

Burying her head in his shoulder she sobs, releasing unrestrained tears.

He cradles her in his arms until she stops, "It'll be all right Kyles!... Nobody knows we are here." He looks toward the road, "The cars can't see us." Gently stroking her hair he pulls her back into his shoulder, "We'll get rid of the fuckin' body!.... I'll make it right!" He nods his head, "You'll see, I'll fuckin' fix it!" Looking down at the body, he has a thought, "Are you sure he's dead?" Feeling her head nod against his chest, he turns, releases her then bends down and feels for a pulse.

He can't feel anything other than his own rapidly beating heart. Removing his hand the man's head flops to one side exposing the other side of his face, 'He certainly looks fuckin' dead!' He tries again, and this time he is sure he can feel just the faintest of pulses under his fingertips, "I think he's still alive Kyles!" Removing his belt he rolls the man over so that he is face down and pulls his arms tightly behind his back wrapping the belt around and around. Pushing the holed end through the metal buckle, he pulls it tight. Straightening he turns to look at her and sees the ring of blood around her neck, "Maybe we should let the bastard die!"

She shrugs.

He points to the man, "Can you give me a hand lifting him into the boot?"

She nods.

As he reaches under Po's arms preparing to drag him to the back of the car, his plastered arm clunks against a pistol holster strapped to Po's chest. Dropping him back onto the ground he pulls open his jacket and unties the holster that is secured around his neck and under the arm. Studying the leather holster embossed with the words 'Smith & Wesson', he blows between puckered lips, "Hullo, hullo, look at this shit, a new fuckin' Smith and Wesson, a silencer and an extra clip!" Turning to Kylie he shakes his head, "This is not your average fuckin' play toy!"

Opening the rear door he throws the holster, pistol and strapping onto the back seat and then turns pointing towards the pistol, "He's a fuckin' hit man hon." Frowning, he shakes his head and looks down at the bound man, "What have we got here?" Closing the door, he bends down and lifts Po under the arms again, but this time drags him around to the rear of the car.

Kylie feels for the boot release button and it pops open, "Lift his feet hon." They dump him into the boot and slam it shut staring at each other as they catch their breath.

Kylie is the first to speak. "If he's a fuckin' hit man, why would he want to kill me?" She shrugs, "I mean, I'm a bloody nobody, why me?... I thought he might have been a pervert or something like that, but a fuckin' hit man!?" She shakes her head, "Maybe that car and this guy have something to do with Johnny and Butch, it doesn't make sense!"

Reaching forward and gently supporting her by the elbow, he guides her to the passenger side, opens the door and helps her in. Shutting the door he returns to the driver's side and lifts the Taser and garrote off the floor. Throwing them onto the back seat beside the holster, he starts the motor. With the air conditioner still on high they are soon bathed with chilled air and Kylie rests her head on the back of the seat and closes her eyes.

After planning his next moves, Joey reaches across and gently touches the ring of blood around her neck.

Her eyes snap open and she grabs his hand pulling it down into her lap, holding it tightly. "It still hurts Joey but I'm okay?" She frowns not being able to rid the question from her mind, "Why would he want to fuckin' kill me?"

"I don't know for sure, but I'm guessing it has something to do with Johnny's drug dealings with the Chinese Triads. I don't know too much about that side of the business but I do know that there was a shit load of money involved!... Huge money, maybe that's it? They would want him silenced now that he is on the run." He shakes his head, "I'm sure they wouldn't want him caught by the cops!" This time he nods his head, "It's the only thing that makes fuckin' sense." He looks over to where the Cruz was parked, "That's why the car is gone, it's following the Toyota."

Kylie shakes her head again. "But why me?"

"That I don't know!"

"What are we going to do now, what if he wakes up, what if he doesn't?. Shit, I'll be a bloody murderer!"

He gives her a wry smile. "Join the fuckin' clan!"

His flippant remark annoys her. Sitting up she turns towards him. "Joey, what are we going to do?,.... Whatever we do we'll have to do it fast! We can't just sit here doing nothing!"

He squeezes her hand and tries to calm her by telling her about his plan. "How about this, we'll take the car to the back of the house, dump the Chinaman in the kitchen and then I'll continue the search for the money." He points towards the Reserve, "You drive to the toilet block and keep watch, if you spot the black Landcruiser or the black Holden Cruz returning let me know.

That will give me time to get out of the house. Can you remember what the cars look like?" She nods, so he continues, "When you get to the toilet block, give me a call so that we know we can connect."

"Okay."

Pointing to the side road, he continues, "Like we planned before, pick me up just past the bus shelter, okay, what do you think?"

She looks at him for a while appreciating his strength, then sighs. "I said that if it became a matter of life or death, or the money, I would choose life and leave the money! Somehow we have gone past that point." She touches her neck, "I've earned half of that money." Frowning, she thinks about another problem, "What about the Chinaman tied up in the kitchen, what happens when Johnny and Butch return? If he's still alive wont we be in more danger than before?"

It is his turn to look at her for a moment and nod, acknowledging the problem.

After a moment he taps her on the leg. "I've got it! Once we have the money.... or not, you're going to phone the police from the call box at the shop and tell them about Johnny's house. Also, tell them that he and Butch are at a dance at Whatipu beach." He gives a wry smile, "That should stir things up at headquarters!"

She shrugs. "Why me, why don't you make the call?"

"I think the first thing Max will do is to run a voice recognition test, I know that my voice is on record at the station, I've made lots of phone calls, but you haven't."

"I have once, when you were in the barn, but that was to Max's cell phone."

He scratches his head. "Yeah you're right, but it is unlikely he would have copied your voice to the computer." Again he studies her for a moment, deep in thought, "Max thinks we're down in Queenstown, if anyone was to make that call he would think it would come from me, not you. Maybe you could change your voice somehow."

"Like in the movies with a cloth over the phone?"

"Why not, should work!" She screws up her face. "Okay, I'll give it a try, how quickly will they come?"

"Max will be onto it pretty fast….. Come on let's go find the fuckin' money!"

Westward from the house, Huia Road continues past the Reserve, over a small bridge, then hugs the coast until the sea squeezes it up against the rocky headland and it becomes a single lane. That's where Whatipu Road starts, winding inland up a steep valley. At the turn off is a sign that warns drivers about the condition of the road. It starts sealed, then deteriorates into loose, dusty gravel. Also at the turn-off is a hand painted sign with an arrow pointing up the valley, it says 'Cave Dance'.

Wi Chun driving the Holden Cruz, points towards the sign.

Feng seated behind him, nods. "That explains the traffic! Must be hundreds going to the dance. I suppose a cave dance is just that a dance in a cave." He smirks, "How Neanderthalic, I shouldn't be surprised!" They both laugh.

Wi asks, "Do you think that Johnny and Butch might be going there as well?"

Feng shrugs. "Maybe, it's their kind of thing!"

They stay in contact with Johnny's Land Cruiser but the frequent twists and turns make it difficult to get closer. When passing slower cars they receive horn blasts, abuse, pumped fists, 'fuck you' middle fingers and a cutlass or two waved out the window. It is the waving swords that convince Wi that the dance is not only a cave dance, but that it is also a fancy dress. The people in the cars in front and behind seem to be dressed as pirates.

Feng agrees, enjoying the irony with Wi that he would be the only true pirate on the road that afternoon. They both laugh. Closing his eyes, he leans back in the seat and thinks about his days as a smuggler on board his father's sampan in the South China Sea. His reverie is short lived, as the sway of the car jolts his eyes open and he watches the billowing dust drift into the unfamiliar vegetation on either side of the road. As he grabs hold of the door handle to steady himself he yearns for his island home on Macau with its ancient stone lined streets and clay tiled dwellings. So different to these raw, bush clad hills at the bottom of the world. A worrying thought crosses his mind, *'Why have I been sent by Shan Chun on a mission that should be handled by any one of his lesser soldiers? Is it a reprimand? Has he found out about the clandestine meetings to depose him?'*

Johnny and Butch are now only a few cars ahead but it is difficult to see in the dust. Feng opens his iPhone clicking on Google Maps. Whatipu Road appears wriggling its way through the ranges to its destination at the beach. He sighs again, tired of this undeveloped colonial country and tired of having to be polite to uncivilized and ignorant gang leaders like Ozzie Clem. Most of all he misses the familiar sights, smells and sounds of his bustling, oriental city. Now at the highest point in the road, he can see in the distance, the bottom of the valley and the black sandy beach beyond. With the increasing congestion of traffic, he becomes aware of how huge this dance is going to be. Smiling to himself he knows that killing in a crowd can be difficult but that the resulting panic can make detection more difficult and escape far easier.

Over the hills, at Huia Bay, Joey is in the kitchen of the house and calls Kylie. "Can you hear me okay Kyles?"

"Yeah, good Joey, how about me?"

"Fine… hey, guess what's on the kitchen table a fuckin' Western Leader open to an advert for the dance. Someone has circled it, they've gone there for sure. It should give me plenty of time." He looks out the window, noticing that it is getting dark, "It'll be dark soon so I'd better get going. I'll call you in ten minutes or sooner if I find the money!"

"Good luck... Hey, how's the Chinaman?"

He looks down at the bound man lying on his side. "Still on the floor in the kitchen,... still breathing but unconscious." He watches him for a moment, "His eyes are puffed up and fuckin' black and blue...... I'll call back in ten." They hang up and Joey starts at one end of the kitchen frantically opening and closing doors and drawers, wiping finger prints, prying into all the corners and trying not to step on the unconscious Po Ling. It is proving easier to search the house than he expected as it is sparsely furnished,

Ten minutes later he calls Kylie and she answers immediately.

"Did you find it?"

"Nah, no fuckin' luck... I even checked the attic..... bugger me, where else?" He looks out the kitchen window again, "I'm going out to the garage might be there."

The side door to the garage is locked but easily opened and he finds the light switch. The interior is large and smelling of old oil and dust. Overhead the trusses support not only the roof but lengths of left over building materials, two old bamboo surf casting rods and in the middle, a dusty and scratched long surf board. It only takes a quick look to know that the bag of money is not there.

Under windows beside the door is an oil and paint stained work bench with a large vice attached. Beneath the bench are a few rusting tins of paint and cans of used engine oil, but nothing else.

At the back is an old wringer type washing machine and a Kelvinator fridge with door ajar, exposing it's rotting rubber seals.

On the wall opposite the side door there are rows of wooden shelving all empty except for dust, cobwebs, and rat droppings.

The front of the garage is only the double sized metal roller door.

Now outside, Joey pulls the side door shut, wipes his finger prints off the door handle and turns wondering where else to look. All that remains is a tin garden shed and an old Hino mobile home resting on concrete blocks beside the driveway. Joey nods, *'Maybe!...... I'll check the fuckin' shed first.'*

It is not locked and the sliding door is held closed by a pull bolt. Inside is a weed eater, a petrol can, cut logs of wood more cobwebs and rotting cardboard boxes full of junk left behind by the previous owners.

Joey turns and studies the mobile home, his last resort, then looks at his watch and dials Kylie, "Hi hon, how you're doin'?"

"Fine! I've moved up the driveway and parked to one side, it gives me a better view of the road. It was a bit freaky being near the loo, you know a girl on her own and in the dark and all!"

"Yeah you're right, can the car be seen from the road?"

"I'm under the flax, it's a pretty good hiding place, what about you, how's it going?"

"Haven't had any luck yet.... Just finished looking in the garage and the garden shed, one more to go, a mobile home!" He shakes his head, "Wouldn't that be a bitch if I can't find the money, maybe Johnny hid the bag somewhere else!.... You'd think that he would want to keep it close by, yeah, it's got to be fuckin' here somewhere! Oh well here goes nothing! Keep watching Kyles I don't want to be surprised.!"

"No problems Joey!"

"I'll call you in ten, kiss, kiss!"

"Love your work... kiss, kiss back at you, bye".

He moves to the mobile home and decides to check the most obvious place for a large sports bag, the exterior luggage compartments on either side of the central doorway. Starting at the left side, he reaches down and turns the chrome handle and is not surprised that it is locked. Once again he uses his small set of lock picks and feels the tumblers click into place. This time the handle turns and the hinged door springs upwards. Exposed is a large spare tire; a heavy duty jack and tools wrapped in a plastic bag. He bends down inspecting the rest of the compartment but it is empty. Pulling the hinged door downwards he locks it again and wipes the handle with a cloth.

Moving past the central door he unlocks the right hand compartment and waits for the hydraulics to push the door up. This time he is sure he will find the money as it is the logical hiding place, but there is nothing inside, not even a mouse nest!

Disappointed, he moves a few paces to his left and studies the lock on the door of the converted bus, *'No problems there.'* He allows himself another thought, *'First time I've broken into a motor home, that's a new one!'*

The door swings open revealing a grey carpeted step leading to the same carpeted interior. It is surprisingly spacious and Joey appreciates the luxury of the old fittings. There is a kitchen with stove and refrigerator and the passenger and driver's swivel chairs face towards the rear. They are covered with mauve leather that matches the three seater lounge filling half the side of the Hino.

Climbing up the step and turning right, he passes the kitchen and stops in front of two floor-to-ceiling cupboards, likely hiding places, but they contain a vacuum cleaner and cleaning equipment in one and a fold out ironing board in the other. The shower is empty as is the small toilet. All that is left is the bedroom at the far end with its double bed with a chest of drawers beneath.

Movement behind the bed startles Joey, until he realises that he is looking at his own reflection in a mirrored head board. It is obvious that the bedroom is too compact to hide a large canvas bag. Frowning, he shakes his head then turns around looking back towards the driver's cabin, *'What have I missed?'* He pulls on the three seater lounge chair but it is firmly attached to the floor and the side wall, *'Unlikely that he would have hidden the money there, too fuckin' difficult!'*

Advancing to the driver's seat, he swivels it one way and then the other, *'It's a large bag, there is just no room for it to be hiding anywhere else in the fuckin' bus!'* He continues to look around, *'The kitchen cupboards are too small. Maybe outside the bus, under the bus?'*

Climbing down the steps, he looks underneath, *'Nothing!'*

He moves to the front of the bus bends down and looks underneath, *'Nothing!'*

Returning to the side of the bus he lies down on the concrete driveway looking under its length, *'Fuckin' nothing!'*

He does the same at the back with the same result. Dejected, he stands facing the engine door and begins to swear, "Shit! Shit! Shit! Where are you bag of fuckin' money, where are you hiding?" Looking at his watch, he realises that his ten minutes is up and he needs to phone Kylie with the bad news.

More in frustration than deliberate intent, he wiggles the chrome handle securing the engine door and is surprised when it unlocks and starts to rise by itself. Stepping backwards, he immediately sees Johnny's large sports bag sitting on top of the engine. His heart jumps and he shouts aloud, "Johnny you sneaky bastard, I've got you now!" The bag is stuffed so tight on top of the engine that he has difficulty pulling it away from the air filter and fuel lines but the anticipation of two million dollars gives him extra strength, even with a reset arm.

With the bag on the ground he looks around to see if anyone is watching. Being the back of the house and the bus, only a nosy pedestrian walking past the driveway to Upland Road would be able to see him, but there is no one about in the fading light.

Picking up the bag he slings it over his shoulder, opens the gate and runs up the driveway depositing it under a ponga tree a few metres from the path.

Next, he returns to the motor home and wipes away all the evidence of his visit. He is eager to call Kylie but hurries into the house to check on the Chinaman and to do a final check.

Po is still in the same place on the floor but is now conscious, he has vomited and his face and hair are covered in smelly, regurgitated food and blood. He turns his head to look at Joey out of his puffed up eyes but they are not focused and he looks confused.

Joey locks the back door, wiping the handle, and runs to the back of the bus closing the door over the motor, then passes through the open gate and runs up the driveway to the ponga tree.

Looking around he makes sure he is not being watched, then bends down and unzips the bag. As it opens he has a terrible thought that it may be full of old clothes or books, but no, exposed are bundles and bundles of red one hundred dollar bills, just as he dreamed there would be! Zipping it up, he slings it once more over his shoulder on top of his backpack and jogs up the few remaining yards to the sidewalk. Before emerging he puts on his floppy hat, then walks as casually as he can down the sidewalk with such a large bag and a backpack to the bus shelter.

Returning to the bushes behind, he drops the bag and at last dials Kylie, "I've got it hon, it's ours, come and get me girl, I'm behind the bus shelter."

"Joey you're a bloody wonder and yes now that you are a millionaire, I will fuckin' marry you!"

He smiles, "Was there any doubt? Come and get me girl!"

"I'm on my way."

CHAPTER 28

Max and Charlie Chang

As soon as Max receives the call from the Coms Centre he leaves his half finished meal and asks Ronnie to join him at headquarters.

Now seated at his desk, he replays Kylie's phone call over and over again. There are too many unanswered questions. First of all, who is the caller? Is it a woman or a man? The voice has been modified somehow and there is no match in their data base. It was traced to a public phone at Huia Bay, so that fits the caller's information. He is convinced it is not a prank although the media have been having a field day with the raids on the P labs and the gang headquarters in West Auckland. There is public awareness triggering that sort of call which usually costs him time and money! He reminds himself, that he has withheld the information that two leaders of the Satan's Sons gang have escaped! That makes the call genuine and although doubting some of its authenticity, it forces him to take immediate action.

Leaning back in his chair, with his arms behind his head, he reviews the facts, *'There is an injured Chinese hitman on the kitchen floor of a gang house, number two thousand one hundred and eleven, Huia Beach Road. That is quite specific but how does that relate to*

Johnny and Butch dressed as pirates at a dance at Whatipu Beach?'
Deep in thought, he takes too large a swallow of hot coffee scolding
the insides of his mouth. Sucking air and trying to ignore the sting,
he returns to his computer and finds the files relating to the dance
at the Whatipu cave. He is well aware of the troublesome dance as
it has already stretched his limited resources. When consulted by
the Auckland City Council his objections were over ruled. They
saw it as a public relations exercise to help the finances of the struggling Huia Museum and to win votes. He saw it as a problematic
law-and-order issue! His thoughts are interrupted by Ronnie who
taps on the open door and enters. "Hi Ronnie, new information,
come and listen."

With Ronnie standing beside him he hands him headphones and
clicks on the 'play' arrow.

Half an hour earlier as Max was driving to his office he sent instructions to the Coms Centre to notify the officers assigned to the
dance to be on the lookout for Johnny and Butch. From his laptop,
he sent a picture of a black Landcruiser as well as a composite of
Johnny and Butch. He is aware that it will be difficult to identify
the two as they will look like all the other pirates going to the
dance.

In a patrol car at Whatipu Beach, Senior Sergeant Mark Richardson
and Senior Constable Andrew Mulligan look at the picture of
Johnny and Butch on the screen on their dashboard.

Andrew nods, "Butch Gueber is the gang guy we booked at the
Waimauku Vets, they must have escaped the raid."

Mark nods, "I wonder how they did that? Max kept that one
quiet." Picking up his mic, he connects with the Coms Centre and
asks for Max.

Within seconds, they hear his gravelly voice. "Hi Mark, are you
at the beach?"

"Yes sir, I'm with Senior Constable Andrew Mulligan, we're
parked beside the Information Booth. Do you want us to start a
search for the Toyota?"

Max thinks it through. "Good idea Mark, but no, it might spook

Johnny and Butch. Also I want you and Andrew to keep the lower car park secure, there is a lot of valuable equipment and vehicles down there. I'll be arriving within the hour with AOS and GTS, this dance has the potential to become a real problem! I've been informed, without verification, that there may be Triads heading your way as well! Of course I'll shut the dance down if I have to. By-the-way, so that you won't be surprised, I will be arriving with five AOS officers, men and women, dressed as pirates. We're going to infiltrate the dance.

It is too much of a stretch for Mark to picture his distinguished boss as a pirate, so he touches his chequered cap with an unseen salute, "Yes sir!"

Back at headquarters, Ronnie removes the head phones and places them on the desk. "Well that's something, when did that arrive?"

"An hour ago."

"It sounds real."

"Yep, I think it's Kylie's voice but she and Joey are supposed to be in Queenstown. They wanted a break. I was about to give them a traced call when you arrived." He points to the computer, "What do you make of the Chinese thing?"

"As you said, it could be Triad connected. They supply drugs to the Satan's Sons."

Max nods, "Why would they be in New Zealand? Maybe something to do with the two million dollars in Rarotonga. Speaking of Rarotonga, have you heard from your brother, what's happening there?"

"Lots... I spoke to him this morning, they've discovered that a Chinese owned coffee company based in Raro is sending drugs to New Zealand in sacks of green coffee beans. They are preparing a report, you should get it soon."

"Why haven't Customs picked that up on x-ray?"

Ronnie shakes his head. "It's almost impossible. The sacks contain a perforated sachet of silica gel, a crystal drying agent. One in ten sachets includes an inner plastic sleeve of ephedrine! It has the same appearance and density as silica gel. Methamphetamine is a powder and would be easier to spot. I've talked to Customs, they tell me green coffee beans may also mask the smell of the drug, making it harder for the sniffer dogs."

"Well that's a break, make a report of what was discussed with your brother, I'll send it to the Commissioner."

"Will do boss."

Max decides not to comment on Ronnie's continuing use of the word, 'boss', which he dislikes. "I suppose they have the Chinese locked up?"

Ronnie shakes his head. "No.... It's very political. Something to do with contracts with China and the Raro Government. They have expelled all the Chinese workers but kept the two responsible for the two Rarotongan deaths."

Max frowns, holding up a finger. "I know of one, Dan Henare, who is the other?"

"Miriama Maana." To emphasise the importance of Miriama's death, he taps his index finger, "Grand-daughter of the Paramount Chief, Leo Maana." Tapping his second finger, he continues, "Daughter of Senior Detective, Albert Maana of the Cook Island Police Force." He taps his third, "Mistress of Ah Chung, manager of the coffee company!"

Max is surprised. "Wow! Really! That will create all sorts of problems. I wouldn't want to be in charge of the prosecutions."

"You might if you knew that Miriama was either strangled by Ah Chung or his Triad henchman Tattoo Chung..." He pauses for a moment, collecting himself, "I knew Miriama, we grew up together as kids. A beautiful woman, she was crowned Miss Rarotonga a few years back.

Max studies Ronnie for a moment, then says, "The crimes against Dan and Miriama are more than just judicial, they are also crimes against the tribes of the Cook Islands, what do they think of that?"

Ronnie nods. "There is huge anger and hurt. Not only is Miriama the granddaughter of the Paramount Chief, but Dan Henare is the grandson of one of the lesser Chiefs."

Max nods, picking up his pen and tapping it twice on the desk. "It's starting to make sense. When you say they have expelled all the Chinese who do you mean by they?"

"The Council of Chiefs."

Max purses his lips. "So the tribes themselves are holding two Chinese, Ah Chung and his henchman, that of course is illegal."

"That's right boss. Ah Chung and Tattoo Chung are cousins. Tattoo is a Triad soldier... You asked how the people of the Cooks are taking the murders. I can tell you that there is a utu placed on both Chinamen by the Council, it is the first utu in a hundred years!"

Max stares at Ronnie for quite some time as he absorbs the information. "So they are not being held by the Cook Island Police?"

"It is not a police matter."

"Really?" After a moment Max nods, "The Chiefs are still powerful aren't they."

Ronnie nods, as Max continues, "You'll keep me informed of any developments won't you? Your brother has done a great job discovering the drugs. I'll give him a call once I receive his report. Keep me informed on the coffee thing."

Ronnie nods. "Yes boss!"

Max pushes himself away from the desk and places his arms behind his head. "I'll bring you up to date. As you heard on the phone call, Johnny and Butch are going to the cave dance at Whatipu dressed as pirates, you know, the one that I tried to stop!"

"Is that happening tonight?"

"It's happening right now! Five hundred tickets have been sold and for some reason Johnny and Butch are right in the middle of it. I've got three courses of action." He holds up a finger, "One, grab them at the dance." He holds up two fingers, "Two, grab them in their vehicle, or three." He changes his fingers to three, "Wait until they return to their beach house." Dropping his hand he continues, "The dance is too risky, the car is a possibility, but the house is the best bet. We'll have to wait and see what happens at the dance." Leaning back in his chair, he points to the computer, "Whoever phoned from Huia talks about a black Honda Cruz leaving a car park at the beach to follow Johnny's Landcruiser. The Honda may or may not contain other Chinese, but I'm guessing that it does! A Chinese hit man is unlikely to travel alone in an unfamiliar country." Looking down at his scribbled notes on his desk he continues, "The house is at two, triple one Huia Road, I've looked it up on

Google Earth. It's a white two storied building with a red roof, easy to see from the road. That's as long as it hasn't been repainted since the photo." He looks at his watch, "The AOS and an ambulance should be there by now! Once we have ID'd that Chinaman we'll know a lot more!"

Ronnie nods, as Max taps his pen again, deep in thought, *'What is he doing in New Zealand? Who tied him up? He wouldn't be alone! Where or who are the others?'* Again his thoughts return to the tip-off by the female voice and wonders again if it's Kylie? *'It certainly smacks of Joey! Are they really in Queenstown?'* Picking up his phone, he looks across at Ronnie, "I'm going to phone Joey, what are they up to?"

For the small amount of eight hundred dollars for two nights, Kylie and Joey have secured the use of the bridal suite on top of the Sheraton Hotel on Symonds Street. They have already had a spa and are now cuddling together with their white terry cloth dressing gowns open, so that their brown naked bodies are locked together, kissing, exploring, touching, stroking and enjoying their quickening passions.

It is the first time Kylie has allowed Joey to touch her after the brutal treatment by Johnny. She is still healing and asks him not to go too far.

Joey respects her wishes and they successfully find other ways of making love.

Now at the point of climax, the phone rings in the pocket of Joey's discarded trousers on the floor at the bottom of the bed. It makes a harsh strident noise, crashing into their euphoric cocoon and shattering the moment.

Sighing, he rolls away from her then strokes her cheek trying to decide whether to answer it or not. *'Who would be calling?... Is it a wrong number?.. Is it Max?'* He shakes his head, "Let it ring, who fuckin' cares?"

Kylie props herself up on an elbow causing one of her brown nipples, still swollen and erect to poke out from under her gown. "I care Joey, it might be about the kids!"

He grimaces. "'Oh yeah forgot about them." By the time he

scrambles to the end of the bed, the phone has stopped ringing. As always, there is an automated message. *'You have missed a call from Max Henderson.'* It gives the number. Joey clicks it off then wraps the bath robe around his waist and ties it closed. Turning towards Kylie, there is a noticeable bulge at his crotch.

She points and laughs, delighted that she has the power to turn him on.

Joey holds out the phone towards her, "It's from Max, what do you reckon hon, shall I call him back? I think he suspects us of making the call. I wonder if he is able to check if we have booked tickets to Queenstown?" He nods, "We could still go you know, what-do-you-reckon?"

"Nah, let's stay put, we've paid for two nights."

"We don't have to think like that anymore."

"Yes we do, I'm not good at wasting fuckin' money, I'll never change, you'd better get used to it Mister Joey Moser!" Laughing, she rolls over onto her back and suggestively pulls the dressing gown away from her legs so that her naked body is framed in the soft white cloth, "Charlotte would have called if there were problems with the kids!" She raises her hand, gesturing, "Come to mumma lover boy."

Joey drops the phone, undoes his belt and his erect penis pokes out between the slits of his gown.

This time Kylie laughs out loud.

Not getting a reply from Joey, Max asks Ronnie to do a check of the airline passengers to Queenstown. Just then his desk phone rings and he is informed by the Coms Centre that the AOS have the Chinaman and that a video is available on his computer. Max looks at the close-up of the bloodied nosed, puff eyed man. *'Who are you?'* He also wonders if Interpol will be able to ID him being so disfigured.

The Coms Centre inform him that a passport was found in his coat pocket and that the AOS have taken finger prints and an eye scan. The passport says he is Len Wong but Max knows that will be a lie. His arrival date and time at Auckland Airport is useful and he requests a copy of the photo taken at Immigration and also a list of names and photos of all the passengers arriving on the same flight.

As he has requested urgency, within ten minutes two attachments arrive from Immigration. One is a clear photo of the so called Len Wong and the other contains five megabytes of thumbnail photos of the three hundred passengers.

Max sends both attachments to Interpol with a brief accompanying email.

Ronnie, who has been phoning from the interview table across the room, approaches Max's desk. "Unless they are using false names, Kylie and Joey are not in Queenstown!"

Max nods. "Just as I thought, hey, take a look at our Chinaman."

Ronnie moves behind him, and looks at the beat up face. "He's not pretty... I wonder who did that to his face?" Just then, a message pops up on the screen, *'Ambos recommend urgent dispatch of Len Wong to Auckland A&E.'*

Max acknowledges the message and instructs his squad leader to assign one of his officers to stay with the injured man, telling him that he will be arriving shortly with reinforcements and to standby for further instructions. Next, he checks on the ETA of the Air Force helicopter and sends a text message to Joey, *'Johnny's Landcruiser, did you purchase? Who from? Licence plate number? This is an order Joey!'* Swiveling around, he looks up at Ronnie, "I've got an unusual job for you. Contact the owner of a fancy dress shop and hire seven large size pirate outfits for immediate delivery. It won't be easy." He looks at his watch, "At this hour, most will be closed. Get the owners at home if you have to. Tell them it's urgent police business."

Ronnie moves over to the interview desk and on his iPad searches for 'Costume Hire Auckland'. While it is searching he looks over at Max. "Do I get one?"

Max looks up from his screen. "Sorry, no. Johnny and Butch know who you are but they don't know me. I want to get as close to them at the dance as I can. I want you to look after the deployment of the troops." Turning back to his computer he scans through a list of available AOS members, selects five, including three of his best women. Two of those being Detective Sergeant Caroline Fatialofa and Detective Ngaire Adams who have already had dealings with the gang. With lateral thinking he adds another name to his three men, Charlie Chang. He is a Chinese speaking Senior Police Officer, on secondment from the Toronto Metropolitan Police.

Charlie, a fourth generation Canadian, takes a ribbing because of his name, but there is no joking when it comes to his knowledge of Hong Kong Triads and North American Tongs. Police organisations around the world know his worth and seek his advice. His diminutive stature and happy disposition hides a deep hatred for the Tongs who murdered his father.

Max thinks about the fun times the three of them have had over the past three weeks. Fishing for schnapper in the Hauraki Gulf and playing golf as often as they can.

Charlie loves those sports, one of the reasons why he agreed to come to New Zealand and lecture at police seminars.

The Toronto Police were glad to release him for a month as he was showing signs of fatigue. Charlie wouldn't agree with that assessment, but he liked the thought of the seminars and to get away from the cold of a Toronto winter. He enjoys New Zealand and especially Ronnie's and Max's company.

Max calls over to Ronnie, "I'm going to ask Charlie Chang to join us, he knows the Triads better than anyone."

Ronnie nods. "None better." Looking at his watch, he adds, "I hope he is sober!"

Max laughs as he dials. The phone is answered. "You sober Charlie?"

"You bet, it's still early, what do you want Max, I hope it's fun."

"Depends what you call fun?... I need your help, of course you can refuse. It's outside our agreement and it could be dangerous!"

"So you think I'm not used to danger? I live with it every day! Stop the bullshit Max, what do you want?"

Once explained, he is relieved. "Shit Max, I'm bored out of my wick in this five star hotel.... I've got wall-to-wall cricket and tennis on TV.... Say, what's with this cricket? A game that lasts five days and ends in a draw, what the hell is that!" It's a statement not a question, so he continues, "I'll be more than happy to help you, old friend, screw the contract. It does sound like you have some of my Triad friends poking around! Send me what you've got to my

Hotmail address, I might be able to ID Mister Len Wong, whoever he is? Do you want me to come to Headquarters?"

"Yes, I'd appreciate that Charlie... I've got a feeling we're going to need you big time, hey, have you eaten yet?

"No!"

"How about a pizza?, I'll order it in!"

"No Chinese food?"

Max pauses, not sure if Charlie is joking. "Sure, if you want."

Charlie laughs. "Just pulling your leg, old buddy, pizza's fine!"

"Hey, enough of this 'old' stuff, oh, by-the-way I've ordered you a pirate costume."

"Say what?"

"I'll explain when you get here, don't be long."

"Send the email, I'll take a look."

Max is relieved on two counts, not only does he have the help of one of the world's most knowledgeable cops, but also an interpreter that is fluent in both Cantonese and Mandarin. He wouldn't admit it, but it will mean that he will also have extra support on this dangerous mission. Opening his top drawer, he removes a small red booklet that has the cell phone numbers of all the Ministers of Parliament. Within minutes he gets permission to use a large NZ Air Force helicopter to fly himself and his band of pirates to Huia Beach.

By now all thoughts of Joey and Kylie have been forgotten, but they return when his phone beeps with a text message, *'Rego is PUREAZ. You like? JS Holdings owns car. Having fun. Lol Joey.'* The message ends with a smiley face.

Max looks up at the ceiling. *'Cheeky bugger, I'm sure you are behind this Chinaman thing, what are you up to?'* He shakes his head, then continues to think about the dance knowing that It will be the first fancy dress he has attended since his teenage years. Like Jean, he has the same thought, *'Bloody hell, now I'm going to a cave dance dressed as a bloody pirate.'*

CHAPTER 29

Thanksgiving Turkey – Bamiyan and a Double Death

As a surprise treat for her Canadian guests, Jean ordered a fresh turkey for their farewell meal. Not having cooked a turkey before, she reads the instructions in an old Edmonds Cookery Book and is pleased to learn that it is all quite simple. Even the bread stuffing, but there is no recipe for pumpkin pie.

A visit to the Titirangi Library provides the information. Short pastry is precooked in a pie dish until hard and lightly browned. When cool, it is filled with a mixture of pumpkin pulp, sweetened condensed milk, brown sugar, eggs and cinnamon, ginger and cloves. After thirty minutes in the oven, this sweet and spicy dessert is left to cool and then topped with whipped cream or vanilla ice cream.

Late Saturday afternoon when all the cooking is done, Jean showers and changes into her costume. Everyone arrives promptly at six, dressed as pirates and are greeted by the commanding presence of Jean as Black Pete.

The girls are surprised to see Jean wearing a black beard and a patch over one eye and to smell roast turkey, and pumpkin pie cooling on the kitchen bench. They knew that Jean would prepare something special but are gob smacked that she has gone to the trouble of preparing a Canadian Thanksgiving Dinner.

On arrival, their gaiety, sparked by their fancy dress, changes to pleasant surprise at her thoughtfulness and then to hugs and tears knowing they will soon depart.

Tane with Emma seated beside him at the big table, is the least affected.

Gary and Mike are wondering how they are going to cope, it will be a wrench!

The pending departure is forgotten by the end of the meal and helped by a round of liqueur, they busy themselves in the kitchen helping Jean with the cleanup.

Late afternoon, leaving the Homestay, they walk one behind the other along the road to the beach and can hear Lady's plaintive yelping.

Robyn turns to Tane. "Can't she come?"

He shakes his head. "I wish she could, but there is a dance rule, no dogs."

Emma, turns to Robyn, "I guess it has something to do with the protected wetlands around the cave. Tane and I talked about it and decided it would be best if she stayed at home."

Julia, wisely stays silent, leaving Robyn and Wendy disappointed that they hadn't been involved in the discussion.

The sun is now low in the sky illuminating everything in a bright orange glow, except the island out in the bay which is a black silhouette.

They are joined by other pirates who are also walking to the dance. Most have backpacks to carry their boots, long socks and hats. With no footpath, they are forced to walk single file beside the narrow road. Crossing over a wooden bridge, they turn right towards the beach and follow a kikuyu grassed track that leads to the sand dunes.

Passing under tall pohutukawa trees, their footsteps crunch on the dry, brown leaves, before they emerge out of the muted light to a clearing.

Set back amongst the trees is a public toilet block. Beside it is a large spreading fig tree and both are bathed in the orange glow of the setting sun.

To the surprise of the locals, who take the tree for granted, the girls walk around the tree marveling at its size. They touch the large leaves and feel the smooth pear shaped fruits on the ends of the branches. They explain that fig trees are stunted and hard to grow in Canada because of the winter. This huge tree is a surprise and they laugh when Emma explains that the tree is thriving because of its proximity to the toilet block.

Now approaching the dunes, the surface of the track soon turns to loose, black, clingy sand, churned by numerous feet. Even the hardy marram grass refuses to grow.

Soon they are over the dunes and onto the wide expanse of the beach.

A century ago, the waves smashed up against the cliffs, but over the years the sand accumulated and now the edge of the water is far in the distance. The expanse of black sand, beyond the tide is dry and still hot from the afternoon sun.

Passing under the towering cliffs to their left, Tane points to two parallel rows of rusting iron spikes. "Those anchored the railway track used by the small bush locomotive, the one we talked about the other day, the one that used to go under the tunnel." Pointing down the coast, southward, towards the head of the Manukau Harbour, he continues, "The track followed the cliff face to the wharf at Paratutai. The hardwood rewarewa sleepers are now used as retainer walls for gardens. It's a shame as the wood is beautiful. Bright yellow with stripes of dark brown grain. When turned on a lathe it makes wonderful fruit or salad bowls, there are quite a few wood carvers living in the Ranges."

Julia comments. "I'd like to buy one as a momento."

Jean, puffing a little as she tries to keep up, adds. "I'll take you shopping before you go."

Wendy says. "Can I come?"

Robyn says. "Me too."

Tane notices that Jean is short of breath so he stops beside the row of rusting spikes.

As the group gather around looking down, Lady comes bounding across the sand, barking a welcome, and not at all apologetic about her escape.

Mike turns to Tane and shakes his head. "She must have got off her lead."

Tane shrugs. "I'm buggered if I know how, I tied it tight!"

Lady heads straight for Robyn who reaches down and strokes her head. They all see the dog lead dragging behind her with a stake still attached.

Tane calls her to him, then reaches down and picks up the lead. Untying the stake he pushes the sharpened end into the sand, "You must have really wanted to come with us girl!" He rubs her behind the ears then bends down and gives her a hug.

Robyn says, "Can't she come with us?... I mean, it doesn't matter does it if you keep her on a lead? I think it would be fun to have her with us."

Emma can see the affection between the girls and Lady and suggests a compromise. "We can tie her up when we get closer to the wetlands, there must be trees or something near the cave. Even a large piece of drift wood."

Tane nods then bends again, giving Lady a vigorous rub.

She responds by lifting her head and giving him a quick lick.

Laughing, he wipes his face with his white pirate sleeve. Turning towards the cliff face he points to his right. "We can shorten our walk by following the old train track close to the cliffs. See that green patch of pohutukawa trees growing on top of that rocky outcrop?"

They all turn and look in the direction he is pointing, "Beneath that is the tunnel, at the other end is a fresh water lake. Lady always likes to have a swim and to have a drink. On the way back we can use the same route." He nods, "It cuts about fifteen minutes off our walk."

Although living nearby, Emma has never walked from Karekare to Whatipu and looking along the broad stretch of flat sand, glowing in the evening sun, it seems to go on forever. "How long will it take to get to Whatipu, Tane?"

"About an hour and a half." He smiles looking at Gary, "Although it depends how fast we walk."

Emma, who enjoys hiking, is looking forward to the exercise, as she has been locked up in her clinic all day. Saturdays are always busy!

It is a beautiful evening, the wind is warm and off the land flattening the usually turbulent waves. The tide is out and the many rivulets, flowing down the black sand, are turned liquid gold by the setting sun.

The group are now closer to the cliffs than the distant sea and the natural amphitheatre makes it seem as if the sound of the surf is coming straight from the cliff face.

Wendy, fascinated by this trick of nature, remembers being told by her Sunday School teacher that even the rocks will cry out. Up until now, she wondered how that could happen!

Moving along the base of the cliffs they soon pass by the first track marker with a plaque that reads, 'Hillary Trail'. The iron railway tracks have long gone but the level, elevated track, provides a perfect walking pathway above the flax. To the left are the towering cliffs and to the right the high sand dunes screening the wide sloping beach and the surf beyond.

For fifteen minutes they stay close to the cliffs surrounded by the pulsing sounds of the surf and the twittering of birds before they enter the silence of the tunnel.

Julia comments. "Not much of a tunnel, I was expecting a real long one. This is just a hole in a rock."

Mike stops and runs his hand over the sharp edges inside the tunnel. "Can you imagine how hard it was cutting this hole with pick axes, chisels and sledge hammers?"

Robyn shakes her head. "Not for me!"

Mike points upward to the low ceiling. "The train driver had to stop and lower the smoke stack so that it could get through. Better than being pounded by the waves at the edge of the surf."

Emerging out on the other side, Lady is released and rushes to enjoy her customary swim and then to lap the clean cool water of the lake.

Mike points across the wet lands, "The railway track was raised on wooden trestles across the lake and marshes. Lots of wood but the settlers were never short of that!"

Robyn remembers the taxi driver's comments about the kauri trees. "Danny, our taxi driver, showed us some of the kauri trees when we drove through the Ranges, they are massive!"

Julia nods. "When we were up in the Bay of Islands, we were shown the largest kauri tree in New Zealand." She shakes her head, "I forget what they called it… a Maori name that means 'God of the Forest', now that is one huge ancient tree, no wonder the settlers wanted its timber."

Still in single file they leave the train track and cut across the flat expanse beyond the lake and the wetlands, then climb up and over the high dunes to the flat of the beach.

An hour later they pass Windy Point and have little energy for conversation being drawn on by the rocky dome of Paratutai island at the head of the harbour. Quickening their steps they can see to their left the large marquee at the Whatipu Beach, lit like a Christmas tree and can hear, faintly, the sound of music.

Mike, Tane and Gary, flip flop along in open jandals, but the girls have tied their walking shoes to their back packs and are enjoying the unfamiliar feel of firm warm sand under their toes.

Lady, like Jean, is puffing, but determined to keep up. Twice they stop to tie Lady to a large piece of driftwood, but each time she looked so forlorn that they agree to wait until the car park at Whatipu beach.

Half an hour later they arrive and she is happy to relieve herself and doesn't have any energy left to complain about being tied to a post, under the puhutukawas, beside the road.

As she flops down, Tane removes a large empty coke bottle from a nearby overflowing garbage bin, cuts it in half and places it beside her, filling it with the last of his drinking water. Then the group walk towards the brightly lit tent and the loud music.

Lady is not happy at being left alone but her leg is beginning to ache and her complaining stops soon after they leave. Resting her head on her paws she watches the never-ending movement of people around her and even though she wants to sleep is kept awake by their noisy drunken chatter.

Up the road from where she is lying a paddock has been mown by the owner and a sign on the gate says, 'Parking $5'. Four parking wardens with yellow florescent jackets wave their torches and direct the vehicles into rows.

The Toyota Land Cruiser that Feng and Wi had been following for the past hour is parked only two vehicles up from their Holden Cruz! In the half light of the evening, they see Johnny and Butch climb out and walk up the paddock towards the gate.

Feng has already decided that the car park is the place for the murders and stays seated in his car, he reasons that Johnny and Butch will return at the end of the dance totally drunk or drugged, or both, and it will be easy targets. The car park is not lit and he knows there will be commotion and noise with engines starting and sudden bursts of headlights. An ideal time to shoot from a silenced pistol. He smiles at the thought of disappearing among the long line of slow moving vehicles leaving the dance, *'By the time their bodies are found, maybe in the morning, I will be on a plane homeward bound! Anyway I'll be long gone with no witnesses.'* His smile broadens, *'Who would be looking for Chinese assassins in a paddock at the bottom of the world?'* He forces himself to return to the unpleasant present and starts planning his next moves.

Watching the waving flashlight of a parking warden, a few cars further down close to the wire fence, he decides, *'We'll need one of those jackets and the torch. Wi can get those once the car park is full and there is no more activity.'* Turning to Wi, he instructs, "Go and get the bag from the boot."

Wi returns and removes camouflaged army fatigues for himself and Feng.

Standing in dim light, beside their car, they quickly change out of their suits and feel more comfortable in their light, Red Army battle dress. Including thin leather gloves and waterproof boots.

Once dressed they meld into the darkness of the interior of the car.

Feng in the back, and Wi in the driver's seat.

Adjusting their night vision glasses, they check their fire arms and fill their trouser pockets with loaded magazines.

Feng tries again and again, to phone Po Ling but there is no answer so he clicks his phone shut with an annoyed sigh. Pushing back against the head rest he closes his eyes. With time to kill he decides to relax.

To the delight of Charlie Chang who was not expecting a night flight, the New Zealand Airforce NH90 helicopter lifts off from the police helipad and heads West. Within a minute they are over the weaving headlights at the Waterview tunnel. Moments later they spook a few horses at the brightly lit Avondale race track, follow the trail of moving red tail lights along Titirangi Road then climb up and over Mount Atkinson. Matching the downward slope of the Waitakere forest, they level off just above the moonlit waters of the Nihotupu dam. Their loud engine noise annoys members of the Auckland Hiking Club relaxing with a cup of tea after a hard day's hike.

Changing direction left at Cornwallis it zooms over a diverse array of people fishing on the long wharf protruding out into the bay and then swings right in a big arc over the Manukau Harbour.

Straightening the pilot slows as they approach Huia Bay and the hills, amplifying the noisy 'chop' 'chop' 'chop' of the blades.

Slowly circling it stops, hovering above the beach Reserve.

Beneath them three STG Nissan Patrols with headlights facing inwards, illuminate the landing zone.

Max knows that if Johnny and Butch hear the chopper, they may take to the hills, or worse hide in the wetlands beside the marquee. He doesn't want to risk that, so he decides he and Charlie will travel over the hills in one of the Patrols. He instructs two of his men to remain at the beach house and the others, including two dog handlers, in their Holden utes to join the convoy to Whatipu. Once there they will begin a systematic search for the black Toyota Landcruiser with the number plate, 'Pureaz'.

Hamish Pasha is going to prove to his security company bosses, that they made the right choice in hiring him. It is his first job after two months internment as an asylum seeker.

At the interview he thought it expedient to tell them that he was fluent in English and not that he was an Honours Graduate in English Language from the University of Kabul! He didn't know it, but Work and Income had already forwarded his qualifications to the company, attaching glowing references from the New Zealand Police who also confirmed that he was their interpreter in Bamiyan for six years.

He was not aware that he was by far the most outstanding applicant for the job and didn't need to be nervous when entering the interview room. Prepared to sell himself, he was confused by their questions about life in war-torn Afghanistan and what it was like working with New Zealanders. Their questions were asked out of curiosity and not whether he was capable of doing the security job! To parry the questions he told them that he was an expert in self-defense which was far from the truth! Hamish is an academic not a warrior and is relieved when they say that he has the job. His training is to start Monday. In the meantime, to give him some extra cash they offer him temporary work as a parking warden at a dance that Saturday night.

After the interview, he sends a silent prayer of thanks to Allah. At last he can live his own life, support his family and leave the Mangere Refugee Resettlement Village that has been his transitional home for the past eight weeks. Happier than he has ever been, he thinks how wonderful it is to be alive and free, far from the horrors of war. Now that he has a job he and his family can start living again.

On duty, earlier in the evening and being farthest from the gate where his boss is stationed, he is sure he is parking his cars more efficiently and straighter than anyone else! With authority he directs the beam of his torch onto the bonnet of a black Holden Cruz and with a sweeping movement pulls it towards him, stopping it exactly in line with the car to his right. Taking three paces to his left, he turns and does the same to the next vehicle. As he shepherds the drivers his thoughts return to his homeland and to his cousin Gul, who only wanted to be a goat herder in the Koh-i-Baba mountains. He smiles an unseen smile, *'Look at me, I'm no different than you, Gul, except I'm herding cars, not goats.'* He shines the torch onto his new work boots and smiles and offers another prayer, *'No land mines here, thanks be to Allah!'*

With the helicopter on standby at the Reserve, Max inside the lead vehicle of the convoy receives an important message from Interpol.

'With reference to the Chinese tourist known as Len Wong, his name is Po Ling, Male, 23 years of age. Birth place Macau. Triad soldier. Known assassin. Right hand man of Feng Tai-Lung, Male, 40 years of age. Also of Macau Island. Triad enforcer. Both are wanted by Interpol for multiple murders and drug related crimes. Feng Tai-Lung and Wi Chu. Male, 20 years of age, Triad soldier, is grandson of Triad Leader, Shan Chu, of Hong Kong. The three were on the same Air China flight as Po Ling. Interpol ID photos attached'

The information confirms his fears and he hands the iPad to Charlie, sitting behind him. Waiting until he finishes reading, he asks. "What do you know about those three?"

Charlie leans forward. "Do you want the long version or the short?"

Max turns and places a ring festooned hand on his shoulder. "We have a five minute flight to Whatipu, give me the long version."

Charlie nods. Like war time soldiers, an unspoken bond exists between them. The more they are involved in life and death situations, the closer the tie. Charlie and Max understand each other completely. Their objectives are the same, rid the world of the bad buggers.

Charlie taps the picture of Feng. "I know a lot about Feng Tai-Lung and even more about Shan Chu, the big boss, but I have little information about either Wi or Po, except that I know they carry the number 49 and are soldiers under Feng's control. Do you know what the numbers mean?"

Max shakes his head, "they are numeric codes used to distinguish between ranks within the gang. They are the street numbers where the gang first took up residence in Hong Kong, after fleeing Communist China. 489 refers to the leader or Dragon Head, that's Shan Chu. 438 is the next level down and refers to three bosses, Operations, Deputy Mountain Master, and the Ceremonies Officer. Feng Tai-Lung the gang's enforcer is the next level down. His number is 426 and his name is the Red Pole. Equal to him is the Head Administrator, 415 and the Liaison Officer, 432." He pauses and looks at Max, "Are you ready for a Chinese history lesson?"

"Is it important?"

Charlie nods, "Very!"

"Okay!"

"You would think that the Enforcer, with all his military power, would be one level below the Dragon Head, but he is not, for a very good reason. Since the early days of the struggle against the Manchu, successive leaders of the gangs have been ousted by their Red Pole! One of the leaders who was a Red Pole himself, relegated the position downward to be equal to the Administrator and the Liaison Officer, both appointed for their loyalty to their leader." He pauses for a moment, gathering his thoughts, "Now this is the important part. I have been told, just recently, that Feng has been agitating for a change at the top, saying that Shan is too old and weak and losing his mind, which are all probably true. Right at this moment there is an impasse within the Triad movement. Feng has the backing for his coup in Hong Kong but Shan's reach is world-wide and he has international support," He counts off on his fingers, "From the Mafioso, the Russkaya Mafiya, Tongs of America, and the Japanese Yakuza. Because of this powerful support, removing Shan is going to be difficult and dangerous for Feng."

Max and Charlie are silent for a moment absorbed in their own thoughts. Max is the first to speak. "Do you think Feng has been sent to New Zealand on some pretext so that he can be killed?"

Charlie nods. "Good a place as any, bottom of the world and all that! It's the only explanation why such a high ranked leader would be sent to New Zealand. You are small fry down here."

Max agrees. "It makes sense, but wouldn't he know something is not right?"

"Probably does, but he must obey orders, it's part of their blood oath! Shan would have sent him on some sort of pretext."

Max rubs the sides of his face with his hands as if that will help him absorb his friend's words. Again he puts his hand on Charlie's shoulder. "It certainly would explain everything! So, you think they have been sent to bump off Johnny and Butch to keep them quiet and then for Wi or Po, or both, to do in Feng?"

Again Charlie nods. "That's the way I see it!"

"Well friend we have our work cut out for us, don't we!" Max picks up the mic off the dashboard and through the Coms Centre, connects with his two officers at A&E and informs them of who they are guarding and asks for a medical update.

The reply comes back that he is in a coma on life support.

The three STG vehicles followed by two cars with the dogs, are almost at the turn off to Whatipu when Max decides it's time to stop pussy footing around Joey and sends him a text message, *Phone me. This is an order. Do it through the Coms Centre. Max.'*

The pink champagne is being expertly poured into their tall crystal flutes by the wine steward, when the phone in Joey's new suit jacket pings its message. He places his silver fork, filled with crayfish mornay, on the side of his plate and then looks questioningly at Kylie. She has just bought the most expensive fish tailed, teal dress in the Gucci shop and after a massage, a pedicure, a manicure and a hair style, she feels and looks beautiful.

For the past four hours she has been in an unreal world of pampering and luxury. She knew it couldn't last, her instincts telling her that the message on Joey's phone will change all that. She has always been pragmatic and as a realist knows that the happenings earlier in the day have left consequences that must be resolved. A moment ago she was ravenous but now that has gone and she crosses her knife and fork on top of the half crayfish shell and nods at Joey. "Answer it hon!"

"It's probably Max!"

She nods again. "We have to deal with it Joey.... we owe it to Max."

"Not the money!"

"No, not the money!"

Sighing he removes the phone and looks at the message then up into Kylie's questioning eyes. "Yes it's from Max, he wants me to call him!"

Leaning forward, she accentuates the peek-a-boo circle in her dress. Reaching across the table she taps her pale blue manicured nails on the white table cloth.

He can smell her Gucci perfume as she pleads. "Do it Joey, it won't go away until we have seen it through. Johnny and Butch are still a threat!"

Looking at her for a moment, he nods. "For you, hon!" He dials Max who answers immediately.

The five minute phone call, with many questions and answers informs Max about their activities. Joey tells him everything, except about the money, explaining the visit to the beach house was to show Kylie her house. He tells him a half truth that they had every intention of going to Queenstown but the Chinaman changed that.

Max doesn't get angry as he is still conscious of the pain he has put Joey through, as well as being preoccupied with keeping on top of the mission, instead, he thanks him, hangs up, then clicks on his mic briefing all staff on who they are dealing with and warns them that this is no longer routine crowd control, but a life threatening situation.

Involuntarily the AOS and STG check their weapons and tighten their flak jackets.

Max's words excite the sixteen STG standing on the running boards and at the sides and rear of their Nissan Patrols. This is what they are trained for, welcoming the challenge and danger of armed conflict. Dressed in their charcoal battle dress and holding on tightly to the overhead hand rails they are ready for battle. They know that they are hurtling towards danger but that is the risk they take as the STG. It is more than just the excitement of the chase, deep down they believe in their oath to protect the community and uphold the law. Trained rigorously by the army they are confident of their physical fitness, weaponry and team work. Each know that they can out manoeuvre and stop any terrorist or gang that threatens the safety of their country.

Max's most important and smart decision, which will have far reaching consequences, is to ask his men assigned to traffic control to talk to the parking wardens and ask them if they have seen either the black Landcruiser or the black Holden Cruz.

Hamish parks the last patron in the far corner of the paddock and speaks into his RT, telling his team leader that the paddock is full. He is told that he has done a great job and that he can now rejoin the others at the gate. As he walks up the hill a car door opens near the fence, throwing light on the car beside it. He can vaguely make out a man standing beside the car beckoning. Changing direction he is guided by his torch, walking between the closely parked cars. He is one row away when his team leader calls him again, this time urging him to hurry as the police want to have a word with the wardens up at the gate.

Obeying an order, Hamish immediately stops, turns around and quickly retraces his steps back towards the gate. As he goes he looks back over his shoulder to the man that is now shouting and still waving his hands. *I wonder what that is all about?... I'll find out after the meeting.'*

Parked beside the gate is a police car with flashing lights. A Sergeant is talking to his Team Leader and the other Parking Wardens. As he approaches, the group turn to face him and his heart misses a beat, *'Have I done something wrong? Can't have, the team leader is smiling.'* The leader beckons with his hand. "Hi Hamish," He points to Mark who is sitting in the car with an elbow resting on the open window, "The police want to know if you have seen a black Toyota Landcruiser or a black Holden Cruz? Do you know what they look like?"

Hamish is probably the best person in New Zealand to be asked such a question. Apart from his years of surveillance where spotting danger is a matter of life or death, he loves cars, particularly new ones like the Landcruiser and the Holden Cruz. The Landcruiser he remembers because they are prohibitively expensive and hard to buy in Afghanistan. The Holden, because of its unfamiliar round lion badge on the front of the grill. They have a similar car, but it is called an Opel. So he remembers seeing both of those vehicles in the car park. Whether they are the ones they want, he doesn't know?

Stepping up to the window, he extends his hand, which is shaken by the Senior Sergeant. It reminds him of his time with the New

Zealand Police, back in Bamiyan. The close contact and the ever present fear of death, bonded the New Zealand Police with their interpreters, so they became close friends. Tying their friendship even closer, Hamish invited his police friends back to his house for an Afghanistan style meal, cooked by his mother, usually slow cooked goat meat in a clay pot with sour cream, garlic, coriander, cumin and lemon juice. Hot baps of tandoor naan bread made a perfect side dish.

The New Zealand troops loved the infrequent visits, not only for the delicious home cooked meals, but to be once again in a family environment and away from their unnatural life in a war zone.

Hamish releases his hand and smiles, "Hi I'm Hamish, I worked with you guys in Afghanistan." He nods, "And yes, I have seen both of those cars, the Toyota Landcruiser and the Holden Cruz." He points towards the car park, "They are down below in the paddock about eighty metres away. I'm trained in surveillance and have a very good memory, so I'm sure I'm right!"

Mark addresses the team leader. "Okay if Hamish stays with us for a while?"

"Sure, no problem."

Mark reaches behind and pushes open the back door.

Once Hamish is seated, he turns towards him. "I'm Senior Sergeant Mark Richardson and this is my side kick Senior Constable Andrew Mulligan, is it okay if you stay with us for a while?"

"Sure, as long as you like!"

Mark smiles briefly at Hamish and then turns and picks up his microphone and connects with the Coms Centre. After identifying himself and his location, he continues, "I have a parking warden with me from SIS Security. Hamish...." He turns, "Do you mind giving me your surname Hamish?"

"Pasha, that's spelt P..A..S..H..A, Pasha."

"Did you get that? Yeah, Hamish Pasha, he tells me that he has seen both of the cars wanted by the Superintendent. Can you put me through to Max please? Over."

There is a moments silence and then they hear Max's voice. "Max here Mark, what have you got for me? Over."

"A parking warden has ID'd the two vehicles, he is with us now and we're at the entrance to a car park a hundred metres above the beach, what do you want me to do? Over."

"I suppose you have your warning lights on? Over."

"Yes sir, over."

"Turn them off, the vehicles may still be occupied, over."

"Yes sir...... Done, over."

"Can your car be seen by the Holden or the Toyota? Over."

"No, they are down a slope about eighty metres away, I'm parked beside the road near the gate, over."

"Good. Make no attempt to approach the two vehicles. Move your car and take position further up the road where you can't be seen from the paddock. I'm in a STG vehicle and will be with you in ten minutes. I repeat, do not try and approach or apprehend anyone in the two vehicles, they are both gang related, is that understood? Over."

Mark looks at Andrew and raises his eyebrows, then turns back to the mic, "Yes sir, I'm moving now and you'll pass by my car a few hundred metres up from the car park, out."

As they drive away Mark turns towards Hamish in the back seat, "How far away from each other are the cars parked?"

Hamish leans forward. "They are almost beside each other up against the fence."

"Did you get a chance to see who was driving?"

"No, sorry, too dark, I'm sure the Holden Cruz is still occupied."

"How do you know that?"

"Someone near one of the cars was waving to me when you asked us to come to the gate.... I was going to see what they wanted! I'm glad that I didn't! Did I hear your boss say something about a gang?"

Mark nods. "It's a good thing you didn't go to the car, eh!"

Hamish enjoys the sound of the kiwi word 'eh'. It is not a word taught at his University, but his best friend in Bamiyan, Sergeant Peter Perry used it all the time.

"Yeah, someone must be watching over me!"

"You'd need someone to survive in Afghanistan."

"I have my religion."

"Are you a Muslim?"

"Yes, it brings me great comfort."

Andrew, driving the car has been looking at Hamish in his rear view mirror and there is just enough light from the dashboard and the communications equipment to illuminate his face. He notes that he is clean shaven with fine features. Not the swarthy dark bearded tribesman that he would have expected. He has been listening to the way he has been speaking, with his choice of words and is surprised that he sounds more English than American and his curiosity is aroused. "You say you were an interpreter with our police in Afghanistan?"

"Yes sir, for six years. I was assigned to Sergeant Peter Perry, we were like brothers. Do you know Peter, he's a wonderful man. When he left Bamiyan he promised me that he would try and get permission for me and my family to come and live in New Zealand." He shrugs, "I knew he would try but I didn't think we'd be allowed." He is quiet for a moment as he fights to control his emotions, looking down at his clasped hands. Looking up he continues, "He brought us all to New Zealand, not just my family, but all the interpreters and their families attached to the New Zealand Police Force in Bamiyan." Again he is silent, looking out the window. Eventually he turns back towards the front seat, "If he hadn't done that we would have all been dead by now!"

Mark turns to Andrew. "We know Peter, you know, out at Otara.... The one that was given a gong for his humanity work overseas." Andrew nods. "Yeah I heard of him, quite a guy! Good on him for bringing the interpreters here, wouldn't have been easy! Can you imagine all the red tape?"

Andrew slows then stops the patrol car just past a steep driveway then reverses back and up, so that he is facing the road.

Mark swivels to face Hamish again. "Why were you in danger, weren't you assigned by your Government?"

"Yes."

"How come they didn't protect you and your family?"

Hamish laughs. "Against the Taliban?" He shakes his head, "We all had a price on our heads, not only myself and the other interpreters but our families as well!... Even our wives and children. How would you like that?"

Mark shakes his head. "I wouldn't."

Andrew turns toward Hamish. "I'm really confused about all the killing over there, aren't you all of the same Islamic religion?"

"Yes, we are Moslems and we believe in the same Islamic laws." Andrew shakes his head. "Isn't it against your beliefs to kill?" Hamish nods. "The Koran, that is our holy book, teaches us to live in peace with our neighbours.... Fanatics will always use religion to justify killing, it has been the same throughout history!"

Mark and Andrew have never thought much about what life must be like in those war torn Middle Eastern countries. Now talking face to face with Hamish they sense the huge moral depth and courage in this small humble man.

Mark nods "I guess you're pretty glad you're here with us now?"

"Yes thank you, I'm more than glad, very grateful."

Further discussion is interrupted by the noise of the approaching convoy.

Andrew turns on the head lights and the flashing lights and the convoy slows, then stops.

Max opens the door and jumps out. Hugging his iPad he jogs briskly up to the patrol car, jangling the gold necklaces around his neck. He has discarded his wig and hat and cutlass, but the large clip-on rings in his ears adds to his incongruous appearance.

Mark and Andrew now standing in front of their car, suppress a smile as they greet him with smart salutes. "Don't mind my outfit!" He looks from one to the other, remembering them from recent police work and their character references. They are both on his short list to become part of the STG. He shakes their hands, "You're Senior Sergeant Mark Richardson and you're Senior Constable Andrew Mulligan?"

They nod, as he looks beyond them towards the car, "You have Hamish, the parking warden in your car?"

Mark nods, "Yes sir, he was an interpreter with our boys in Afghanistan. He's very bright, seems to know his stuff."

"Is he one of those that have recently immigrated to New Zealand?"

"Yes sir."

"Fancy that.... let's keep him out of harm's way, wouldn't look good on my resume if anything was to happen to him." He looks from one to the other, "I'm assigning him to you, keep him safe until this is over. Okay?"

They say "Yes sir." Together.

Max moves towards the patrol car and opens the rear door and gets in. He shakes Hamish's hand. "Hamish, I'm Superintendent Max Henderson, sorry about my costume, I don't usually dress like this, but I'm going to the dance undercover. There are some gang members who could cause trouble."

Hamish nods, having already figured it out.

Max continues, "So you're the man who has spotted the two wanted vehicles?"

Hamish nods again, as Max opens his iPad selecting a picture of the two vehicles and turns it towards him, "Are these the two cars?"

"Yes sir!".

Max goes to 'Google Maps' and zooms in on the area that is being used for parking, "Is this your parking lot?"

Hamish studies it closely then answers. "Yes sir" again. He is impressed with Max's use of the internet, particularly as he seems quite old. Hamish reminds himself that he is in New Zealand and not in an ancient country like Afghanistan where the internet is deliberately stifled by religious orthodoxy.

Max hands him the iPad, "Show me where the cars are parked?"

Again Hamish studies the map for a moment, then places his finger on the screen. "This is the entrance." He traces an irregular rectangle, "There is a wire fence all the way around the perimeter." Tapping the screen, he continues, "The two cars are parked half way down this fence, closest to the beach." He looks up at Max, "I think there is someone in the black Holden, it is below the other car you are looking for."

"Why do you think there is someone in the Holden?"

"A man was standing by the side of the car with the door open, waving at me to come over."

Max selects a picture of Feng, then changes it to Wi. "Did he look like one of these?"

Hamish shakes his head. "The light from the car only allowed me to see his legs and his arms waving at me." He pauses as he tries to remember as much as he can, "Maybe he was having car trouble." He shrugs, "I don't know."

Max sees a frown cross his face,

"I can't be sure, but I think he was wearing camouflaged pants!"

Max nods and snaps the iPad shut. "Thanks Hamish, you have been more than helpful!" He looks at him straight in the eyes, "Work hard at your security job, when you get your citizenship, come and visit me at Police Headquarters, maybe we can fit you in somewhere. We can always do with a bright fellow like you who knows a lot about the Middle East." He shakes his hand, "Hamish Pasha, I'll be interested in talking to you again once you have settled in."

As Max gets out of the car, Hamish presses his hands together in prayer and thanks Allah again for bringing him safely to a land of such great opportunity.

Max calls the Coms Centre from the Patrol, and asks to be connected with the head of SIS security at the dance. He tells her about Hamish and about the potential trouble. He asks her to arrange for his pirate team to be admitted, discreetly, into the marquee.

Sending a Patrol to the beach, with its driver and five pirates, Max, Charlie and Ronnie drive towards the car park in the paddock, accompanied by two squads of STGs, all armed with fully automatic Bushmaster carbines.

Earlier, when the parking warden abruptly turned and walked away, Wi called out but was ignored, so he looked down towards Feng. "Shall I go and get him?"

Feng shook his head. "No, we'll wait for him to return."

Nodding, Wi reached into the car and put on his night glasses. In shades of green and grey, he watched Hamish disappear over the top of the hill towards the entrance. Just then, catching his attention, were flashes of light reflecting off the tops of trees. Bending down to be level with Feng, he said "There are flashing lights up by the road."

Feng put on his night glasses, opened the door and got out.

Looking up he saw only parked cars, the fence, dark irregular shapes of tree tops near the road, but no flashing lights. Removing his glasses he ordered Wi back into the car. "We've got plenty of time, Johnny and Butch won't be back for a few hours. Keep a look out for that parking warden, we want his jacket and torch." Feng returned to the front seat and shut his eyes.

Wi seated himself behind the steering wheel and began tapping on the wheel with his gloved hand.

Feng frowned and opened his eyes, "Take it easy Wi, why are you so nervous? I'm trying to sleep…. Keep quiet!"

He would not have shut his eyes if he had known that Wi was trying to decide whether to kill him now, or later. He decided *'later'*, and stopped tapping the steering wheel.

On the far side of the fence two STG scouts with night glasses, are screened by the long stalks of thick paspalum and oioi reeds as they wriggle downwards towards the two vehicles.

Once in position they look toward the front of the Holden Cruz.

Four rows up from the Holden, two other Scouts dart from car to car until they are opposite, crawling under two SUVs with high axels. One scout is above the Toyota and the other, above the Holden.

As the four scouts are wearing night vision cameras on their helmets, Max, Charlie and Ronnie follow their progress on a multi picture monitor. The two cameras show the rear of the Toyota and Holden, up to the bottom of the doors. The scouts, behind the fence, also send clear pictures of Feng and Wi sitting in the front seat of the Holden, but there is no one in the Toyota. With this information, Max instructs the scouts behind the fence to retreat back up the hill in case of crossfire. He tells the two under the cars to hold their positions. Next he spreads his troops in a 'V' formation, so that the Toyota and the Holden are in the centre of the V. Once in position, he instructs the two Nissan Patrols to move as slowly and quietly as they can, with lights out, each one row over from the Toyota and Holden. Once they are on the downward slope, they switch off their engines and silently free wheel until they are opposite the Holden. The door of the closest Patrol opens and Charlie climbs down with a megaphone in his hand.

In the still of the night, his voice booms out in Cantonese. "Feng Po-Ling and Wi Chu, this is Police Inspector Charlie Chang of the Toronto Metropolitan Police, you know who I am and I know who you are! You are surrounded by armed police ready to fire. There is no escape! Come out of your vehicle with your hands above your heads! Do not have weapons! I repeat, do not have weapons! If you have weapons or anything that looks like a weapon, you will be shot!"

There is no movement so Max instructs everyone to remove their night glasses and powerful spot lights bathe the Holden and the Toyota with blinding light. Max asks Charlie to repeat the message in Mandarin and then again in English.

At the first burst of Cantonese, Feng and Wi shocked, jerk their heads around towards the booming voice. The fact that it is their old adversary Charlie Chang calling them to surrender does not register. What does shock them is that the police know them by name and know that they are here in the car park. How? Feng's first thought is that Ozzie Clem has double crossed him, but he instantly rejects that.

When the spotlights light up the interior of the car, he flings his pistol out of the window and commands Wi to do the same. Wi ignores the order and continues to point his pistol at the closest lights.

When Charlie repeats the demand to surrender, this time in Mandarin, again Feng orders Wi to throw his pistol out of the window, instead he cradles it even closer to his chest.

Feng tries to reason with him. "Wi, they don't have anything on us, other than illegal entry and possession of automatic firearms. We will surrender and after a period in detention we will be returned to Hong Kong!" He tries a reassuring smile, "That wouldn't be so bad, would it?" He pushes his hand towards Wi, "Give me your pistol!"

Wi looks at Feng and shakes his head.

Feng is outraged and becomes angry, "Wi Chu, I'm ordering you as the Red Pole to give me your pistol."

Wi's wide eyed, agitated stare, suddenly changes to a sneer. "I do not take my orders from you any more Feng, I take them from the Mountain Master, and his orders are to kill you." As he says, "kill you." he shoots Feng twice in the face splattering blood over the passenger window.

Pushing the driver's door open he drops to the ground rolls twice so that he is up against the next car. Springing to his feet, in a crouch, he sprints towards the fence.

All the STG hear the two pistol shots and the squad at the fence see the blood splatter against the inside of the window.

Max sees the car door open and a man in military uniform sprint towards the fence and he gives the order to shoot.

Wi can see the fence and the long grass beyond. *Five paces more and then I'm free!'* He launches himself upwards diving head first over the top wire but his body doesn't roll when it hits the ground, instead, it thumps down in a torn mess riddled with bullets.

Wi Chun and Feng Tai-Lung who live by the bullet, die by the bullet!

CHAPTER 30

The Dance at the Whatipu Cave

When Lady hears the unexpected sound of a megaphone, she opens her eyes and pricks up her ears. At the muffled 'crack', 'crack' of pistol shots, she lifts her head off her paws and looks up the road. At the louder 'snap' of rifle fire she is on her feet growling. Alert now, she concentrates all her senses, but the night has returned to its expected sounds and smells and she flops back down again and tries to sleep.

It is not long before she is back on her feet again, tugging at her lead and barking when an ambulance races past and up the road. Upset and agitated, she turns around, looking towards the brightly lit tent and the faint sounds of music, wondering when Tane will return. She would prefer to be back home, something is wrong with this night.

There is nothing wrong however with the dance, it's a roaring success! Everywhere happy pirates perform their own rhythmical interpretations of Dave Dobbyn's song, 'A Slice of Heaven'. The band members of DD Smash have been re-united for this one-off charity and are in the cave on a raised stage facing outward towards the jerking mass, under the canopy of the brightly lit marquee. The song ends to loud applause and Dave, with sweat dripping off his face, swings into the opening chords of his iconic, 'Loyal' song. The applause, which started to subside, swells again and then stops as the crowd sway together with hands above their heads. So strong is national pride that even the worst singers will not be denied and shout out the words.

It is hard to hear and even harder to be heard, frustrating Charlie and Max.

Max's ear piece and mic are on full volume under his long black wig and pirate hat, while Charlie's are under his red bandana.

The billowing sleeves and leather vests conceal Glocks, strapped to the side of their chests.

Although difficult, Max has made audio contact with the other five police pirates who are standing close to Johnny and Butch seated at a table.

Earlier, Max on his first circuit of the tent was surprised to see the Canadian girls with their boyfriends dancing as a group not far from the gang members.

Now, observing them discretely, from a distance, he also checks Johnny and Butch for potential weapons. The decorative cutlasses dangling from their waists are ignored but like his own loose fitting costume, he knows they could be concealing anything! Of immediate concern is that they have full jugs of beer on the table and are already very drunk. As Max and Charlie sip mugs of ginger beer, they see Johnny bend down and remove a small plastic bag from the top of his boot, pour white powder onto the table then pinch some up each nostril.

Butch does the same and starts to sneeze.

Max knows that he could make an arrest, but is still not sure if there are any other Satan's Sons at the dance. Also, the drunken environment means innocent people could be hurt. While he watches Johnny and Butch getting high, he is aware that they have been watching Julia with prolonged and unnatural intensity.

Careful with his own surveillance, he can tell that they are fixated on the tall, beautiful girl, who is in a threesome with Jean and an unknown male. Watching Julia, he is reminded of her connection with the gang leader. *That's the pool player that humiliated Johnny.* Turning to Charlie, he holds up his mug. Charlie does the same and they 'clink' together. After drinking, Charlie stares at Max, knowing it's play acting for a reason.

Max leans closer, so that he can be heard above the noise, "Close to Johnny and Butch there is a group dancing, you can't miss the tall blonde girl. With her is a stout lady with a black beard and a man with a purple bandana."

Charlie takes a drink and then casually turns, then just as casually, turns back again. "The tall blonde is a honey!"

"Yeah she is …. she's also a Canadian!"

"How do you know that?"

"She and two Canadian girlfriends and their Kiwi boyfriends clashed with the Satan's Sons gang in a pub two weekends ago. They escaped and were chased by Johnny and his gang through a forest. They were lucky to escape with only minor injuries. Some of the gang were killed, bike accidents. The local police filed a report as well as the Ambos, so I visited the girls and their boyfriends at a Homestay not far from this beach. I wanted to try and quash any personal charges against the gang, as I was preparing to raid their headquarters."

Charlie nods, absorbing the information, well aware that the close proximity of the Canadians and the gang members creates a new dangerous dimension. "What are the Canadians doing here, are they on holiday?"

"Yeah, they're due to fly out on Monday. This is a real surprise to see them here, it adds another unwanted level of danger."

Charlie nods again as Max continues, "I didn't tell you about the girls because I didn't expect to see them again. Now it's important to brief you fully, can you hear me okay?"

Again Charlie nods, moving a little closer to Max.

"Julia challenged Johnny to a game of pool in a pub, not only did she thrash him, but taunted him in front of his gang, according to the bar manager. Johnny will want revenge and I don't think it's a coincidence that the Canadians and their boyfriends and the gang leaders are here at the dance. Somehow Johnny must have found out they were going. I'm sure if the girls had known, they wouldn't have come. Obviously they haven't recognised Johnny and Butch, else they wouldn't have stayed."

Charlie studies Julia and Jean for a moment, "Where are the boyfriends?"

"Just behind them. Tane is part Maori and muscular and he's with the local Vet, Emma Swift. She's tall and blonde like Julia. Can you see them?"

Charlie turns again, then nods.

"The rest are in that group… There's Mike, tall and fair with a moustache, fit looking, he's with his girl, Wendy, short and pretty with tight black curls."

Charlie continues to watch, storing away their names and appearance.

"Gary is the big guy and he's with Robyn with the ginger hair, she's the third Canadian."

Charlie studies each dancer carefully, but is interrupted by Max tapping him on the arm,

"I should have told you that the girls are from your home town, Toronto! This is just what I don't want right now. The death of the Chinese assassins will give me a month of paper work and God knows how many top level meetings down in Wellington."

Charlie nods. "I'm sure it will!" Turning, he looks at the three Canadians with renewed interest. It is his duty to protect them even though they are in a foreign country. Turning, he asks. "How can I help Max?"

"I have nothing for you at the moment…. I might want you to act as my go between, I'm sure Johnny and Butch know who I am, but I doubt that they know what I look like, I can't risk that. They are wanted for murder and that makes them unpredictable and dangerous. If they suspect that they are going to be caught they will grab a hostage or hostages." He looks around at the partying crowd, "Innocent people could die in this tent!"

Charlie studies Johnny and Butch for a moment and then turns back to Max. "This is a security nightmare."

Max points with his finger towards Jean. "I'm going to warn the group through Jean, she's the older one dancing with Julia, she's a local, the owner of their Homestay. It was only two weeks ago that Ronnie and I interviewed them, including Emma the Vet. I can remember them all very well."

Charlie nods.

Max watches Jean and Julia moving rhythmically to the music, "Jean is really smart a straight talker, she was helpful at the interview, kept every one calm." He turns back to Charlie, "Stay close to me I'll need you if all hell breaks loose. I'm going to brief the officers."

Moving to the side of the tent he searches for his pirates among the dancers. Raising his mug to hide his mouth he alerts them of the potential attack on the girls and their location in the tent. He asks them to hold up their left arm and wave it in time with the music so that he knows they have heard and to identify their location, they all respond. Next he calls Ronnie who is busy securing the shooting scene at the car park and alerting the medical team, "Ronnie, we've ID'd Johnny and Butch, they're stalking Julia and her Canadian girlfriends, they are all here, their Kiwi boyfriends and Jean Farley from the Karekare Homestay, over."

Like Max, Ronnie is surprised. "What are they doing at the dance? That complicates things big time! Over."

"You bet, changes everything. I'm going to try and sneak them away bit by bit. You can do something for me, contact Sergeant Mark Richardson at the lower car park and ask him to arrange transport for eight of them to Karekare, I want them safely out of the way, over."

"Sure boss, do you want us to break into the Toyota and check for arms or drugs or do you want to leave it clean for forensics? If we do we'll have to kill the alarm, over."

"Go for it, I'm not worried about forensics, we're past that."

Pausing for a moment he adds, "Put the dogs through the Toyota so they know Johnny and Butch's scent. Let them sniff clothing and items like that. The dogs will be our best weapon if they do a runner, over"

"Will do boss, over"

The repetitive use of the word, 'boss', irritates Max again and he snaps back. "Jeez Ronnie, stop calling me boss! We're a bloody police team not a sweat shop!. Call me Max, supe, chief, or sir, if you must, but not boss, over."

"Okay......... supe, over."

Max is immediately sorry for losing his temper. He reminds

himself that it is never right no matter what the provocation as it interferes with rational thought. Something that he has told his own men and women on numerous occasions. Remaining quiet for a few moments he considers the deployment of his troops, "Send twelve men to the car park by the beach but tell them to stay out of sight, over."

"Okay......... chief, over."

Max realising that he's still on edge softens his voice. "How's your end Inspector? Over."

"The Toyota and Cruz have been roped off and I've sent the chopper to pick up the Coroner from HQ. I told the pilot to come in low from the harbour side to a paddock next to the car park. The Ambos confirm that both Chinese are dead... I've ordered two tow trucks from Titirangi, what have I missed, sir? Over."

"All good, thanks!... I don't really know what is going to happen… I'll play it by ear!"

Again he pauses as he tries to think through all the possibilities, "Go and talk to the dog handlers, yeah we may need those dogs! Out."

Jean is sweating under her wig as she tries to keep up with her energetic boarders. Even Robyn is hopping around Gary like a teenager. They are all having fun except her. She knows now that it was a mistake to come because as she suspected, the dance is for the young. The night is dragging and she feels trapped and would rather be tucked up in bed with a novel. That sort of excitement she can handle. She is happy that her new found friends and her boys are enjoying themselves doing their own dance interpretations of Dobbyn's music.

Wendy is looking the least regal of all and it doesn't surprise her that the lovely Julia is the centre of attention. It is Julia that keeps encouraging her to dance as a three-some, to the annoyance of her ever changing partners. In her thigh length black boots, Julia is the sexiest pirate at the dance and knows it, but doesn't care, she's here to have a good time, not to find a soul mate!

Jean smiles at Julia, trying to hide her discomfort as she stamps and hops and does the occasional turn-a-round. She knows she will miss Julia when she is gone.

It has been a long time since Jean has had a male dancing partner and is slightly flummoxed when a short oriental pirate approaches her and asks if he can join her as a threesome.

Julia agrees immediately while Jean turns a bright pink under her black beard and renews her efforts to look like she is enjoying herself.

When he seems to be dancing closer than he should, she takes a step backwards frowning.

Leaning forward, Charlie whispers. "Jean, don't take fright but I'm a policeman. Superintendent Max Henderson is not far away and asked me to come and speak to you. We are both in disguise as pirates because you and your Canadian guests are in real danger."

She immediately stops dancing.

Charlie leans forward again, "Keep dancing Jean.

Halfheartedly she starts to stomp again.

When he tells her that they are being watched by two gang leaders, she stumbles and he catches her under the arm.

Releasing her, he raises his hands above his head clapping loudly in time to Dobbyn's 'Whaling' song.

She forces a smile, and does the same.

Charlie returns the smile, "You're doing great Jean! Max didn't want to come over and talk because he may be spotted by the gang. He wants you and the others to leave the dance as soon as you can. Don't be afraid we have men and woman on duty in the tent, you are protected!" Spinning around, he claps his hands again above his head, "At the end of this song go back to your table and tell the others what is happening. Don't leave as a group, but four first, then two.... You and Julia go last. That's important!" He leans closer and this time Jean doesn't back away, "Don't look around, but Johnny Schmidt who is the gang leader and his Sergeant, Butch Gueber are sitting two tables back from us. They have been watching you and Julia for quite some time. Tell the others not to look at them either, act as naturally as you can, that is also important! If they suspect that they are being watched, I don't know what they will do. They are high on drugs and drunk." Again he spins around clapping his hands and Jean tries to do the same. When they are facing each other again he reminds her, "Keep smiling and dancing Jean. At the next dance, four of your group will be met just outside the entrance by two police women dressed as pirates, have you got that?"

"Yes, but I'm afraid!"

"Of course you are. Just think of the safety of your guests and their men friends... Max tells me that you can be relied on to stay calm, is he right?"

She smiles and nods. "Yes!"

He smiles back, "Good, I'll leave you now, but we'll be watching. Don't look behind you, tell the others." He does another swing around as the electric violin plays its final jig and then he moves away quickly as the clapping starts.

Johnny and Butch are so preoccupied watching Julia that they don't notice Charlie's comings and goings.

Earlier they followed Julia to the port-a-loos behind the marquee but she had the company of girlfriends and the toilet area was brightly lit. They are in no hurry as they enjoy stalking their prey and they know the game will continue when they leave the dance and walk back along the beach to Karekare. The night is theirs and the thoughts of what they are going to do to Julia is exciting foreplay.

Johnny is already fantasizing as he watches her dance. He can't wait to see her arrogant, carefree face change to submissive fear. Stimulated by cocaine and P that he inhaled back at the beach house he has been aroused for over an hour and his crotch is beginning to ache. Shifting positions in the plastic chair he adjusts his pantaloons. Distracted by erotic thoughts he has not noticed the departure of her friends.

After another drink of beer, he reaches down and again withdraws his plastic bag of heroin from inside his pirate boot, tips some of the powder into his palm and then hands the bag to Butch.

The bag started as half a gram, but now most has gone. It is while he is sniffing that Julia and Jean meld into the dancers and quickly leave the tent.

As Charlie advised, they are met at the marquee entrance by two large female pirates who introduce themselves as Detective Sergeant Caroline Fatialofa and Detective Ngaire Adams and together they move quickly down the track.

It is Butch who first notices that Julia has gone.

Now on their feet, they search the dancers close by and then push their way through the crowd, crisscrossing until they give up.

Moving to the tent entrance they see the illuminated track disappearing around the protruding cliff face towards the car park. No one is on the track.

Johnny points towards the surf beyond the swamp. "They wouldn't have gone out there, too fucking wet!" He points towards the track, "They're either down that way, or they've gone to the shit houses, let's check those first!"

There is a steady flow of patrons heading to and from the port-a-loos, but Julia is not one of them, or in the lineups, so they are forced to wait until all the toilets discharge their occupants. She is not one of those either! As Johnny looks back towards the tent he is sure he is being watched. It is a sixth sense that has saved him many times. As casually as he can, he scans the area around the tent and the lighted track where people are standing. There are clumps of pirates at the entrance smoking, but none of them look his way. There is a tall guy beside a short guy with their backs to him, standing next to the marquee, nothing there. Opposite them are two hefty male pirates who make frequent glances their way. Johnny leans close to Butch. "I think we're being watched."

"Where?"

"Two big bastards near the entrance to the tent, they're not smoking, just standing there, not even yakking, they're fuckin' watchin' us all right!"

Casually, Butch pulls a packet of cigarettes from his pocket, hands one to Johnny. Flicking a lighter, he lights Johnny's first, then his own. As he drops it back into his vest pocket, he glances nonchalantly towards the men and blows smoke up into the night sky. "Fuck you're right, they're both looking! Something's up for sure. Who do you think they are boss?"

"Fuckin' security maybe?" He shakes his head, "The fuckin' cops don't know we are here. Shit, this is the last place they'd think of looking!" He sneaks another look, "Yeah they're fuckin' watching, one has just looked away. This is what we'll do, that blonde bitch and those other fuckers must have left the dance and will be on the track to the car park, they wouldn't have gotten far. If we hurry we'll be able to grab that bitch somewhere down in the flax." He places his ringed hand over his crutch and squeezes, "My cock wants some pussy, here pussy, pussy." They laugh, "Fuck I'm horny!" He puts his hand inside his vest and taps his pistol, "And nobody's gonna stop me, come-on let's go get ourselves a fuck!" They pass the marquee entrance and Max signals the two policemen to follow.

The track is sandy near the cliff face but it gets muddy when it gets closer to the creek and the swamp. Giant flax bushes thrive in the damp and Johnny and Butch are soon lost under an overhanging canopy of its tendril like leaves.

As Max watches them disappear he hears a voice in his ear. "This is Ronnie sir, just reporting that two Canadian girls and Emma the Vet are in one patrol car and their boyfriends and Hamish with a dog, in the other, shall I send them home or do you want me to wait for the others? Over."

"No, get them out of there as soon as you can. Johnny and Butch are heading your way along the track, they'll be there in about ten minutes."

Ronnie looks at his watch, as Max continues, "Julia, the blonde girl and Jean, the owner of the Homestay should be with you very soon, they are being escorted by Detectives Caroline Fatialofa and Ngaire Adams, over."

"I've commandeered an SIS car for their transport, is that okay? Over"

"Under the circumstances, perfectly okay. What have you done about the deployment of the troops? Over."

"They are positioned around the Toyota and the Cruz and on the sides of the road leading to the upper car park. The dog handlers are on standby waiting your instructions. Do you want any troops at the lower car park? Over."

"Yes but they must be out of sight. I want the arrests of Johnny and Butch to take place in the upper car park near their car, it's the safest place.... We are going to have some action pretty soon. They don't know we are here yet, both are high and very drunk, so expect the unexpected. Charlie and I are on our way, over."

"Okay sir... See you soon, out."

Johnny and Butch, moving under a long row of flax, stop, then turn and look back up the track towards the marquee. The two large pirates that they think are security guards, are making their way towards them.

Butch whispers to Johnny. "Shall we take them here, or hide?"

Johnny shakes his head. "No, I don't want to fuckin hide, we'll lose the girl and this is too close to the tent." He gestures, "Come on let's get a fuckin' move on."

They soon leave the shelter of the flax and approach a projection of cliff that intrudes into the swamp. Near the cliff the flax is replaced by cutty grass, blackberry and gorse and as they run it scratches their arms and tears at their pantaloons. Slowing, they pick their way over a rough made bridge of logs that spans a small creek flowing around the outcrop of rock. To avoid the creek, the track climbs up and over the corner foot of the cliff face, before it turns right and follows flat land to the car park on the other side of the creek.

Now standing above the swamp, at the highest point, on the foot of the cliff, Johnny and Butch can see the hurrying backs of four people in front of them. Illuminated by the solar lamps on either side, they can see Julia's long blonde hair and can also see, in the distance, the brightly lit car park.

Johnny points. "That's her, that's the bitch."

They scramble and slither down the track but stop when they hear the 'clunk' of boots on the wooden bridge behind them.

Johnny makes the decision, "We'll do it here, I'll take the first, you take the second."

They hide in the thick ferns and creepers at the bottom of the cliff, where the track turns right towards the car park.

Screwing silencers onto the ends of their Baikal pistols, they release the safety catches and crouch waiting.

A moment later the two large policemen slip and slide down the track, turn right, pausing to look down at the two rows of solar lights and yellow plastic ribbons marking the track immediately in front of them, before it bends around the curve of the creek.

They were expecting to see Johnny and Butch but no one is on the track. They knew they could hear them, just a moment ago.

Johnny touches Butch on the arm then points to the man on the left and then at himself. Then to the man on the right and then to Butch.

Butch nods.

Johnny motions for them to stand. With the policemen five paces in front, they raise their pistols, aim, and shoot at point blank range.

Each policeman is shot in the back of the head and the resulting 'crash' of falling bodies into the undergrowth is louder than the sound of the silenced pistols.

Quickly they drag the bodies by their boots back into the ferns and move down the sloping track to emerge a few moments later a hundred metres behind the girls.

Caroline and Ngaire, hearing the shots and the sounds of breaking branches behind them, stop and turn and listen for a few seconds.

Caroline turns to Julia and Jean and asks them to stay still and quiet.

They all turn and look back towards the cliff face. There are no further noises, only the return of the insect sounds and the croaking of bullfrogs.

Peering along the softly lit track, winding its way towards the dark of the cliff face, they cannot see any movement.

Caroline, frowning, turns to Ngaire. "What do you make of that?"

"Sounded like pistol shots!"

"Yeah that's what I thought!... Strange, I'll call Max."

"Hi Mister Henderson, this is Caroline Fatialofa, did you hear pistol shots? Is everything okay your end? Over."

Max who is puffing, trying to keep up with Charlie, replies. "No, I didn't hear anything Detective, although my hearing's a bit off... I'm still deafened by the band! You guys all right? Over."

"Sure, no problems, over."

"Have you seen anything of Johnny or Butch, they must be close to you by now. How far are you from the car park? Over."

She turns and looks back up the track again, "Nothing of the gang guys yet. We are almost at the carpark." Turning, she looks towards the car park. "I can see the car park lights, maybe five minutes, over."

"Good, talk to you soon, out"

The bends in the track and the thick bushes thriving by the creek have concealed Johnny and Butch as they hurry towards the ladies.

The Detectives would have liked to move their charges faster, but Jean is puffing and struggling to keep up.

Now fifty metres behind them, Johnny and Butch are jogging, spurred on by the chatter and Julia's distinctive, North American twang and by P and heroin. Their blood is pumping through their veins and they are no longer rational human beings but predators. Like hunters at the chase.

Stopping briefly to take off their boots, they run silently until they are as close to the ladies as they dare, without being seen.

Just before the kikuyu grass of the Whatipu Reserve, the track is forced to make a large detour around a bend in the creek.

This is the opportunity Johnny has been waiting for. Holding his pistol in front of him and concealed by the bend, he races up to Julia and grabs her roughly by the arm before she can react. Pushing the pistol hard against her neck, he shouts for the others to lie face down on the ground with legs and arms spread wide.

They all freeze, shocked and surprised and seeing the pistol at Julia's neck, instantly obey.

Caroline as she lowers herself to the ground, has the presence of mind to turn her mic on, so that Johnny's aggressive voice can be heard by Max and all the police. "Don't look up. Don't move a fucking hair, else I will shoot you! Shut your fucking eyes now, if you don't, I'll shoot this pretty little lady first!"

Julia winches as she feels the silencer being pressed hard into her neck, "Tell them Yankee bitch what I'm doing with the pistol. Tell them how much it fuckin' hurts."

Julia is too afraid and too traumatized to say anything, so Johnny releases the pressure of the barrel in her neck and then cracks it against the side of her ear. It is a soft blow, but it is painful and her knees give way.

Johnny easily holds her up, and snarls into her ear, "Hot shot fucking pool player, how do you feel now?... Bitch!" He pushes the pistol hard into her neck again, "Tell them where my gun is pointing!"

Julia's muffled reply is not heard by any of the police who are now galvanised into action.

Without waiting for instructions, Ronnie has his three STG at the beach carpark on the run, through the tall grass and the flax and the tea tree above the track. That is when the Airforce helicopter arrives with the Coroner and hovers with its searchlight blasting above the upper car park.

The distant, 'chop', 'chop, 'chop' of the blades stops Johnny cold. He thinks it is the Police Eagle and that forces him to change his plans. Still holding Julia with the pistol to her neck, he shouts at Butch. "Fucking hell, the cops know we are here!" He points up the valley with his left hand, "That fucking police chopper is at our car park we can't get to the car!"

Although lying on her stomach with eyes closed, Detective Sergeant Caroline Fatialofa is still aware of what is happening. True to her upbringing, her faith has always been a comfort and she prays for guidance.

After a moment, she knows what she has to do, even though it will risk her own life. The ladies are entrusted to her care and she must do her duty! She decides to become a distraction and a major player in this pantomime from hell!

Surprising Johnny and Butch she rolls over, sits up and speaks to them with as much authority as she can muster, without appearing frightened. "Johnny Schmidt I'm Detective Sergeant Caroline Fatialofa of the Henderson Police.... You are surrounded by the STG. It will be better for you and Butch Gueber to surrender to me right now!" She holds out her hand, "Give me your pistols!"

Johnny glares down at her. Her demand is not only preposterous but insulting and he becomes enraged. "Look at you, sitting on your fat fuckin' black police arse telling me to hand over my fuckin' gun... I'm the one who decides who lives and who dies, not you!

You fuckin' black sow!" His face is contorted with rage as he walks towards her dragging Julia with the pistol still pressed into her neck.

Behind him, Butch calls out. "Do you want me to shoot her boss?"

Shaking his head slowly, he sneers down at her. "So Detective Sergeant Caroline Fatia-something-or-other, you're going to arrest me?"

"Yes!"

"I don't fuckin' think so, you're coming with me and Butch and this pretty little lady, what do you think of that?"

Caroline says nothing, so he turns to Butch, "She's yours Butch, you've got yourself some black arse!" As he laughs, Caroline places her hands behind her and pushes forward, preparing to stand. She is stopped when Johnny points his pistol at one of her knee caps, "Which fuckin' knee cap do you want to lose?" He waves it backwards and forwards, "Left or right, how about both?"

She sits down again knowing she has gained some time, but even more aware of how crazy he is and that frightens her even more.

Johnny, satisfied that he has now regained control, returns the pistol to Julia's neck, then turns to Butch, "These two fuckers will be our ticket out of here, a Yank and a cop, what-do-you-know!" looking down at Caroline again he smiles, "Specially for you and our Yankee tourist, we're taking the scenic route to Karekare through the swamp!" He turns and points towards the beach and then back towards her, "You are going to be our lead." He points again, this time to the creek beside the track. "We go that way. Butch, make two long ropes of that plastic tape." He points to the side of the track, "Tie them tight around their waists, then to our belts, that will keep them from fuckin' running away." He points to Caroline, "Shoot her if she's a fuckin' problem. Up you get bitch!"

Using a switch blade that he had concealed in his jacket, Butch cuts a length of the yellow tape, twists it and then ties it around Julia's waist and hands the end to Johnny. He does the same to Caroline. While pushing it around her, he contacts her battery pack still connected to her mic and earphones. Ripping the wires off, he holds it up toward Johnny. "Look what I found boss, she's wired."

Butch glares down at her again, "Sneaky fuckin' bitch, you'd better not have any other tricks else I'll blow your brains out!" He waves his pistol upward making a 'poofing' sound, then turns to Johnny, "What shall I do with this stuff boss?"

"Chuck it in the creek... Come on, we've got to get the fuck out of here!"

As the battery pack, mic and ear piece, splash into the water, Butch pushes his pistol into Caroline's ear and tells her to move towards the creek.

She knows that she has to obey to survive, so she lifts the yellow ribbon on the creek side of the track, pushes the cutty grass aside and then slides down the bank into the water with Butch close behind.

Johnny looks down at Jean and Ngaire still face down on the dirt, "You bitches stay where you are, keep your eyes shut, if you move, I'll shoot blondie."

Pushing Julia ahead of him, they are soon up to their waists in the cold water that smells of mud, eels and wild mint.

Following the flow of the creek, they are quickly lost in the darkness and all that can be heard is the 'swish' 'swish' of their legs moving through the water.

CHAPTER 31

The Tunnel

Superintendent Max Henderson faced with an unexpected hostage crisis orders all his troops to back off.

Wearing their night vision glasses the STG are close enough to hear Johnny but the tall bushes on either side of the track obscure their view.

After repeated attempts Max has not been able to make contact with the two policemen he dispatched earlier. Already he fears the worst, one battery pack could be faulty but not two. He knows them both and their families and his intuition tells him that they are probably dead. Pushing aside feelings of remorse and guilt he concentrates on saving Julia and Jean and his two Detectives.

Hurrying forward, he and Charlie have already crossed the bridge and have unknowingly passed by the murdered officers and are now on the winding track close to the creek.

Three hundred metres away in the dark of the wet lands, Johnny, Butch and their hostages have left the creek, leaving behind the small lakes and their contributing streams. Now on firmer land, the undulating black sand is covered with sea buckthorn, blackberry, cutty-grass and the reed like oioi.

With little light to see, Caroline, leading the way, often stumbles into the thorny bushes and soon all of her flimsy pirate costume is torn and the skin on her arms and legs scratched and bleeding. She discarded her soggy boots back in the creek and now bare legged is the worst affected.

Johnny loses patience with her slow progress ordering Julia to take the lead. Luckily she is still wearing her thigh length boots.

Seeing Caroline stop in the creek and pull off her pirate boots, she decided against it preferring the extra weight to feeling the slimy unknown under her toes.

Now as they weave between the clumps of vegetation towards the dunes and the sea beyond, a huge golden moon rises above the headlands to their left, lighting the way.

They are too far into the wet lands to be heard by anyone other than surprised swamp birds that scurry or waddle away, quacking and squawking their annoyance.

Inland, on the track to the car park, after rounding a bend, Max and Charlie see Jean and Ngaire lying face down on the ground. Fearing the worst they sprint towards them and are relieved to see them lift their heads and turn in their direction.

When they see that it is Max and Charlie, they scramble to their feet.

Charlie is first to arrive and Jean hugs him with tears streaming down her face.

When Max arrives, a moment later, Ngaire approaches him, stands to attention and salutes. "They have Caroline and the Canadian girl sir, there was nothing we could do to stop them,... they had guns. Johnny had one pushed into Julia's neck. Butch had his pointing at Caroline." She shakes her head, "I couldn't do anything!" She pauses for a moment trying to regain control. Her voice is steady but tears flow down her face, "Sorry sir, but we were forced to lie down on the track!"

Against protocol Max steps forward and wraps his arms around her large frame giving her a comforting hug. He pats her on the back and then releases her. "We heard it all Detective. One of you must have been smart enough to turn on their mic, was it you?"

"No sir, must have been Caroline!"

Max shakes his head. "Don't blame yourself for anything Ngaire, in the circumstances you did exactly what you should have done."

Turning, he studies Jean, "You okay Jean, did they hurt you?"

Shaking her head, she brushes dirt off her clothes, as Max continues, "I'm sorry that you have been placed in danger, at least it's over now and we can make sure you get home safe and sound."

Jean smiles, nodding, then frowns. "I'm okay, but it's not over for Julia or Caroline, it is terrible, those two evil men have the girls. What can you do Superintendent? I'm really afraid for them!" She shakes her head again, "They're like wild animals Max!"

"Don't I know it! The good thing is that I have the resources to stop them, hostage situations are never easy!" He looks from one to the other, "I'll do my best to get Julia and Caroline out of this mess."

Jean, reaching forward, pats Max on the arm. "You're the best man for the job Max, I know you'll do it!"

Although intended as a morale booster, it actually has made his job a little bit harder.

"As I said, I'll do my best." Turning, he looks out into the wetlands, guessing that's where they would have gone. After a moment he looks at Ngaire, "Which way did they go, did you see?"

She nods and walks over to the creek with him following. "We were told to keep our eyes shut, but I took a quick peak." She lifts up the yellow track marker and points towards the broken bank where they slid into the water. Reaching forward she pulls a piece of white cloth off a blackberry bush and holds it towards Max, "They went in here. Julia and Caroline were tied to the men with strips of this track marker, they're both on a leash." She turns and looks out toward the beach, "They're out there somewhere in the swamp, I heard Johnny say that they are going to Karekare."

Max nods, then turns on his mic and updates everyone.

Within minutes, the STG troops surround Max and rest their arms on their downward pointing rifles.

Max takes the small piece of cloth from Ngaire's hand and approaches the team leader. "Organise an escort for the two ladies, there's a car waiting at the car park." He returns the salute and then turns on his mic and calls Ronny, "Hi Ronnie have the dogs been inside the Toyota yet? Over"

"Yes... mmm.... Max, we found a leather jacket with Satan's Sons patches and we are sure it's Johnny's, over."

"Have you got it? Over."

"The dog handlers have it, over."

"Good, send the jacket and the dogs down to me, over."

There is a pause while Ronnie facilitates the order, then apologises. "Sorry about the chopper chief, bad timing, over."

"Not your fault. Send the chopper to the beach car park, the Coroner can stay with her dead bodies." He looks out again towards the swamp, "Get the dogs down here as soon as you can, okay? Over."

"Five minutes, boss.... I mean chief, over."

"I want you to head out onto the beach with two of the Patrols and their troops, smash the barrier if you have to, I will be in the chopper with Charlie. We'll keep you informed of the hostage situation as soon as we locate them. There is a chance that Johnny may leave the swamp and walk along the beach to Karekare, I'll be in touch, out!"

For the first time, he realises that his hat is an annoyance and he flings it and his wig into the bushes and then bare headed stares out into the black of the wetlands.

With Charlie standing beside him they both have the same thoughts, *'I wonder if we can get them out alive?'*

Within minutes two large Alsatian dogs appear on the run and behind them their handlers holding onto long leashes.

The dogs sniff the jacket and the remnant of cloth left on the blackberry thorns and soon locate where the group entered the water. They strain on their leashes, pulling hard towards the edge of the creek. With only the briefest of commands they are into the water dragging their handlers with them.

The remaining STG follow immediately, without hesitation, jumping into the creek, as Max and Charlie head for the helicopter that has just landed beside the car park.

The dogs miss where Johnny and Butch and the girls left the creek and it's not until fifteen minutes later, pushing through boggy mud near the edge of the lake that they realise their mistake and double back finding the correct exit point.

Everyone knows they have just lost twenty minutes of valuable time.

The low gearing and the independent suspension of the four-wheel drive Patrols make short work of the undulating sandy track, leading to the beach.

The six troopers, on each of the vehicles are forced to hold on tight as the vehicles sway, twist, and turn. The soft sand causes the tyres to lose traction one moment and then bite hard into clumps of reeds the next.

The two vehicles are in a hurry knowing that their quarry has a lead and heading in a direct line to Karekare Beach while they are forced to take a large arc four times the distance!

Accelerating once they hit the hard sand, they know that the gang and their hostages must be ahead of them somewhere to their right between the swamp and the steep cliffs.

Prodded forward, Julia soon becomes exhausted. She stumbles into rabbit holes and patches of soft sand but she is not allowed to slow and has to dig deep to find new energy. Angry words and hard pushes keep her on the move.

It is easier terrain now being close to the high dunes and well past the swampy ground near the marquee.

They are moving at speed when the helicopter passes them by, low to the ground, half a mile inland with its powerful searchlights probing left and right.

Johnny calls a halt and pushes Julia under the spreading stalks of a clump of toitoi, telling Butch to do the same. Hidden under the canopy of long thin leaves they watch the military helicopter move away as it continues to search close to the cliffs.

Johnny, pressing up against Julia's back becomes aroused and she can feel him swelling against her buttocks. Her hair is under his nose and he can smell her perfume and sweat. Afraid, she tries to squirm away but he reaches over and roughly grasps one of her breasts.

Pushing up close once more his hand continues to crush her breast and she cries out in pain and fear. This excites him, and he rolls on top of her and tries to kiss her on the lips but she thrashes her head from side to side.

Squeezing her jaw with his other hand, he stops her movement and crushes his lips hard against hers.

It is a brutal kiss and she can feel his tongue probing between her lips so she unclenches her teeth and bites down hard. She tastes blood as he jerks his head backwards sits up and then back hands her so hard that her face snaps into the sand.

Raising his hand, he is about to strike her again, when he hears dogs barking, not too far to their rear, so he scrambles to his feet, reaches down and effortlessly yanks her up by her vest and shoves her forward spitting blood from his mouth.

Julia knows that at some point in time he will sexually assault her again and she uses that fear to keep her legs moving.

The extreme exertion has her aching in every part of her body. She wants to stop but deep down is a driving instinct to survive. Harsh Canadian winters have taught her to call on untapped reserves and she keeps going. Almost in a trance, her legs propel her forward as her mind returns to thoughts of how she survived the freezing blizzards in the cabin by the lake. Delirious, her father is there beside her telling her that everything will be all right as long as she keeps moving. Tears blind her and she crashes headlong into the middle of a buckthorn bush puncturing holes in her face and arms.

Johnny, holding her lead and close behind is pulled headfirst into the long needles and backs out swearing. "You fuckin' stupid bitch!" He is furious but again is reminded by the excited barking of the dogs, that they are closing fast.

He wants to inflict pain, but self preservation keeps him on the move. Reaching down and ignoring the thorns, he drags her upright then pulls on her leash to get her moving again. When she falters he punches her hard in the back, knocking her to the ground again. Turning to Caroline he orders her to take the lead.

Caroline is physically much stronger than Julia and much fitter than either of the two men. Her gym work and netball training keeps her fit for her job. She can tell that Butch and Johnny are also struggling with the pace. The tugs on her back are more and more frequent now and she knows that it is her strength that is keeping Butch moving.

Sometime soon she will make her move.

Glancing back toward Julia and Johnny she is sure that his drug driven body is starting to slow as well.

Suddenly Johnny calls a halt and then turns towards the sound of the yelping dogs at their rear and figures that they have about a three hundred metre lead. He can tell that they are getting closer, and decides to take evasive action. The lakes by the cliffs are again his best option to hide their scent, even though it increases the chances of being seen from the air.

The moon, now higher in the sky, is a smaller globe, but it still sheds enough light for them to increase to a jog.

Soon they are wading up to their armpits in the middle of a shallow lake.

The water is lapping under their chins before it becomes progressively shallower and they are able to scramble out the other side.

The vegetation on this side of the lake is thicker and it slows their progress, but it also hides them better than the open sands near the beach.

Now standing between two tall flax bushes and dripping wet, they pause to catch their breath.

Johnny's tongue is hurting and he pulls the plastic bag of heroin out of the side of his boot empties all its contents into his cupped hand, raises it to his nose and then sniffs until it is all gone. He has just taken a dose far greater than he has ever taken before.

His brain demands more oxygen and his heart is forced to pump even harder. A mere mortal would have over dosed, but his years of drug abuse has built an unnatural tolerance and he survives for the moment, but his vital organs have been compromised.

With heroin, methamphetamine, beer and bourbon coursing through his blood, he almost faints and he holds his pounding head in his hands and rocks from side to side in agony until the pain goes. His brain tells his body that he has been poisoned and his stomach contracts, forcing him to vomit. Doubled over with his head down, bile runs out his mouth and nostrils but he still has a firm grasp on Julia's lead! Shaking his head, he feels his pounding heart subside and opening his eyes he looks around, everything is as it should be, he's still in charge, but something is wrong with the sounds around him. The helicopter is still 'chop' 'chopping' in the distance but the dogs are no longer barking!

Max and Charlie with the aid of an infra-red camera and monitor on the chopper, have been watching the group's progress. They have also been receiving on-going reports from the dog handlers.

At the beginning of the search, when the dogs lost the scent and were forced to double back, they concentrated on the swampy ground by the marquee. Once the dogs found them again, they have been able to keep them constantly insight, even when they hid under the toitoi, or as now, under the flax, close to the cliffs.

Max's plan is to shepherd them forward, until they are out of the wet lands before attempting to free the hostages. He doesn't know where or how, but at least the odds will be better. From years of hostage experience, Max and Charlie know that the dogs are their best weapon and he wants Johnny and Butch out in the open.

Right now, while the group is sheltering under the thick flax, they can plainly see the four heat signatures of the dogs and their handlers moving through the water. Max instructs them to slow their chase and then to stop once they reach the opposite bank. Next he sends one of the Nissan Patrols ahead to Karekare Beach to block that exit and then advances the other along the beach until it is parallel with the group. Max also decides that the helicopter is too close and instructs the pilot to move away from the lake and to appear to search near the beach.

With the departure of the helicopter, Johnny is sure that they haven't been seen and is thankful that they are now close to the cliffs where it has already searched. There is enough moonlight to allow him to see, far in the distance, the rocky outcrop that he knows is near Karekare Beach and beneath it the old railway tunnel. He has been there before and knows it is a perfect hiding place. With shallow lakes and joining creeks all the way, he is hoping he can stay ahead of the dogs, even lose their scent. He is also hoping that once in the tunnel it will appear as if they have vanished. Hiding in the tunnel is his trump card!

Buoyed by this strategy and ignoring the strange erratic beating of his heart, he decides to double their speed.

Taking the lead, he pulls Julia behind him. Soon after they hear the dogs again and they know that they must have crossed the big lake and are now heading their way.

Staying close to the cliffs on higher ground between the swamp and the sea, they make rapid progress but they are all slowing as they reach varying degrees of exhaustion.

Caroline is still the fittest and is able to conserve energy.

Johnny is suffering, but is driven on by his maniacal will power and fear.

Julia is in a stupor, her legs propelled forward by her subconscious and encouragement from Caroline.

Butch just wants to stop and rest.

Many times they are tripped by the shoots of the marram grass or patches of reeds, but at last they see the expanse of the shallow lake before the rocky out crop and beneath it the tunnel.

Johnny leads the way through the vegetation on the edge of the lake scattering nesting sea birds. Some fly, some run and some swim away and he hopes that the dogs can't hear.

The bottom of the lake is covered in a grass like weed, so although they don't get bogged down it is still hard going. At each step the hind foot has to be pulled out of the sucking sand and weed.

Julia is delirious and stumbles often, falling head first into the shallow lake. Swallowing brackish water, she coughs and spits, when Johnny pulls her upright by her plastic tether.

Still driven by the large dose of heroin, he yanks her forward. Each step is now excruciating and she is not sure she will be able to continue much further.

Caroline, whose strong Samoan physique and natural athleticism enables her to endure the pace, is concerned about Julia's exhaustion. Pulling Butch forward she walks alongside her encouraging her to keep going, helping her to keep moving.

Julia turns to her with a whispered, "thanks."

Caroline gives her a pat on the back before Johnny yanks Julia forward again.

Instinctively Caroline knows that the longer they continue the greater the opportunity for them to escape.

The helicopter pilot, positioning his plane above the wide stretch of the West Coast beach, turns to Max. "They're heading for the tunnel." He points towards the cliffs with its grey sandstone surface contrasting with the black of the forest above, and the black sands below, "See that dark patch of trees forming a triangle down the cliff face?"

Max nods, "the old tunnel is under there."

Max nods again and taps him on the leg. "Take us up higher and closer to the tunnel, I want to see the lay of the land, but I don't want Johnny to know what I'm looking at.

The helicopter immediately turns and climbs higher over the rolling surf before swinging towards the beach and racing inland towards the cliffs. Rapidly approaching is the northern entrance to the tunnel surrounded by the natural amphitheatre of the cliffs and the raised track leading to and from the tunnel.

Both Max and Charlie know that this is an ideal location for an ambush! Max instructs the helicopter pilot to leave the tunnel area and head out over the surf. Next, he contacts Ronnie, in the Patrol at Karekare Beach and instructs him to take up positions, stealthily, around the tunnel's exit.

The other Patrol is directed to move inland and follow the dunes on the sea side until they see the entrance to the tunnel.

The trap is closing and the dogs are becoming increasingly excited as they get closer and closer to their prey. They want to be freed from their restraining leashes, but Max orders the handlers to muzzle the dogs and push forward across the small lake.

In the middle of the same lake, Johnny halts the group and with concern looks up at the helicopter hovering high over-head. He is relieved that it hasn't got its search lights on and is more relieved when it moves away out over the sea again. He can't hear any barking from the tracking dogs, on the other side of the lake and hopes they have lost their scent.

Moving forward again they are soon on the edge of the lake and close to the tunnel entrance.

Bent over, Julia is on the point of collapse, as she staggers forward into the dark of the tunnel.

Now inside, she stops, sinks to the ground, not caring that Johnny is tugging on her lead. Her clothes are in tatters and her hair is wet, sticking to her face. The puncture holes and the scratches all over her body are stinging from her sweat. The mosquitos smell the blood and attack, but she doesn't feel their bites.

Butch is also in trouble. Being an unfit, overweight man, he leans up against the wall, head down, panting.

Caroline watches both Johnny and Butch, she knows that she is stronger than either of them right now, but without a weapon she must choose her time carefully.

Johnny, with his chest heaving and sweat poring off his forehead, reaches inside his tunic and pulls out his pistol and points it at Julia's head. "Get up bitch!" He motions upward with the pistol.

Terribly afraid, Julia uses the sharp rocks on the side of the tunnel to pull herself up, sobbing with the effort. Once standing she pleads with Johnny, "I can't go any further Johnny.... I'm done.... I can't go on."

He moves forward and raises his pistol to strike her across the face when Caroline moves to her side. "Hit me you big brave bastard, not her.... Shit you're a bloody coward!.... I bet you used to be a bully at school.... I know your type mister bloody Johnny Schmidt, gang leader, ruler by intimidation and fear! Just one big bloody coward that's what you are!" Her words were meant to shock and throw him off balance, it works.

Glaring at her with uncontrollable and maniacal fury his eyes water making it hard to see and his head starts to pound. Swinging the pistol, first at Caroline then back to Julia, he tries to decide who he is going to shoot first.

Julia collapses onto the ground and moaning, covers her head with her arms which commands his attention. Looking at her at his feet, he regains his composure realising that he is in control again. Nodding, he turns toward Caroline. "One fucking hostage is all we need bitch, so who's it going to be? A fuckin' drama queen or you a fuckin' big fat black cop?" Again he asks, "You or her?" As he swings the pistol from one to the other the tracker dogs bound out of the water near the entrance to the tunnel. Their muzzles have been removed and they are in full voice and ready for the kill. Although still constrained by their long leads there is no doubt about their intent and there is nothing more ferocious than a trained wolf.

Johnny swears and summoning the last of his remaining energy, roughly pulls Julia to her feet, and drags her, stumbling behind him, as he runs out of the tunnel.

A few moments before, in the helicopter over the bay, the pilot, Max and Charlie, watched on their screen the small infra-red images of the group as they left the lake and ran into the tunnel. Immediately Max ordered the pilot to accelerate back to the tunnel and take up position above the exit.

The dog handlers at the same time, requested permission to release their dogs but Max refused, not knowing whether that would cause the death of Julia or Caroline. He did give them permission to remove the dog's muzzles as he knows that angry barking can cause fear and act as a distraction.

Now hovering above the cliff, the helicopter bathes the exit with bright light just as Johnny and Julia emerge and run along the elevated track.

A moment later Butch also appears behind them.

Max reaches for the megaphone, leans out the side of the helicopter and calls out to Johnny to surrender.

Johnny stops and turns, pointing his pistol towards the blinding light but he fires only two shots, knocking out one of the search lights.

The sudden appearance of the STG rising out of the kikuyu grass on either side, pointing there rifles directly at him, makes him abruptly change plans. Grabbing Julia around the waist he pushes his pistol, once again, hard into her neck.

Max immediately orders the STG to lower their rifles and retreat back into the undergrowth. Next, he instructs the pilot to slowly gain height, but to keep the searchlight on the hostage scene below.

Johnny swings Julia backwards and forwards like a rag doll with the pistol still in her neck, shouting out into the blinding light. "Don't try and stop me, else she will fuckin' die!" He starts to advance along the track dragging her behind him when he hears Butch cry out in pain.

When the dogs, barking, splashed out of the lake, Butch panicked, dropped Caroline's lead and followed Johnny out of the tunnel.

Caroline at last free, saw her chance! All her years of back yard rugby with her brothers came into play and she sprinted out of the tunnel into the bright light and the loud 'chop', 'chop', 'chop' of the helicopter blades and hit him with a perfect crash tackle into his back. His pistol jolted out of his hand and he was driven hard into the ground. With all her weight on top of him he was pinned, face down. Reaching forward, she grabbed his long black hair in both hands, lifted his head, then slammed it hard into the track.

That's when he cried out in pain and Johnny took his pistol out of Julia's neck and aimed it at Caroline sitting on Butch.

A quarter of an hour earlier, not far away at the Homestay, Lady, tired of waiting for Tane and Mike to leave the house, decided to return to her kennel on her own. It had been a strange old night, quite confusing with all the music and people and gun shots and she was more than ready to go to sleep.

Inside her kennel she circled her blanket a couple of times, as she always did, before flopping down. Tucking her tail under, she rested her head on her paws. One big yawn and a sigh and she was almost asleep, that's when she heard the helicopter and she pricked up her ears. Next she heard a vehicle racing along the beach and that made her rise and go to investigate. There were too many noises that she had never heard before at the beach. With her head cocked to one side, she heard the faint baying of dogs on the hunt. That was too much for her curiosity and she quickly made her way down the track towards the beach.

At the beach, in the moonlight, she saw a Nissan Patrol with black helmeted soldiers clinging to the side race towards the cliffs and then disappear behind the dunes. When a second vehicle appeared, further up the beach, she decided to go and see for herself and galloped towards the walking track by the cliffs.

The now frenetic baying of the Alsatian dogs seemed to be coming from the direction of the tunnel and she knew the fastest route. Running and jumping over the loose rocks at the base of the cliff she was soon close to the entrance and she could hear that there were people inside.

Sinking down into the grass, she watched and waited. To her right she could hear the careful approach of soldiers and on the other side of the tunnel, the baying of the dogs out in the lake.

Frightening her with its loud noise, a helicopter zoomed in towards her then hovered above, bathing the area with its bright light. She sunk lower into the kikuyu grass. Turning her head towards the tunnel she heard a man's voice, then she heard Julia's voice, in pain.

Being part of her family, she decided to investigate. Moving towards the tunnel, close to the ground, she stopped when she heard an angry female voice, so she slunk closer to the tunnel on her belly. From the fury of the barking, she could tell that the dogs had now left the lake and were approaching the tunnel, that is when a man rushed out with Julia close behind, then a second man, chased by a woman.

Up above her, on the track, Julia cried out in pain as she was roughly grabbed by a man.

A low growl started deep inside Lady's belly and she launched herself forward through the kikuyu grass and up onto the track with teeth barred. Now on the track, she can see that Julia is being attacked so she races forward and bites the man hard on his ankle, at the same time knocking him over with her charge. A gun goes off above her, as he crashes to the ground.

Johnny, instead of shooting Caroline, shoots Butch's up turned face, leaving Caroline with a handful of hair and scalp.

Horrified, she releases her grip and what is left of his face, flops down into the dirt.

Johnny, landing heavily on his arm, still has the pistol in his hand.

Lady is again onto him in a flash, snapping at his throat and he throws his other arm around his neck to protect himself. Trying to raise the pistol, his arm suddenly sears with pain. The intense pain spreads to his chest and then a vice like hand squeezes his heart and it stops beating. He convulses twice and then lies still, killed by a massive seizure.

Racing forward, an STG trooper reaches down and pulls Lady away by her collar. Her eyes are wide and white and she is barking furiously as she strains towards the man on the ground.

Julia slowly gets up off the track and moves over to Lady. Kneeling beside her, she strokes her head and body trying to calm her. Then taking her quivering body in her arms, she speaks softly, close to her ears, "You brave, brave, dog." She hugs her again, "You saved my life Lady!... I'll never forget you.

The Alsatians, still waiting for the command to attack and by now quite confused, have to satisfy themselves by sniffing around Butch and Johnny's dead bodies.

Caroline comes over and taps Julia on the shoulder, she stands and the two hug each other crying with relief.

Overhead, the helicopter slowly descends to one side of the track and Max and Charlie walk with Ronnie towards the macabre scene.

Julia flings herself into Max's arms, sobbing uncontrollably against his chest and he gently strokes her tangled wet hair. Although a hard bitten, tough, career cop, there is moisture in his eyes and he is glad about the concealing darkness. He continues to hold her tightly until he can tell that she is more composed and then escorts them all back to the helicopter and flies them to the nearby sanctuary of Jean's kitchen.

It is the first time a helicopter has landed at her car park and being late at night, all the lights come on in the houses and cottages. They don't know it yet, but this night is going to be talked about for many years to come.

Julia is helped by Caroline to climb the front steps of the Homestay.

In Jean's kitchen she hugs everyone and requests a whisky on the rocks.

Charlie asks for one as well. They are joined by Max, Ronnie and the Airforce pilot who settle for one of Jean's perked coffees, while Lady is already asleep in her kennel, dreaming about her first ride in a helicopter.

CHAPTER 32

Sacred Drums

There has not been a sacrificial death in Rarotonga since the Missionaries arrived in eighteen twenty-one. Tonight there are going to be two, and there is an expectant buzz around the island.

After sunset, flaming torches mark the track leading to the sacrificial stone, high on the mountain side near the old Marae. The drums are beating as the barefooted and bare chested Ah and Tattoo Chung with plaited ropes around their necks are pulled toward the stone.

Six days before, the Tangihanga for Dan Henare and Miriama Maana commenced and being the most significant funeral in Rarotonga for many years, it lasted five days.

The open invitation attracted a few curious tourists who found themselves listening, but not understanding, the koreros and the supporting waiatas.

The Chiefs, wearing their spectacular feathered head dresses, were too great a temptation for many of the photo hungry tourists, who soon found themselves hustled off the premises, no one regretting their departure.

It takes days through oratory, for the kaumatua to tell the history of the tribes and their connection with Dan and Miriama. Stories were retold right back to the earliest settlers from the Marquesas and Society Islands to the arrival of the ocean going vakas, from Tahiti, Tonga and Samoa. Day after day and into the night the large crowd inside the Marae listened with respect to the tohungas who spoke with authority, punctuated with dramatic gestures, about the mystical world of the old Gods. With rapt attention, they were transported into the cosmos of the Supreme Being and the Sky Father and the Earth Mother. That takes time and a huge amount of kai and koha, but all the outpouring of words did not lessen the loss of their loved ones, in open coffins, lying in the centre of the hall.

It is the Islanders' belief that the Tangihanga frees the spirits of Dan and Miriama to depart on their final journeys. They also know that until the utu is honoured their spirits will remain earth bound in the Marae. Every one of importance was in attendance, although not for the whole five days. Only family members stayed close to the bodies throughout, sleeping in shifts until the day of the burials. Even the Prime Minister, Tusi Pisi and all his Cabinet were there, including the pakeha Catholic Bishop who eventually presided over the Christian burial service at his church by the sea.

That was yesterday and now there are no more tears to shed! Tonight the utu will be lifted and the spirits released. Only the Paramount Chief, the lesser Chiefs, the tohungas, close family members, the warriors and the drummers are allowed to witness the deaths.

Earlier in the morning a strong opiate had been added to Ah and Tattoo's water cooler and they are now compliant.

Before that they were violent, throwing food trays and smashing furniture against the walls. Moving them to separate cells helped, but they still demanded their right to make phone calls, which were denied.

Now they are being led, roped by the neck, one behind the other, with their hands tied behind their backs.

Two bare chested warriors, in full war regalia, pull them from the front, while two restrain them at the rear. On either side, warriors keep them moving, lifting them up if they fall.

The tohunga from Dan's tribe leads the procession and the tohunga from Miriama's is at the rear. In between are the drummers, at the front and rear, and the rhythms they beat on their hollow wooden drums, are ancient ones, handed down through the ages. It is not a happy beat but slow and sinister and it has not been heard in the forest for nearly two hundred years.

As if the Gods are mourning, it starts to rain and the track, lit by the flickering flames, becomes slippery and wet.

Ah and Tattoo often slip but are held up by the warriors and pulled forward by the ropes around their necks.

The procession zig zags higher and higher up the side of Mount Maugaroa. Nearing the top it emerges from under the overhanging branches onto a small clearing of long grass. In the middle is the ancient sacrificial stone. Behind the stone, on a make shift stage, are two carved wooden chairs. The Paramount Chief, Leo Maana is seated on the left and beside him, George Henare on his right. Behind them are their immediate families and the families of their two slain grandchildren.

Leo and George are resplendent in chiefly trappings and radiate authority.

The drummers stop beating as they enter the clearing and the grandmothers, mothers, sisters and aunties of Dan and Miriama start wailing a karakia, the sound is neither musical or rhythmical, it is a sound that comes from deep within the soul and it tells of extreme anguish and loss and it can only be made by a human throat. It stabs the hearts of all that hear, except Ah and Tattoo Chung who are forced to kneel in front of the two Chiefs, Ah, in front of Leo, grandfather of Miriama, and Tattoo, in front of George, grandfather of Dan.

The kneeling Chinese still roped and restrained by the warriors, do not resist.

The wailing fades away after one final, sustained, high pitched note.

Leo, Ariki of all of the Cook Islands stands and looks down at Ah who is immediately jerked to his feet. Leo has an ancient whip in his hand. The shaft, woven from tanned human skin, stripped from the body of a Chief of yesteryear, is topped with the Chief's plaited hair. The holder of this whip has immense power, the power over life or death.

Leo moves forward to the edge of the stage, stopping in front of Ah who tries to defiantly stare back. The opiate is making him light headed and he is unable to hold his head up. After a moment his head drops and he stares at the ground.

Leo weaves in and out of the warriors who are holding him with the ropes, tapping around Ah's body until he is facing him again. This time he speaks. "Ah Chung you sent Miriama off on her long journey, now I'm going to send you on that same journey, but you will be her slave, if she hurts, you will hurt, if she is hungry, you will feed her, if she thirsts, you will bring her water, you will never rest! I send you now to be her slave forever." Turning, he places his whip on his chair and then holds out his hand to his tohunga who gives him a long shafted, heavy wooden club, with spikes carved onto its bulbous head.

As the drums start beating again, the Tohunga chants a prayer and behind them the women start to wail. Summoning all his remaining strength, Ah lunges backwards and forwards but he is held securely by the ropes.

With both of his hands on the handle of the club, Leo points it towards the stone and Ah is dragged, still struggling, until he is pulled head first over the smooth indented top.

Approaching Ah from the rear, he swings the club effortlessly over his head and then down hard onto the back of his skull.

As the club swung, the wailing reached a crescendo, then faded away. The beat of the drums having climaxed with the 'crunch' of the club, are now silent as Ah's lifeless body is dragged away.

In silence, Leo turns and walks back to the platform towards his son, Albert, who is not in his police uniform, but wearing his full ceremonial head dress.

Approaching Albert, Leo stops and bows his head then hands the club to George Henare. As George stands the women renew their wailing and his tohunga starts an incantation and the drums start to beat again.

Tattoo Chung does not die easily, his large sumo like body is harder to restrain than the tall, lithe, Ah. Ropes are removed from Ah's body and tied around Tattoo's kicking legs and flailing arms until he is trussed up like an Egyptian mummy and dragged to the stone.

George for all his age, swings the club almost as vigorously as his Ariki and Tattoo at last is still.

That night, a fierce fire completely destroys Ah Chung's house and in the morning the Coroner documents that two bodies, Chinese Nationals, are discovered in the ashes.

Two days later, the sun is shining and it is another glorious day in paradise.

At the Tamarind restaurant car park, the Police Commissioner's modest car is parked alongside the Prime Minister's black Cadillac and Leo Maana's shiny red Holden ute.

Robert Afaai, Foreign Affairs Minister, who is the last to arrive, is forced to park his rusty van, further away from the entrance. Picking up his black leather satchel from off the seat, he makes his way up the stairs where he is greeted by the owners, who usher him to their best round table, in the corner, closest to the sea.

The most powerful people in the Cook Islands, rise to greet him and after handshakes all around, he places his satchel on the table, opens it, and removes an official looking leather bound book that is stamped with the insignias of the New Zealand Government on the top left corner, the seal of the United States of America, on the right, and on the bottom, in the middle, their own, the Monarchy of the Cook Islands.

Robert smiles at Tusi Pisi before handing him the book.

Tusi opens it and reads the gold leaf lettering. 'Agreement between the Governments of New Zealand and the United States of America and the Monarchy of the Cook Islands, for future Economic Development and Aid.'

The Prime Minister looks up at Robert. "Is it as good as the Chinese offer?"

Robert smiles. "Better!"

Tusi reaches across the table and shakes hands, first with Leo Maana, the Paramount Chief and then with Carlos Vaiili, Commissioner of Police and finally with Robert Afaai himself, Minister of Foreign Affairs. After signaling the wine waiter to fill all the glasses, he raises his, and proposes a toast. "To the future prosperity of the Cook Islands." Four crystal glasses 'clink' together.

Acknowledgements

Thanks to my son Paul, graphic designer,
for creating the book cover.

To my daughter Kiri for suggesting the cave
at Whatipu as the climax of the story.

To my brother Greg who kept me company while
walking the locations at Karekare beach and joining
me afterwards for a spot of surf casting.

To my sister, Nina Elliott for correcting the manuscript
and brave enough to advise where the story dragged.

To Peter Ben and his knowledge of pool.

To Robert Va'ai, and Leo Tasi who encouraged
me when I was writing about life in the Pacific
Islands and the destructive power of P.

To a number of people of the New Zealand
Police Force, too many to name, and Megan
Fairley of the St. John Ambulance Service.

Thank you Waimauku and the Auckland Veterinary
Clinics for being so gracious with your advice. To
all of the above, please forgive me for fictionalising
then simplifying your professional skills.

To Pudding who is a wizz tech!

Finally, thanks to my Canadian reviewers,
Dean Walker and the late Tom Briggs.

Epilogue

Methamphetamine

Junkies give it many names, meth, ice, shard, shabu, crystal, glass, tweak, tina, crank, yaba and P. It is not a new drug as its precursor ephedrine is an active ingredient in ancient Chinese medicines. In eighteen ninety-three, Nagai Nagayoshi, a Japanese chemist, found a way of modifying ephedrine so that the resulting compound resembled a naturally produced psycho-stimulant. Even a small amount of methamphetamine will trick the brain into producing massive doses of synaptic dopamine and serotonin. The user feels like a super human, but the brain is hurt by the resulting hyper activity. Excessive and repeated use usually causes irreversible damage to the central nervous system.

The worlds' military knew its potential. Nazi Germany dispensing it under the trade name Pervitin. Their armoured brigades called it 'Tank Chocolates' and the Luftwaffe, 'Herman Goering pills' or 'Stuka tablets'. In Japan it was known as Philopon. At the conclusion of the war, occupational forces discovered large stockpiles of the drug. It was cheap and soon found its way into the worlds' markets.

In the U.S. nineteen fifty, a pharmaceutical company called Obetrol marketed methamphetamine as an effective weight control drug. The users, unaware that they were becoming addicted, experienced two unexpected side effects, feelings of wellbeing and enhanced sexual prowess. The escalating addiction statistics forced the U.S. government in nineteen seventy to remove Obetrol from the market.

This neurotoxin and potent psycho-stimulant has a good side! Medical practitioners use it sparingly in the treatment of ADHD, obesity and sleep disorders. However, when used repeatedly as a recreational drug, it has a dark side that is shaking the foundations of the worlds' health organisations.

Triads

One hundred and fifty-six years of British rule of Hong Kong is a mere flash in its thirty-thousand-year history. Many Chinese dynasties had come and gone before eighteen forty-one. The last of those was the Quing, also known as the Manchu. Even though a minority, they imposed their Manchurian laws and Confucianism on the Buddhist Ming. Fearing their Shaolin Monks, they ordered their death. Only five Monks survived finding refuge in the Sacred Mountains. Over time they became known as The Triad Five Elders and founded the martial art of Ng Jo Kuen. The warrior monks had many names over the next two hundred years as they fought to survive. They were called, the Hung Mun, White Lotus, Cudgels, Big Swords, Red Fists, Green Tang and the Three Harmonies Society. Their collective name today, with their triangular insignia is the Triads.

With hundreds of thousands of members over the years successive Chinese and foreign powers have made use of this underground society to subvert and force change. The Triads with their unholy beginnings offered their services to any government that was willing to pay. In nineteen forty-one they sided with one of their own, the Nationalist's General Chiang Kai-Shek. A short time later, a civil uprising led by Mao Tse-Tung forced the Triads to seek refuge in Hong Kong.

The British Government, during its tenure until 1997 tried to eliminate the nine gangs but they still exist today with tentacles out into the criminal underworld where drug trafficking is estimated to be worth, annually, over two hundred billion dollars.

Fictional Characters

Tane Lendic	Maori mother. Father of Dalmation and Maori descent. Potter. Lives with Mike Robinson. Artist, rugby player.
Lady	Tane's dog. A Border Collie.
Mike Robinson	European. Artist. Lives with Tane.
Gregory Robinson	Mike's wealthy father.
Raechel Robinson	Mike's athletic mother.
Gary Reilly	European. Rugby friend of Mike and Tane. Lives at Karekare beach.
Jean Fahey	Owner of the Karekare Beach Homestay.
Danny Topu	Maori. Taxi driver. Encyclopedic knowledge of New Zealand fauna and flora and Maori protocols.
Max Henderson	District Superintendent Auckland, New Zealand Police.
Ronnie Vaiili	Inspector. Head of Gang Control Auckland, New Zealand Police.
Mary Clarke	Police Communications Officer
Mark Richardson	Senior Sergeant, Waitakere, New Zealand Police.
Andrew Mulligan	Senior Constable, Waitakere, New Zealand Police.
Caroline Fatialofa	Detective Sergeant, Waitakere, New Zealand Police.
Ngaire Adams	Detective, Waitakere, New Zealand Police.
Emma Swift	Waimauku Veterinarian.

Paul Swift	Emma's father.
Jan Swift	Emma's mother.
Johnny Ray Schmidt	Satan's Sons gang leader.
Butch Gueber	Satan's Sons gang. Sergeant and Enforcer.
Carla Rae	Johnny's sex slave, live in cook and house keeper.
Keaton O'Nally QC	Satan's Sons lawyer.
Kylie Temata	Johnny's sex slave, live in cook and house keeper.
Wiremu Temata	Kylie's son.
Caitlin Temata	Kylie's daughter.
Hailey Temata	Kylie's sister. Looks after Kylie's kids.
Karl	Gang member. Hailey's partner.
Rueben	Gang member.
Megan Farley	Saint John Ambulance, Senior Paramedic
Ross	Saint John Ambulance, Paramedic
Ozzie Clem	The Pit Bull Motor Cycle Club leader.
Hinemoa	Parakai pub cook.
Hamish Pasha	Parking Warden. Refugee from Bamiyan.
Andrew Schollum	Puhoi pub owner.
Mark Elias	Ex All Black
Jenny	Tane and Mike's agent.

RAROTONGA

Ah Chung	Rarotonga based, Chinese manager of Chang Chemicals and the Chung Coffee Company. Has family connections to the Triad movement of Hong Kong.
Tattoo Chung	Cousin of Ah. Supervisor at the Chung Coffee Company. A Triad and skilled assassin.
Ah Ting	Supervisor at Chung Coffee Company. Triad

Wah Lee	Ah Chung's cook.
Miriama Maana	Grand-daughter of the Paramount Chief and Ah Chung's personal assistant at Chang Chemicals. Ah Chung's partner.
Leo Maana	Paramount Chief. The Ariki of Rarotonga
Albert Maana	Son of Leo. Senior Detective, Cook Islands Police Force.
George Henare	Chief. Grandfather of Dan.
Dan Henare	Gang member. Grandson of George.
Leilani Henare	Sister of Dan and granddaughter of George. Kitchen hand at Ah Chung's house.
Pita Henare	Guard at Ah Chung's House. Cousin of Leilani.
Carlos Vaiili	Commissioner of Police for the Cook Islands. Brother of Ronnie, Inspector with the New Zealand Police.
Tusi Pisi	Prime Minister of the Cook Islands.
Leo Pasi	Minister of Justice for the Cook Islands.
Ray Gandhi QC	Council to the Government of the Cook Islands.
Robert Afaai	Minister of Foreign Affairs for the Cook Islands
Selwyn and Rua	Constables, Cook Island Police.

AUSTRALIA

Joey Moser	Half Aborigine, half Israeli. Petty criminal and money man for the Satan's Sons gang.
Alinga Moser	Joey's mother. Half Aborigine, half European.

CANADA

Julia Johansson	Scandinavian descent. Anglophone mother. Legal Executive. Lives with Wendy.

Lady Wendy Howard	Born at Howard's Castle, England. Works as a Production Assistant for TorontoTV. Lives with Julia.
Robyn Petheridge	Insurance Clerk. Close friend of Julia and Wendy.
Charlie Chang	Third generation Canadian of Chinese descent. A specialist in Triad and Tong gangs. Works for the Toronto Metropolitan Police Force.

HONG KONG

Shan Chun	Leader of the Triad movement. Code name 489. Called Mountain Master or Head of the Dragon.
Feng Tai-Lung	Feared enforcer of the Triad movement. Code name 426. Known as the Red Pole.
Wi Chun	Soldier in the Triad movement. Code name 49. Related to the leader, Shan Chun.
Po Ling	Soldier in the Triad movement. Code name 49.

REAL PEOPLE (FICTIONAL USAGE)

| Dave Dobbyn |
| DD Smash |
| Suzanne Prentice |
| Johnny Cash |
| Tim McGraw |
| Pete Murray |
| Tere, George and Arbs |

About the Author

Peter Pedrotti
peterbpedrotti@gmail.com

Born in Paparoa New Zealand, Peter is married to Janet of Kitchener, Canada. They have two children, Kiri and Paul and four grandchildren.

Living in New Zealand, this is his first novel, something he promised himself after a career of forty two years in television.

Highlights of his career include being the News Director on the night of the Wahine disaster. Co-ordinating Producer for CBC-TV of the first moon walk. The first Expo baseball game from Montreal; The Flip Wilson Show, Carol Burnett and Laugh-in.

After eleven years in Canada, on his return to New Zealand he wrote and produced a documentary series called Our Heritage. A DVD of the series is available at libraries throughout New Zealand.